ON THE HEARTH, above a basket piled with yarns and threads, a stand held an antique wooden embroidery hoop. The words stitched on the enclosed sampler read: "This is no metaphor, it is a simple fact. We start out of Nothingness, take figure and are apparitions." Below the yellowing cloth a silver needle swung back and forth on its skein of scarlet thread as if some invisible hand had just released it.

And a painting hung beside the bulge of the chimney. Its surface gleamed, gilded by an aging coat of varnish. Lauren glanced at it, then stiffened and strained forward. It was the original of the dull, drab photo in Bremner's book. It was "Catherine's Destiny." Or was the second word inscribed on a tarnished plaque beneath the portrait, the word after the possessive name, "destiny"? The large "D" and trailing letters might, Lauren saw with yet another prickle, be the word "Dream."

Subtle ridges and whorls of paint beneath the varnish traced the still vibrant colors, from the scarlet of the woman's dress to the amber-gray stone framing the window behind her to the lapis lazuli of the sea swells she overlooked. The swells that bore a galleon brave with gold trim and scarlet pennons helplessly forward, as though to deposit it at her feet like a cat its prey.

Her—Catherine's—hair flowed brown and russet and gold, a thick curtain down her back and around her face. A face with a long nose, a generous mouth parted in eagerness, deep-set brown eyes wide with caution, even fear. A face too strong for contemporary tastes. A face that was Lauren's own.

BLACKNESS TOWER

LILLIAN STEWART CARL

JUNO

Blackness Tower
Copyright © 2008 by Lillian Stewart Carl

Cover art copyright © 2008 by Timothy Lantz
www.stygiandarkness.com

ISBN: 978-0-8095-7202-1

Juno Books
Rockville, MD
www.juno-books.com
info@juno-books.com

FOR MY MOTHER.

CHAPTER ONE

Lauren Reay had come to the end of the world. Across the sea she glimpsed the blue-tinted hills of the next. White gulls called. The wind and the waves whispered, *The water is wide, I can't cross o'er* . . .

Rational thought swam up from the depths of her mind, informing her she had only come to the northern end of Britain, and now stood on the coast of Scotland looking across to Orkney.

Only? She was here at last. She seemed to be standing outside her own body. And yet she was very much in her body, hyperventilating with the excitement, with the jet-lag, with the fear of what would happen now. She should have followed the advice of her distant cousin and native guide, Emily, and waited until tomorrow to finish her journey. But Lauren could never have made Emily understand why she couldn't wait another minute, let alone another day. Why coming here wasn't finishing her journey at all.

This day was still, the sun warm, the air moist, and a dark haze like a deep blue shadow hung low over the sea, so the smooth peaks of the islands seemed to be suspended in midair, unsupported as a dream.

In her dream, Lauren had never smelled this north wind, scoured clean by salt and ice and yet, on this August afternoon, no more than a sigh against her cheek, soft as a lover's caress. And perhaps as false.

Her lips tightened in a scowl of impatience. Taking a firm step to her right, she eyed Blackness Tower planted atop the low green hillock of its "ness", a word meaning "headland" in the ancient Norse language once spoken here.

The original L-shaped tower house, built in the sixteenth century, was crowded by later additions, stone walls and slate roofs sticking out at odd angles. Its flanks were coated by harling, a sort of stucco that, instead of glinting black or even gray, glowed a delicate rosy gold in the late afternoon sun. The walls were capped by gables and turrets and a saw-toothed parapet that was more likely Victorian imitation than medieval. If the tower had ever had a moat and drawbridge, they were long gone. Now it was encircled by a stone wall, a barricade holding back the rolling turf of the headland.

In Lauren's dream, the windows of the tower were empty sockets, dark and deep. Now she saw the small antique panes, each one reflecting the sunshine in watery ripples of light, so bright they appeared opaque. If he stood behind that glass, gazing out at Lauren and Emily, she couldn't see him. Him, the mysterious David Sutherland, who refused to return her calls or answer her letters.

Fine. Be that way. She'd get into Blackness Tower. She'd ask her questions. She'd find her answers.

"Well then, is it what you were expecting?" asked Emily's voice with its lilting accent.

Lauren jumped, startled out of her—not a dream. She knew dreams, and this wasn't one. "I'm not sure what I expected. Pictures aren't, well, they're just pictures." From her shoulder bag she pulled out a page cut from a wall calendar and enclosed in a plastic sleeve, and handed it over.

The seams of Emily's face pursed less in curiosity than caution, no doubt taking the measure of this stranger from another generation, who had arrived on her doorstep like an explorer on the shore of a mythical land.

The photo of the tower had been taken from this angle, revealing two faces of the building. It had been taken at this time of year, when the wall barely restrained the flowers and leaves of a garden. Even the sky in the picture was the same, a blue so deep it had an almost purplish tinge, so solid it seemed as though, if she could only reach it, Lauren could flick it with her fingernail and produce the trembling chime of crystal.

Printed beneath the photo were the words *Blackness Tower, Reay, Caithness*. If those words weren't yet carved on her tombstone, she had at least felt footsteps crossing her grave the moment she first saw them.

She remembered the stack of mail addressed to Donald Reay. The same name on a hospital door, beside a janitor's trash bin filled with wilted poinsettias. The man laid out on a bed, his fragile shell monitored, chained up by wires, tied down like a technological sacrifice. *Grandpa, I have your mail.* Said in the artificially bright voice used to children and invalids. *Look, it's a calendar from Scotland. Look, March is Edinburgh Castle, April is Loch Lomond, June is Ardnamurchan Lighthouse.*

Look. August. Blackness Tower. Reay. Caithness.

Her heart hanging in her chest, a diver poised at the edge, dizzy with vertigo and anticipation. The acrid, antiseptic air catching in her throat. The old man's foggy eyes meeting hers and the thin gray lips emitting a ghostly whisper. *Is that it, Lauren? Blackness Tower? Is that the place you've been dreaming about?*

Yes. It was the place in her recurring dream, the one that had haunted her for a decade now. Only Grandpa knew about that dream. Who else could she trust with it?

Craig? "You've got a heck of an imagination there, honeybunch," her ex-fiancé would have said, affection cut with impatience.

Her mother? "You studied history in college, you work with books, you've seen a picture of that place before. Like grandfather, like father, like daughter," she would have said, affection cut with rue, not needing to add her usual, *all three of you, away with the fairies*.

If the fairies lived here, so be it.

With a slow nod and hint of a frown Emily returned the photo. Her clear blue-gray eyes fixed on Lauren's face.

Lauren attempted an innocuous smile. "I can always blame this on you, you know, sending Grandpa the calendar."

"I didna send him a calendar," Emily replied.

"What?" Lauren glanced back at the tower, half-expecting an upper window to shiver in a wink, acknowledging her as fate's fool. Not that fate normally sent packages via Royal Mail. "The envelope was postmarked Thurso, and you're the only person Grandpa was writing to there."

"He was likely corresponding with someone else as well."

Then why hadn't he said so? But Lauren couldn't ask him, not now.

She went on, hoping Emily wouldn't notice the strain in her voice, the tension that suggested falsehood when in reality it was simply—reality. "Grandpa always wanted me to pick up the genealogical baton, so to speak. The photo in the calendar, it was a sign, an omen. There, in the hospital, two days before he died, he made me promise I'd finish the family tree. I hadn't intended to do it just a few months later. But the publisher I was working for went under, and my fiancé bailed out on me, so it's not like I had anything else to do."

"Things happen," Emily told her. "Things change, through no fault of our own."

"Yeah." And some things stayed the same. Like her dream. Lauren slipped the photo and its plastic shroud back into her bag. Salt-sweet air filled her chest. She was here. Here at last. Atop the cliffs, the sea foaming at their feet.

Her fingertips touched velvet. She fished a blood-red jeweler's box from her bag and balanced it on her palm. "Grandpa left me a request, that I go on a quest, and he left me a bequest . . ." She puzzled over that, then decided she was punch-drunk. "He left me this."

She opened the box. Inside, nested on a bed of crimson silk, lay a metal skull a bit smaller than her fist. It glinted in the sun like treasure trove. Mottos and sketches were engraved on its polished surface, and a band of decorative openwork ran from temple to temple.

Emily gasped. "Well now, you've got a bonny wee bauble there, and no mistake! That's never gold!"

"It's silver gilt."

"A pocket watch, is it?"

Good for Emily! No one else had ever guessed its use—most people turned away with a grimace or a lame joke . . . *Oh.* "Grandpa told you about it, right?"

"That he did. Said it was by way of being a family heirloom." Another frown, like a reflection from the watch, raced across Emily's face and vanished. "Interesting, what will come down in families."

"You've got that right," Lauren stated, even as she wondered, why the frown? There was no problem with Grandpa telling Emily about the watch. He'd never have betrayed Lauren's confidence by telling Emily or anyone else about her dream.

Lauren upended the skull, evoking a faint silvery tinkle, and flipped open the hinged jaw. Inside, a clock face marked with Roman numerals was bordered with more engraving. An inscription read, *Gloria in excelsis Deo, et in terra pax, bonae voluntatis.* "It's a watch, but it's never kept time, not that I know of. It still chimes when you joggle it."

"Well then." Emily turned her curious, cautious—concerned—gaze from the watch's face back to Lauren's. "A wee bit grisly, it is. A work of art, but grisly."

"The Victorians really knew how to romanticize death. At least, I assume it's Victorian. It belonged to Grandpa's grandmother."

"Susanna Mackay. She's buried in yon graveyard." Emily gestured over her shoulder.

Lauren closed the box on the watch, on the *memento mori,* a souvenir of death—*remember that you, too, will die*—and tucked it into her bag. "Grandpa knew who his grandmother was. The question is, who was his grandfather?"

"There's a question worth the asking."

"That's why I'm here, to ask questions."

"To find answers." Emily's features, plain as pudding but considerably more intelligent, crumpled again.

Okay, Lauren thought, what do you think I don't know? That she stood on uncertain genealogical ground? Saying, "Well yeah, of course," she made a deliberate about-face away from Emily's scrutiny and from the impassive facade of the tower as well. Her back prickled. But then, what part of her body didn't?

Before her, atop a green swell of land tufted with sheep, sat the ruins of a tiny chapel. The slender stone slabs of its walls and the bulkier ones framing its trapezoidal doorways hinted of prehistoric chambered tombs and ceremonies conducted by torchlight. And yet the structure was probably medieval, a Christian foundation.

Grave monuments huddled to one side of the roofless ruin like a frightened congregation. Some of the carved stones were lichen-splotched and worn by wind and rain, others were so polished and pale Lauren wondered if they glowed in the night. In the real night, not the one of her dream.

In her dream, she walked down from the tower, beside a stream with its whiskey-colored water, and up this hill to the chapel. Sometimes she walked in daylight, when the sea rolled away billow upon gleaming blue billow past the islands to the edge of sight. Sometimes she walked in rain, cloud and mist hiding the cliffs and magnifying the low roar of the waves. Sometimes she walked at night, a light hanging about her even though she carried no lamp or flashlight, and with every step she drew as close to the peril of the cliffs as to the sanctuary of the chapel.

Now she walked up the hill for real, consciously, if not quite awake. When she slipped on a muddy patch, Emily grabbed her arm. Lauren barely felt the older woman's solid grasp.

Her dream was non-corporeal, as though she walked through a painting, without sound or smell or touch—as though she glided, her feet not touching the ground. But now she heard the nervous scamper of sheep, felt the sun hot on her cheeks and the turf spongy beneath her shoes, smelled the tang of mildewed stone. Still, even with her senses overflowing, she felt unreal.

So what was real?

Lauren stopped at the low wall made of stacked slabs of stone that surrounded the chapel. A rabbit shot out of a burrow almost beneath her feet and bounded away. She jerked back and again Emily steadied her.

The rabbit was an ordinary brown one, not white. It wasn't wearing a waistcoat and carrying a pocket watch.

She was the one carrying a watch. A broken watch, no longer counting the hours and the years, still as death, assuming death was indeed still.

Lauren set her hands on the triangular stones topping the wall. Beneath their gritty warmth she sensed a damp cold, like that proverbial long dark night of the soul. Which grave was Susanna's? The one topped by the statue of an angel, its features eroded into blandness, a cancer of orange lichen marring the smoothness of its wings?

Wait a minute. In the graveyard, rows of small, neon plastic flags marked off a grid pattern, as though a Lilliputian circus was setting up a show. Two shovels leaned against the inside of the wall. Surely no one was planning to build here. The chapel was a listed ancient monument.

Spinning back around, Lauren glared at Blackness Tower. What was Sutherland up to? He might own the tower, but Historic Scotland owned the chapel . . . That agency cared for a long list of ruinous buildings, many in more populated and accessible areas. In this far northern county, Sutherland could probably get away with anything short of tearing the chapel down and building a McDonald's on its ancient foundations.

Lauren told herself to be fair, fairness being as elusive these days as it had always been. She'd developed a prejudice against David Sutherland and his curt, British answering-machine voice. Just because he'd gone to the trouble and expense of fixing up the tower didn't mean he owed anything to curious descendants of its earlier inhabitants.

She asked Emily, "Do they still have funerals here? I know the chapel's been decommissioned or deconsecrated or whatever, but people have family ties to old graveyards. I have family ties to this old graveyard, with Susanna, at least."

She imagined Susanna Mackay's funeral: a black glassed-in coach and horses wearing black plumes, or black-clad pallbearers struggling down the path with a coffin. Her grandfather's grandmother had died at the age of thirty-seven, ten years older than Lauren was now. "How did Susanna die? Disease? Accident? Murder? That might explain a little inter-generational trauma."

"Murder, is it?" Emily darted her a sharp glance.

Lauren backpedaled. "That's way too dramatic. Never mind."

"Mind you, history is dramatic." Emily turned back to the graveyard. Her strong, stubby hands grasped the wall as if she planned to dismantle the stones and rebuild. After a moment, she said, "I saw in the newspaper, there's to be a dig here."

"Oh. Archaeology. That's okay, then. That's cool."

"A fine coincidence, your arriving just now."

"Grandpa used to say there was no such thing as coinci—" Lauren bit back her words.

"Important archaeological site, Black Ness, with a long history and longer tradition. Ghost stories and the like."

"Ghost stories," Lauren repeated. Dreams seen by other people. Or Seen, with the capital-S of Second Sight, Celtic ESP.

Swaying, she clutched at the wall—any minute now she'd float up and over the headland and out to sea, only to be lost forever in some undiscovered country.

Again Emily gripped Lauren's arm. She laughed and shook her head, probably forgiving Lauren for not being what she'd expected. And what had she expected, a character from *Sex and the City?* "You've had yourself a look at the place. There's time enough to be getting on with your plans. Just now you'll be wanting your tea and a good night's sleep."

No kidding. Lauren hadn't slept for thirty-six hours. Her last meal had been a paper cup of lukewarm tea on the flight from London to Aberdeen, and a protein bar from her bag on the flight from Aberdeen to Wick.

She smiled, and the smile spread into a laugh of her own. She might as well laugh. She'd spent enough time in tears. "Plans? What plans? I'm making this up as I go along."

"We're all after doing that. Come along now." Emily led the way down the grassy hillside and onto the walkway that ran beside the stream, then up a long slope.

Placing her feet very carefully, Lauren followed. She couldn't cross a small bridge and take the path toward Blackness Tower, not now. But she looked toward it even so—it pulled at her the way a magnet pulls at iron filings, an invisible but undeniable current.

Something flashed like a signal from high on the tower, like the way the silver skull had glinted in Lauren's hand.

She stopped. Had David Sutherland opened a window to see who was encroaching on his territory? No, the windows were still opaque, even secretive. The flash had come from the roof walk.

A small gargoyle sat on the parapet. It hadn't been there before. At least, Lauren didn't think it had been there before. And was that a woman standing behind it, in the shadow of the topmost turret? Her hair cascaded over her shoulders and she wore a long white dress that reminded Lauren of her own never-used wedding dress, now buried in her mother's back closet.

Lauren closed her grainy eyes and opened them again. The gargoyle sat motionless. But what she'd thought was a woman was a doorway in the shadowed side of the turret, its discolored paint suggesting wraiths of lace.

Taking a deep breath, she turned away. And heard music, so faint at first she thought it was a lingering jet-engine resonance in her ears.

Then the melody strengthened, high, clear notes played on a flute or a whistle, rising and falling, growing and fading, circling around so that they went in where they came out, rousing her senses like a lover's kiss on the back of her neck. She almost recognized the tune, she knew it . . . It died away into the murmur of wind and wave.

The nerve endings in her mind, along her spine, in the pit of her stomach, quivered with a similar, more familiar song. *The water is wide, I can't cross o'er, And neither have I wings to fly, Give me a boat that can carry two, And we shall row, my love and I.*

My love and I, she thought. Right.

And "crossing over" was a synonym for dying.

"Lauren?" called Emily from the top of the slope. The top of the brae. "Come along. You're looking a wee bit peaky."

Peaky? Meaning what? Stubborn? In need of a keeper? "I'm coming," Lauren replied, and set her feet into motion once again, walking away from Blackness Tower like she did in her dream.

In her dream, she never reached the Tower, and yet she kept returning to it.

Once she might have doubted either dream or tower had meaning, and believed the people who told her both were nothing more than imagination, as though imagination was ever nothing.

Then she'd discovered the tower was real. And now, here, today . . .

Now she knew her dream was, too.

CHAPTER TWO

Lauren sat at Emily's kitchen table, all the usual domestic objects and a few unusual ones—was that a toast rack?—rotating slowly around her, caught in a perceptual eddy. "What does 'peaky' mean?" she asked.

"Puny. Sickly. No offense." Emily splashed milk into a mug, filled it with black tea, and added sugar. She pressed the resulting brew into Lauren's hands. "Drink up. Tea will be ready in a tick."

But this *was* tea. Oh. The meal Emily was cooking was called "tea." Check.

Lauren drank, scalding her tongue but charging up her brain, and inhaled the scent of baking scones. Her mouth watered. Food was good. Appetite was good.

She had sat both stunned and hyper-alert as Emily drove through the village of Reay—blink and you miss it—and back toward the east, the road paralleling the shadows cast by the lowering sun and pointing toward a pale, slightly flattened moon, the gibbous moon beloved of poets.

Trying not to cringe every time a car passed them on the right, Lauren had told herself that being in a mirror-image of reality made as much sense as dreaming about a place she'd never seen. But then, her definition of "sense" was taking a beating.

Now she looked out Emily's kitchen window, past her garden teeming with flowers, to where the slow swells of

Thurso Bay shone a deeper blue than the sky. They were shielded on the left by the green arm of Holborn Head, a white lighthouse tucked into its elbow. And why wasn't that a "ness," too, Lauren wondered.

Beyond the bay, the waves rippled toward a horizon closed by the hills of Orkney. The islands rose above the haze like the grayish blue humps of a great sea monster, with the stark vertical of The Old Man of Hoy—a pinnacle of rock separated from the mainland—forming either the head or the tail. Imagine waking up every morning with that view instead of the vista of office buildings and steel-choked highways Lauren saw from her apartment complex in Dallas.

Emily plunked a plate in front of her. "With the heat I'd normally be having a salad or cold sandwich, but you'll be wanting more than that."

"Heat?" Lauren asked, picking up her fork. "It's barely seventy."

Smiling at the outlander and her strange notions, Emily removed a sheet of scones from the oven. She scooped them into a basket and, with a squeal of chair legs across linoleum, sat down.

The older woman was getting the raw end of the deal, facing Lauren's pale, sagging face rather than the window. At least, Lauren assumed her face was pale and sagging. She hadn't dared check herself out in the mirror when she unpacked in the cozy bedroom upstairs.

She forked up a chunk of yellow omelet oozing golden cheese. The salt-savory flavors melted on her tongue. The scone was crusty and airy both, and the red jam was sweet with the memory of ripe strawberries. Bliss. Paradise. Valhalla. Or, since this was Scotland, Tir nan Og, the Celtic Otherworld, island of eternal youth and beauty.

Lauren was young, although she was catching glimpses of her thirtieth birthday like a storm cloud on the horizon. As for beauty, her long nose, generous mouth, and deep-set brown eyes were too strong for contemporary tastes, and despite the application of diet and exercise, her body was shaped more like an old-fashioned hourglass than a trendy stick.

And her hair! Stylishly sleek and smooth it wasn't. The thick russet-brown waves hung like a theater curtain down her neck, pulling her chin up and her head back. She might as well wear it long. Short, it made her look like she'd crawled off Dr. Frankenstein's electric operating table.

Both her father and her grandfather had hair as bright and unruly. Men of their respective generations, the one had worn his in a crew-cut even into the hirsute eighties, and the other had pasted his down with the contemporary equivalent of bear-grease. Although at the end, Grandpa's hair had lost its texture and color and become spider webs clinging to his naked skull.

Between her appearance and her imagination, not to mention a tendency toward gravity beyond her years, Lauren had spent her adolescence half-paralyzed by self-consciousness. Then, in college, she'd discovered art history. The ever-changing images of beauty and varieties of imagination proved that the times were out of joint, not her. Encouraged, she'd stumbled into a part-time job sitting for Life Drawing classes, not in the nude—she hadn't abandoned all her inhibitions—but in garments and draperies that would have swallowed a lesser woman.

The rustle of paper, the soft scrape of pencils, the teacher's murmured instructions reminded her of medieval monks copying their psalms beside the cloister walk. Posing was meditation, not vanity, she assured herself. And the finished sketches were a revelation, the images not capturing her soul but releasing it.

Her mother, as mothers did, told her to straighten to her full five foot nine and carry herself like a queen. But it wasn't until she saw the lush, romantic sketches of herself as Guinevere, or Cleopatra, or Helen of Troy, that Lauren felt regal instead of ungainly. Not that she intended to launch any ships, but she supposed that Helen hadn't intended to, either.

Then there were the sketches that she laughed about with her girlfriends, the ones that made her resemble a clown or a cow, Nicole would say, or Picasso's worst nightmare, Rachel teased.

Well, the occasional reality check factored into self-acceptance. Like the occasional scone, calories be damned. By the time Lauren mopped up the last morsels and drained her second cup of tea—strong life-giving caffeine and carbs, none of this lettuce leaf fear-of-food business—sanity was in her grasp.

She put down her fork and looked up at Emily. Who was, once again, looking at her.

It was Emily who was sane. No make-up concealed the jovial creases of her cousin's apple cheeks or the clarity of her blue-gray eyes. Her wiry silver hair was cut short and her blocky body was swathed in a loose blouse and canvas pants. She wore no jewelry except for a wedding band, worn and scratched, that she probably couldn't remove over the chapped knuckles and plain, square-cut nails of hands, she'd told Lauren, that had sheared sheep and stacked hay bales.

Her appearance was every bit as no-nonsense as her personality, well-grounded. Like Lauren's mother, Emily would never allow anything weird to sneak up on her. Lauren had to satisfy Emily's conspicuous curiosity about her young relative without revealing the metaphysical facet of her persona, her recurring dream. Emily wouldn't believe that. She might even retreat with a shudder of revulsion and a dismissive sneer.

"Thank you for taking me in like this," Lauren said. "Nothing like having a second cousin or whatever it is appear out of nowhere."

"My granny was Susanna's sister Florence, meaning we're second cousins twice removed or something of that nature. No matter. I'm delighted you've come. Donald mentioned your name in his first letter—you're his only grandchild, aren't you now?"

"Yes. My father was an only child, and so am I. The family tree's more of a shrub."

"You're using the past tense about your own father, now."

"He's been gone a long time." Lauren stuck to the facts and just the facts. "Grandpa was my father, he always came to my piano recitals and spelling bees."

"That was very good of him."

"I think he felt responsible for . . ."

Emily let the unfinished sentence twist slowly between them.

"Well," said Lauren, with what she meant to be a casual shrug but was more of a galvanic jerk, "even Grandpa used to say that my dad was away with the fairies. That's a Scottish idiom, isn't it? He probably got it from his own father. Away with the fairies, you know, a little too, um, imaginative."

"Ah," Emily said under her breath, and then, louder, "Oh aye, it's meaning that, right enough. Though the young people nowadays are using 'away with the fairies' meaning 'drunk' or 'drugged'."

The last crumbs of the scone turned to ashes in Lauren's mouth. Surely Grandpa didn't know the more recent transatlantic version. Surely his "away with the fairies" was not the equivalent of telling a child that the stork brought babies, a fable covering an inconvenient truth. Her mother's despairing "nuts" was bad enough, cutting too close to the bone. To add "drunk" . . .

An electronic bleat made her look around. Emily reached across to a sideboard, plucked a portable phone from its combination base and answering machine, and responded with her number.

Lauren cleared her throat by draining her cup of tea down it. Saved by the bleat from revealing the details of Donny's—Donald Junior's—disappearance when she had been all of nine years old.

He and his father had never gotten along. They were too much alike, her mother said, although even she thought Donald was charmingly eccentric, while Donny's alcohol-fueled music-and-poetry weirdness had been the contributing factor in the divorce. Whether recent advances in drug or cognitive therapy might have helped him didn't matter. Neither did it matter whether Mom's practicality was a response to, or a contributing factor in, Donny's madness. He was gone, as completely as though he'd been abducted by aliens. Or fairies.

"Oh aye, she's arrived," Emily was saying. "Genealogy and Blackness Tower, right enough." And, a moment later, "I'll be telling her. Cheers." Punching a button on the phone, she laid it on the table and explained to Lauren, "Rosemary Gillock, she's a librarian at the public library. She's saying she'd be pleased to help you with your inquiries, refer you to the Local Family History group and the like, accustomed as she is to colonials looking out their ancestors."

So Emily had been telling her friends that Lauren was coming. Her visit was a big event. *Okay. No problem.*

She smiled at "colonials." "That's nice of her. Although I don't have much to go on. Grandpa knew squat about his family, as we'd say in Texas. His father, John, flat refused to talk about his parents. He didn't have any photos, he never got any letters, nothing. All he said was that he'd come from the Auld Country, Scotland, in 1907, and good riddance to it. He might just as well have been conceived in a Petri dish."

"I'm sorry I exchanged no more than three letters with Donald before he passed on. A fine old chap, he seemed to be."

"A shame he never got the hang of e-mail. Y'all could have gotten to know each other. But then, you don't have e-mail either."

"The computers, they're mysterious creatures. I've learned the workings of the till at the shop, and the calculator, and the remote for the telly. Those will do. That telephone, I have troubles enough with that."

And Lauren felt empty-handed without her computer and cell phone. No calls, no instant messaging, no texting. No keeping in touch with friends who were willing to cut her—call it dreaminess—some slack. But her phone wasn't set up to work here and her laptop didn't need to be dragged a quarter of the way around the world.

That world had changed more in a hundred years than it had in centuries before that. Being out of touch for two weeks wasn't comparable to immigrants never seeing their friends and relatives again. For them, heading out to another country was almost like dying.

"What of the skull watch, then?" Emily prompted, her head tilted like a bird's.

Her pose made Lauren feel like a worm. "During the Depression, Grandpa and his older sister were scouring the house for things to sell. They found the watch in John's wardrobe. Their mother didn't even know about it. John wouldn't sell it, even though the money would have tided them over some hard times. Grandpa said that was the only time John ever said anything about his mother, when he told them the skull had been hers."

"That's all?" Emily asked quickly. "There's no more than that?"

"That's all. Grandpa figured there'd been a scandal or a tragedy in Susanna's life. But he didn't have the time and resources to do any research until recently, and then he didn't have the energy to travel. I found some stuff on the Internet about Clan Mackay, but it wasn't until Grandpa hired a guy named Hawkins at Scotland's Folk in Edinburgh that he got anything about Susanna herself."

Emily's gaze didn't waver from Lauren's face.

Maybe the older woman was having more trouble understanding Lauren's accent than Lauren was understanding hers—not for nothing had she been watching A&E and BBC America. She tried to speak more clearly. "What got Grandpa going was finding out John wasn't born a Reay. He changed his name from Mackay when he got to the U.S. in July of 1907. Since his birthday's the same as mine, May 7, he was barely fifteen. Just a kid, all alone. His birth certificate, registry entry, whatever, listed his mother as Susanna Mackay." Lauren pronounced the name the way Emily had, as *muhkeye*, to rhyme with the organ of sight. "By the way, do you even know how Susanna died?"

"She died." Emily glanced down only long enough to line her fork and her knife diagonally across her plate.

"Oh. Well, John's birth certificate says she was a spinster of Reay Parish. That's it."

"Aye," said Emily with a sigh, "John was illegitimate. And the shame of it on his head as well as his mother's, that being the custom in the old days. He might have wished for that Petri dish, had he known about such things."

That was it, Lauren told herself. Emily thought she'd be sensitive about John. But she wasn't in her seventies and nostalgic for the fifties. "No wonder he headed out for less judgmental climates. It wasn't like today, when having a baby without getting married is standard procedure."

"That changed round and about the time 'spinster' became 'bachelorette'," Emily said, not betraying any nostalgia, either. "It looks like being scandal and tragedy both. Donald was a wee bit embarrassed about that, I'm thinking."

"I'm thinking so, too." Lauren was embarrassed about her own father's scandal, tragedy, mystery—she changed her opinion of it daily. Some days she was angry and resentful. Some days she felt compassion. But no reaction, positive or negative, would bring Donny back.

Emily drained the teapot into Lauren's cup and nudged the milk pitcher and sugar bowl in her direction.

"Susanna was born July 12, 1870, died February 2, 1907, and was buried at St. Bride's Chapel, Black Ness," Lauren recited. "Grandpa liked to think she was a lady of good breeding since she was descended from the James Mackay who built Blackness Tower, especially since *he* was related to the branch of the Mackays that was the Lords Reay. I bet John chose his last name from the village, though. Of course one of the early Lords Reay was reputed to be a wizard, which makes sense . . ." *Oops*. Once again she'd almost said too much. Damn her tiredness, and Emily's kindness, and a full stomach.

"Quite so." Emily leaned forward. "That's likely why another Lord Reay busied himself studying Highland Second Sight. The Seeing Gift, it's called. He exchanged some right interesting letters with Samuel Pepys on the subject, round and about 1700 or so."

"Oh." Leaning back, Lauren picked up her cup and this time drank the tea straight up, straight down, letting its astringency clear away any lingering fat—and any lingering fancies as well.

Emily waited a moment, then, when Lauren offered nothing else, started clearing the table. "Any road, by the time Susanna came along, the Mackay lands in Strathnaver had been sold to the Lords Sutherland."

"That's how David Sutherland got Blackness Tower? He inherited it?"

"No, he bought the place from Caithness County Council on the cheap, agreeing to restore it."

"You know him?"

"He stops by the shop for the odd soup spoon and the like. An officer and a gentleman, he is, though he keeps himself to himself, no matter the lasses making eyes at him."

The man must be attractive in appearance, then, if not in personality. And she'd been expecting a grizzled old goat.

Well, he had to be at least middle-aged, to be retired. He was probably one of those crusty military types. And wealthy enough to make him attractive. No matter, Lauren would be knocking on his door tomorrow. Or staking it out, if he tried to keep on ignoring her, although there was always the possibility he didn't know anything that would help her.

Gathering together her plate and cup, Lauren stood up. "I interrupted you. By the time Susanna came along . . ."

"The Mackay lands were sold, the Reay title had gone to a relative in the Netherlands, and the family was known mostly for its piety."

The zeal of the convert? Or protective coloring? Lauren knew about protective coloring.

Maybe the weirdness in the family tree had blown like a dead leaf to America and landed, tickling, on the back of her own neck. Highland Second Sight. The Seeing Gift. That part of her that was her mother's child said, *don't go there*. But her father's child, a Reay, a Mackay, was long accustomed to going on treks over the hills and far away.

She laid her dishes beside the sink, then walked over to the window. The light was thinning, tinting land, sea, and sky with pastel colors. A couple strolled along the walkway that edged the bay. With a distant buzz like a mosquito, a jet-ski sliced across the water, trailing a white plume that rained down to puncture the lazy blue swells.

Lauren slumped against the sill. She was a long way from home, she was tired, she was alone with a woman who seemed kindly enough, but who kept looking at her with the intensity of a cat waiting at a mouse hole.

Maybe, unlike her friend at the library, Emily had never met an American before. Or maybe there was some dark secret perched like a raven in the branches of the family tree that Emily didn't want her to find out.

Right. Lauren herself was the one with the dark secret. Speaking of which . . .

She turned away from the window, picked up the dishtowel, and asked casually, "Second Sight. That's like ESP, right? Except the seers only see the future. And they have, er, waking visions, not dreams."

"Sometimes having the Sight simply means seeing the invisible," Emily replied, "whether backwards, forwards, or sideways. Visions, dreams, call it what you like. Supposedly families passed on Second Sight, generation to generation. Your Donald was right interested in that, wasn't he?"

"Well . . ." She tried a dismissive laugh, but it barely passed her lips. "He said he never dreamed, though I think he just never remembered his dreams. Maybe that was in self-defense—his father had nightmares that he never talked about. And then there was my dad, he was a musician, a poet. You—ah—you have to wonder what a modern psychotherapist would have done with the old seers."

"You canna reason away the uncanny, it's with us always."

The uncanny was with some people more than others, Lauren thought, only to have a sudden beeping noise jerk her around.

Emily grabbed the phone and jabbed at it, her expression that of a bomb-disposal expert ripping out a trigger. The beeping stopped. With a frustrated sigh, she restored the phone to its docking port. "Punched the wrong button and didn't sever the connection. As I was saying, these modern electronic devices are a bit much for me." She returned to the sink, rescued a wet plate, and held it out.

Taking a deep breath—*calm down*—Lauren burnished the dish until it shone. The circular motion of her cloth made her head spin. Tired. Depressed, even. Well, that was jet lag.

She found something else to say. "Thanks for turning up that old book, the one that says Susanna lived at Blackness Tower the same time as Francis Weir and Rupert Beckwith, the painters. Grandpa was thrilled about that. Or as thrilled as he could be, when he was fading so fast."

"Ah, it's Charles Innes in the shop next to mine who needs thanking. Mind you, he thinks himself no small beer, but he's a dab hand with the old books. There's me, thinking he might have a source, and right enough, he recognized Susanna's name straightaway. He swapped me the old book for a new carving knife. Quite a nice one, Solingen steel. It's in the sitting room, you can have a go at it after the washing-up."

Lauren assumed she meant the book, not the knife, was waiting in the sitting room. Good. Burying her head in a book meant she could avoid any more conversation without being rude.

"I've not had the time to read more than a few pages," Emily went on. "Slow going it is, and then some. Still, there's Susanna sitting for paintings as Guinevere and as Helen of Troy and—there was another. Morgan le Fay. Her sitting might have been a wee bit scandal itself, if she was a lady rather than a woman."

Lauren grinned. Emily should teach a Women's Studies course . . . *Oh*.

Susanna, too, had sat for paintings of Guinevere and Helen of Troy.

CHAPTER THREE

That Lauren herself sat for sketches, not paintings, and for students, not for professional artists, was a distinction so feeble that it didn't begin to stop those psychic feet from pacing again across her grave. This time, though, it wasn't a chill that trickled down her spine but sweat, as though she'd fallen into a fever . . .

Dream.

She wasn't feverish. Seventy degrees *was* warm, when the house was built to keep the heat in. Only two small panels atop the kitchen window could be opened, and they admitted no more than a periodic cool breath. Lauren forced her attention back to Emily.

"Near as I can tell, everyone in my branch of the family led lives of unsurpassed propriety, so dull no one could be bothered to write about them, Lord Reay or no Lord Reay stirring his newts like Macbeth's witches in the family tree. And yet . . ."

Lauren had to ask. "And yet?"

"My granny told stories of Blackness Tower. Of Black Ness itself, come to that, and St. Bride's Hope, the bay just behind, though she only rarely ever mentioned Susanna. An unlucky place, Black Ness, she'd say. It still is—my cousin Tam's farmhouse burned to the ground not five years since."

"Things happen." Lauren repeated Emily's own words.

"Aye, they do that. Like as not my cousin left his cigarette smoldering. Still, folk are never falling over the cliffs or boats smashing against the rocks by chance, no, it's all ghosts, fairies, selkies. The usual tales, if not so usual when you've got a personal connection to . . ." Well." Not looking at Lauren—very carefully not looking at Lauren, for once—Emily took the dishtowel and draped it over a rack. "There. Let's have us a sit-down."

Ghosts, fairies, selkies. Washing them down the drain was an exercise in futility. They'd peer out at you from the P-trap, beady eyes glistening. Maybe Emily could see them, after all. Her practical acceptance of the uncanny, if that's what it was, might open up new vistas, hints of unexplored lands and strange customs. But Lauren wasn't about to ask. That would be like asking a new acquaintance how much she weighed, or what she liked in the way of sex.

Silently, she let Emily guide her into a living room and seat her on a couch. From there she eyed the modest, comfortable furnishings and their patina of personal items, photos of Emily and her late husband and the children, vacation souvenirs, books and magazines, plants on the windowsill that reflected in the glass like ghosts of the bushes and flowers outside. A clock ticked on the mantelpiece, above an electric fire and below a framed print of Highlanders dancing in swirls of tartan. The room was pleasant. Domestic. Tidy, more so than Lauren's apartment with its nests of books and stashes of chocolate. More so than Lauren's life right now.

Emily handed her a book, switched on a lamp, and, murmuring excuses about accounts to settle, sat down at a desk in the corner.

Lauren pried the musty pages apart. Even when she turned them toward the light, the type crowded onto the sepia-edged paper swam before her eyes. The name "Susanna" did not jump out at her, although the name "Francis Weir" did. A faded black and white photograph tipped into the book was labeled in microscopic type as one of his paintings. Lauren turned the book from side to side, and finally decided that the title was "Catherine's Destiny."

Catherine? Of Aragon? De Medici? The Great? She remembered no mythological Catherines, unless you counted two saints, one known for being martyred on a wheel, the other for starving herself for God. The painting must depict some private-citizen Catherine.

Lauren could see little more than a woman's figure clothed in a long gown, hair streaming over her shoulders, framed by an archway. Judging by the angle of her head and set of her shoulders, she was peering intently and yet warily outwards, like a diver debating her leap. She lifted a rounded object in her outstretched hands. A large egg? An apple? Probably not a baseball.

What was she looking at? All Lauren could make out were a few faint lines against a murky background.

Francis Weir and his colleague, poet and painter Rupert Beckwith, had been late disciples of the Pre-Raphaelite movement, devoted to idealizing nature and romanticizing the past. Perhaps with the revival of artists such as Rossetti, Millais, Holman Hunt, Waterhouse, and Burne-Jones, Weir and Beckwith's reputations would be rehabilitated. Although that wasn't going to produce any information about Susanna in the next two weeks, before the return date on Lauren's plane ticket.

She closed the book. Its title and author had been embossed in gilded letters on the binding, but now only a dusting of gold looked like King Midas's acne on the disintegrating leather. Squinting, she read, *Life and Times*, by Gideon Bremner.

The title was dull, the book far past its prime. Still, the book dealer might have been able to sell it for a lot more than a carving knife was worth. "Why did Mr. Innes agree to a swap?" Lauren asked. "This book is pretty valuable."

"Eh? Is it then?" Emily asked. Her reading glasses glinted in the evening's glow. "Charles is keen on the history of Blackness Tower and was right pleased to hear you were coming. And he's a wee bit eccentric as well."

That kind of eccentricity wouldn't cause a blip on Lauren's normality radar. "Let me pay you for the book."

"Ah no, lass, it's yours. A welcome home gift."

Home? "Oh. Well, thank you very much." Lauren made a mental note to send Emily a book of Ansel Adams photos or something similar and turned back to the book she held.

Who was Gideon Bremner, anyway? What was he to Susanna and the artists, and what life had he led that he felt compelled to write about it, the compulsion to write about it being unrelated to anyone's wanting to read it? Although Lauren did want to read it, her eyelids were lead-weighted, and her head seemed too heavy for her neck.

She made one last effort. The flyleaf was water-stained but otherwise pristine, not inscribed. She recognized the publisher as one long out of business. Laboriously she converted the date of publication, "MDCCCXCVIII," to "1898." The chapters were listed by numbers, except for an appendix with the intriguing title of "Superstitions of the Scottish Highlands."

Intriguing, yes. Maybe even important to her quest. But she'd lapsed into illiteracy for the moment. Setting the book down on the coffee table, Lauren considered her options.

Grandpa's agent in Edinburgh had milked the public records for all they were worth, or so he had said when Lauren contacted him, but she had multiple sources in

Thurso. Maybe, she thought with a yawn, she should just take out an ad in the local newspaper: "Bewildered American searching for dirty linen."

"Have a look at the telly," said Emily.

"Thank you." Lauren surfed through the four available channels but saw nothing except her own thoughts. Conscious thoughts, under her control, not visions. She wondered if Emily had actually met anyone with the Sight. If, confronted with the loose cannon of such awareness, she would retreat toward the drugstore and the psychotherapist's couch.

Grandpa had discussed Lauren's dream with her, even whether it was ESP, the Sight, whatever. But he was gone now. A lot was gone. There should be a statute of limitations on how many parts of your life you could lose in the space of less than a year—Grandpa, Craig, her job.

Although, to be brutally honest—and she'd gotten good at brutal honesty, like a cold shower after an erotic dream—she might have formatted high school yearbooks and coffee-table art and photography tomes until she withered and blew away like the flowers on Grandpa's grave. After all, gainful employment was nothing to be abandoned lightly, not even to fulfill her promise, and most especially not to chase the wild goose of her dream.

And, while she was being honest, she admitted it was easier to have lost Grandpa to death than to have lost Craig when he dumped her a couple of months before the wedding, telling her she was too shy, too spooky, too screwed up. Even though she'd never been entirely honest with him.

On the television, dissolving images of castles, standing stones, and antique portraits indicated the beginning of a history show. *Sweet!* Lauren pried her eyelids further open.

The camera panned past the sagging black and white facade of a half-timbered house to a man wearing a pricey leather bomber jacket. "I'm Magnus Anderson," he said in a deep, unmistakably North American, voice. "This week we've brought our instruments to Mumford Manor in Sussex, where legends of a ghostly nun have persisted for almost five centuries."

Magnus. Odd name for an American or Canadian. He was of Orcadian ancestry, maybe, with St. Magnus and everything. His features were craggy, assembled from disparate and assertive elements: an arched nose, a wide mouth, ears peeking coyly from carrot-red hair. A tidy goatee provided the centrifugal force that held his face together and framed a grin that was neither innocent nor ironic.

"Later on in the program, we'll investigate Glastonbury Tor, supposedly shaped into a three-dimensional labyrinth by the same ancient hands that built Stonehenge and Avebury stone circles. This is *The Paranormal Files*, where science meets superstition. Spooks and specters, haunts and hags, bogles, boggarts, and blights—we have them all in our sights."

What, Lauren thought, no fairies? And what was a blight? Like the blighted heath where Macbeth met the three witches? Or was that a blasted heath? A yawn almost split her face in two.

Tomorrow and tomorrow and tomorrow was another day, another chance to get in touch with her uncanny side. Lauren switched off the TV and heaved herself off the couch. "I'm turning in before I pass out and you need a fork-lift to get me into bed."

"Good night, then. Sleep well," Emily returned with a smile free of the—expectation?—that had been its subtext the rest of the day.

Upstairs, Lauren levered the bedroom window outward and tasted the cool air and its strange scents, smoke, fish, salt, frying bacon. A car drove past. Several people strolled along the walkway. A trailing skein of music faded into the thrum of the sea and the slow blink of the lighthouse watched over the bay. The crest of each parallel wave was edged with pink or peach, so that the sea shimmered like watered silk, the fabric of fairy banners, perhaps. Above the indistinct smudge of Orkney the sky glowed a clear indigo sheened with silver.

Morgan le Fay, the witch, the enchantress, a relative of King Arthur's as well as his nemesis. Hadn't she come from Orkney? Maybe the "Fay" meant "fairy," signaling her occult powers, as well as "fey," that antique word that meant knowing your fate, knowing you were doomed. But then, "doom" circled back to fate or destiny. Like Catherine's destiny. Like walking in a dream, unreal.

Lauren collapsed gratefully onto the bed. The pillowcase smelled of fresh air. She closed her eyes . . .

. . . and was walking down from Blackness Tower, the wind whipping at her, tugging her hair loose from its bindings and setting her skirts to flapping madly around her legs. She stumbled over stones and heather roots, slipping in the mud, drawn toward the precipice overlooking the sea.

Cold salt spray stung her cheeks and her eyes watered. Mountainous gray-green waves dashed themselves to froth on the shelves of slate below, were sucked back into the depths, hurled themselves forward again. They thundered in invisible caverns beneath her feet, so that the rock itself shuddered, threatening to throw her over the rim of earth into the tormented water.

Shouts echoed from the cliffs. Then a beam of sunlight broke through clouds as turbulent as the sea, picking out a ship wallowing in the waves. Its high stern glinted with furtive bits of gold still clinging to weathered and stained wood. Its masts were broken, their jagged tips reeling against the sky. Human figures clung to its heeling deck.

The waves drove the ship against the rocks, slowly, slowly, crushing the smooth curve of the hull, overthrowing and splintering the stumps of the masts, casting the men into the water or against the rocks like so many gutted fish. The shriek of rending wood, the cries of the doomed men, the howl of the wind mingled in Lauren's ears and swirled inside her skull.

And the ground she stood on fell away, sending her spiraling down the glassy sides of a whirlpool into blue-green depths where deformed creatures swam. She screamed but made no sound, or else she screamed but her cry was swallowed by the other noises . . .

The dream drained into an abyssal silence and she woke up with a gasp, drenched in sweat cold as the sea spray. The static air felt clammy against her skin. The last echo of that wail of lost souls twisted in her gut like a demon taking possession of her body.

She lay blinking into the darkness until her breaths lengthened and her heartbeat slowed. She was in Emily's house. She was in Scotland. She was here at last. She was alone.

She had dreamed the familiar dream. But now it wasn't of a mysterious landscape, tinted with melancholy, it was of pain and horror so immediate, so personal, that her head spun.

It was only a dream, she told herself. It was only a nightmare. It wasn't real.

A repetitive noise broke the silence. The rhythmic drip of water from a faucet? No, the bathroom was down the hall. It wasn't raining outside. The sound was muffled but unmistakably there, close by.

A sudden silvery chime, like a ripple of crystal, jerked Lauren to her feet, toes curling on the cool carpeted floor and every follicle erect. Slowly, fearfully, knowing she had no option but to look, she sidled across the room to the dresser and opened the bottom drawer. She lifted out the red velvet box and, standing in the attitude of the woman in the painting, posed like Catherine at her door or window, she flipped up its lid.

The watch was ticking, beating a cadence steadier than that of her own heart. It had chimed midnight, the witching hour.

She lifted her forefinger as if to touch the silver gilt forehead—*who are you, what are you?*

Lauren curled her forefinger back against her palm, slammed the box and thrust it into the drawer. She closed the window, darting only one glance toward the smoked-glass swells of the bay. She saw the slow, wise blink of the lighthouse on its far side. She did not see the galleon, gliding silently, illuminated not by stars or moon but by the ashen faces of its doomed crew.

The ship hadn't raced to destruction in the bay, though, but in the open sea, on the windward side of Black Ness.

Shivering with more than cold, she threw herself back into the bed and pulled the covers up to her nose. The watch had been activated by joggling around in her bag, that was all. Not by her dream. Not by her arrival here. Besides, the bedside clock said one-twenty, not midnight. The watch was wrong. So there.

And something deep in her mind seemed to whisper back, *no, here.*

CHAPTER FOUR

Lauren edged Emily's small car onto the main road, making a right turn more than wide enough to end up in the left lane. Left correct, she instructed herself. Right wrong.

Righting a wrong was why she was here. Reclaiming the family ties denied John Reay, born Mackay, illegitimate son. Redeeming the shame visited upon Susanna, who had not, after all, conceived her child without the aid and abetment of a man.

At least, righting a wrong seemed a less self-centered justification than assaying the truth of her dream. Than searching for her identity.

Lauren could cope with the steering wheel on the right and driving on the left. If concentration wasn't exactly her strong point, then tenacity was, even if Craig had called it stubbornness. But thank goodness the brake pedal was in its accustomed spot on the left and the accelerator on the right.

After a mile without mishap, she spared a glance past her white knuckles and the bumper of the car ahead. Great puffs of clouds like whipped-cream galleons sailed the depths of heaven, trailing shadows across the green and gold of the fields. To her right the deep blue of the sea was empty of ships, whether dream-sailed or diesel-powered. To her left rose blue-tinted mountains, their horizon so distant they seemed as unattainable as the peaks of Orkney. Blotches of purplish-pink brushed the low rolling hills ahead—the blooming heather of song and story, no doubt.

Past Dounreay Nuclear Reactor with its science-fictional buildings, and Reay with its antique cottages, Lauren made another perilous, across-traffic turn onto the lane leading to Black Ness. There stood the blackened shell of a stone farmhouse, overgrown with weeds, that must belong to Emily's luckless cousin Tam.

With a sympathetic shake of her head, Lauren drove on between fences of lichened stone slabs set on end, and stopped at the patch of asphalt where the road ended.

The Range Rover that had been parked there yesterday was gone. *Great.* If Sutherland wasn't home, there went any chance of talking her way into the Tower. So much for her dress-to-impress tailored wool pants and coordinating jacket over a silk blouse and chunky necklace. She might just as well have worn jeans and an art school tee.

Three new vehicles occupied the puddle-pocked blacktop, one of them a battered panel van. The archaeologists must have arrived, then. Well, that was some compensation. Lauren hoisted her bag, whether of tricks or treats—and now including Gideon Bremner's peeling testament—and climbed the hill.

In the field beside the path a dozen black and white birds sat in a circle looking like avian dignitaries at a summit meeting, except for the orange soda straws they had for beaks. The tower posed against its backdrop of sky, sea, and island, the morning sunlight casting its shadow like a pointing finger toward the chapel.

A cool, brisk breeze rippled the hair she had bundled back with a silk scarf. Behind her, the black and white birds took to the air, their repetitive cries less harsh than a gull's and more insistent than a dove's. The sound strummed her senses with something that was both memory and dread, and inside her bag the watch trilled, evoking ghostly church bells.

It was no longer ticking this morning, if it ever had been.

She couldn't see the breakers frothing at the feet of the cliffs, but she didn't have to. The galleon rending on the rocks, the desperate cries of the men, the cold gale and the colder water sucking her down—the scene rubbed a blister on her senses. Had any of the men caught between stone and sea survived?

Had the wreck actually happened?

Ships often came to grief in the Pentland Firth, the narrow passage between Orkney and the mainland. These waters betrayed ships with tidal rips and whirlpools rumored to be witches' cauldrons, and with foul winds generated by those same witches. No surprise she'd dream about a wreck. Or hallucinate about a spooky watch, for that matter. Her new dream meant only that she'd been overwhelmed yesterday, short on sleep and long on fat and salt and emotion.

Rationality might be as much a default as having the brake pedal on the left, she told herself, but she was still driving on the wrong side of the road.

She looked toward the chapel to see several people standing outside its wall, their youthful, casually posed bodies clothed in windbreakers and jeans, their faces turned toward a man wearing a wide-brimmed, slouch-style hat. His right hand made gestures as though with chalk on a blackboard. His left held a canvas bag, tapping it against legs clad in well-worn jeans.

With a glance and a promise at the tower, Lauren took the path to the chapel.

Today the sheep gathered at the far end of the field, woolly shoulders turned to the proceedings. A bedraggled gray bundle against the slate fence might be a dead one, although Lauren tried to convince herself it was asleep and dreaming it was running across a bluebonnet-filled pasture in Texas.

A couple of the students, dig team, whatever, looked around at her, then back at the man with the hat. He took no notice. With his jeans, knit pullover, and muddy boots, he didn't appear any different from the others, except for the greater breadth of his shoulders and depth of his chest. Those, and his attitude—erect, even formal—signaled Alpha Male, Leader of the Pack.

He was saying, ". . . Caithness might have been a foreign country, so far as the rest of Scotland was concerned. The politicians in Edinburgh were thinking we were all barbarians wearing blue paint instead of proper trews. They're still thinking that, mind."

Lauren snickered along with the rest of the group.

The lecturer darted a glance in her direction, revealing two oddly pale eyes gleaming in the shadow of the hat. Pitching his Scots-accented voice not loudly but more deeply, cutting through the murmur of wind and wave, he went on, "Till quite recently, most travel in these parts was by ship. No surprise Orkney was a territory of Norway. So was this northern coast, as the names reveal. We've got the Norse 'ness' for headland, 'hope' for bay, and the like. Academically, names can only contribute so much, but they're evidence, just the same."

Names, Lauren thought, had power. Magic. A *glamour*, to use the fine old Scottish word.

"This chapel is twelfth century, the earliest ecclesiastical foundation in Caithness. A Norse foundation, though dedicated to which saint we dinna ken, nor are we likely to, save by a miraculous apparition." The lecturer snorted his opinion of miracles and/or apparitions. "The Celts sharing these parts with the Norse dedicated the chapel to St. Bride, Bridget of Ireland, who was perhaps the pagan goddess Brighid, who in turn has roots in the Celtic triple goddess—maiden, mother, crone. No, you canna tell the players in these stories even with a program. The attribution explains why the chapel's known as Ladykirk, and the bay behind Black Ness is St. Bride's Hope."

Rats, Lauren thought. She'd seen "Bride's Hope" on the map and imagined all sorts of romantic backstories. But it was just a trick of nomenclature, like Reay, like Mackay. Next he'd say that "Black Ness" itself . . .

"The 'black' of Black Ness comes from the Norse 'flaik', meaning 'fence'. A prehistoric fort occupied this headland. You can see bits of stone walls or fences in the turf, if you've got a good eye and wee bit imagination. I'm planning a go at one of the mounds or cairns, but just now it's the chapel that needs digging." The lecturer— the commander-in-chief—began to issue orders.

Lauren scanned the headland. Yes, low ridges rose, fell, curved around tumbled mounds covering—what? Ancient graves giving rise to Emily's ghost stories? The occasional damp stone peered from beneath the grass thatch like an animal from its den.

As much as she wanted the name "Black Ness"—and by the mutation of the English language, "Blackness"—to refer to fell deeds and hair-raising legends, she'd long ago decided that the name came from something as simple as the color of the slate forming the cliffs. That, however, was a honey-gray. A name referring back to the original inhabitants was just as good. The faceless, voiceless prehistoric men hadn't lacked deeds, not to mention legend.

She saw them huddling behind their walls, around a fire that drove back the cold as well as the unnamable fears of the surrounding darkness, telling stories. Dreaming dreams. Searching for meaning and identity.

A male voice as crisp and cold as the ice crust on old snow spoke in her ear. "So you're here already, are you now? Well then, you're obliged to wait your turn."

Lauren spun around to face the man in the hat, staring into a square face, broad of brow, strong of chin. The wrinkles edging his ash-gray eyes and the ruddiness of his cheeks testified to the hours he'd spent outside in the wind and sun, while the furrows in his forehead beneath his tilted-back hat bore witness to the hours he'd spent crouched over computers and microscopes. She assumed he had a mouth, since he'd spoken with it, but now his lips were compressed to a horizontal line.

Just her luck, to find her way blocked by someone with a highly developed territorial imperative. How could he possibly know who she was and what she wanted?

She drew herself up. "I'm Lauren Reay. I'm a cousin of Emily Brodie from Thurso. I'm here doing genealogical research. My grandfather's grandmother is buried in the graveyard. Her name was Susanna Mackay."

"Ah," he said, with a subtle tremor of his facial muscles. "You're not with the TV swine, then."

Lauren tilted her head, but he looked just the same from that angle—not at all embarrassed, as though his mistake was her problem. "TV?"

"Ewan Calder, archaeologist," he interrupted. He seized her hand, squeezed it, let it go. "My assistant, Bryony, she looked you out, did she?"

"What?" Lauren's hand tingled from the pressure of his, work-roughened, warm, and solid. She tucked it into her pocket.

"We were after getting permission before we made a start on the dig."

"Permission?"

The muscle coiled in his jaw. He was getting more and more impatient with her, when it was his own assumptions that were causing the problem.

Lauren seized her wits, sat them down, and told them to behave. "You're excavating the cemetery. You need permission from the families of the people buried there."

"The folk most recently buried—your Susanna's one of the oldest." A subtle shift in Calder's expression, less a softening of his jaw than a re-alignment, signaled his impatience turning back on itself. "We've missed you out, then, you and your cousin as well. I'm a lecturer at the University of Stirling, thinking, for my sins, that this would make a fine learning opportunity for my students."

Some people, Lauren thought, might interpret excavating a cemetery as grave-robbing, not opportunity. His students wouldn't dig up broken pots but the bones of her own great-great grandmother, the remnants of a lived-in body, the cast-off shell of a mind, a spirit, a soul.

Because of that interpretation, she had power over him. He didn't have to know that digging up Susanna's grave might serve her own purpose. Maybe, for example, she'd been buried with a locket containing a picture of her lover.

Lauren summoned her most gracious smile. "No problem. I can see how you didn't find us."

"We've checked over the records and made the geophysical surveys. I've laid out the trenches. There's nowt left but the hard labor, the actual digging of the graves. What's left of them." Calder gestured a command toward the students.

She hadn't realized how square he was holding his shoulders until they relaxed, although even relaxed they didn't come close to resembling the curving spines of the youths, male and female, who filed by carrying shovels, sieves, plastic bins, and wooden boxes.

Behind the students came a not-quite-so-young black-haired woman carrying a computer and a couple of clipboards. Eyeing Lauren curiously, she repeated Calder's peremptory wave.

Lauren looked back at him. He was looking at her, his eyes in the shade of his hat as neutral as sunglasses. He was middling height for a man, but still he seemed to be viewing her from a height—one of importance, perhaps, reminding her he was not a petitioner, but an expert, a professional. His lips appeared, stretched into a small, stiff smile. He took a step back.

He wasn't going to get away that easily. Not once she'd found the chink in his armor—her family connections. "Which grave is Susanna's? The one with the angel statue?"

"That's marking the Bremner plot. Susanna's stone is just outwith the door of the chapel."

So she hadn't been part of the family. But then, the pre-Raphaelite artists had delighted in using working women as their models, probably all too aware of Emily's distinction between "lady" and "woman." "Gideon Bremner," Lauren repeated. "He owned Blackness Tower. Who was he?"

"Merchant and manufacturer. Descended from boatbuilders on his father's side and Glasgow tobacco lords on his mother's, with an English cotton mill or two for extras. He bought the Tower near to collapsing, repaired it, invited in his artist friends from the south, and finally died there."

"So he wasn't intimidated by the tales of fairies and ghosts and everything?"

"Not a bit of it. He and his salon, they made a meal of those."

Did they believe them? Lauren wondered. Or did they simply exploit them? She asked, "Why did you choose to excavate this cemetery out of the hundreds of old cemeteries in Scotland?"

"Rabbits."

"Rabbits?" she repeated, thinking she'd run aground on dialect.

"The wee burrowing rodents. They've been turning up bits of bone, coffin hardware, and the like. The folk with relations buried here are after having them re-interred, being a bit choosey about their family associations. We're collecting and labeling the remains, placing them in new containers along with any associated artifacts, and transporting the lot to the Thurso cemetery. We've got a local minister standing by to perform a service. Nae worries, it's all gey respectful."

"I'm not worried. I'm four generations removed from Susanna." Lauren looked over the fence into the cemetery with its lichen-mottled, weather-worn stones. Small mounds of upturned earth marked dark apertures, especially beneath the horizontal table tombs. Maybe what seemed to be bits of brownish stone half-concealed in the grass were actually bones, so old and remote that they seemed sad instead of grisly. And yet . . . There was always an *and yet.*

Calder frowned, not at her but over her shoulder. "Eh! Jason!" he shouted to a husky, tawny-haired young man who was raising a small mattock, one end a pick-axe, the other a narrow shovel. "You're not digging a ditch. Cut along the edge of the trench and then peel back the turf. Gently, so you're feeling in your palms if the point of the mattock's touching anything."

"Right." Jason made several small chops and jerked forward as the tool dropped into a burrow. Calder winced.

Lauren was beginning to see what he meant by *for my sins*, although what his sins were, she couldn't imagine.

"Well then." Calder took another step back. "If you'll leave an address, my assistant will be posting you the proper permission forms."

In other words, go away. Fine. She shouldn't wear out her welcome. Reluctantly, Lauren scrounged in her bag for notebook and pen. She copied down Emily's particulars, tore out the paper, and handed it over.

"That's all right then. Thanks." Calder jammed the paper into his pocket without looking at it and took a third step back. His hand shook the canvas bag impatiently against his leg. "If you'll excuse me."

She replaced the notebook. Her hand jarred the velvet box holding the skull watch. The vibration of its chime traveled up her arm and fired a spark across her mind. *Bait.* Something to keep this mutual-ingratiation encounter going a little longer.

She pulled out the box. "I have an artifact here that belonged to Susanna."

"Oh aye?" Calder was still watching Jason. Beyond him other students set a sieve on two sawhorses, spread out boxes and equipment inside the roofless chapel, and applied a plumb bob to an obelisk that listed to the side, undermined by rabbit sappers.

Lauren opened the box. The silver-gilt cranium flashed. Calder glanced around. His entire body turned from flesh to stone. Only his eyes still moved, opening so widely the silvery flash was repeated in his gray irises.

Yes, Lauren thought, the artifact was startling, but . . .

With a deep inhalation, Calder returned to life. He shot a glance at Lauren as swift and sharp as a blow from one of his tools. Then he reached into his own bag, extracted a white box, and let the bag drop to the ground, where it caught a puff of wind and inched away. Opening his box, he held it up next to hers.

Inside, on a bed of cotton, lay another silver skull.

CHAPTER FIVE

This time the icy wave of petrifaction tingled along Lauren's limbs and down her back. The sounds of the wind, the ocean, the voices of the students, even a distant thud like that of a car door, all faded to a buzz in her own living skull.

Blinking, she saw that Calder had only a cranium, more like a cap than the top of a skull. The dented silver-gilt arch, the fretwork band around the bottom, and a broken hinge at the back still bore traces of tarnish. If Lauren set it onto the face and jaw of her own watch, crowning the works beneath, it would have fit perfectly.

Et in terra pax, bonae voluntatis. She wasn't feeling any peace, not on this earth, whether this man was of good will or not. Logically there were other skull watches, yes, but . . . "What the hell?" Lauren raised her stunned stare to Calder's face. "Did you find that here?"

His gaze was still sharp, even accusatory. "In a rabbit's burrow, amongst the bits of bone, wood, coffin brass, even prehistoric pottery, whilst surveying. There's no way of knowing where it was originally buried, if it was that at all. I cleaned it up a bit. And I worked out its original provenance."

"It—mine—this watch was Susanna's," Lauren stammered, as though that explained anything. "Victorian sentimentalism. Death imagery. The pre-Raphaelite artists."

"Not a bit of it. The skull pocket watches are six-teenth century, the both of them. The three of them. There's one other."

"One other?" Lauren barely heard her own voice.

Calder leaned so close she smelled the wool of his pullover. "Oh aye, in a private collection in Spain, by way of belonging to the descendants of the Duke of Medina Sidonia, commander of the Spanish Armada in 1588. He survived the battles and the foul winds in the Channel and went leading the remains of his fleet the long way round the British Isles, aiming to return to Spain. They met rough seas round Orkney in August. Ships went down at Fair Isle, and at Mull, and loads of them along the Irish coast. And some vanished."

His words whined in her ears, ebbing and flooding like the sea itself—the sea that had dashed a galleon against the cliffs as casually as if it had been a log.

The wind had tugged at her hair and her long skirts wrapped damply about her legs—she had been there, she had seen it, she had heard it, she had felt it.

1588.

A sudden cold gust sent Calder's hat rolling down the hillside. Lauren's scarf slithered off her head and took wing. Her hair billowed over her shoulders and into her face, each lock dancing.

The short ends of Calder's blond hair stood up like antennae. Ignoring his hat, he said, "A local legend's saying the captain of one of the ships, *El Castillo Negro,* had himself a copy of Alexander Lindsay's 1540 *Rutter of the Scottish Seas,* a pilot's chart. It's saying he tried a shortcut through the Pentland Firth and wrecked here at Black Ness."

"Yeah, I know. That there's a legend, I mean." But she didn't know about the legend, only about her dream.

Her new dream. If that one was a glimpse of the past, then what about the old one?

El Castillo Negro, she repeated to herself. *The Black Castle*. Well, of course.

With one hand, Lauren scooped the mass of her hair away from her face, so that it streamed out behind her. Her other fumbled the velvet box and the watch jangled a warning. Calder's free hand caught hers and steadied it. His fingers were long, with prominent knuckles, like strong but flexible bamboo poles, and were no longer warm but hot. So were his eyes, silver as the skulls but heated by—what? The artifact she held, what she'd said, who she was?

With her own deep inhalation, she released her hair, snapped down the lid, and extracted hand and box both from Calder's rock-steady grasp. She ducked his eyes, knowing that her own were about to reveal too much. He was an academic, a scientist, a stranger. She could never explain how she knew so much and at the same time so little. Like where Susanna had gotten a three-hundred-year old artifact, and why her son had carried it with him across the sea to a new world, and why this place and this artifact haunted her, waking as well as sleeping.

A second watch. A third.

A second dream . . .

Calder retrieved the canvas bag from its resting place against the wall and placed the box inside, his back turned toward her as though after that moment of weird connection, almost of intimacy, he was trying to re-establish the proper boundaries.

Yes. Boundaries. Boundaries did have their moments. But what she had were questions.

"Hullo, Calder," said a refined tenor behind Lauren's back. "Your hat's got away from you, I see. And here's your girlfriend's scarf."

Again Lauren jerked, startled. She crammed her confusion into her rationality the same way she crammed the velvet box into her bag, as though confusion and box alike were something to be ashamed of, and spun around.

A man stood on the path below her, her scarf fluttering in his outstretched hand like a flag from the mast of a ship just setting out on its journey.

He was tall enough that his face was at the same level as hers, lean enough that he had to stand braced against the wind, tilting forward. His long dark hair, held in a pony tail, floated behind him. Several day's worth of whiskers smeared but didn't conceal a square jaw below high cheekbones and a tall, pale forehead.

The gaze of his blue eyes fixed on Lauren's features, widened, and intensified from dispassionate courtesy to astonishment as abruptly as twin searchlights piercing a sea mist. His hand, clenched around the scarf, fell back to his side. His skin flushed. And those eyes didn't blink.

She saw herself in them, her hair rippling brown and russet and gold in the wind and the sunlight that flared and retreated again, her full lips parted and her brows drawn down in puzzlement and something else, a recognition deeper than the simple realization that this man, this was David Sutherland.

But, unless he'd been modeling for the covers of romance novels, she'd never seen him before. And there was no way he could have seen her, even though he was staring at her face as though, he, too, was feeling an army march across his grave.

Calder picked up his hat and jammed it onto his head. He jerked the scarf from the other man's hand and held it out to Lauren, once again his look accusing her of, of something. But Sutherland's "girlfriend" wasn't her fault.

Gritting her teeth, she squeezed out "Thanks," and reclaimed her scarf. She turned back to Sutherland and said, with the same wary courtesy Calder had used to deal with her, "Hello. I'm Lauren Reay."

The man was now staring at his feet, clad in hiking boots beneath military camouflage pants and planted firmly on the turf. His body quivered in one slow oscillation from head to toe, so that she expected to hear a note of music. "How do you do, Miss Reay. David Sutherland," he said, his voice every bit as brusque as it was on his answering machine. Without offering to shake her hand, never mind giving her a second look, he plunged down the path and almost ran across the bridge and up toward the castle.

What? she thought again. Was he a hermit in general, or was she in particular a threat to his territory, his boundaries?

The shadow of a cloud raced over the chapel and the field. The cries of the gulls echoed. Lauren's silk scarf felt slick and chill as ice. She stuffed it in her pocket.

Tight-lipped, Calder watched Sutherland withdraw toward his battlements. Then he said, "Please excuse me, Miss Reay. I've got work to do." And with that irrefutable if frustrating fact, he turned toward the graveyard and its expectant audience, living and dead.

Fine, Lauren thought again. She was accustomed to working alone, to holding her own hand, to providing her own counsel. A good thing, too. Her quest was off to a rocky start, caught between a temperamental archaeologist and a stubborn landowner. Neither of whom seemed to have time for each other, to say nothing of her.

Sutherland must have been embarrassed he hadn't answered her messages—although he had made quite a leap of inference, to know who she was before she introduced herself. Calder realized she could make trouble for him, if not as the—reporter?—he'd first taken her for, then as a relation of the honored dead. She was above both men's courtesy horizons, then.

Calder knelt beside one of the tombstones, two acolytes receiving objects from his knobby, dirty hands. The older woman stood over them, her short black hair lying sleekly on either side of a small, pert face. As if feeling Lauren's gaze, she looked up. She considered the interloper with an expression cool to the point of cold. Before Lauren reacted with either a smile or a quizzical return stare, the woman turned the back of her Celtic-interlace design tee and knelt down beside Calder, shoulder to shoulder. Closing ranks.

That must be his assistant, Bryony. Her pose implied a territorial imperative that had nothing to do with land, graves, or bones no longer clothed with flesh. *Don't worry,* Lauren beamed silently at her, and by extension, Calder, even as her hand remembered the firm clasp of his fingers.

Clenching that hand into a fist and the other on the strap of her bag, she walked down the path, across the bridge, and up the opposite slope.

At the crest of the hill stood a small hillock, where the blanket of the turf stretched and tore over several flat boulders with jagged edges. The stones and the surrounding grass were blackened by fire, as though someone's weenie roast had gotten away.

Lauren imagined wreckers building a beacon atop the headland, drawing a ship into the cliffs with false promises of safety. Any ship would carry plunder. *El*

Castillo Negro had carried two silver skull watches—or so it seemed.

As if in answer, the Reay family talisman chimed again, its music muted by the heavy fabric of her bag.

The path segued from wooden planks to stone flags. Lauren stopped to catch her breath, not that it was climbing the path that had taken it away.

Out to sea, a red oil tanker plowed through the glassy blue swells, its wake a bridal train of white foam. Something old. Something new. Something borrowed, something blue. She looked toward the top of the tower, to the door in the turret that yesterday afternoon had appeared to be a ghostly woman in a wedding gown. In the morning sun, the door's mottled paint was just that.

And the gargoyle was gone, even though that had been no illusion of sun and shadow. It could well have been a cat, however. The castle was playing with her, bells and whistles, smoke and mirrors.

And this was a surprise how? she asked herself, and walked on. Maybe those family connections that had opened the chapel door would open the castle portcullis, too. Not that she was going to tell Sutherland, either, about her dreams or the curious incident of the calendar.

Through the wrought-iron curlicues of the gate in the perimeter wall, she saw the door of the tower. It was set into an alcove in the angle where two sheer walls met. Except for the dappled paint of the turret door, a stain or two on the stucco-like coating of the walls, and the wavy old glass of the window panes, the tower seemed newly built. Maybe the door would open and an Elizabethan gallant would step through, ruff at his neck and sword at his side.

No. The latter part of the sixteenth century had never been Elizabethan in Scotland, where Elizabeth I never ruled. And Sutherland's restoration, let alone Bremner's, might not have been even remotely sympathetic to James Mackay's building. The only representation of the original that Grandpa's agent had been able to find was a rudimentary sketch on the border of an old map, where cartographers should have written *hic sunt dracones*: here be dragons.

Now that she saw the tower itself, not a drawing, not a photograph—and not a dream—she thought that a dragon or two in the dungeon would be just the right touch. Not a cartoon Day-Glo green dragon, though. A small one with dark gleaming scales, very fierce.

If any flying creatures lived in the tower, though, they would be bats and ravens, evocative but hardly fantastical. No dragons. No fairies with gossamer wings. Not even a gargoyle.

Mildly disappointed, Lauren pushed against one of the iron leaf-and-tendrils of the gate and stepped into a cobbled courtyard. A lush herbaceous border lay in the lee of the wall, close against the sun-warmed stone. She recognized roses in several shades of red and a few herbs. Other than those, her botanical knowledge ran to cactus and mesquite. She couldn't even grow pots of tomatoes on her back porch. The little yellow blossoms would fall to the hot concrete without ever coming to fruition. There had to be something symbolic in that.

She stepped up into the alcove. The front door was constructed of wide wooden slabs and held together with iron brackets, that, despite their decorative whorls, were obviously intended to repel battering rams, let alone inquisitive visitors.

The door was ajar. Had he seen her coming? "Hello," she called.

Silence, except for the wind and raised voices from the chapel—Calder barking at his students, probably—and a strain of music . . . She pricked her ears. No. No music. And no greeting from the darkness behind the door, either.

In his hurry, Sutherland must not have shut the door properly. The wind had blown it open. Lauren looked for a bell or a knocker shaped like a mermaid, at least, but there was nothing. She rapped her knuckles against the wood, producing a weak little tap-tap-tap, not even loud enough to be Poe's raven rapping at his chamber door.

Silence.

She pushed the door open. Like the gate, it glided without creak or squeal. "Hello? Mr. Sutherland?"

Silence.

She'd made a promise, not just to Grandpa but to herself. She wasn't turning back now.

Lauren stepped inside, every nerve ending alert. Her parted lips, her dilated nostrils, detected damp and musty books, wood, smoke, and stone—the scent of time itself—as well as the aroma of coffee and something that might be potpourri or even incense. She heard only the scuff of her own feet on the stone floor of a small, still room. An ordinary antechamber, not a decayed Victorian parlor or Renaissance hall draped in cobwebs, guttered candles gone to gloom.

She left the door open, the better to make her escape if necessary. In the light spilling through it, she saw an arched doorway, half-covered by rich fabric, opening onto a gleam of sunlight. Two closed doors stood next to a spiral staircase that wound upward into more sunlight, with its white-painted walls resembling the inside of a nautilus shell. On a marble-topped table sat an old oil lamp and a bell jar, a round object dangling from its dome that might have been the White Rabbit's—very ordinary—pocket watch. A plastic bag labeled "Charles Innes, Book Dealer" spilled books across the table top.

Was Sutherland studying up on masonry or gardening? Did he like best-selling thrillers? Lauren suspected none of the books was *How to Win Friends and Influence People*, but you never knew.

The glossy protective covers of the books shimmered, ghost-like. The labels wrapping their spines were printed with the codes of the Dewey Decimal system. Sutherland patronized the library as well as Innes's bookstore, then.

The book on top was titled, *The Last Pre-Raphaelites*. Next came *Prehistoric Landscapes of Scotland*. Beneath that was what looked like a psychology textbook . . . She really was hearing music, the same tune she'd heard yesterday played on a flute or whistle, played now on a piano.

And she remembered where she'd heard that melody before. Her father had sat at the piano in their suburban living room, playing Scottish songs such as "The Water is Wide" and composing melodies as slow and subtle as laments, music to soothe his disordered mind. This was one of them. It rose and fell, grew and faded, circled around so that it went in where it had come out and tied a knot in the back of Lauren's throat.

With a long, trembling breath, she shoved aside the damask curtain and stepped into a sitting room. A deserted sitting room.

The music stopped. The morning light, reflected through the small, wavy windowpanes, cast ripples of luminescence on white walls, dark wood, printed fabrics. An antique upright piano sat against one wall. Its yellowed ivory teeth gleamed, untouched by human hands. Perhaps some resonance of the melody lingered in the piano's encoffined strings. Perhaps it lingered only in Lauren's ears, now accompanied by the thud of her own pulse.

Now accompanied by the uneven thud of footsteps coming down the stairs and across the anteroom. She heard the front door slam shut, as solidly as a prison door. She heard the swish of the curtain and a startled gasp.

Still staring at the piano, as though taking her eyes from it would cause it to start playing again, she said dully, "The door was open. I heard music."

"Music," said Sutherland's cool voice behind her back.

"It's not a player piano, unless you've got something electronic hidden inside." But then, she added to herself, how would he know to tantalize her with Donny's composition?

"I didn't know you'd come walking in uninvited, did I?" And, after a long silence in which Lauren heard him take another step toward her, he murmured, "The place is full of noises, sounds and sweet airs that delight and hurt not."

"That might work for Shakespeare but . . ." She frowned. "Please don't tell me the place is haunted."

"Very well then, I shan't tell you Blackness Tower is haunted."

"But it is, isn't it?" She forced herself to turn her back on the piano, to face Sutherland's high clear forehead, carved cheekbones, clouded blue eyes, his unblinking gaze so strong she felt it pressing against her.

Again a rosy tide flooded his face above the shadowy beard. His voice dropped to a husky vibrato. "Yes. And you're the ghost that's haunting it."

CHAPTER SIX

Lauren had expected a denial, even derision. But no. *You're the ghost that's haunting it.* Said as though it were a confession dragged from him at gunpoint. Said as though it were fact.

He watched her, his hands knotted at his sides, his cheeks flushed. Waiting for a response, she felt. For her own confession.

His thick dark lashes fell, concealing his eyes.

Released from that gaze, Lauren took a clumsy step backward. Funny, she was dizzy. Hyperventilating again. But the floor wasn't really buckling beneath her feet—the flagstones were uneven. She croaked, "You're joking. You're teasing. You're trying to scare me away."

"Why should I do that, any of it?"

"You never answered my letters or my messages. You didn't have to call me back, overseas. You didn't have to use paper and a stamp. I gave you my e-mail address. You could just have said something to my cousin Emily in Thurso. Emily Brodie, you know her, she runs the housewares shop."

"Next to Charles's book shop. Yes, I know." He turned away from her and eyed the piano, his jaw clenched, as though the music had somehow given him away.

What it had done, Lauren thought, was give her away. And at the same time give her an opening in Sutherland's stone wall, one she could chip away, very slowly, very carefully, until she found answers.

Allowing herself a moment to steady her hand, Lauren looked around. The room was shaped like a blunted, uneven star, deep bays of windows and doors cut in the thickness of the walls. Furniture and fabrics alike had an Arts and Crafts feel, appropriate to Bremner's time and tastes, and yet seemed new. The lamps *were* new. So was a computer, and a television set and its electronic appendages, including a rack of DVDs topped by the most recent avatar of *Dr. Who*. The fireplace was the only sixteenth-century feature in the room, its stone hood protecting a blackened grate.

On the hearth, above a basket piled with yarns and threads, a stand held an antique wooden embroidery hoop. The words stitched on the enclosed sampler read: "This is no metaphor, it is a simple fact. We start out of Nothingness, take figure and are apparitions." Below the yellowing cloth a silver needle swung back and forth on its skein of scarlet thread as if some invisible hand had just released it.

And a painting hung beside the bulge of the chimney. Its surface gleamed, gilded by an aging coat of varnish. Lauren glanced at it, then stiffened and strained forward. It was the original of the dull, drab photo in Bremner's book. It was "Catherine's Destiny." Or was the second word inscribed on a tarnished plaque beneath the portrait, the word after the possessive name, "destiny"? The large "D" and trailing letters might, Lauren saw with yet another prickle, be the word "Dream."

Subtle ridges and whorls of paint beneath the varnish traced the still vibrant colors, from the scarlet of the woman's dress to the amber-gray stone framing the window behind her to the lapis lazuli of the sea swells she overlooked. The swells that bore a galleon brave with gold trim and scarlet pennons helplessly forward, as though to deposit it at her feet like a cat its prey.

Her—Catherine's—hair flowed brown and russet and gold, a thick curtain down her back and around her face. A face with a long nose, a generous mouth parted in eagerness, deep-set brown eyes wide with caution, even fear. A face too strong for contemporary tastes. A face that was Lauren's own.

Fairy fingernails tickled the back of her neck and traced the length of her spine. Her skin puckering, she lurched closer to the picture.

The object Catherine held in her uplifted right hand was silvery, so bright the light of it leaked between the bars of her fingers and gathered in a halo. A giant golden egg. A crystal ball. Or a silver watch shaped like a skull.

Lauren couldn't remember where she'd put her bag. If the watch was chiming a response, she couldn't hear it over the roaring in her own ears. She raised her own hand in the same gesture, like a supplicant before an altar. *Stop the world, let me get off.* . . . That was what the men on the ship had prayed, as the sea hurled them headlong into the unforgiving cliffs.

Long limber fingers closed on her upper arms. A grasp that wasn't entirely steady drew her back to a chair and seated her in it. Then the hands slipped upward to her shoulders and fixed themselves there, both offering support and holding her down.

A polished tenor said, "James Mackay built the Tower in 1579 on the foundations of a Norse tower, with stone that had lain here since time beyond memory. He married Catherine Sinclair in 1585. Their marriage was one of convenience, a dynastic alliance. Business, nothing personal. Catherine gave her pent-up love to a selkie, a supernatural being, part man, part seal. James murdered her for it. Or so the stories say."

Lauren opened her mouth, found no words in it, and shut it with a pop. She pressed her right hand against her chest, ready to catch her heart when it leaped through her ribs and plummeted into deep water. In Celtic belief, if you saw your own double you were doomed to die.

"That's one of Francis Weir's paintings, based on a poem by Rupert Beckwith. Susanna Mackay sat for it. She was your great-great grandmother."

So he had read her letters, after all. Is that what he meant by her being a ghost, her weird—Weir, weird, hah!—resemblance to long-dead Susanna?

"We are such stuff as dreams are made on, and our little lives are rounded with a sleep." She felt his breath stirring her hair. His voice was British, not specifically Scottish, modulated cadences over an undertow of strong emotion, emotion she couldn't quite identify. Fear? What did he have to fear from her? She was the one who should be afraid, and not just of the unknown. Perhaps she should be afraid of him. He was talking about dreams as though he read her mind.

"To sleep," he murmured, "perchance to dream, but in that sleep of death what dreams may come?"

His hands were cool, and strong like the strings of the piano were strong. His fingertips both kneaded and caressed the taut flesh of her shoulders. This time her shiver had a very physical origin, part pleasure, part dismay. What, had this melancholy Brit been sitting in his tower of solitude reading his classics for so long he'd lost touch with reality?

As if her own reality was at all rational. *This is no metaphor.*

She wasn't going to be afraid, she wasn't going to simper and vapor, not here, not now. Gently she pulled herself away from his hands.

"I'll make a pot of tea, shall I?" he asked.

Her voice was thin, but it worked. "That would be good. Thanks."

Footsteps paced away.

Lauren took a deep breath. Her shoulders ached where his hands had rested. Either the blood was now flowing back into the prints of his palms, or else she craved more of his touch. And she'd thought Ewan Calder's steadying clasp of her hand was intimate. Now she should be lying back in the chair smoking a cigarette. Not that tobacco was one of her vices.

Somewhere dishes rattled. She shouldn't just sit here and let him fetch and carry for her, now that she'd broken not just into the tower but into his armor. Although it wasn't Susanna's name that had gotten her in, but Susanna's face. No wonder Sutherland—David, maybe Dave or Davy—no wonder the man had looked at her, there by the chapel, with startled recognition. No wonder he seemed almost frightened of her.

Again Lauren inspected the painting, this time more calmly, calm being relative. She wasn't seeing her own double but a family member. People in the same family tended to favor each other. Her own mother looked enough like her younger sister to be her twin.

But then, her mother and her aunt weren't several generations apart.

Lauren stood up. The flat stones of the floor were steady, if asymmetrical beneath a bright Persian carpet. Without looking again at the painting, she found her bag on the piano stool and followed the domestic clatter into the antechamber. One of the doors next to the staircase was now standing open.

Inside, past a small dining room, lay a modern kitchen, its satiny blond wood cabinets and rust-red laminate-covered counter tops ranged below a medieval barrel-vaulted ceiling. Flowerpots lined a windowsill. In a block of sun, on a throw rug, reclined a gray striped cat with a metal tag dangling from its collar. It raised its head, registered Lauren's entrance with the usual feline shrug of indifference, and lay back down.

At least her guess about the identity of the gargoyle had been correct, for what that was worth. Whether any of her guesses about her reluctant host were correct remained to be seen.

He was standing, more or less at parade rest, staring at an electric kettle, a watched pot more interesting than his uninvited guest. He didn't look around as she walked in and helped herself to a chair at a wooden table.

He wore not only camouflage pants, but a slightly threadbare army sweater, with nylon patches on the shoulders and elbows. Maybe his stance had less to do with nervous tension than with military training. Maybe too long a time doing close-order drill had driven him to his hermitage here at the world's rim.

A half-full bottle of Scotch whisky stood on the counter. And had something driven him to drink as well? *An officer and a gentleman*, Emily had said. But he was young to have retired from a career.

A small bulletin board above the table held only a few items—a couple of receipts, a postcard of the Taj Mahal, a photo of three young men wearing suits and ties and standing in front of a church doorway. At a wedding, Lauren guessed by the rosebuds in each lapel. David stood on the left, his short dark hair tousled, his smile half-formed, as though the photographer had snapped off a shot while the men goofed around before the ceremony.

She tried to think of something clever to say, that would draw him out. She tried, "Nice cat," and then cursed herself.

"Her name's Persie."

"Her? But Percy's a male name."

"P-e-r-s-i-e." He spelled it out. Steam issued from the kettle and he went to work with tea and pot.

"Oh." So much for that ploy. Lauren considered the cups, sugar bowl, and creamer on the table. Plain, pottery dishes, the sort Bremner's servants probably used. She wondered whether Susanna had been considered a servant.

David set the teapot on a brass trivet and himself in the chair across the table. When he poured, Lauren saw that his hand was shaking. But then, so was hers. He pushed a plate of chocolate-covered oatmeal cookies toward her, and then sat with his elbows braced on the table and his cup clutched between his hands. Watching her. Waiting. Through the steam his face wavered as though it were under water.

Lauren sipped. The tea was blazing hot and stiff enough to strip paint. She added more milk and sugar and started in on a cookie—a biscuit, she translated— while it cooled.

"Why have you come here?" he asked, just as she asked, "What was that about me haunting the place?"

After a moment of mutual silence, the deep curve of his lips flattened into something between a grimace and a smile. Creases in his cheeks made Lauren wonder if he was as young as she'd originally thought. "It's your face in the portrait," he said. "Gave me a bit of a turn." His eyes above the rim of the cup were steadier than his hands.

No, she replied silently. *There's more to it than that.*

She must have shaken her head slightly, conveying her thought. He looked suddenly down at his cup, then poured its contents down his throat—it must be lined with asbestos—and without missing a beat asked again, "Why did you come here?"

"I'm researching my genealogy," she replied, giving an easy answer to a hard question. "My grandfather wanted to know who his own grandfather was. Who was the father of Susanna's child, John Mackay, who changed his name to Reay."

"John Mackay? Illegitimate, was he?"

"His birth certificate says Susanna wasn't married." She swallowed the last soothingly sweet bite and almost licked her fingertips, then thought better of that particular gesture and brushed the crumbs off into her saucer.

"Sounds a proper scandal, then, but it's nothing to do with me. I live here, that's all."

Right. If he wasn't lying, he was hiding the truth. Time to deploy her ticket of admittance. Lauren pulled the jeweler's box from her bag, opened it, and set it next to David's elbow. The light reflected from the curve of the silver skull onto his downturned face, making his skin look ashen.

Or maybe it was ashen. "Ah," he said, in a long sigh. Slowly he put down his tea. Slowly his supple hands cupped over the skull and lifted it from the box, raising it like a soothsayer cradling a crystal ball. "That's it, then. That's what she's holding in the painting."

"Was the watch Catherine's? Did it come off the Armada ship? Ewan Calder, the archaeologist, he says there's a legend about an Armada ship wrecking here. He has the cranium from another watch. He says it's Spanish, and there's a third one."

"In Spain. Oh yes, I've heard Ewan Calder performing his song and dance about *El Castillo Negro*. No other historian believes a Spanish ship tried navigating the Pentland Firth. If Calder can prove one did, he'll make his reputation. A visitor center, loads of tourists, plastic ships made in Taiwan, tea towels, tartan tat, and Calder holding court. That's not right, not for Black Ness. Not for the Tower. Not for the powers that . . ." He left his sentence dangling.

Well yes, the men were in the midst of a power struggle. The battle lines were staked out across that uneasy ground where ambition met reticence. Maybe where science met superstition, for that matter.

An appendix to Bremner's book referred to superstition. Nowadays paranormal beliefs made popular TV shows. Maybe David meant, *powers*.

The watch chimed. Lauren couldn't tell whether he shook it deliberately or whether his hands still trembled. The cat rose from the rug and stretched upward, forepaws resting on the man's lean thigh, ears pricked toward the shiny object.

David's gaze hit Lauren's face. Not hostile, not like Calder's. Not curious and expectant, like Emily's. David's eyes challenged her, dissected her emotions, gauged her every reaction, and tried to read her thoughts, eager and yet resentful.

"You were called here, weren't you?" he asked. "How? Why?"

Called. Yes. By powers.

Another minute and she'd be babbling her dreams and fears, uncertainties and griefs. But one ambivalent grip and a few perceptive questions didn't a confidant make. Neither did David's spooky vibe, which was not only like her own, it was like her father's. Her vanished father, the musician, the poet, the melancholy Scot.

Outing any number of skeletons in the Reay ancestral family closet would be better than confessing those in her own. Than admitting her reason for coming here was to find out whether her dream and all its implications was a gift or a curse.

She shrank back, pressing against the hard, cold wood of the chair. "What about those sounds and sweet airs, the music that I heard? What about me looking so much like that portrait? What about Susanna's child?"

He answered one of her questions. "His father was Weir or Beckwith, like as not."

Like as not, considering her father's artistic tastes. Considering the old question of nature versus nurture. But likelihood wasn't proof. It was Calder who knew that.

Still his gaze probed her, like a doctor, like a lover. The horizontal lines of his eyebrows tightened at the inner ends. "Why did you come here, Lauren?"

All this time she thought she'd look around, ask some questions, and get her answers, one two three. She should have known it wasn't going to be so easy. Nothing about her dreams, her Sight, whatever it was, was easy.

She was going to have to give as well as take. The question was how much, and to whom, and to what end.

Fear gripped her chest and groped her vitals. Scooping the skull from David's hands—cool hands still, but with a hum beneath the skin—she replaced it in the box and the box in her bag. "I'll do some research in town. If you think of something you want to tell me, I'm staying with Emily."

He inspected his hands, still cupped, empty. Whatever he wanted from Lauren, she hadn't provided it. Even Persie cast her own version of a sharp look across the table, then hopped down and trotted away.

"Thanks for the tea," Lauren said.

"Come back tomorrow and I'll give you the grand tour. I shan't bite, I promise you that." And David looked up at her, his swift, lopsided grin so rueful, ironic, self-aware, so compelling she almost sat back down again and leaned trustingly across the table toward him.

No. Not now. Not a flying leap over the cliffs, but a gradual and difficult scramble down an escarpment, pebbles slipping underfoot. "Thank you," she said, and added, "I'll see myself out," even though he made no move to stand up.

She beat a retreat into the anteroom. The glass dome on the marble-topped table shone in a beam of light reflected from some shiny surface in the kitchen. Inside hung not a pocket watch, but an ornate brooch, gold filigree edging a clear compartment that contained a tiny braid of amber-red hair. A mourning brooch with a lock of Susanna's hair. With her great-great grandmother's hair, so much like her own.

Without turning her back on the brooch twinkling inside its glass sarcophagus, Lauren grabbed the handle of the front door, pressed the latch, and hauled it open. She couldn't leave. She had to leave.

In her dream, she walked down from the Tower. In her dream, she always returned.

She spun around and threw herself straight into the arms of a red-bearded man.

CHAPTER SEVEN

"Whoa!" the man exclaimed. He grabbed Lauren's elbows and peeled her from his broad, leather-jacketed chest. "What's your hurry? Ghoulies and ghosties in the castle?"

Grinding, Lauren's brain switched gears. She knew this man. Who was he? His deep voice had an odd ring to it. His hands rested lightly on her elbows, poised, so that she had the feeling he could have thrown her across the courtyard.

He grinned down at her from his six inches of greater height, what looked like a mouth and a half of teeth glinting in his tidy beard. Carrot-red locks lifted and fell in a chill eddy of air. She couldn't see his eyes behind his reflecting sunglasses, just her own startled face.

"Hello?" he asked.

Oh. "I saw you on TV." She managed to extricate herself from his grasp.

His hands remained open, ready to seize her again if necessary. God only knew how crazed she must look. "Yep," he said. "That's me. *The Paranormal Files.* Magnus Anderson at your service. That's Mag-nus. Don't call me Maggie."

That was why his voice sounded odd. He was speaking with an American drawl that even after only twenty-four hours in the UK hit Lauren's ear like a pancake, flat and bland. "Hi. Lauren Reay. Sorry to run into you like that."

"No problem. But I've got to ask—what's a nice American girl like you doing in a place like this?"

"Genealogical research. My great-great grandmother lived here." Lauren gestured over her shoulder, at the still-open door. "She's buried at the chapel."

"The woman that guy Calder is digging up?"

"He's digging up everyone, he said."

"Oh yeah." Magnus at last removed his glasses, revealing coffee-brown eyes lit with an avid sparkle. Reaching into his jacket, he stowed his glasses and produced a thick cell phone. Cool, it was one of those that was also a PDA—he thumbed in a note. "This'll be a great story. A castle with spooky legends that have been documented at least back to the sixteenth century. A cemetery giving up its dead."

Silver skulls and discomforting portraits. "I thought TV people sent out scouts and advance teams and, you know."

"I'm not just talent," he told her. "It's my show. It's my magazine, my blog, my empire."

"Oh," she replied, without adding that his empire apparently didn't extend across the Atlantic.

Magnus stowed his electronic secondary memory. "My local contact says that Mr. Sutherland, esquire, is bit of a hermit. You got your foot in the door, though. How about an introduction? Or was he chasing you away with a broadsword?"

"No, I was just . . ." Lauren didn't have the foggiest idea how to finish her sentence. *Running away?*

She didn't have to finish it. From behind her came David's voice, no longer cool but positively chill. "Well then. This is my day for visitors, is it?"

Magnus whipped out an ingratiating smile and his right hand. He didn't exactly shove Lauren aside. She dodged as he lunged toward the door, seized David's hand, and pumped it up and down. "Magnus Anderson. *The Paranormal Files*. Rosemary Gillock says she forwarded my message to you."

David retrieved his hand, crossed his arms across his chest, and did not move out of the doorway. "Yes."

"I thought maybe we could scare up some manifestations," Magnus went on, "if you'll pardon the expression. I hear some really odd things have happened up here. Though it's funny how many odd things are exorcized the minute I turn up with my instruments."

"Who told you about these odd things? Rosemary? Or was it Ewan Calder?"

Rosemary Gillock, Lauren repeated, and remembered the library books on the table. Rosemary was Emily's friend the librarian.

"Never met Calder until today, though I've talked with his people, the lovely Bryony Duff, more than was necessary. Bryony Duff, sounds like one of those quirky British desserts." Magnus grinned again, so disarmingly Lauren forgave him for flirting with "cupcake" or "crumpet" or some other objectification of the attractive Bryony.

He went on, "Ms. Gillock contacted me through the *Paranormal Files* website and said I should do a show on Blackness Tower."

"You'll do one whether I cooperate or not, is that it?" asked David.

"Hey." Magnus raised his hands—*nothing up my sleeve*. "If you've got secrets to hide, buried treasure, dungeons, whatever, far be it from me to start poking around."

David's eye turned toward Lauren, as though wondering whether Magnus, her fellow American, had sent her ahead to soften him up. Grimacing, she shrugged a denial.

If David caught her message, he didn't react. He stepped back from the doorway and gestured, if not a welcome, at least a tolerance. "You have me at a disadvantage, Mr. Anderson."

"Magnus." He started for the door, then spun toward Lauren. "Whoa—where're my manners? It was nice meeting you, Lauren. Good luck with the research. Keep me posted if you turn up anything really cool."

"Sure," she said, only too aware she had something really cool in her bag at that very moment.

Funny how she was starting to sympathize with David's desire for privacy. Funny how she felt that if she appeared sympathetic, he might eventually share the secrets he did have. Ones that intersected her own secrets the way his gaze kept intersecting hers.

She offered him a wave as he stepped back to let Magnus cross the threshold. He didn't notice. His profile against the shadows of the antechamber might have been carved on the cold metal of a coin. His hand grasped the side of the door, knuckles white as bone and as immobile. Moments earlier, he had been looking at her with such strong emotion his hand trembled.

"Well then," Lauren overheard him say, "you've blackmailed your way inside."

"Blackmail?" asked Magnus's voice.

"You're as keen on exposing my past as that of the Tower, I expect. Don't waste your time —the newspapers, especially the Irish ones, already made a meal of the incident."

"Yeah, I checked you out. That's part of the shtick, the personalities of the owners, locals, whatever. If I can catch one of them picking his nose, so much the better. Not that there's anything wrong with that." Magnus chuckled. David did not. "But I'm genuinely interested in the stories of the Tower. I'd like to find just one fricking site that actually checks out as a disturbance in the Force."

"Well then." David's hand vanished. The door shut with a clunk that echoed off the battlements. A couple of gulls screeched.

Lauren laced her arms across her jacket, realized she was imitating David's protective stance, and let them drop to her sides. She saw not the courtyard but the ends of her thoughts, dangling like the needle on its red thread. Susanna. Catherine. Her own appearance, which must be the cause of Emily's scrutiny. Her dreams. David and the deeps of his eyes and his slightly off-balance smile. Whatever she wanted from him—and it was more than Grandpa's grandfather's name—he hadn't provided it. If she answered his questions, though . . .

Do this now, she told herself, *or forever hold your peace.*

Lauren turned away from the door wondering just what David's incident was. Something in Northern Ireland? He might have served in the army there, as a soldier who was either occupier or protector, depending on who you asked and who held the weapon.

As for Magnus, she'd thought his program was one of the credulous ones, but he might be as much of a skeptic as Ewan Calder. Although she shouldn't deduce Calder's position on the paranormal from one joking remark. At least she now knew that by saying "all my sins," he was confessing as subtly as possible to ambition.

Calder. That was it. Fooled by her professional appearance, he had thought she was working for Magnus Anderson. He'd known the man was coming, but was no happier than David about it.

She scuffed toward the gate, shoulders hunched, elbows flexed at odd angles, hands swinging clumsily. Calder, Sutherland, Anderson—she'd been touched by more men in the last couple of hours than in the last six months. You'd think that would loosen her up, but no. She was going the other direction, fitting herself for her own personal suit of armor.

Lauren trudged out of the courtyard into the wind and the low rolling thunder of the sea. The light failed as the clouds thickened, the color of the ocean dulling from blue to gray and the green of the grass muted. She stopped beside the burned patch and looked back at the tower.

Susanna's tower had looked like that, mostly. Catherine's, without the appended rooms, had appeared even more sheer, stony, and stern. Even more of a masculine imperative thrusting up from the gentle mounds of Mother Earth.

Once again the door in the turret looked like a phantom bride, her gown gray with age.

Catherine had been a bride. Susanna had not. Lauren split the difference, in a way. Perhaps Susanna, too, had been cheated of marriage, while Catherine found marriage unendurable.

Instead of vanishing once Lauren looked closely at it, the human shape atop the Tower stepped forward, into the sunlight, completely solid. It was not woman but a man wearing dark clothing, his similarly dark hair waving around a pallid, indefinite blotch of a face. It might have been David, if he'd galloped up the stairs donning a cloak and releasing his ponytail. But Magnus seemed more the trickster than David, and it sure wasn't him.

The stranger behind the parapet, the sentinel on the tower, raised his arm in a gesture that might have been a greeting—*come on in, the water's fine*—or a warning—*riptides, swim at your own risk.*

She took a step, not looking away, not even blinking. She felt the air on her eyeballs, drying them out . . . He dissolved into a beam of sunlight and was gone.

This isn't happening.

But it was.

It hadn't been Persie posing as a gargoyle, the light catching her tag, not this time. Lauren had seen a ghost, or so it appeared. So he appeared, rather. And yet David had said *she* was haunting Blackness Tower.

What she was doing was having waking dreams. Seeing the invisible, whether backwards, forwards, or sideways. Either that, or she was losing her grip on what passed for reality. Going nuts, like her father.

Here, in Caithness, where the very air was tinged with the dust of her ancestors' decomposed bodies— here, where their voices lingered on, murmuring in the calls of the birds, in the wind, in the sea—her Sight had reached critical mass. Maybe Magnus could use physics to explain the non-physical, but she wasn't holding her breath. Not for that, anyway.

No vapors, she reminded herself, and forced a deep breath of the salt-sweet air into the iron maiden of her chest. Taking one step at a time, she walked on down to the footbridge, and only then allowed herself a glance at the chapel.

The students were ranged along the perimeter wall munching on sandwiches and drinking from bottles and cans. A youth sporting a bandage on his left hand was declaiming, ". . . barely touched the soddin' stone and it fell bang on ma finger . . ."

It hadn't taken long, Lauren thought, for the local unluckiness to catch up with the crew.

Bryony—Calder's people, staff, the cupcake acting as though she was jealous—wasn't there. Neither was Calder himself. Lauren saw the top of his apparently disembodied hat just outside the chapel door.

He knew about the pocket watch and the Armada ship. Perhaps he knew something about Catherine

Sinclair and either her destiny or her dream . . . Wait a
minute. The hat was rising and falling above the site of
Susanna's grave.

Magnus said Calder was digging up her grave. Did he
mean exactly that? Changing course, Lauren climbed the
hill, brushed by the row of students, passed the gateway
in the low stone wall.

And stopped so abruptly she almost lost her balance.

She saw fewer gravestones, the tall ones standing
upright, the inscriptions on the low ones newly cut.
Fresh flowers lay beside the Bremner monument, a ray
of sun glinting off their dewy-fresh petals. By the chapel
door yawned a black, oozing gash in the earth, an open
grave.

Beside it stood a man wearing a dark cloak, a touch
of white at his throat and at his wrists. He glanced back
over his shoulder. His face was a blur, with no more than
shadows for eyes. But the silver flare in his hand was
clearly defined, the filigree, the engraved words, and the
arch of the cranium.

So was the silk scarf half-wrapped around hand
and skull both, the same one the wind had blown from
Lauren's hair into David's grasp.

CHAPTER EIGHT

"You've come back, have you?" The voice was familiar, if distorted, the first words coming from a long way away, the last close by, with a sort of Doppler effect in between.

Lauren fluttered her lashes, fanning away the cobwebs. Clouds blocked the sun. The sea rolled sullenly toward the horizon. Fungus, crumbling rock—everything inside the wall was decayed except the massive stones of the chapel. Only weeds lay against the monument with the decomposing angel. *Margaret Bremner*, read the inscription on this side, *wife of Gideon Bremner. Who can find a virtuous woman? For her price is far above rubies. 1862 -1912.*

Bryony knelt beside the black gash in the earth, now only one slit of several cut in a grid pattern across the cemetery. Calder stood between the re-opened grave and a monolithic doorjamb. The silver wedge of his trowel repeated the sheen of his eyes. His face in the shade of his hat wasn't scowling, but it wasn't smiling either.

Again Lauren grasped at her wits, which by now were positively nauseated. She'd seen another ghost. Or the same one in a different context. Who he was, *when* he was, what he was trying to tell her . . . She checked her pocket. Her scarf was still there. And the skull watch lay heavy in her bag next to the old book.

Bryony sat back on her haunches and looked around, tapping her own smaller trowel against a lump of stone so that it made a tinny *dink dink* like the tick of a stop watch.

"May I help you, Miss Reay?" Calder asked loudly.

Lauren found her voice. "You've gone straight to Susanna Mackay's grave."

"Oh aye," he replied. "Looks to be a right interesting site."

One where there was a hell of a disturbance in the Force. "Were you planning to start with her grave all along? You thought she didn't have any relatives to ask questions."

Calder's face turned toward his canvas bag, lying on the hollowed threshold of the chapel. A dark furrow ran around that stone, too, exposing what might have been carved shapes or letters now packed with black muck and root tendrils like capillaries.

"Or is it my own fault?" Lauren almost said, *for my sins.* "I showed you her skull watch, and now you're looking for the rest of the one you found here."

Dink dink.

"You were saying you had nae worries, being four generations removed and all," Calder replied without looking around.

"I know, it's just that . . ." Once again, Lauren didn't know how to finish her sentence. Calder was even less likely than David to understand if she said, "That skull might be a thread tying everything together, and I need to know what the everything is."

Dink dink.

"Bryony, give it a rest," snapped Calder.

Frowning, Bryony leaned over the grave, reached, and scraped. "I'm seeing what looks to be bones, Ewan. Not so deep at all. You'd expect a coffin, wouldn't you now? Coffin hardware at the least, and the stain of the rotted wood."

Calder dropped into a crouch beside the hole. Careful not to break down the rim of any of the trenches, Lauren hopscotched around the broken monuments and stepped up beside Bryony.

She saw the ruler-straight part in the woman's hair, the top of Calder's hat, and two trowels flashing in the trench. A small exploratory trench, only about two feet long and one wide, driven expertly toward the heart of the grave and finding it mere inches below the tangled roots of the wildflowers and weeds. A chill breath flavored with mold oozed upward.

"Oh aye," said Calder, his crispness melting in a warm breath of enthusiasm, "we've got a clavicle just here, and the tip of the sternum. There's the ridge of the jawbone. And what looks to be a clasp, with fabric attached." His trowel indicated what appeared to Lauren like nothing more than a small tangle of blackened twigs and a dark, sodden rag.

Her great-great grandmother's bones. The remains of the body that had posed for a painting wearing a scarlet dress. The breathing, sensing, tasting body that through art and imagination had traveled into other places and played other personae. Her flesh with its receptors of both pleasure and pain, her brain, with every impulse to both appetite and rue. This ruin was everyone's destiny, coming in the end not to dust but to mud.

Bryony's practically short but fashionably crimson fingernails pointed to a thin running gleam in the muck of the grave. "Gold thread. She was buried in something real posh."

"Buried without a coffin?" asked Calder. "And that fabric's never a shroud. The grave's not so deep as most . . . Stop just there, Bryony, and fetch the camera. Muggins here left it in the van, thinking we'd not be needing it the day."

Gracefully, Bryony rose, sidled around Lauren leaving as wide a gap as possible, then sped toward the gate. The black fringe of her bangs came to Lauren's chin. She could have wrapped one of Lauren's belts twice around her waist.

Calder sat up less gracefully, took off his hat, and wiped his forearm across his brow. His gaze at Lauren was almost as intense as David's, as though he, too, was waiting for answers she either didn't have or wasn't prepared to give. At least David accepted that some answers were personal. Calder seemed to think she was withholding those answers to thwart his ambitions.

Then, he, too, smiled up at her, a starched little quirk of his lips complemented by a crumple of his eyebrows that reminded Lauren of a schoolboy called to the principal's office. She wondered if his weather-beaten appearance and constipated demeanor had fooled her into thinking he was older than he really was.

"We've got ourselves a bit of a riddle here, it seems," he said.

"We? You and your crew?"

"You and I, Miss Reay. Your great-great granny's grave. Your complete skull. My partial skull. If you've got a problem with my excavating just here and now . . ."

"No," Lauren replied. "No problem. I'll sign whatever permission you need. Just as long as you keep me informed and answer my questions. I have a lot of them, about more than Susanna."

"You're not working with that TV presenter, are you now?" Calder's smile contracted.

"No. It's just coincidence that we both turned up today."

"I was telling him to leave well alone, but he'd not have himself a telly program if he did that."

And I wouldn't be here at all. Lauren found herself sympathizing with this man, too. And perhaps if she were seen to sympathize with him . . . "Mr, er, Dr. Calder . . ."

"Ewan," he said.

"I'm Lauren, then," she returned. "Ewan, what do you know about Susanna? What do you know about Catherine Sinclair and James Mackay?"

"Susanna worked as an artist's model for Bremner and his salon. Amongst other paintings, she sat for a portrait of Catherine. Of a sort." He cast a jaundiced glance toward the tower.

Lauren waited, but he didn't add anything about her resemblance to Susanna. He hadn't recognized her when she first appeared, for that matter. At least, not in the way David had recognized her. "Have you seen the portrait?"

"There's a bad copy by some hack-handed art student hanging in the wee book shop in Thurso. The owner got right shirty when I asked about it, though, said no more than that the original's at the tower. It's a fine picture, looks to be, but not historical. The ship's like no ship that's ever sailed, and the dress is all wrong, not as constructed as garments in either the sixteenth or the nineteenth century."

"It's art, not history," Lauren told him. "It's romance. The scarlet dress might be symbolic."

Ewan shrugged that notion away. "I'm a scientist. I'm needing ground truth."

"Is Catherine buried here, too?"

"She was, like as not, but there's nothing so old still here. I'm surprised we're finding remains a century gone, in this acid soil. There's nothing left."

"Except for the cranium of a skull watch."

He nodded. "Not fair, is it, that the artifacts outlast the hands making them? Like the tower. James Mackay built it in 1579 atop old Norse ruins, re-using the older stones lying about the headland. Recycling's not a modern-day concept, not at all."

David had said that, if more poetically. "But the chapel was already here."

"Twelfth century, near as we can tell. Also built of older stones." He tapped on the huge slab of the threshold. "See the marks of weathering, sun and frost, here on the buried face? It was above ground for a right long time before it was set down here."

"Aren't those carved semi-circles beneath the weathering? And what about that circular thing in the middle, the one that looks like a giant thumb print?"

"The curving lines are by way of being no more than decoration, to us, at the least, since we've not got the vocabulary to understand their meaning."

No kidding. "So what about James and Catherine? Their marriage was a dynastic alliance, wasn't it?"

"Like as not. The Sinclairs and the Mackays, they're still powerful families in these parts."

"David Sutherland says Catherine had an affair with a selkie, and James killed her out of jealousy, or possessiveness, or revenge. The usual motives."

"Huh." Ewan rolled his eyes, replaced his hat, and peered again into the grave. "Sutherland's away with the fairies, and no mistake. Makes him a good fit with that Anderson chap and his Paranormal Rolodex, or whatever it is."

Lauren half-smiled at his joke and half-frowned, wondering just how he intended "away with the fairies." She could retort, *you came this far from saying yourself that archaeologists need active imaginations*. But she knew what he meant. David's spooky vibe.

No need to make herself collateral damage in Ewan's skirmishes with David. Neither did she intend to play either end against the middle, alienating both. She was just a neutral observer, if not exactly a dispassionate one. "Magnus was enthused about the local legends."

"He's saying there's never a ghost or a fairy he couldna explain," said Bryony's breathless voice from behind Lauren's back. "Here you are, Ewan."

The red-taloned hand extended a small digital camera over the grave. Ewan took it and started pushing buttons. Almost kneeling on Lauren's feet, Bryony began to lay out meter sticks and other markers in the dark but not so deep grave.

Magnus had said he'd talked more than necessary with Bryony. Maybe he could woo her away from Calder. Maybe that was none of Lauren's business.

A low rustle of footsteps, like the approach of a herd of hoofed beasts, made her look around. No, the sheep hadn't gotten in, but Jason and the other students had, still chewing their lunches. They were no doubt wondering what had made the boss call for his camera so soon. It was time for her to back off, let the man work.

"Thank you, Ewan," she called over Bryony's head. "I'll be back out here tomorrow to see what you've turned up."

He glanced up from beneath his hat brim. "If you're keen on the facts of the place as well as the fancies, ask at the Thurso library for Rosemary Gillock. She's by way of being the local expert."

"Thank you. I will." So all roads led to Ms. Gillock, Lauren told herself. Not to mention Charles Innes, the book dealer. Good. She could have her genealogy and her—well, they weren't exactly fancies—as well.

She zigzagged through the oncoming youthful bodies, catching a whiff of meat here and cheese there. Her stomach rumbled. There was another reason to get back into town, to get some nourishment before she mugged one of these kids for his sandwich.

"Gather round," Ewan told his flock. "What we've got here, I'm thinking just now, is a silver clasp holding a very fine bit of fabric, likely a cloak."

In mid-growl, Lauren's stomach clenched. A cloak. She'd had a vision of, Seen, a man in a cloak. *Right*. Up until only a few decades ago, everyone had worn cloaks. No surprise Susanna had been buried in one. A high-quality one, woven with gold threads and clasped in silver.

But she'd been buried without so much as a shroud, in a shallow grave. Ewan was right, that was a riddle, for both of them. For all of them, Bryony, students, and all.

Lauren stopped at the opposite side of the Bremner monument. *Gideon Bremner 1842-1907. A man's a man for a' that*. Not a scriptural admonition like the one for Margaret, the wife, but a line from a Robert Burns poem about honest men, a rather egalitarian verse for a wealthy, powerful man's grave. She'd have expected something about buried Caesars.

1907.

That was the same year Susanna died. The same year her son John had left the Auld Sod. A lot had happened in 1907. And in 1588. And recently, too. When it came to leads to follow, she'd gone from too few to too many.

Lauren walked back through the narrow gateway, bracing herself for what Magnus had called manifestations. But the world was just the same outside the wall of the cemetery as within it. Birds called, the sea advanced and retreated, the sky filled with clouds. Blackness Tower rose from its headland. From its foundations of ancient stone.

And a very contemporary Magnus bounced down the opposite slope. His thick-soled shoes thudded across the bridge. He shot a curious glance toward the chapel, saw Lauren, and stopped. As soon as she got into earshot he offered her a knowing grin, every tooth gleaming. "You were holding out on me, Lauren. If I buy you lunch back in town, will you spill the beans about that painting? Just not on my lap, please."

He'd recognized her in the portrait. He'd probably made a note on his PDA.

Suddenly Lauren wanted him to hurry and set up his instrumentation. Thermometers, infra-red cameras, anything that would help dispel what was getting to be a permanent pucker in the back of her neck. Assuming any instrument in existence could explain or dispel her walk between worlds.

"Sure," she said. "Let's do lunch."

CHAPTER NINE

Lauren leaned back in her chair so the waitress could set a plate in front of her. Breaded and deep fried bits of haggis, Magnus had assured her, made a great appetizer.

He hadn't said much else to her, not yet. It had taken him all the way to the Black Ness parking area just to give her directions to the restaurant, considering she knew Thurso like the back of the moon. She'd pulled out onto the main highway right behind his sports car, but within moments he'd whisked around a lumbering farm tractor and vanished. Too nervous about her passing skills to follow his lead, she'd poked along for miles behind the tractor and its trailer piled with huge taut black cylinders—hay bales, she deduced, harvest being earlier and wetter in this climate.

Just getting both herself and the car safely back to Emily's house had been an accomplishment. Her face in the bathroom mirror had been pink, not pale, and so far from sagging she looked as though she'd had a face lift, brows riding high and eyes glazed with the glare of oncoming headlights, no matter that those headlights were symbolic.

Leaving a note for Emily, she'd walked the rest of the way, and arrived at the small, stylish restaurant to find Magnus in control of a table by the window. And in demand. In the ten minutes since he and Lauren placed their orders, he'd had three phone calls. Each time he'd skipped outside and paced past the window, gesturing so expansively that once he'd almost socked a woman pushing a baby pram.

Now he made a show of switching off the phone and tucking it into a pocket of his cargo pants. "Okay. I really am here this time. Whaddya think of the haggis?"

Lauren sniffed at the little brown bundles. The odor was earthy, but not to the point it reminded her of cemetery mud. She pried off a bit of breading and meat paste, dabbed it in mustard sauce, and ate. It was both rich and subtle, mouth-filling, the culinary equivalent of Ewan's Scots accent. "Mm, good."

"You don't come to the UK to eat ball park nachos." Magnus started consuming his own haggis, using his knife and fork British-style, as pusher and conveyor respectively.

It was just as well she'd run into him, Lauren thought. Otherwise she'd have gone back to Emily's house and assumed a duck-and-cover pose in the kneehole of her dressing table, her head in her hands, the teeth of the skull watch chattering away beside her.

She'd told Ewan that Magnus's arrival was coincidence. She hadn't told him what her grandfather said about coincidence.

The restaurant's sound system segued from light jazz to Norah Jones singing "Come Away with Me." Lauren retrieved the last crumbs from beneath the lettuce-leaf garnish, consigned them to the no longer echoing pit of her stomach, and looked up at Magnus. She had to hand it to him—he'd cleaned his plate without leaving traces of food on his facial hair. "So why's an American guy doing a program on British TV?"

"I was born here in Scotland, but my folks headed out for greener pastures in California when I was just

a kid. I kept flying back and forth visiting the relatives
and switching schools and so on, then finally found me a
job with the BBC. That didn't last long," he added with a
grin, inviting her to imagine him ushered out by security
after threatening the Queen with a cream pie.

"Do you get back to California very often?"

"Naw. My folks are gone now, my friends are here.
And I'm pretty good at hosting the woo-woo stuff."

"Do you like the woo-woo stuff, or are you just
catering to public taste?"

"Both. I cut my teeth on stories of gray ladies, fairy
hills, earth energy—you know, Stonehenge as a giant
electricity conductor, site of fertility rites, whatever."

"Yeah, if historians and archaeologists can't explain
something, they default to 'ritual use' and 'fertility rite'.
And if the occultists want an explanation, 'earth energy'
covers a lot of ground. If not what Ewan Calder calls
ground truth."

Magnus grinned. "Absolutely. But these ancient
people have to have been doing *something* with all the
earth-moving and stone-dragging. Charting the seasons,
sure, that makes sense. But what else?"

"Wishful thinking?" suggested Lauren. "We're all
guilty of that."

"No kidding. There's been an uptick of interest in
the paranormal recently. A hunger for otherworldliness,
whether you call it woo-woo or spirituality. Maybe it's
millennialism. Maybe the real, physical, bite-you-on-
the-ass world's just too much with us. Who knows? Here
ya go." He handed his empty plate to the waitress.

He was "on," giving Lauren his spiel. "Do *you* believe
in the woo-woo stuff?" she asked.

"I've never found any place that lived up to its
reputation. Especially not Stonehenge."

Like David, he didn't answer her question. Maybe she was asking too many. She saw them as a pre-emptive strike, although if he wanted to interpret them as her collecting his references, great. "But you'd like to find such a place, wouldn't you?"

His forehead crinkled. "Sure I'd like to find such a place," he said. "One with verifiable paranormal phenomena, wouldn't that be a kick in the head? And, before you say it, yeah, it would sure as Hell's a town in Norway put me on the front pages of the papers."

He was an ambitious soul like Ewan, then, if grasping at straws rather than old bones and older stones. "Not so long ago it would have gotten you burned at the stake."

"No kidding. Even though proof that the soul survives death is what religion is all about."

She conceded that with a nod. "The hunger for ghosts as a hunger for spirituality. Fine. But isn't verifiable paranormal phenomena a contradiction in terms?"

"That's what I'm working on." Magnus leaned confidingly across the table, his gaze unwavering.

When David's gaze had been steady, she'd sensed he was lying. Magnus, though, lied for a living, more or less. Perhaps there was a faint glitter in the depths of his eyes. Perhaps that was merely the reflection from his glossy shell. Above the unbuttoned placket of his knit shirt, beneath the fringe of his beard, his Adam's apple jumped in the white expanse of his throat.

Would he be able to tell she was . . . Not lying. Just protecting her privacy.

"So what's up with that portrait?" he asked. "You're a dead ringer for it. But Sutherland isn't talking, not about you, anyway."

What *was* he talking about? Lauren wondered. "Susanna Mackay sat for the portrait. She was my great-great-grandmother. And she was descended from Catherine Sinclair."

"Kind of weird, isn't it, that you look just like her? Susanna, that is, although who's to say whether you look like Catherine?"

It's more than kind of weird. She answered, "Yes."

"What do you know about Susanna?"

"Year of birth, year of death. And that her only child, my grandfather's father, John Reay, was illegitimate and didn't want to talk about it."

"Tracking down the mystery of your ancestry, huh? There's a story in there."

"Not really." She took a drink of her Coke, that had arrived cool but without ice.

"How about . . ." Magnus was interrupted by the waitress, who doled out soup and bacon sandwiches.

Lauren considered the white, glutinous mass in her bowl. "Excuse me, I ordered chicken noodle soup."

"That's it, right enough," said the waitress. "If you've changed your mind . . ."

"No, no problem." Lauren dipped her spoon and tasted. Yes, there were some nubbins of chicken and a few noodles suspended in the cream and butter.

"Eat up," said Magnus, retracting into his own personal space. "Don't be fooled by a few brief bouts of sunshine. In this climate you need all the fat you can get. Insulation."

She assumed he wasn't commenting on her body shape, and ate up. The bacon was heavy and salty, and the bread was much more solid than the cottony stuff she was used to, like the handsome stone houses of Thurso were more solid than her jerry-built apartment complex. "What kind of soup do you have?" she asked after a while.

"Spicy Mulligatawny. Try some." He shoved the remains of a bowl of chunky liquid, red as his hair, in her direction.

Delicately, she spooned up a bite. A good thing he hadn't offered her some on his own spoon—that would have been too intimate a gesture. "Oooh. Nice burn. Picante, like a good salsa."

"Salsa? Consider yourself warned—they do great Indian food here, Mexican, not so much. At least, not out here in the boondocks. There are some places in London . . ."

"I won't be here long enough to go anywhere else." Lauren put down her utensils and wiped her lips, feeling a little less tender around the nerves. Now, though, it was time to get down to business, see if he could help her pursue her quest. Bearing in mind that every take required a give.

He beat her to the punch. "So what is she—Susanna pretending to be Catherine in that portrait—what's she holding in her hand?"

"I think it's a sixteenth century watch shaped like a silver skull. One came down in my family from Susanna herself."

His eyes widened so far the whites glinted. "Why that's—that . . . Cool! Do you have it with you?"

"Yes, but I'm not showing and telling here." She glanced meaningfully around at the crowded tables.

"Let's go up to the library after lunch, then. You were going there anyway, to look at the genealogical records. I'll introduce you to Rosemary Gillock. She's into the wee folk and ESP and all that good stuff. She's been a big help with my research. Seems there have been juicy legends about Black Ness for ages—no surprise, with the ancient stones and everything. Though the really grim and dark legends started in the sixteenth century, like the one about musicians and dancers changed to stone for playing on the Sabbath. There's your echo of the old religions—it's one of the more common explanations of ancient stone structures up and down the UK."

"The sixteenth century," Lauren repeated. "People happily torturing and killing each other over points of doctrine. And Shakespeare, da Vinci, Copernicus on the side of civilization."

"Sounds like modern times." Magnus was leaning over the table again. If he'd been wearing a tie, its end would be dragging in his empty bowl. "I'm doing a show about Robert Kirk of Aberfoyle. Know who I'm talking about?"

"The minister who said a nearby hill was a fairy mound, right?"

"Right. Considering this went down in the 1680s, religious conflict, witch hunts, and all, he was either nuts or onto something so weird he couldn't hide it. He wrote *The Secret Commonwealth of Elves, Fauns, and Fairies.* Not Tolkien's tall, gorgeous elves, like Liv Tyler in the movies, whoa."

"Orlando Bloom's not so bad, either. But I know what you mean, I did my homework."

"Elves. Fauns. Fairies. The little people." The glitter grew in Magnus's eyes. "Pre-Celtic, pre Iron-age people, driven underground, perhaps literally as well as metaphorically."

"Or the Celts interpreted their burial mounds as underground communities. Houses of the dead."

"The fairies were indigenous people who passed into legend as well as into the gene pool. The dark Celts, we call their descendants today. You and me, we're the big bright Celts. Plus I've got Scandinavian ancestry. Vikings, Picts, Scots, Gaels, Britons—by now the Brits and their descendants are a motley crew. All this being greatly simplified. I've learned to do that for the customers."

"Of course," Lauren said. Her mother's family came from Brittany and Normandy, on the Celtic fringe, another land where Viking and Celt met and mingled.

Magnus's eyes were an even darker brown than hers. It was dark-haired David who had the sea-blue eyes, gene pools being more like whirlpools than millponds.

She, too, leaned over the table, the buzz of conversation, the clink of cutlery, the sound system fading to a hum behind Magnus's voice with its familiar accent. An almost exaggerated accent, that probably being part of his shtick as well.

"Anyway," said Magnus. "Robert Kirk was either found dead on the fairy mound in his nightshirt, or he just disappeared and his grave contains a box of rocks rather than his coffin. Either way, rumor had it the fairies or elves or little green men kidnapped him for revealing their secrets."

"Most of us like to keep our secrets," Lauren stated.

"Kirk's apparition appeared to a cousin, and told him he could break Kirk out of the fairy pen by throwing an iron dagger over his head. But the cousin was so startled to see him, he didn't do it. You'd expect iron to have power in an ancient culture that was defeated by it."

"People taken alive into fairy mounds—that's another common story."

"With lots of variations, like Rip van Winkle. No fairies in that story though, he just fell asleep and woke up years later."

Had he dreamed during those years? "You think fairies are real, then? What else? Pixies? Selkies?"

Lauren knew she was channeling Ewan, but she suspected Magnus enjoyed a challenge.

"Selkies and mermaids are easy to explain with anything from optical illusion to outright lies. Fairies, though. Think about it. Burial mounds. Fairy mounds. Most people who go under the earth don't come out again, forget Kirk and van Winkle."

"Fairies are the spirits of the dead, you mean? Ghosts?"

Magnus spread his hands—*ta da!* "That's an old Celtic belief, Rosemary says."

"What is a ghost, then? Some sort of echo or resonance in time?" One that few people sensed, Lauren added to herself. Humanity went about its business hip deep in shades but oblivious to them, like sea creatures perceiving the surface of the water as the end of the world. She'd been that near-sighted, once. Ah, for those days of innocence.

"There are different kinds of ghosts. Some are spirits hanging around because of unfinished business, like wanting decent burial for their remains, so that their souls can then go on to, well, wherever souls go."

"Into that peace that passes all understanding."

"I hope so," said Magnus. "Then there are the ones that are no more than a recording. Any of them should show up on sensors. But that's where it gets tricksy. Murphy's Law—you go looking for a ghost and it won't perform. Most of the good photos are accidental, like the ghost video from Hampton Court."

The waitress was standing over them, pad poised. "Afters?"

"Dessert?" Magnus translated, a waggle of his eyebrows suggesting a double-entendre.

"No thank you." Lauren smiled. Yeah, the afterglow of food resembled that of sex, didn't it? The slow seeping calm. The threat of heartburn. No problem, though—she liked Magnus, for all his glossy verbal armor.

She made a gesture toward her bag. "Let me."

"No, this was my idea. Damn good one, too." He presented his credit card to the waitress and then leaned on the table again. "So what do you want from me, Lauren?"

Bushwhacked, she stammered, "What?"

"What's your agenda?"

"To find the identity of my grandfather's grandfather," she recited.

"Right," he said, and for a long moment considered her face, almost watchful as David, almost expressionless as Ewan.

The credit card and its accompanying slip returned in the hand of a man—the manager, probably—wearing a white shirt, a striped tie, and the stretched smile of the celebrity hound. "Thank you for stopping in again, Mr. Anderson. If we could just have your autograph here, ha ha."

"Good to be back." Magnus returned the smile by exposing all his teeth, then took his time with the credit slip, totaling the numbers and figuring out a tip, until at last the man drifted away. Only then did he sign the slip and tuck it beneath the edge of his bread plate.

When he looked up at Lauren, she was ready for him. "So what's *your* agenda?"

"My agenda?" The puzzlement on his face was a bit overdone.

"What do you want from me?"

"A story," he answered. "Part of the story of Blackness Tower."

"And what do you want from Blackness Tower? Just a story?"

He looked at the watch riding his forearm like an archer's vambrace. "It's past two. If we're going to the library for show and tell . . ." He got to his feet, slipped on his jacket, pulled out her chair.

"Good save there," Lauren told him.

"I thought so," he returned, and annotated his grin with a wink.

She grinned back at him, wondering which of them was more the stranger in a strange land here. And she didn't mean the strange land of Scotland.

She started toward the door, Magnus guarding her back. And only then did she register that the sound system was playing "The Water is Wide."

For love is gentle, and love is kind, The sweetest flower when first it's new, But love grows old and waxes cold, And fades away like morning dew.

CHAPTER TEN

So much for hoping that a good meal, let alone several miles between her and Blackness Tower, would numb the rise and fall of gooseflesh like a tide up and down Lauren's body. The uncanny was getting to be with her much more than she'd bargained for.

Oblivious to her discomfort, Magnus closed the door of the restaurant and surveyed the street, the buildings, the gray sky. A couple of sea gulls atop a light pole made choked grating noises that Lauren supposed were squawks, and a cold, damp wind caught her hair and the tails of her jacket. Funny, she'd taken that calendar photo as gospel truth, assumed "August" meant "warm," and brought only medium-weight clothing. At least she'd left behind her strappy sandals and flirty chiffon tops.

"Nice town, for boondocks," she said, hoping Magnus couldn't detect the mini-quaver in her voice.

"Yeah, there's something to be said for slower-paced. Library's up this way."

She walked along beside him, craning her neck toward his sharp profile and mischievous grin that made him look less like a Viking than a leprechaun on steroids. "You live in London?"

"Yep. Costs the earth, but then, it's the center of the earth."

"You don't miss the USA?"

"I miss the space. Everything's smaller here. Cramped. But then, I'm a big guy."

No kidding, Lauren thought. She didn't meet too many men who made her feel sylph-like. She should start hanging out in locker rooms instead of art studios.

"Eventually I'll sell *Paranormal Files* to the American market and go back. Civil War battlefields, Indian burial mounds, that sort of thing." He reached into his pants pocket and pulled out his phone. "'Scuse me while I check for messages."

They paused in front of what Lauren saw was Emily's housewares store—the name painted on a plaque above the door was the simple, straightforward, "Brodie's." The window displayed everything from cutlery sets to plastic toys to tartan-bedecked boxes of shortbread.

If this was Emily's place, then the bookstore . . . Lauren stepped further down the sidewalk.

Behind her a truck rumbled up the street. Magnus's voice rumbled more quietly, but not quietly enough. Between the clarity of diction he'd learned working on television and Lauren's increased sensitivity, she heard every word. "I told you I'd bring her in. What's your rush, Mare, she was coming there anyway. Yes, in a few minutes. Keep your shirt on. Please."

Mare? Rosemary?

Lauren's already heavy stomach sank a bit further down her torso. Magnus hadn't guessed she intended to go to the library to do genealogical research. He'd stated it, because he'd already known it. Emily had told Rosemary, and Rosemary must have told Magnus, and— what? Lauren tried to make her qualm into a joke by telling herself she sure didn't get that level of service from her library back home.

The dingy window beside her was painted with the words, "Charles Innes. Bookseller." Books were fanned, face up, across the windowsill, their covers ranging from 1930's drab to contemporary lurid. Beyond them, shelves partially closed off a cubbyhole furnished with a desk and a filing cabinet. You'd almost need to unspool a thread to find your way, like Theseus in the Labyrinth.

A light glared from a naked bulb above the desk, illuminating a wizened old man, presumably Charles Innes himself. His scalp gleaming through thin strands of hair, his stooped shoulders, and his long, angular limbs, reminded Lauren of her grandfather.

The wall behind him was filled with framed pictures of various sizes, some as large as an average-sized art print, others small as a school photo. Several pictures were covered by glass that reflected the harsh light. Others were, from Lauren's angle, no more than smudges of color and suggestive shapes. If one of those was the copy of "Catherine's Dream" that Ewan had mentioned, she couldn't make it out.

Innes' sharp features turned right and left, as though sensing a mouse among the stacks, then turned toward her. In the overhead light his glasses looked opaque and his cheeks hollow, and now Lauren was reminded of the silver skull.

She balanced on one leg—go on down the street, or go inside . . .

A warm hand the size of a baseball glove fell across her shoulder blades and guided her away. "Great shop," said Magnus. "There's stuff in there that's probably worth a fortune on eBay, if you didn't die of dust inhalation looking for it. Charles is a great guy, too. Veddy British. Got a few loose brain cells, but who doesn't? Library's up this way."

Lauren cast one quick look back. The light was still shining, but Innes was gone. Eccentric, loose brain cells, whatever, he was inked on her schedule.

Despite her sudden misgiving about Magnus—she was entitled to a little misgiving, by this time—his hand on her back felt soothing. She hadn't realized how much she'd missed Craig's embraces. Just your average, comforting embrace, sexual rapture simply a side benefit.

Magnus kept his hand on her back until they'd crossed the intersection where the main road turned south and headed out of town. Then his hand fell away and indicated a small park and a statue in front of a church. "Sir John Sinclair," he said. "Very important historical figure. We're walking down Sinclair Street. That's St. Peter's church behind him—the new one, not even two hundred years old. The *old* one is near the harbor, a picturesque ruin suitable for photo ops. The oldest one is buried beneath that."

"And in my part of the world, we think the Alamo is ancient." Lauren's back felt cold. She stepped a little closer to Magnus's side, like a ship seeking calmer waters off a lee shore.

"There's the library. Used to be part of a school." He pointed toward a white-painted building embellished with columns and a tall cupola.

"I gather this isn't your first visit to Thurso," she said as they mounted the low steps.

"I'm always scouting for good locations, and the local library's the place to start. It was just serendipity that I fell over Rosemary there. She's the local expert on Black Ness."

Wait a minute. He'd told David he first learned about Blackness Tower when Rosemary e-mailed him. Now he was implying he'd come here first, and then met

Rosemary, who he knew well enough to nickname. Who he knew well enough to plot with, sort of. Maybe.

Lauren reminded herself not to let Magnus's larger-than-life charms inflate the benefit of her doubt.

Stepping into the building was like stepping into another century, going from the nineteenth-century elegance of the exterior to the tidy modern library inside, not one quill pen or inkstand in sight. Along with the heady aroma of books, Lauren smelled the acrid scent of an overworked photocopier.

Before Magnus could approach the youth at the front desk, a woman of what was once called "a certain age" appeared through a doorway. She peered at them over, rather than through, narrow bifocals. "Mr. Anderson," she called quietly, as behooved a librarian. "It's lovely to see you again."

"Hey," said Magnus diffidently, and Lauren took a step away from his shadow.

Rosemary raised the files she held so that they made a shield in front of her upholstered but not over-stuffed chest. Twin spots of color on her cheekbones flared like traffic lights and then drained away. Her rounded chin dropped and then snapped upward again, so firmly it pressed her mouth into a fixed smile that encouraged no familiarities. Without having blinked once, she said, "I don't believe we've met."

Lauren didn't reply, "You know darn well who I am," or even "Weren't you expecting me?" She said, "I'm Lauren Reay, Emily Brodie's cousin."

"Oh my. So you are. Susanna Mackay's descendent. You do look like, well . . . I'm Rosemary Gillock." Each syllable was expelled past small, very white, teeth and thin, very red, lips. "Genealogical research, is it? We're well set up for you, then. This way."

Lauren shot a glance at Magnus in time to catch his look toward Rosemary, a narrow, toothless smile. He hadn't told her, then, that Lauren looked like the portrait. Talk about playing both ends against the middle. Magnus and "Mare" weren't exactly plotting as one. Not that there was any point to subterfuge. Why would anyone want to be less than honest with her?

Maybe because she wanted to be less than honest with them. And yet her dreams weren't affecting anyone else but herself. They couldn't be. They were dreams.

Magnus lagging behind, Lauren followed Rosemary between the shelves, racks, and tables, past a rank of microfilm readers. The library was as much a maze as the bookstore, except larger and better lit, light streaming in through the tall windows even on this increasingly cloudy day.

Rosemary's dark hair was symmetrically curled and her eyebrows penciled. Her white blouse, black skirt, and low-heeled shoes were leavened by a paisley scarf draped and apparently glued in pleats over one shoulder. She carried herself as though she'd been wearing a corset all her life, waist in, chest out, straight and tall, even though her height was closer to Bryony's than to Lauren's. She appeared to be the sort of person who card-catalogued the spices in her kitchen. If she had any spices in her kitchen.

But appearances were deceiving, Lauren told herself. Even her own.

Rosemary led them to a small, quiet side room. Lauren had half-expected it to be teeming with "colonials," but no, she had the place to herself. Well, to herself and Magnus, who was standing uncharacteristically both in the background and silent.

"Census records, wills and testaments, parish records." Rosemary's hand indicated each item on the surrounding shelves. "That notebook contains an index of further resources, including microfilm copies of local newspapers going back a century or more. We've got bound paper copies as well, but you're obliged to request those at the front desk."

Her gesture pulled the cuff of her blouse away from her wrist, revealing what looked like a burn, a tapering red streak mottled with scab, stark against the lily white skin.

Quickly lowering her hand, she set it on one of the files in the crook of her left arm. "These sources on Lord Reay and Highland Second Sight will answer some of your questions. Have you been out to Black Ness at all?"

"Yes," Lauren replied. "Yesterday and this morning as well."

"Then you've met Dr. Calder, I expect. These references are the ones I've collected for him." Rosemary patted the second file envelope and then placed both on a table as though placing ritual objects on an altar.

"What about David Sutherland?" asked Lauren. "Have you collected references for him, too?"

"No. I have not. If I can be of any further assistance, please ask. The library closes at five today." And with one last stare at Lauren, her blue eyes aloof beneath flaccid lids, Rosemary strolled away. She pulled the door shut behind her.

So did that mean that David had never asked for her help, or that he had and she'd refused him, for whatever reason? Maybe the same reason she was picking at David's shell by sending Magnus to besiege his fortress of solitude.

And here she'd thought, Lauren told herself, that the only issues she'd be investigating were those of the dead.

She dumped her bag next to the files and rooted around inside for her notebook and pen. And for the skull watch, even though she was now less than enthused about showing it to Magnus. She couldn't back out, though, without revealing her suspicions of him. And he was hovering expectantly, as much as a man of his size could hover.

Even when she shook the red velvet box it emitted not one tick-tock, just a ripple of chimes. "Here you go," she said, and placed it in Magnus's outstretched hand.

With a long sigh, as if steeling himself to the task, he lifted the lid and then the watch itself. Gently he turned it over, opened it, closed it. Quick reflections ran over his rapt face like water over stones. His forefinger tapped the words inscribed on the inside of the skull like thoughts moving in the brain. "*Et in terra pax* and so forth. Peace on Earth, good will to men, right?"

"More like peace to men of good will, my grandfather used to say."

"Yeah. And what about this?" He turned the watch upright, indicating the figure of Death and his scythe engraved on the forehead. "*Pallida mors aequo . . .*"

"Something about pale death knocking at the doors of peasants and kings equally."

"Yeah, nobody's a wallflower at the dance of death." He grimaced. "Ewan Calder found a piece of another one of these in the cemetery. No wonder he's going through the place like a hot knife through butter. You got a handkerchief?"

"What?"

"Fingerprints. Those are Sutherland's, aren't they? And yours and mine. The oils in your fingers can cause corrosion on silver, you know, where it gets all black and ratty-looking."

Like the bundle of twigs in Susanna's grave that Ewan identified as the clasp of a cloak. Lauren dived back into her bag and produced a tissue. "Here."

"Thanks. Your family's been keeping the watch clean all this time, but not polished to where the details are rubbed out. Good going."

Every month or so Grandpa had wiped the skull watch with a soft cloth he kept for just that purpose, and cleaned the openwork and the watch workings with a cotton swab. He'd always hummed tunelessly along with the slow repeated chime, as though he and the artifact shared a unique duet. As though he and the watch and the puddle of light from his desk lamp were in a separate world, his own personal Tir nan Og. He was there permanently, now.

A quick scrape caused Lauren to spin around. Chill eyes gleamed between edge of the door and the frame. Then they were gone, and with them a quick flick of paisley and a tap of heels.

Rosemary. Lauren whirled back around to Magnus. But he was wiping the skull as meticulously as he probably polished the chrome on his car, his tongue caught between his teeth in concentration.

Had he phoned Rosemary to tell her about the skull? Or was she listening at the door on general principles?

Lauren glanced down at the files. The bottom one was labeled, "Lord Reay and Second Sight." Maybe Rosemary had guessed that, with her descent from the Mackays, Lauren would be interested in the subject. And yet she'd said, "that will answer some of your questions." Like Magnus, she knew more than she should about Lauren's intentions and motivations.

From the front of the library came the sound of a phone bleating. And suddenly Lauren knew. Last night, at Emily's, Rosemary had called. Emily hadn't shut off the phone. But it had taken a lot of conversation about Seeing and the skull and Lauren's family before the phone had emitted its warning beep. Before Rosemary had finally tired of listening on the open line, and broken the connection.

So what? Rosemary was Emily's friend. She was being helpful. And besides, like verifiable paranormal phenomena, a sinister librarian was a contradiction in terms.

As for how Magnus figured into the plot, assuming there was a plot on his no doubt crowded but not entirely public agenda, he himself had admitted he wanted to expand his media empire.

He set the skull back into the box, and the box on the table next to the files. With a gesture like a caress, he closed the lid. "There you go, old fella. You realize, Lauren, that this thing would bring a bundle at an art and antiquities auction."

"I know it's valuable. But it's a family heirloom."

"That's why I need to get you on the show, holding the watch up next to the painting in the same pose. In a similar dress, with your hair streaming down. I can just see it, the camera panning in from Catherine-Susanna's face to yours. Great stuff."

No, it wasn't great. A shudder wracked Lauren from crown to toe and stem to stern. She grimaced. "I don't think so."

"What? Did you feel someone walk over your grave?" He grinned. "Never mind. We'll figure out the details later. Right now I've gotta work the phone, get my technician up here before Sutherland goes back on our deal and Calder cleans out the cemetery."

Never mind? He didn't have a clue, did he? Lauren's patience, stretched to this utmost on this day of doubt and revelation, snapped. "What do you have on him, anyway?"

"Who, Calder?"

"David Sutherland. Something about an incident, and the Irish papers. He thought you were threatening to blackmail him."

That dashed the grin from Magnus's face. He raised his hands in the same *who me?* gesture he used on David's doorstep. "Whoa. Listening outside doors isn't exactly kosher, you know."

"Tell that to your friend Rosemary. She was watching you play with the skull."

Magnus glanced sharply at the door, then back to Lauren. Now his eyes were guarded, dark as dungeons hiding fell deeds. "I thought we were gonna be friends. Help each other out."

"That's what I thought, too. But there's some funny stuff going on here. And until you're ready to come clean . . ." *Yeah, look who's talking.* She sat down in the nearest chair and opened her notebook to a blank page.

He leaned over her shoulder, a warm presence that still, even now, seemed reassuring. She forced herself to shrink away. But he didn't touch her. His massive hand picked up her pen and wrote a number at the top of the page. "Call me. Any time. I'm as eager to work through the funny stuff as you are, believe me."

He strode across the room and had shut the door behind him before she found her voice, and murmured into the warm, close air of the room, "I believe that. I just don't know what else to believe."

CHAPTER ELEVEN

Lauren walked through a brassy twilight, over the billows of turf toward Blackness Tower. Through the gateway rolled a death coach, a Victorian hearse with glass sides gleaming and black plumes waving. The hooves of the horses rose and fell in utter silence, while the cry of a flock of black and white birds haunted the air.

The coach drew near. She stepped aside from the path, long scarlet skirts clutched in her hands, long hair hanging lank in the windless dusk. Through the glass panels she saw the coffin.

Its lid opened. A dark-haired, dark-bearded man with a white ruff at his neck, wrapped in a cloak, sat up and stared out at her with David Sutherland's sea-blue, smoke-blue, stone-blue eyes.

His hand rose, passed through the glass as though it was mist, grasped her hair and pulled her toward him, into the hearse, into the coffin itself . . .

With a small cry, she jerked back into wakefulness.

Okay. That was it. The heavy meal, the lingering jet lag, page after page of small type and crabbed handwriting, the stuffy, musty air of the room, had made her doze off twice already. Now, third time being the charm, she'd slipped into her usual dream. Except, like the shipwreck, it wasn't her usual dream at all. It was nightmare.

With a creak as much of her muscles as the chair, she stood up and shook herself like an animal shedding water droplets.

The building was so quiet she wondered whether she'd accidentally been locked in. As much as she loved libraries, a dark deserted one would be kind of creepy. Especially if Rosemary Gillock was lurking there, armed with . . . What? A rubber stamp?

The woman was a busybody was all. If she'd wanted to keep Lauren from looking for answers, she'd be refusing her admittance to the library, not loading her down with way too much information.

Lauren glanced at her watch, the one on her arm, and saw that it was four-fifteen. Good, she could make her escape before closing time. Observing library etiquette, she piled the books and rolls of microfilm on the end of a table for Rosemary or, more likely, a flunkey, to replace.

As for what she'd learned from her afternoon's slog through the quicksands of historiography, well, she hadn't expected to find a complete narrative of events. Neither had she expected, though, to find such a mess, like several thousand-piece jigsaw puzzles mixed in together, with no borders and only a few pictures— including the one from the calendar, for what that was worth—to guide her in assembling the one she wanted.

She leafed through her pages of names, dates, phrases, the tidbits she'd gleaned from newspaper articles and registers to supplement the bare facts supplied by Hawkins at Scotland's Folk in Edinburgh.

Such as the census of 1891, taken the night of April 5, that listed name, age, place of birth, and relationship to the head of the household. In the instance of Blackness Tower, that had been Gideon Bremner, age 49, born in Glasgow. Margaret Bremner—no maiden name given—

was "wife," aged 29 and born in Ross-shire, just down the road.

Rupert Beckwith was 26 and born in County Wicklow, Ireland, perhaps, Lauren thought, the child of English landowners like those who were perceived as oppressors or civilizers, depending.

And there was Susanna Mackay, 21, a spinster—and by 1891 that no longer meant that she spun for a living. She had been born in Strathnaver, Mackay Central. So had Florence Simison, age 28, her sister.

Harold Simison, age 31, had seen the light of day in Thurso. They were listed as housekeeper and ghillie—servants. Lauren wondered again whether Susanna had been the equivalent of a servant, or whether she'd occupied that special class allotted to artists, children, and madmen.

In the 1901 census the household was ten years older and minus Beckwith, but with Francis Weir, age 46, Suffolk, England. The Simisons now had two children—the younger would in time become Emily's father. And there was Lauren's great-grandfather, John, age 8, no relation to Gideon.

But then, just because Gideon Bremner was married didn't mean he couldn't be John's father. Now there was a theory worth considering.

The next page was crammed with notes from the columns of the Thurso and Wick newspapers. The more discreet media of the late Victorian era had reported nothing juicy about either scandals or seers at Blackness Tower, just the dinners, picnics, and hunting parties of the gentry and their artistic guests: Andrew Carnegie, the Duke of Argyll, Alfred, Lord Tennyson, Oscar Wilde, William Morris, Arthur Conan Doyle.

There were other names Lauren didn't recognize, but must have been of people the newspaper reporters felt were celebrities. She imagined them all sitting around discoursing on the romantic aspects of the Highland landscape and the backwardness of the aboriginal inhabitants.

Voices and the soft rumble of a book cart sounded through the room's closed door. Good, Lauren thought. She hadn't been abandoned here after all.

Some of the newspaper accounts were illustrated by low-resolution photographs. One showed workmen toiling at the shell of Blackness Tower. Another showed a team of oxen hauling a huge slab of stone toward it—recycling one of Magnus's dancers and musicians petrified for levity on the Sabbath, or, in other words, for observing the last remnant of a discredited rite. *Great.*

Small articles in different papers told of a worker's legs crushed by a toppling stone and another's arm broken in a fall. Three others had been felled by typhus. Were the accidents and disease caused by the miasma of bad luck gathered around the tower, or by the lack of occupational and sanitation police?

Also small were the photos of the principal characters. Margaret's huge hat and Gideon's shrubbery of a beard obscured their features. A fingerprint-sized face peering out from behind several others was identified as Miss Susanna Mackay, but might just as well be Queen Victoria, so far as Lauren could tell.

Even photos of Weir and Beckwith told her little she didn't already know. Their casual hats, soft collars, and languid attitudes proclaimed their aesthetic tendencies, but their faces were little more than blurs, not unlike the faces of the—ghosts—she'd seen on the tower and in the cemetery.

Maybe one of them was the ghost. Maybe one of them was her great-great-grandfather.

Lauren ran her hands through her hair and rolled her shoulders. She was getting few enough facts about Gideon himself. She was not going to find a shortcut through the cramped typeface of his autobiography after all.

Life and Times still squatted like a brick in her bag. The next time she used her lip gloss she'd taste the book's musty odor. She was going to have to hunker down and read it, tonight, hopefully with one of Emily's scones nearby for support.

Here, now, the most intriguing factoids she'd found concerned not Gideon but Margaret.

A newspaper article dated 1895 mentioned a tea to honor a small chapbook written by Mrs. Gideon Bremner. The reporter's every word choice dismissed Margaret's accomplishment. At least he—the article was uncredited, but the reporter had to have been a he—had given the title and subject matter of the book in the very last paragraph, where the least hiccup of a printing press would have blown it off the page.

Catherine Sinclair and the Matter of The Seeing Gift: Notes Provided to the Society for Psychical Research. Maybe, Lauren thought, just maybe, Charles Innes had a copy of that book as well. Or there might be one in the library. She should look up the enticingly named Society, too.

And what about Rupert Beckwith's poem about Catherine, the one that David told her had inspired Weir's portrait? Was a copy lying around in an old book or magazine? What was the source material behind both Beckwith's poem and Margaret's book? Local legend? Old letters?

The register of Reay parish church duly recorded John's baptism—no father listed—and the funerals of Margaret, Gideon, and Susanna at Ladykirk, St. Bride's Chapel.

But Margaret's body wasn't buried beneath the monument with decaying angel and the suitable but rather sexist Bible verse. An article dated April, 1912, detailed how she'd gone down with the *Titanic*. No surviving family members were listed—she and Gideon had had no children, and he had pre-deceased her.

A car started up just outside the window. Some of the library staff must already be taking off for the evening. *So many questions, so little time.* And Susanna herself was maddeningly elusive, just a ghostly face and a name whispered in passing.

With a huff of frustration, Lauren turned back to the two file envelopes and their contents, crisp photocopies of old manuscript pages. One more time, in case she'd missed anything. Although when it came to answering her questions about Lord Reay and Highland Second Sight, the material in the first folder had been both too little and too much.

The Seeing Gift went back, like the foundations of Blackness Tower, into the mists of time. You had the artistic, nature-worshiping Celts—sort of a society of pre-Raphaelites, Lauren thought, except for the head-hunting and human sacrifice—mingling with the ancient Neolithic people with their strange burial rituals. Which only seemed strange, Ewan would probably say, because modern man didn't know the secret handshakes.

Then you had Christian rituals and beliefs imported by early Irish missionaries, like the ones who'd named the chapel for St. Bridget. To those were added the paganism of the invading Vikings. Therefore—Lauren wrote *Ta Da!* in her margin—Neolithic man's burial rites, Celtic mysticism, and Christian and Norse beliefs were knotted like an intricate interlace design into Second Sight. Knotted here, in northern Scotland, the way Harris tweed was woven in the Hebrides.

That was all well and good, if a little academic. What had really made her sit up and take notice was a letter from a Walter Mackay, dated 1901 and typed, thank goodness, if on a primitive typewriter that smudged every other letter.

He wrote that a caste of Seers, perhaps descended from the Celtic priests called Druids—and there was a name that remained evocative throughout the currents of history—survived in the north of Scotland until at least the seventeenth century. Some of his own family, an eighteenth-century Lord Reay in particular, were prone to visions. Mackay never mentioned the supposed Wizard Reay, who seemed to inhabit legend rather than a particular time and place.

"The Sight always renders true visions," wrote Mackay, "but those visions must never be used for selfish reasons, or to do harm." Were ghosts visions? Lauren wondered. Or did visions merely pick up quantum waves or something—well, that was Magnus's territory.

Mackay went on psychoanalyzing the Celt, with his savage fury and dark depressive moods, and the Norseman with his fatalism, and presumably the Englishman with his bowler and umbrella, but Lauren had had enough. Her brain was out of disk space.

Sliding the paper back into the folder, she rubbed her eyes. Again she heard voices from the main part of the library. It was almost five. She'd have to come back tomorrow . . . No, she was going back to Blackness Tower tomorrow, before, as Magnus had said, David went back on their deal.

Magnus had never answered her question about David, not that she'd given him much of an opening. To be fair, Magnus had been a little slick with David, but had never actually threatened blackmail. It was David who'd used that word.

And now it was too late to use the library computer to do an Internet search on him. Amazing, how people used to have nothing but scraps of paper for information.

No surprise David was guarding his privacy. He seemed to be the strong but sensitive type. Craig claimed those traits were mutually exclusive, which explained a lot about their failed relationship.

Smothering a yawn, Lauren turned her attention to the second folder, the one that Rosemary had assembled for Ewan.

She'd thought the century-old handwriting in the first collection of papers was hard to decipher, but the sixteenth-century writing in this one was as bad as code. Several pages had transcriptions, such as *A True Account of the Natives of Northern Scotland* by Alexander Lindsay, he of the 1540 chart of the Pentland Firth, but even with Lindsay's handwritten manuscript rendered into contemporary type, the period Scots dialect was almost incomprehensible.

A letter from James Mackay, Catherine's husband, written in January, 1589, had not been translated. Lauren peered at it, but all she made out was the chilling passage: ". . . since it has pleased God, by his hand, upon the rocks to drown the rest, I will, with his favor, be his soldier for the dispatching of that rag that yet remains." Was he writing of *El Castillo Negro*, or of some criminals making their getaway, or what? She set the paper aside.

Then there was a second-generation copy of a page written in a language even more bewildering than four-hundred-year-old Scots, four-hundred-year-old Spanish. The original paper, stamped with the logo of a library in Madrid, had been torn and stained. Contorted letters above narrow columns of words indicated that it was the manifest of *El Castillo Negro*, which had sailed with the Armada to conquer England in 1588, only to come to grief—well, it was just Ewan's theory that it had wrecked at Black Ness. And Lauren's own dream.

She lowered the paper to replace it in the folder when one line caught her eye. Amid the Miguels and Diegos was the name Patricio Onella. Beneath that, in another hand, was written the English version: Patrick O'Neill. Now that was interesting.

On the principle that the enemy of my enemy is my friend, Irish Catholics had supported their Catholic Spanish cousins in 1588. It wasn't unlikely that an Irishman had joined the Armada, for God, for glory, for booty—or maybe just to hitch a ride home.

She held the paper up. Next to many of the names were the words *marino* or *soldado*, sailor or soldier. Next to O'Neill's was the word *platero*.

Silversmith.

You wouldn't think there would have been much work for a silversmith on a warship, although O'Neill could also have repaired metal fittings of various kinds. And yet . . .

She reached over to the jeweler's box still sitting next to her bag and gave it an experimental jiggle. Was it possible that amidst all the intricacies of the engraving and molding on the silver skull was a tiny *Patricius me fecit*, Patrick made me?

The skull watch duly emitted its muffled chime, but no answers.

Okay, that was it, Lauren told herself again, and this time she meant it. Quitting time. She stacked the remaining photocopies and inserted them into their respective files.

A paper creased into quarters slipped from the Second Sight folder. Not copy paper, it was thick, ivory-colored rag paper. She'd glanced at it earlier, but hadn't wanted to spend precious minutes deciphering the cramped and cautious handwriting.

Still she unfolded it, the paper smooth and chill against her fingertips, and this time the elegant coils of letters resolved themselves into words: "Sweep away the illusion of time; compress our threescore years into three minutes . . . Are we not spirits, that are shaped into a body, into an Appearance; and that fade away into air and invisibility?"

The pen had spluttered, throwing tiny blots of ink across the page like blood spatters at a crime scene.

A prickle crawled from Lauren's hairline down the back of her neck and vanished beneath her collar. She saw again the words stitched on the sampler set before the hearth at Blackness Tower. *This is no metaphor, it is a simple fact. We start out of Nothingness, take figure and are apparitions.*

She swept the paper into the file and slapped both envelopes down on the table. She needed to get out of there, into the free air, away from . . .

She'd never get away from herself.

From outside the door came hurried footsteps and insistent voices. Rosemary's words were short and precise. "We've just closed. Come back tomorrow, and I'll furnish you with new copies."

"I'm sorry to be troubling you," said Ewan Calder's thistle-strewn voice, "but my assistant here, she's misplaced the file, and I'm after having the references soon as may be."

"I never," Bryony insisted, her voice climbing an irritated octave. "Someone's pinched that folder, I never lost it."

"I'm hoping you've got more copies, Mrs. Gillock," said Ewan, louder.

"I've made copies for an American lass," Rosemary told him. "She's in the Quiet Room."

"An American? Lauren Reay? You've given her my reference material?"

"Don't you agree, Dr. Calder, that knowledge is power?"

Three sets of footsteps clumped and clicked. The door opened so quickly it crashed back against the wall.

Ewan was wearing his muddy pants and pullover. His only concession to the library was his shoeless, thick-socked, feet, and his hat held in his hand. His expression was suffused with nervous energy, mouth compressed and eyes blazing. Bryony's black bob and pouting lips looked around one of his shoulders and Rosemary's curled perm and slightly reptilian gaze the other.

Lauren stood up, feeling as though she'd been caught in some sort of act. "Hello."

Muttering something beneath his breath that she hoped was not a variety of *turned up again like a bad penny*, Ewan brushed past her so closely she smelled the peaty earth in his garments. He rejected the first folder, snatched up the second, and leafed through it. "That's it, right enough."

He turned toward her. His features slid to one side, forming what would have been a sheepish smile if the pressure from beneath hadn't squeezed it into a grimace. "I'm sorry. You're right welcome to share my resources. It's just that we've had a bit of turn-up at the dig."

"And that's no joke," said Bryony from the doorway.

Whatever it was, Lauren thought, it had nothing to do with Susanna, not if he needed the Armada material.

"The bones buried in your great-great-granny's grave," Ewan said. "They're a man's. A man from the sixteenth century, judging by the associated artifacts."

Lauren felt her own expression contort. "You mean, Susanna's not there?"

"Oh, she's there, right enough. Tucked well away in her coffin. Beneath the body of a man who lived and died three hundred years before."

CHAPTER TWELVE

Stratigraphy, Lauren thought. One of the principles of archaeology was stratigraphy. The stuff on the bottom was older than the stuff on top.

Except when it came to Black Ness, where space and time didn't seem to work the way they did everywhere else.

Anticipating questions she'd had neither the time nor the space to formulate, Ewan said, "There's a logical explanation, has to be, but as yet I've got no clue. Nor to what I'm expecting to find in this lot, either—" His hand with its dirt-rimmed fingernails flapped the folder. "—save details of *El Castillo Negro* and Alexander Lindsay's journal."

"The body was buried with a silver crucifix," said Bryony. "Ewan's thinking it's Spanish, evidence for his theory of the shipwreck."

"Your theory's why you accepted the job at the cemetery," Rosemary added, "despite that unfortunate edict from the University. Good job, finding anything at all to support it."

"Any excuse to dig at Black Ness, when there's loads of better jobs in the south." Bryony set her hands on her hips and gazed, head lowered, at Ewan.

So they were digging bones of contention as well as human bones, Lauren thought. Or had Ewan and Bryony's affair—they had to have had one, those barbs were too edged for a business discussion—soured to the point that everything was contentious?

And what was behind that crack of Rosemary's? Lack of support for his theory from the university? What business was it of hers anyway?

Ewan's relationship with his academic peers was just as much Rosemary's business as Bryony and Ewan's relationship was Lauren's. She had puzzles of her own, already.

She shoved her notebook and pen into her bag, then reached for the velvet box. Instead of chiming, it jangled harshly as she thrust it away, loud in the quiet room where they all seemed to be holding their breaths.

Rosemary's lips turned up at the ends, but her expression was no smile. "Miss Reay, the library's closed. Dr. Calder. Miss Duff . . ."

Bryony spun around and fled. Ewan jammed his hat down on his head and headed for the door, Lauren on his heels.

The main room was dark, shadows gathered behind the shelves. Perhaps the characters from the books were waiting, poised, until the living souls were gone and they could spill from their pages, Elizabeth Bennett curtseying to Gandalf the Grey, Willy Wonka bowing to Anna Karenina, Genghis Khan riding down on Mary, Queen of Scots. Why not? This was the country that rationality had forgotten.

With a longing look at the computer terminals—her e-mail was stacking up, she was out of touch—Lauren let Rosemary urge her toward the front door. Which Bryony was holding open, her slender body outlined against the daylight. Lauren pushed past her.

Outside, thick gray banks of cloud were sinking lower and lower, smearing the hard edges of steeples and roofs. A cold blast blew Lauren's hair into her face. Through its strands she saw Bryony replacing her shoes. Ewan slipped on his boots while clinging to his hat and keeping the file envelope clenched beneath his arm.

Behind them, Rosemary locked up, and, with one last sharp glance through the glass pane of the door, faded back into the building. This time she really was smiling, her eyebrows above the dagger-thin glasses raised in something like satisfaction. Concluding a job well done.

Lauren assumed Rosemary had a home to go to, and didn't simply lie in state beneath the circulation desk like Dracula in his coffin.

She glanced up the street. Maybe she had time to visit the bookstore. No reason to hang around here. Ewan had already said he had no answers for her. Yet. And it wasn't as though she had a home to go to, although Emily's house made a good alternate.

"I never misplaced that folder," Bryony hissed.

"One of our super brilliant students pinched it, is that it?" Ewan replied.

"Maybe it was that television chap, Magnus."

"He was chatting you up, all right, but I'm not thinking it was the folder he was after. Nor what you were offering."

Lauren took a step backward and barely caught herself before she fell down the steps. "Good night, um, I'll be back out at Black Ness tomorrow . . ."

Bryony glanced over her shoulder. "Good night then." And she snapped to Ewan, "Good night to you as well, Dr. Calder." The title and last name came out as an insult.

Bryony stamped down the steps and a few paces up the street, then slowed. She was, Lauren estimated, waiting for Ewan to call her back and proffer a few verbal flowers and chocolates.

Ewan hung like grim death onto his hat and the files. "Lauren, the rain's coming on. I'll drive you to Mrs. Brodie's house."

Bryony's shoulders jerked back. Speeding her pace, she almost ran across the street and around a corner.

Lauren's first impulse was to tell Ewan not to use her as a weapon. Her second was, maybe he had answers to *something*. The wind blowing icy droplets into her face finalized her decision. "Thank you, but how do you know . . . Duh, I gave you the address this morning. That seems like a month ago."

"Mrs. Brodie's home's no more than a block from my hotel. Come along, the van's just down the street." He led the way to the battered panel van that Lauren had seen that morning, opened the door, and levered her into the seat with almost too firm a grasp of her upper arm.

Lauren installed her seatbelt and noted the tools of the archaeologist's trade, from trowels to cameras, ranked behind Ewan's canvas bag like soldiers on parade. He leaped into the driver's seat, opened the folder, and considered several pages, among them the manifest. The corpse was wearing a silver crucifix and a silver clasp.

"Did you notice the Irish name on the list?" she asked. "Patrick O'Neill. And he was a *platero*. That's silversmith. Maybe he's the body in the grave. Maybe he made my—our—skull watches. Coincidences happen."

Ewan's snort had no humor in it. "Aye, that they do, and more often than the pseudo-science, ghost-and-goblin lot are admitting. But coincidence is one thing and stratigraphy another. Perhaps the body's one of Bremner's friends, done to death at a fancy dress ball . . . Ah. Never mind. The lab work lasts gey longer than the dig, but it answers more questions." He tucked the folder into the glove compartment, his hand almost brushing Lauren's knees—unwittingly, she assumed—and started the engine. He didn't exactly pull away from the curb with a squeal of tires, but he didn't hesitate, either.

"I guess Bryony's staying near here."

"Aye, she's found herself a hotel in town." His *this time* hung in the air like the condensation gathering inside the windshield.

Her loss was Lauren's gain, then, although she was hardly going to say so aloud.

"Sorry. Bryony and me, we were a bit over the top, there." Ewan guided the van up Sinclair Street and stopped at a red light in front of the church.

"No problem. Been there, done that." In her and Craig's case, the issue had been serving alcohol at the wedding. Her mother wanted to economize with punch. Craig said his friends would be insulted without an open bar. Over the next couple of months, that one disagreement had escalated slowly but surely into so many more that the stress fractures in the foundation of their relationship broke open. And the walls had come tumbling down.

She had more in common with Ewan than just an interest in history. She hazarded, "I bet Bryony was just trying to make you jealous by flirting with Magnus."

"Anderson's a wee tumshie," said Ewan. "A turnip. Flash and cash. She's welcome to him."

Magnus was flashy, yeah, and not short of cash, but a turnip? Well, the jury was still out. Lauren changed the subject as the light changed to green. "I was going to stop at the bookstore, right along here."

"It's gone five—the book shop's closed as well."

"Oh. I'll stop in tomorrow morning."

"It's closed Thursday morning, stays open late that evening."

"Oh. Okay. I'll tackle Innes after I tackle David, then."

She realized she was thinking out loud when Ewan's gray eyes flashed in her direction. Perhaps the flash was in response to her American dialect, it taking him a moment to realize she didn't mean "tackle" literally. Or he could be wondering why she was already on a first name basis with David. He still didn't know about the portrait, did he? *Coincidence*.

"The ghost-and-goblin lot" he'd said, and not in the almost affectionate way Magnus had said "woo-woo stuff."

The front window of the book shop was so dark Lauren saw the reflection of the van coasting past like the death coach of her dream. On the floor above, though, three tall windows shone with light. A wizened figure was just drawing the drapes, his bespectacled face turning to follow the van up the street. Innes didn't have a long commute to work, then.

The van turned the corner in front of the restaurant where she'd eaten lunch with Magnus, at least a week ago, it seemed. Now the same waitress was setting a tea tray on the window table, lights reflecting off the metal pots and pitchers.

Lauren huddled into the chill seat, her stomach rumbling. Raindrops spattered across the windshield. "You know Charles Innes?"

"Oh aye. Bloody-minded old soul. If he takes a dislike to you—and I'm thinking he'd take a dislike to Mother Teresa—you're not getting one of his books, even with ready money. He had the cheek to call me a toe-rag."

"A what?" she asked, thinking of the dismissive "rag" in James Mackay's letter.

"Tramp, more or less. I'd been excavating a fine chambered tomb at the Yarrows, and walked into his shop in my working clothes. I've met maitre d's in London less pernickety."

Lauren laughed, rather surprised she remembered how. "He gets along all right with . . ." she almost said Magnus, and diverted to, "Emily, but then, they're neighbors. She traded him a knife for a biography of Gideon Bremner."

"*Life and Times*?" Ewan slammed on the brakes, throwing Lauren against her seat belt.

This time she couldn't mistake the glint in his eye, which was less a quick flash than a slow glow. "Yes. I've got it right here in my bag."

The driver of the car behind the van tooted its horn politely. Ewan faced front and started up again. As they drew away from the closely spaced buildings of the town proper, Lauren glimpsed the bay, heaving with waves that surged towards the beach, tripped, and shattered into froth on the sand. Light winked from the lighthouse, but Orkney had vanished into murk and mist. If she had just now arrived, she wouldn't know the islands existed.

"I offered him fifty pounds simply to borrow the book long enough to scan it," Ewan said, the words squeezed between his teeth. "Daft old bugger, to hand it over so cheap!"

"It's rare, then?"

"The British Library and the Ashmolean have copies, and a few others are scattered about. I've managed to get bits and pieces photocopied."

"Because Bremner might have written about the Armada ship?"

"Rosemary and Bryony, they're not wrong that I took up the cemetery project to dig at Black Ness. It's a grand site, with the Neolithic remains and all, even if I never turn up evidence for the ship."

"What was that about the University? If you don't mind my asking, that is."

Ewan expelled another humorless snort. "My Head's saying I'd have better luck finding the Loch Ness monster than *El Castillo Negro*. That like as not the *Castillo* went down in the open sea. That no captain would have risked his ship in the Firth, charts or no charts—the fleet, such as it was by then, sailed north round Orkney. But we know the ships were separated by storms. We know *El Gran Grifon* went aground on Fair Isle, north of Orkney. Perhaps the *Castillo* went round Orkney with the others, then dropped back south, whether voluntarily or not." He guided the van into a right turn, followed by another.

"And what happened to the men who were on the ships that wrecked?" Lauren asked.

"Scotland being an independent country at the time, and not so fond of England if not openly at war, the Spaniards wrecked in Scots territory were treated well and eventually returned home. Not so the ones landed in Ireland. The English officials and their soldiers made the survivors wish they'd drowned, fast and clean."

"But what about James Mackay? If he was Protestant . . .'"

"You've found that letter of his, have you? Aye, he might well have seen the way the political winds were blowing, pushing Scotland into the ungrateful arms of England, and set about murdering any survivors that came dripping onto his doorstep. The lairds in these parts, they were by way of being judge and jury."

The sixteenth-century was no more inventive with its methods of torture and murder than any other century, Lauren supposed, human progress being a matter more of place than time.

Emily's white-stuccoed house materialized from what was now a steady rain, its porch light shining like that of the lighthouse. "You're staying at that hotel?" Lauren asked, looking back at a big box of a building on the corner.

"In one of the wee lodges behind the posh part. Academics, mind, we're never flush with funds. Here you are." He stopped the van, then reached behind him and produced the long padded pole of a furled umbrella. "Hang on a tick, I'll walk you to the door."

Lauren was fumbling in her bag for the key when he opened the door of the car, the dark dome of the umbrella held ready. This time his grip on her upper arm was just as unshakable, but not painful. She thought again how much she'd missed the touch of a man, even a neutral, no more than polite, one like this.

The rain drumming on the taut fabric overhead, she walked in Ewan's pleasantly earthy aura up the sidewalk, and stepped into the pocket-sized alcove of the porch. The light illuminated his chest and his hands, but his features were shadowed by the umbrella. Lauren saw little of his expression except the gleam of his eyes, his gaze moving from her face to the bag on her shoulder.

On the one hand, she wanted nothing more than to go to ground on a corner of Emily's couch. On the other hand, Ewan had driven her home, and he knew a lot about Black Ness, and he had similar battle scars. "Come on in. I'm sure Emily won't mind. She makes a great cup of tea. I'll share Bremner's book with you."

He swayed forward, so that the umbrella's teeth nicked the corners of the porch, then pulled himself back again. "Thank you just the same, but no, I'll not be going in, not like this, dirty as a coal miner."

"Well, okay. I was planning to look at the book tonight, but I'll bring it with me tomorrow and you can borrow it."

"You're going back to the tower, are you? Have a care, then."

"What?"

"Sutherland. He's more than a bit loony."

"Kind of depends on how you define loony," Lauren returned.

"Nuts," Ewan said. "Crackers. Round the bend. Off the rails."

She still couldn't see his expression. "Well, living at Blackness Tower all by yourself . . ."

"There's more to it than a wee bit of eccentricity." Ewan grasped her wrist and shook it, so that the key in her hand clinked. His voice fell to a gravelly whisper. "Lauren, David Sutherland's been called a murderer."

CHAPTER THIRTEEN

Murderer. The trailing syllables slipped like cold drops of rain through Lauren's mind and down her back. "What?"

"Aye, the court-martial ruled he didna actually murder the woman, he killed her by accident—and aye, I'll grant that's the case, no surprise soldiers under pressure can go a bit trigger-happy." A gossamer curtain of water wetted Ewan's arm, each droplet a jewel on the wool of his sweater. Releasing Lauren's wrist, he subtracted himself into the shelter of the umbrella. In its shadow, not only his eyes caught the light but also a thin wedge of teeth.

Lauren took a step away, so that her back touched the door. "That's not fair. You've taken a dislike to David the way Charles Innes has to you."

"I've never done wrong by Innes, he's got no call for that chip on his shoulder. But Sutherland, he's either slamming his door in my face, or lecturing me on my business, or rabbiting on about ghosts and strange powers and fate. Magic," he spat. "It's like to drive a normal person mad. I'm thinking his tour in Northern Ireland's left him—damaged."

Then, Lauren thought, by Ewan's standards, *she* wasn't normal. Maybe her dreams had left her damaged. If he knew about them, he'd sneer at her, too. Maybe she had more in common with David than she'd thought.

That's what happened in Northern Ireland. That's what Magnus had checked into. David killed a woman. No, it hadn't been murder, but when it came to death, meanings got muddled.

Lauren unlocked the door and opened it. Light and the scent of food leaked into the gloom. "Thanks for the ride," she said.

Ewan retreated several steps down the walk, so that the light shone full on his face. The abbreviated ends of his hair were tangled every which way above his sturdy but otherwise unremarkable features. Only his mouth, lips curving like the outline of islands on the horizon, suggested anything beyond regular. Average. *Normal.* "Dinna mind me, Lauren. At times I go a bit loony myself."

If Magnus's goal was to find the paranormal, then Ewan's goal was not to find it. Maybe Black Ness scared him. It had certainly scared her. So had David, whose goal she didn't know. But she could at least be fair to him.

Aloud she called, "Good night," her delivery much softer than Bryony's snap and snarl.

"Good night," returned Ewan. The light inside the van flashed and the slam of the door reverberated off the front of the house.

Stepping inside, Lauren closed the door on the dark, wet evening. Sanctuary.

From the kitchen Emily called, "There you are! You're soaking, poor lamb."

"I'm okay. I got a ride from the library with Ewan Calder. He's the archaeologist working at the old chapel." Shivering—she hadn't realized how cold she was until warmth enfolded her—Lauren set her bag by the staircase and walked into the kitchen.

Tonight the curtains were drawn over the large window, making the room a snug, private place. Emily stood at the stove, where pans emitted frizzling sounds and the delectable odor of fried potatoes. A cozy covered a pot of tea on the table. Without standing on ceremony, Lauren sat down and helped herself, adding milk and sugar to her cup. At home, she never used milk and sugar in her tea. But Magnus was right, here you needed insulation.

She wondered whether he was staying in the main building of the hotel on the corner. She wondered whether he and Bryony would get together. She wondered whether she cared.

She told Emily, "It's not just a dig at Black Ness. The cemetery's being moved into town. We need to give Ewan permission to exhume Susanna's bones. Would you believe that a man's bones are in the grave with her?" Lauren recapped the events of her day, skirting any mention of what Magnus would have called woo-woo and Ewan, with contempt, magic.

Emily stirred, scraped, and listened, occasionally shooting a sharp glance at Lauren, her steel-wool eyebrows arched. She said at last, "I'm not properly a relative of Susanna's, not like you. Till Donald began writing me, I didna even know she was buried at Black Ness—my granny and granddad are in the Thurso cemetery. And now you're telling me Susanna's not on her own at all. That's a tale and no mistake."

"I just hope I'm here long enough to see how it all plays out. Ewan wants to excavate some of the prehistoric remains, too, and Magnus Anderson's here to do a story on it all."

"Oh aye, the television presenter. Rosemary rang, and was telling me you arrived at the library with him, though I was one step ahead, thanks to your note . . . Oh!" Emily jerked back from the stove.

"Are you all right?" Lauren half-rose.

"The grease splashed my jersey. Good job, it might have burned my arm."

"Rosemary has a burn on her arm."

Emily shook her head. "Bad luck, that."

"It looks as though she brushed it against the edge of a hot oven." Or else lashed it with her over-active tongue, Lauren added silently, and glanced at the guileless face of the portable phone in its answering machine base. "You remember when you didn't get the phone turned off last night, how it took the alarm a long time to go off? I think Rosemary was listening while we talked."

"Was she, now?" Emily shot an alarmed glance over her shoulder.

"And she was looking through the keyhole, more or less, when I showed Magnus the skull watch. But . . ." Lauren in-haled. "No harm done. She's a good friend of yours, right?"

"Not especially. We meet at the monthly book club is all. She's—curious, I reckon." Emily's utensils moved more slowly.

"Yeah, well, 'curious' has two meanings, inquisitive and peculiar."

"So it does, aye. And Rosemary's both."

"She doesn't have the same accent the local people do."

"No, she was born and raised down south. She's lived here no more than two years. Divorced or widowed, she's never said, just that now she's on her own."

Lauren tried to excuse Rosemary's prying and to visualize Mr. Gillock, but failed on both counts. She moved on to a less discomforting topic. Or one that was discomforting for a different reason. "David Sutherland doesn't have a Scottish accent at all."

"You've had yourself a blether with him, eh?" Emily's approving nod was more likely meant for David's looks than for Lauren's initiative.

"You've seen that portrait in his living room, haven't you? No wonder you were looking at me so funny yesterday. Why didn't you tell me?"

The utensils stopped moving. After a long, immobile moment, as though she was running a mental comparison between woman and portrait, Emily said, "You'd not have believed me, would you now? The likeness is astonishing. I reckon David was gobsmacked."

"Blown away? Oh yeah, he was," Lauren understated. "I was, too. Neither one of us believed our own eyes, you're right about that."

Emily's spatula whanged against the skillet.

I'm as eager to work through the funny stuff as you are, believe me, Magnus had said. David was a lot less eager and a lot more enigmatic. "What's David's background, anyway?"

"His folk have an estate near Edinburgh, Charles is saying. They're not shy of a bob or two. David attended the sort of posh schools where they strip away your native dialect as being beneath your station, and install one with less character but more commercial appeal."

Whereas Ewan, Lauren thought, had the education but not the class distinction or the money. And he had issues with David. "Ewan said David killed a woman in Northern Ireland. Is that true?"

"It is that. The way I'm hearing it, he went out leading a patrol after a bomb scare, and shot a young woman breaking the curfew fetching milk for her baby. You canna blame him for being a bit quick on the trigger, though he was blamed, loudly. Tragic situation all round."

He'd have been better off shooting himself. And Ewan said *his* sins had brought him to Black Ness. "Did they throw David out of the army?"

"Not directly. His superiors suggested he resign his commission. Too much bad publicity, making the natives restless, or so the English would have said about us Scots, not so long ago."

David was still wearing his military clothing. In defiance? Or in contrition, it being his version of a hair shirt? Lauren was beginning to suspect that the man was less a hermit than an outcast. Again she felt a stirring of sympathy for him—and reminded herself that the wounded warrior types were more appealing in theory than in fact, when the dashing unshaven chin turned to sandpaper against your cheeks.

Emily set two plates brimming with fish and chips and green peas on the table. "Eat. The scones are just coming."

Lauren didn't have to be told twice. She picked up her fork and dug in.

The planks of fish were battered and fried until they looked as though they were encased in gold leaf, crunchy on the outside and flaky on the inside, emitting a fragrant steam. The thick slabs of the potatoes were full-bodied and melted in her mouth. The peas—well, they were the size of small marbles and had just about the same taste. But Lauren wasn't complaining. She only put down her fork long enough to smear butter and jelly on a scone.

After a while—a long while—Emily said, "I hope that television presenter's not planning to harass the poor man. David, that is to say."

"Magnus wants to do a program about Blackness Tower, which is something David might count as harassment."

"Ghosts, fairies, selkies, all that lot, is it? Good stories there, good stories. Nothing like the tickle of the uncanny to ginger you up a bit."

They're not just stories. Not any more. Lauren didn't feel at all gingery, if by that Emily meant that pleasant shiver caused by a scary story or exciting movie.

She drained the dregs of her cup. She needed insulation, yes, not just from the meteorological cold, but from that insistent chill on the back of her neck and the creeping sensation between her shoulder blades, the caress of invisible fingertips. And then there were David's very physical hands pressing into her shoulders. Into her flesh, as though no fabric had cushioned his touch. Ginger. Paprika, curry, and chili powder. *Whoa.*

Emily started to clear the table. "Your researches are getting on well, then."

"Not really. I'm getting a lot more questions than answers."

"That's the way of life, isn't it now? Loads of questions, and wondering whether we're asking the right ones." Emily's smile was calm, pleasant, and slightly fixed. Beneath her composure something was troubling her, like her distant cousin's strange resemblance to a woman long dead.

Lauren wasn't too happy about that, either. But since she couldn't help it, she helped Emily wash the dishes and clean the kitchen. Normality had its points, just as boundaries had theirs, both concepts being very flexible right now.

Retrieving her bag from the front hall, Lauren sat down in the sitting room, where the electric fire glowed soothingly—although you could probably burn yourself on that, too—and the mantel clock counted out the receding minutes of the day.

For ten of those minutes, she and Emily inspected the skull watch, from cranium to jaw of the case to the catgut mechanism inside—now that, Emily offered, had to have been replaced in the last four hundred years. Even when Emily brought a magnifying glass from her desk, they found no maker's mark amid the intricacies of design and metaphor. *Where did you come from, Patrick O'Neill? Where did you go?*

Emily at last gave it up and went upstairs for a bath, leaving Lauren alone with her notebook, pen, Bremner's autobiography, and the skull perched on the end table. Her talisman. Charm. Or maybe even her family fetish.

Remember that you, too, will die.

Charms could also be unlucky, Lauren thought, and set her jaw as though it, too, was cast in metal, if in something less attractive than silver gilt.

She picked up *Life and Times*.

CHAPTER FOURTEEN

Trying to close her nostrils against the odor of decay, Lauren opened the book. It had no index, not that she'd really expected one. The only photographs were the foggy one of "Catherine's Word-beginning-with-D," tipped in towards the end, and a clearer one of the man himself as the frontispiece.

Gideon Bremner was seated in an ornately carved chair, his bony right hand braced on the top of a walking stick like a lion's paw clutching a decorative finial. His dark suit was unbuttoned, exposing a waistcoat and a watch fob dangling several insignia which were too badly defined to identify.

Lauren assumed his blindingly white shirt had the high stiff collar of 1898, but she couldn't see it—his beard started at his cheeks, cascaded over his chin, and tapered out at the upper part of his chest. The whiskers were darker on the ends than around his face, where they blended into the gray hair climbing past his ears and around the back of his balding head. Even by the hirsute standards of the time, that was a heck of a beard. Was he compensating for the smooth skin shining through the few strands of hair still covering his skull?

He'd been born in 1842. He'd been fifty-six when the book was published, and, presumably, the photo had been made. Old for that day and age, if not for today, when the Boomers of her mother's generation were still rocking around the clock.

But Gideon exuded the gravity of maturity and wealth. His gaze from beneath shaggy brows was bellicose, as though he dared anyone to dispute his potency, age or no age.

Lauren stared back at those printed eyes, tiny full stops, wondering if this man was her grandfather's grandfather. But she saw nothing of the Grandpa she'd known and loved in Gideon's truculent expression.

She turned to the text of the book. The antique typeface crammed onto each stained and brittle leaf made her eyes ache before she'd read more than the pages detailing his family background, his birth, and his school days, all of a respectability approaching hidebound. Not unlike David's, she supposed, respectability not immunizing anyone from either drama or trauma.

Within moments of launching into Gideon's analysis of capitalism and the evils of labor laws, a headache swelled in her temples. ". . . the means of production and exchange upon which the foundation of our prosperity rests, the rules of property and indeed of propriety itself, rest upon principles . . ."

As a child of trade and industry, Gideon wasn't likely to man the barricades alongside les miserables. One of his ancestors had even worked for the Duke of Sutherland, clearing the land of its infestation of peasants, the better to "improve" it. If brutality was required to accomplish the task, so be it—the dirty, ignorant, superstitious, and above all poor tenants had brought it on themselves.

Lauren got the idea. But Gideon as social Neanderthal wasn't on her agenda. If she skimmed ahead, maybe happenstance—to say nothing of coincidence—might lead her to the information she wanted. At least she was getting used to the smell.

The telephone rang. She looked up, wondering if Emily was in the bathroom. But no—she heard her cousin's voice upstairs, a quick hello, an affirmative, and something about Lauren herself. Footsteps retreated and a door shut.

Lauren told herself to be glad she was providing so much amusement for everyone.

Her ears filled with the swish of falling rain, like the curl of the sea, she turned page after page. Her eyes rolled back as Gideon's economic and social rant rolled on . . . Aha! She found it! In 1883, Blackness Tower was standing derelict, a monument to great men of the past, James Mackay, reformer, and so forth. It would make a summer retreat sufficient to escape from worldly duties.

The denigrated but ever-useful working classes rebuilt the interior of the tower to contemporary standards and cleared the area of a litter of rock and stone, the last wretched remnants of our primitive ancestors. Lauren made a face. That figured. Gideon had tidied away not just a few loose stones but all the remaining prehistoric structures, unspecified, left after James had done his own tidying, the better to build Blackness Tower atop the Norse foundations.

James could be forgiven, maybe—to him, the stones were evidence of a mythical and pagan past, of devilish forces that threatened the community he led. Gideon should have known better. Was he trying to also clear away the ghosts with the stones? But the stories had attracted artists, poets, and other raffish characters.

"Mrs. Bremner . . ." Lauren flipped back a few pages. Where had Gideon met Margaret? Well, suffice it that they did meet and marry. With her being twenty years younger, the match had probably been a business arrangement. She might even be his second wife. Whatever, Gideon had no children. No legitimate children.

"Mrs. Bremner having taken a fancy to the works of Calliope, Terpsichore, Erato, and the other muses, I have indulged her whims by inviting practitioners of the arts to form a salon. And pleasant it is, on a quiet August afternoon, to enjoy the more creative talents of mankind, for it is such that elevate us above the apes that Mr. Darwin in his foolishness would have as our relations."

So the artists and their foolishness were all the little woman's fault. Lauren expected Gideon to go on with snide remarks about the creative class's fixation on myth and legend, the romance of. But what he derided as superstition in the peasantry he celebrated as inspiration in his pet artists, never mind that art criticism was by 1900 moving on from the idealized images of the pre-Raphaelites.

Maybe the salon was an excuse for Gideon to decorate his house with pictures of attractive young women rather than stiff, gory classical tableaux. Maybe some of those attractive young women even posed undraped.

She didn't know whether Gideon had any paintings of undraped women—while the pre-Raphaelites had no objection to skin, they preferred clothing it with lush fabrics, lovingly rendered. She hadn't even found any mention of Susanna, yet, but then, Gideon wouldn't be admitting to an affair with her. And if Susanna had been getting it on with one of the artists, Gideon must have turned a blind eye. He sure hadn't thrown her and her son out into the gutter, not when both were listed in the 1901 census.

Whether or not Susanna had been the scandal and the caution of August 1891, the month her son had been conceived, the conception had had nothing to do with Petri dishes. Whether it had had anything to do with passion, for art, for flesh, for that murky strand between, Lauren was beginning to suspect she might never know.

Emily padded down the stairs and into the living room, wrapped in a snug terry-cloth robe and looking so comfortable Lauren's head hurt even worse, with envy.

"Do you mind if I watch the telly?" Emily asked.

"Oh no, go right ahead," replied Lauren. *The Paranormal Files* had better not be on again, the last thing she wanted to see was Magnus's grin.

Emily tuned in the last part of *Time Team*. This week the group was digging at a hill fort in England, with a side trip to the ancient stone circle at Avebury. There, the narrator explained, the medieval villagers had been so frightened by the great sarsen stones they'd undermined, tipped over, and buried more than a few of them. That excavators had found a medieval barber crushed beneath one of the stones seemed no more than poetic justice, although Gideon, whose workman had almost met the same fate, had no doubt thought nothing of the sort.

Massaging her temples—her brain seemed to be swelling—Lauren looked back at the book. She also had yet to find any mention of the specific legends of Black Ness, never mind that of the Armada ship, unless the Appendix . . .

Yes. Tonight she noticed the tiny footnote at the bottom of the first page of *Superstitions of the Scottish Highlands*: "With thanks to my wife, Margaret, for her assistance."

Margaret had written her own book, *Catherine Sinclair and the Matter of The Seeing Gift: Notes Provided to the Society for Psychical Research*. She might have done more than assist Gideon in writing this section of his book, she might have ghost-written the parts about the artistic salon in the main text, accounting for the change in tone.

Lauren squinted at the even more cramped typeface of the appendix. The Society for Psychical Research had been founded in 1882. A woman named Ada Goodrich Freer had investigated Highland Second Sight, or The Seeing Gift, on their behalf. Lauren pulled out her notebook. Yes, Freer had visited Blackness Tower several times.

Her investigation had been compromised by charges of manipulation of the evidence, but that was calumny heaped upon the very able members of the Society who had been of great help in investigating the stories of Black Ness. Bremner, sir or madam, did protest too much, Lauren thought. Hah, she channeled Shakespeare as well as David, if in a less classy accent.

And there, at long last, was something about Catherine Sinclair. She had come from a long line of Seers . . . Back to the notebook. Yep, a caste of Seers, that was in Walter Mackay's letter. Catherine's family, ostensibly Catholic, had married her to another Seer, James Mackay, who professed the new Protestant religion.

Many lay Catholics with their saints and relics and reverence for the Virgin Mary had been, or so Lauren seemed to remember, kindly disposed towards the old ways of magical thinking. But some of the new Protestants had discouraged free thought by a variety of methods ranging from nasty to downright sickening. As Magnus said, that was probably why the legends of Black Ness had turned grim and dark in the sixteenth century. Nature spirits, fairies, whatever, had become tools of the devil.

Although, people being people and prejudice being prejudice, terrible things had been done in the name of God, singular or plural, back to the dawn of Christianity and beyond, in Caithness as everywhere else.

Catherine's marriage to James was, as David said, difficult. Nothing like a disparity in religious beliefs to cause conflict, no matter how much else they may have had in common, woo-woo or mundane. Catherine did her duty and bore James a son and heir. Then she fell in love with a selkie, a seal-man—again, as David said. She met her lover secretly, helped by her maidservant, Mariota Simison.

Another Simison? Cool! Lauren glanced up at Emily, who was knitting a tiny garment while she watched her program.

And what happened to Catherine? Had she owned the skull pocket watch? Had James murdered her? Lauren forced her gritty eyes down the next page.

Damn! Catherine's story was merely the segue from The Society for Psychical Research into tales of selkies, ghosts, and fairy abductions. Juicy tidbits, yeah, but all presented as amusing yarns at best and superstitious nonsense at worse. Maybe Margaret adopted a more credulous viewpoint in her own book, whereas in this one she'd modified her views to fit her spouse's comfort level.

Lauren would have to find a copy of Margaret's book, either in the shop or the library. And that was assuming Margaret had been able to express herself freely even in her own little, insignificant, too-female, no doubt, work.

As for Rupert Beckwith, he'd been allowed plenty of poetic license in relating Catherine's life and loves. That was probably where David's bit about the selkie came from. Or so Ewan would say, declaring that if Catherine had had a lover at all, he was a mere mortal man.

A man from the sea? A sailor from *El Castillo Negro*? A *platero* with samples of his wares?

Lauren sat up straight, staring into the eye sockets of the skull watch beneath their heavy brow ridges, cast by the lamplight into shadowed and secret caverns.

There was a thought. There was also a screaming coincidence, if one that might explain . . . No. The unforeseen body couldn't be Patrick's. It was in Susanna's grave, not Catherine's. Catherine's body had long gone to its component chemicals including, Lauren supposed, traces of silver.

Was it Catherine who was haunting Blackness Tower? If David based his idea of what she looked like on the portrait, that would explain his saying Lauren was haunting the place.

Wow, a rational explanation for something. She should quit while she was ahead.

On top of the pressure building inside her head, the skin of her temples was stinging. She'd rubbed bits of the decaying leather binding into them, probably, not to mention the dust of ages. Groaning and yawning both, she returned *Life and Times* to her bag. She wouldn't go back on her offer to share it with Ewan, just as long as she stayed out of the line of his fire.

She considered the to-do list in her notebook with its paltry two items—one, genealogy, two, dreams—and added several more: Margaret's book. Beckwith's poem. Book shop. What really happened in 1588. In 1891. In 1907. Talk to David. Talk to Ewan. Talk to Magnus.

All three of them, focused on their own agendas, jostling for precedence, using her or sweeping her aside as their purposes dictated. *Men!*

She stowed the notebook and pen in her bag, closed the velvet box and tucked the skull watch away, too. She couldn't sit up all night afraid it would start talking to her again. Better to leave it downstairs, where it could talk to itself, for all her benumbed brain cared now. Setting her bag next to Emily's desk, she stood up and stretched.

"Away up to bed, are you?"

"Yes. It's been a long day. A really long day."

"Good night then," Emily said with a smile, and went back to her knitting.

Lauren washed her hair, rubbing her scalp beneath the hot water until the muscles loosened. Then she let the water trickle down her shoulders and back, drip off her breasts, lick the sensitive places of her body, until she finally relaxed. Sleek as a seal, she turned off the water and toweled herself off, trying not to feel guilty about using so much water. Here, they had lots of water.

Enveloped in the fragrance of her shampoo, she peered through her bedroom window into the last lusterless light of the evening. Sky, land, and sea were no more than shades of gray. Even the white-topped breakers looked like used soapsuds. The buildings ranged around the harbor, beside the lighthouse, appeared as the sum of their windows, nothing but an irregularly spaced row of lights like will-o'-the-wisps in the shadows.

So that was one day down. Now what?

Not any cozy conversations with her friends, via voice or text, that was for sure. She might as well be on a desert island.

She stretched out on the bed, and closed her eyes, and thought of David walking through the tower in the darkness, alone. Long winter nights, short summer nights—no difference, dark was dark. No matter how many lights he switched on, there would still be shadowed corners, and strange drafts, and his sounds and sweet airs. The cat, Persie, would still stare into nothingness, as cats had always done—one reason they were seen as occult familiars . . .

She was walking not away from the Tower, but towards it, through a night so wet and thick she couldn't tell where the ground ended and the sky began. But lights shone from the tower, arched lights, square lights, depending on the shape of the window, and beckoned her—home.

She stepped through the gateway and past the plants that rubbed their leaves together and murmured behind her back.

Her nape shrank in the cold night air, exposed between the low neckline of her dress and the piled-up mass of her hair, heavy hair tilting her head back and her chin up.

The door was ajar. Without knocking, without calling out, she pushed it open and stepped into the antechamber. It was furnished by only a wooden chest with ornate iron hinges, and illuminated by two candles. They guttered, flames flaring, so that the shadows reeled against the stone wall. She smelled a rich, coppery odor, like mulled wine or spilled blood.

A step behind her, a breath on her neck. She spun around. The man who watched her from the doorway stood in shadow, so that all she saw of him was the dark suit and white shirt and watch fobs dangling, each a tiny silver skull.

He raised his hand to her, palm up, inviting. And she stepped forward to place her hand in his.

Long limber fingers closed over hers. Flesh touched flesh. His thumb teased the hills and hollows of her palm, the friction sending a warm thrill up her arm. She gasped, her entire body rippling with pleasure.

And shadows flowed through the doorway, swirled around them, tore their hands apart, and swallowed them in silence and the dark.

Lauren woke up, her scream no more than a whimper of loss.

With a sigh, she rolled over and went back to sleep, dozing and waking and dozing again, free of imagery, until she jerked into full wakefulness and peered around the room. Daylight leaked past the curtains, the ash-gray light of an overcast day. A car drove by. A dog barked.

And she heard again the sound that had waked her up, Emily's sharp, urgent voice calling her name.

CHAPTER FIFTEEN

Lauren rolled out of the bed and bundled on her robe, clumsily, the last remnants of her dream tying knots in her thoughts. Another new dream, variations on a theme. Another nightmare. But she couldn't be in danger from a dream.

"Lauren!" Emily called. "Please come down!"

"Coming!" Lauren returned, and headed down the stairs, her sock-covered feet soundless on the carpeted treads, the cold air heavy on her skin still warm from sleep.

Emily stood in the living room looking down at Lauren's bag. Which was now no longer sitting beside the desk but on top of it, gaping open. Mingled with Emily's papers and pencils were *Life and Times*, Lauren's notebook, her lip gloss, her hairbrush, her iPod and its earbuds, her passport and plane ticket in their vinyl folder, her British money . . . *No. No way.*

"The skull watch," Emily said, her voice taut. "It's gone."

"No!" Frantically Lauren dug through the bag, raked the top of the desk, dropped to the floor and crawled around the carpet. She even dumped out Emily's wastebasket, producing nothing but empty envelopes and paper scraps. "No!"

"One of the glass panes in the kitchen door's been broken in. Easy enough to reach through and turn the key. I'm always leaving the key in the lock. Not a high-crime area, Thurso. And here's me, sleeping the sleep of the virtuous, never hearing a thing."

Lauren sat on the carpet, her arms around her knees, her head hanging. The family talisman, stolen. Some evil-minded stranger slipping soundlessly into Emily's house, searching.

But it couldn't have been a stranger. It was someone she'd seen yesterday. Someone who knew her address—or how to find it. Someone who didn't care how badly Lauren got hurt.

"Damn it! There I was being careful about not showing it at the restaurant, but I had it out at the dig—Ewan, Bryony, all the students saw it. I showed it to David. I showed it to Magnus at the library, and the creepy librarian . . . I'm sorry, I don't mean to imply Rosemary . . ." The watch. Men of good will. Right.

"No, I'm sorry I let this happen." Emily patted Lauren's shoulder.

"You didn't let anything happen," Lauren said with a heavy sigh, and squeezed Emily's hand. It was trembling. "I should be apologizing to you for dragging you into—whatever this is."

"I've rung the police. A constable will be here straightaway. Get yourself properly dressed whilst I make the tea."

Lauren hauled herself to her feet and by rote did as she was told, knowing that neither clothes nor food would soothe the fear that crawled beneath her flesh and the ache that quivered in her blood. Grandpa, polishing the watch. Susanna, holding it up. The ship wrecking on the unforgiving coast. The one actual physical object she had to inspire her, to guide her.

Gone. Taken by an enemy.

She allowed herself a sob, wrenched from deep in her gut—if only she'd carried the bag upstairs with her, if only she hadn't so cavalierly dismissed the watch last night—and yet the thief might have violated her bedroom.

The dream itself wasn't dangerous. As for the place the dream had led her . . . Shuddering, she splashed cold water on her face and headed back downstairs, walking carefully so as not to jar the bruise beneath her heart.

The odor of toast wafted through the house and the doorbell rang.

The constable introduced himself as P.C. Liddell. He was tall, spare, and as businesslike in manner as his uniform was in color, black broken by bits of insignia. His cap tucked politely beneath his arm, he considered the broken window and the turned-out bag, made some notes, and only let his professional demeanor slip when Lauren described the object of the theft.

"A sixteenth-century silver-gilt pocket watch shaped like a human skull," he repeated, pen poised, eyes wide. "Not the sort of thing easily fenced, I'm thinking."

"Not hardly," Emily agreed.

"And yet the thief left the money and passport and all behind."

"He couldn't have made it any clearer just what it was he was after, could he?"

No one answered Emily's statement. After a moment, Liddell shut his notebook. "Right, then. We'll be in touch."

Lauren refrained from telling him to give Rosemary Gillock the third degree. If the librarian had wanted the watch, she could have dropped by with a batch of cookies and taken it by sleight of hand. She didn't have to break in. But then, no one *had* to break in.

Magnus had something to prove. Ewan had something to prove. Bryony had something to prove. Even David must have something to prove. And what about the students? Who wanted the watch badly enough to commit a crime to get it?

Or, for that matter, who wanted Lauren not to have it? There was a thought, and not an encouraging one.

Beyond the *who* was the *why*. And *why* was something Lauren hadn't even figured out for herself yet. Maybe, like David's cat, someone had simply been attracted to something shiny. She'd rather think that than follow her dream into nightmare.

Equally businesslike, Emily conducted Liddell to the door, tacked a piece of cardboard over the broken window pane, then carried on with breakfast. But all Lauren forced into the clenched fist of her stomach was some toast and part of a scrambled egg. And the tea, like mother's milk, always comforting.

She helped Emily tidy up the kitchen as usual, but not as usual, neither woman spoke.

She'd counted her pennies, thought Lauren, bided her time, made her plans. Now she was here, and her plans disintegrated in her hands. Where was her Sight, if that's what it was, when she'd needed it? If she'd known what was going to happen—ghosts, graves, burglars . . . No. Even if her courage had failed her, her stubbornness would have brought her here. To answer the call, David said.

David. In her dream, it was his hand holding hers. It was his hand swept away from hers by a torrent of shadow. He'd invited her back to Blackness Tower, where the watch had once been safe. Or had it?

What Emily was thinking, Lauren had no idea. The tautness had drained from her face, and she was no longer trembling, but her clear blue eyes were somber and her face sagged, overloaded. At last she gathered up her own bag. "That's me away, then. The shop needs opening. And keeping open late, 'til seven. And there's the stock-taking, meaning dinner's catch as catch can tonight."

"I'll get myself something, no need for you to cook for me every night."

"Nae worries, dear. Oh, and if you're away back to Black Ness," she added, "best you wear one of my coats."

"I will, thanks. And thanks again for letting me use your car. I can't believe I brought all this on you, I didn't mean . . ."

"Nae worries," Emily replied, and went on her way.

"Yes, worries," Lauren called into the hush of the house. Nothing answered. But then, this house wasn't the one that was haunted. Profaned, no longer a sanctuary, but not haunted.

Quickly she changed from her jeans into a tidier pants and sweater combination, the warmest garments she had, and chose a coat from Emily's hall closet. It smelled faintly of either damp wool or wool on the hoof, sheep, but it was waterproof and warm.

She crammed her belongings back into her bag as though they could fill the velvet box-shaped void, and considered the calendar photo in its plastic sleeve. August. Blackness Tower. Reay. Caithness. And the days of the month, last year's month, all in order.

No photographer's byline tagged the photo. The back of the page was blank. She remembered the original calendar, its cover the perennial Scottish tourist icon, Eilean Donan Castle, with the legend, "Compliments of The Scottish Tourist Authority." And its brown manila envelope, a small typed label with Grandpa's address, stamps, and the Thurso postmark looking like bandages on its battered face—its Atlantic crossing had not been smooth.

Who had sent the calendar to Grandpa? His Edinburgh researcher hadn't ordered it sent from the Tourist people—she'd asked. Besides, there was the postmark.

A human being had sent the calendar, just as a human being had stolen the watch, here, in Thurso.

Venting a four-letter word, Lauren slipped the photo inside the bag and headed out into the chilly morning. Third time's the charm, she thought as she started the car. She was going to Blackness Tower for the third time, and this time she was going to find answers. Any answers.

Lauren's preoccupation with everything from the skull to the artists' salon to Susanna's grave kept her from stressing out over driving, even when she was caught in a traffic jam at the gates of Dounreay Reactor, one caused by an accident that seemed to be more than fender bender but less than a catastrophe. Way to ruin your day, though, she thought. Like having someone steal your heirloom and your security, both at once.

She parked next to Ewan's van and walked over the hill to see Blackness Tower rising from its headland. In the morning's fragile light, against a sky part gray cloud and part quicksilver mist, it appeared a Fata Morgana, a mirage.

At the chapel, the bright jackets of the students seemed sacrilegious. Lauren made out Ewan's hat bobbing and weaving beside the doorway, Bryony's head close by. Had the missing file turned up? Or were they simply setting aside their personal relationship and acting professionally?

Four young men, including beefy Jason, walked out of the cemetery carrying a dirt-stained oblong box. A recent coffin, not yet so rotted it couldn't be moved intact. To the accompaniment of gull calls, the youths carried it gingerly around the corner of the wall and set it down, out of Lauren's sight. But she guessed what was lined up beside that wall. Maybe Susanna was there, too. She'd have to pay her respects.

Later. Right now she wanted to deal with Susanna's life, not her death. And it wasn't as though she was able to help Ewan, considering she wasn't normal.

With a narrow look at the students—were there window glass particles in someone's cuffs?—Lauren strode across the bridge, up the hillside, and past the patch of burned turf. Several rabbits lolloped away and disappeared into the ground like fur-covered fairies vanishing into their secret kingdom. She saw nothing on top of the tower, no ghosts, no gargoyles, no phantom brides. The gateway stood open, the gate with its iron tendrils pushed back and stopped with a flowerpot. The leaves of the plants within the wall's embrace hung just as still, like decorative metal rather than living tissue.

I could get used to walking up to Blackness Tower for real, Lauren told herself, and pounded on the door.

A window above her head squeaked. "It's you, then," said David's disembodied voice.

She stepped back far enough to look up, but he was gone. Had that been a welcome? He'd had all the hours of darkness to have second thoughts.

The door opened. Today he was clean-shaven, the angles of his face crisp as Black Ness slate. He wore jeans and an open-necked shirt beneath a green V-necked cable-knit sweater, trading the military look for preppie. "Good morning," he said, with the same lopsided smile, self-aware, ironic, rueful, that she remembered. "Fancy a coffee?"

"Yes, thanks." She stepped into the antechamber and sure enough smelled the delectable odors of brewing coffee and baking cookies. The marble-topped table stood against the wall as it had yesterday, except now the books were stacked atop Innes's bag and blocked her view of the bell jar and its mourning brooch. "It looks as though you had a fire back there, at the top of the hill."

"I didn't, no. The local teenagers had their annual Lammastide party here last week, the first of August."

"Lammas? One of the old Celtic quarter days? I didn't think anyone outside of a few New Agers and Wiccans cared about that sort of thing any more."

"They don't. It's no more than an excuse for a bonfire and a rave-up. Women shrieking like banshees—set themselves on fire, I daresay—and me clearing away the beer cans and crisp packets the next day."

David took her coat and folded it over his arm. She thought for a moment he was going to offer to brush it off for her, but no, he laid it over a chest at the foot of the stairs. Over intricately curled iron hinges and lock black as scorch marks against wood dried by time into a silvery gray.

It was the chest from her dream.

CHAPTER SIXTEEN

"Where did the chest come from?" Lauren asked, keeping her voice as steady as she could.

But apparently not steady enough. David's eyes, changeable as the sea, targeted her. "It's a sixteenth-century Spanish pay chest. I found it here when I began the renovations. I've got no clue as to its provenance. Gideon Bremner might have bought it from an antiquities dealer, to illustrate the Armada fable."

Fable? "What's in it?"

"Letters and drawings from Bremner's day, regarding *his* renovation work. I didn't turn them up until I'd spent hours in the Thurso library looking out early architectural plans and drawings."

Lauren's fingers itched and she folded them into her palms.

"There's someone's amateur archaeological collection as well, and sketches of the ancient earthworks James Mackay destroyed, more shame to him. But then, he was afraid, and fear makes us . . ." David's voice died away, whetted into nothingness.

Yeah, fear broke down boundaries. "Does Ewan Calder know all that's here? He'd be interested in the chest alone, as evidence for the *Castillo Negro.*"

"Calder knows it's here, Rosemary Gillock having ever so helpfully told him."

So had Rosemary helped herself to the skull watch?

"He was at my door first thing this morning," David went on, "meaning to have it tested, seeing as how he's found a sixteenth-century body in Susanna's grave."

"Yeah, he told me about that. Evidence for his theory, but weird."

"Plenty of weird to go round, here. Still, the grave's a fine and private place . . ."

"But none, I think, do there embrace," Lauren concluded.

David's nod was footnoted by a trace of his smile. "I told Calder to send his lads along, and I'd hand over the chest peacefully. I—ah—I've spoken with Charles, and decided it's all meant to happen this way."

No surprise David rose to Charles's standards. "The philosophical viewpoint works as well as any," Lauren told him, without feeling particularly philosophical herself. "What else did you find in the tower?"

"Loads of things. The painting, for example. Your painting."

"It's not my painting." She glanced toward the sitting room, but all she saw past the hanging curtain was shadow. Not the portrait, not the piano, not the sampler with its cryptic message. "It's just coincidence that I look like Susanna. And who knows if she looked like Catherine . . ." He'd never suggested that, had he?

"Shall we sit in the kitchen?" he asked.

"Yes, please." Neutral ground, kitchens.

He seated her at the table, brought her a cup of coffee, offered her sugar and cream, and placed a platter of shortbread triangles in front of her. They were still warm from the oven, and their buttery, sugary crumbs melted on her tongue.

She and David were retracing a pattern—the modern kitchen, something hot, something sweet. But then, breaking bread together was a time-honored method of establishing detente. In fact, for someone who'd ignored her as long as he had, he was sure trying to make a good impression. Now that he'd seen her resemblance to the portrait. Now that she was dreaming about him, or aspects of him—she'd seen his eyes in the face of the man in the funeral coach and his hands on an image of Gideon Bremner, in dreams that had turned to nightmare.

His physical hands rested on either side of his cup, and his almost-physical gaze rested on her face. She watched him watching her, and wondered who was the cat and who the mouse. "Where's your cat?" she asked.

"Persie's upstairs, playing slug-a-bed. No sun to lure her out this morning."

"Did you work out a deal with Magnus Anderson?"

The deep curve of his lips crimped, but his voice remained mild. "Since I'm not so keen on his entire crew tramping about the place, we worked out a bargain. One assistant with a camera and other detectoring toys. And Magnus himself to ask questions, not that I'm promising to answer them. Cheeky sod, turning up on my doorstep, but he seems genuinely interested."

"He's looking for verifiable paranormal phenomena. You have phenomena to spare, I know that for myself. Everyone around here knows that. As much as you can *know* that."

"Everyone knows, yes. For living on my own, I'm a public figure, more's the pity."

"The woman . . ." Lauren began, meaning to go on with ". . . at the library, Rosemary, she sent Magnus here."

But David said, "They'll have told you about the incident in Northern Ireland, I expect. The woman I killed. Bridget O'Neill, her name was. My own fear of dying caused her death." He looked down at his hands, as though calculating how much blood was smeared on them.

Lauren considered his downturned face, his lashes lowered, and his hair scooped back from the crown of his head and tied by a length of yarn into a thick coil at his nape.

Bridget O'Neill.

There were probably hundreds, even thousands, of Irishwomen named Bridget O'Neill. Even if Patrick O'Neill the sailor, the soldier, the silversmith, came ashore in St. Bride's Hope four hundred years ago . . . Just coincidence, Ewan would say. David would disagree.

He felt he had to tell her that. Why? To gain her sympathy? To clear the air? "I'm sorry," Lauren said, and she was.

After a long moment, David looked up, and once more searched her face as though trying to memorize her features. But he had already memorized her features, long before he met her.

"Verifiable paranormal phenomena," he repeated. "Rosemary sent Anderson here as well as Calder. 'Knowledge is power', she's fond of saying. Her sort of knowledge is more than historical or literary. It's— personal."

"So I gathered. She eavesdropped when I was talking to Emily. She was spying when I showed Magnus the silver skull pocket watch. And now . . ." Her voice caught on something sharp, like a thorn, in her throat. "The watch is gone. It was stolen from Emily's house during the night."

A flash of lightning darted across the sky-blue of his eyes. "The watch, stolen? Ah, hell. I'm sorry."

And he was. Lauren *knew* it.

"You're not implying Rosemary's a housebreaker as well as a gossip?" he went on.

"I don't know what to think, David." His name filled her mouth like the ambrosial flavors of shortbread and coffee with cream, easing the acrid tastes of anger, fear, and grief. A stolen watch, she told herself, didn't rise to the ghastliness of an accidental death. Everyone had to die, but no one had to steal. "A lot of people know I had the watch—Ewan, Bryony, the students, Magnus."

"And me."

"I can't see you breaking and entering."

"Thank you." His lips wobbled, if not quite into a smile.

Watch out for that benefit of the doubt, she reminded herself. "What I'd like to know is why anyone stole the skull. It's a valuable artifact, it has sentimental value to my family, but as the cop said, it would be a bit hard to sell."

"In the portrait, Catherine's holding the watch. Susanna as Catherine's holding the watch. It's important to this place. And you've brought it back."

"I did bring it back, yeah, but now . . ." The thorn in her throat twisted, and from her lips spilled the most important questions of all. "Why does it matter? Who does it matter to? Why does my even coming here matter?"

He drained the contents of his cup and then looked into it so intently she wondered if the answer was hidden in the coffee grounds.

She plunged on. "Right at first you thought I was cheeky, too. You wouldn't answer my letters or anything. Then, once you saw me, you said I was called here. For myself, or as some kind of echo of Susanna or even Catherine? Or as a vehicle for the skull watch? In which case, whoever—" she refused to say whatever, whatevers didn't break windows "—wanted it has it back."

"Does someone want the watch for himself, or is he trying to keep it from you?" David asked the cup.

"Yeah, I thought of that one, too. I've got lots of questions and damn few answers."

"As do I. The theft, the portrait, come to that—it's all a puzzle, one that needs assembling. You and me, we . . ." He began toying with his spoon, flicking it between cup and saucer like a pendulum, so that the china emitted a chime reminiscent of the watch.

You and me. We're the weird ones. Pixilated, her mother would have said. Haunted.

Lauren took a detour along the scenic route. "How long have you lived here?"

"Four years."

"Four years alone?"

"Not a bit of it. When I first arrived, and set about restoring the tower, Charles gave me Persie. Persephone, her name is, but that's a mouthful for daily use."

"I'm sure Persie's a great cat, but she's probably not much of a conversationalist."

He shrugged. "I go to the shops, buy food at Safeway's or the Co-op, books from Charles, odd items from Emily. I met a bit of resentment at first. Sutherland's not a respected name in these parts, with the Clearances. I'm not related to the Duke, though. My family, well, my father's got a long, frightfully distinguished military record. We're estranged."

Had scholarly David been strong-armed into his military career to begin with? Wincing—an estranged father was worse than a vanished father—Lauren snagged another piece of shortbread for solace. "And your mother?"

"She visits occasionally, murmuring about men being obstinate."

Lauren smiled at that.

"My friends have holidays here. The occasional art or architectural historian has stopped in, as well an unpleasant chap from an auction house. I had workmen until the spring—plumbing, electric flex, masonry, floor joists, windows re-glazed, doors re-hung, the contents sorted and moved about. Finding workmen who'd agree to come here took a bit of doing, with Black Ness's reputation. And then one chap fell from a ladder and dislocated his shoulder, and another dropped a sledge on his foot. Thank goodness for steel-toed boots."

Bremner's workmen, Emily's cousin, Ewan's student—maybe the unluckiness was spreading, Lauren thought, and remembered the accident outside Dounreay. Just as long as there were no accidents inside Dounreay.

"I suppose," David concluded, "it was only a matter of time until a television presenter like Anderson turned up. But I'm not all that alone."

"Not if you have those sounds and sweet airs," she told him.

The corners of his mouth tucked themselves into something that wasn't quite a smile, and emphasized the creases in his cheeks. Setting down his spoon, he looked up at Lauren, still questioning, still challenging, and yet somewhat more at ease.

Again she took the plunge. "If you've had all those people coming and going, what was so intimidating about letters from an American woman doing genealogical research?"

"I apologize," he said with a quick bow. "I intended keeping the paintings and the history to myself. But I see now—I see they concern you as well."

No kidding. And "concern" was an understatement. Lauren asked, "There were paintings, plural, still here? Well, the pre-Raphaelites were only resurrected recently. Hence your auction guy."

"The salon began withering in 1891, the year Beckwith left for a grand tour of the Mediterranean and never came back. Soon after, Weir returned to England and a career as a minor art critic, notable for dismissing the Impressionists as a passing fancy of low minds."

She smiled again. "Weir was there for the 1901 census—reliving old glories, maybe. Then Susanna died young, and Gideon old, and Margaret Bremner took a cruise on the *Titanic*."

"Leaving no children. Any valuable and portable goods went to distant relatives, who had no use for a drafty Gothic tower at the edge of the world when they could have the Macintosh-design house in Glasgow and the pied-à-terre in London."

"And the tower sat empty for almost a century?"

"A local family leased it, first as a farmhouse, then as storage. By the 1970s, even the Simisons had had their fill of the place, and abandoned it and all its contents to the mercies of the weather, birds, rats, the odd vandal."

"Simison?" she asked, with an Emily-like tilt of her head.

"There have been Simisons looking after Blackness Tower since time immemorial, or so I hear from Rosemary. Despite her snooping—or because of it—she knows her local history."

"So why are you here?" Lauren aimed the piece of shortbread toward her mouth.

David leaned forward, head cocked one way, smile the other. His chest rose and fell with a deep breath. He answered, "A dream."

The shortbread went dry on her lips. "What?"

Ducking her shocked stare, David stood up. "I promised you the penny tour. Or the pound tour, considering what I and several historical preservation agencies have spent on the place."

"A dream?" she repeated, trailing him past the dining room into the antechamber.

"There are more things in Heaven and Earth, Lauren, than are dreamt of in your philosophy."

"Give me a straight answer, will you?"

He stopped, his foot on the bottom tread of the spiral staircase and his hand on the banister, a thick rope strung alongside the steps. He looked as off-balance as Lauren felt. "I will do," he said without looking around. "First let's have that tour."

With a grimace of frustration, Lauren wiped sweet crumbs from her mouth, squared her shoulders, and followed him up the stairs.

Even on the murky day, the view from the top of the tower was amazing, islands, sea, mountains swept by sheer curtains of rain. Inside, corridors twisted and turned over bumps, around corners, up steps. Alcoves and closets formed dead ends. One short passage led to a stone-blocked door. In a contemporary bedroom, Persie was asleep in the middle of a contemporary bed, the comforter smoothed around her but not actually made up, so as not to disrupt her slumber. She opened an eye at the human intrusion—*we are not amused*.

A photo on a dresser showed David in the full kilt, belt, and bonnet of a Highland regiment. He stood between an older man dressed in a more highly decorated uniform, his gray moustache sharp as his features, and an older woman wearing the sort of suit and hat that shouted of money and aristocracy even without the jewelry she wore. Her face was pinched, starched and ironed, her smile fixed. And the photo had to have been taken before Northern Ireland.

All Lauren said was, "So you're an only child, like me?"

"Carrying the family expectations, yes," was all he replied.

Several less-renovated rooms were lined with paneling, or Victorian wallpaper, or contained bits of furniture or other odds and ends. All were filled by shadow, the frail daylight barely seeping past the drapes and shutters that closed the deep window recesses. Whiffs of potpourri or pine cleanser reached Lauren's nostrils, softening rather than masking the scents of age and decay that no amount of restoration could exorcize.

She expected David to pull something about time's winged chariots from his literary reservoir, but he merely muttered the occasional, "Mind your head."

Then from the depths of the tower a melody began, piano notes echoing the reverberation of shoe against creaking floor, starting when they walked, stopping when they paused. If David heard the music, he didn't react.

By the time he led her down another flight of steps and around another corner, this one freshly plastered, Lauren was convinced the tower hadn't been built, it had grown. "This place is a maze in three dimensions," she said. "Four dimensions, counting Time. Lots of dead ends and places you have to double back."

"So it is," David agreed. "And if there's a center at all, then it's here." He opened a door and stepped into a darkened room.

Sensing more than seeing objects in the gloom before her, Lauren waited while he found his way, surefooted as a cat, to the window. A shutter squealed, admitting tenuous light.

In her dream the night before, she'd seen every window blazing. But then, in the uncompromising glare of electric light, that antique mirror propped against the far wall might not be stained with age, but positively opaque. And that vast bed, its massive posts draped with embroidered fabric, its wooden canopy carved and painted, might turn out to have worm holes, splinters, loose threads.

There was a reason you made love in the shadows. Especially if you were doing so with a mirror turned toward the bed.

"Are the bed and mirror Victorian?" she asked.

"Sixteenth-century," replied David. "Original to Blackness Tower, according to Margaret Bremner. Susanna's brother-in-law, Harold Simison, found them in a shed, and Margaret had them restored."

"So this was the Bremners' bedroom?"

"No, it was the artists' studio." He indicated several shrouded rectangles leaning against the panels of the wall opposite the bed, but instead of stepping toward them, he backed away.

Lauren didn't. She lifted the corner of the closest covering-sheet. Dust particles rose into the air. David didn't check these over every five minutes, but then, he probably had them memorized.

Suppressing a sniffle, Lauren gazed down at a painting of Morgan le Fay, the sorceress, the temptress, who might or might not have been a local girl. Susanna had most certainly been a local girl, and yet here she looked every inch a queen.

Her hair flowed gold, russet, brown, entwined with a golden cord. Her hands were raised gracefully over a flaming brazier, dropping rose petals redder than fire. Draperies the blue and turquoise of the sea, stitched with arcane symbols, swirled around her body and exposed hints of white flesh. Her bare feet were poised just inside a circle traced on the turf with fire or knife, black against the green. Behind her, on its headland, rose Blackness Tower, flanks glowing in a brassy twilight.

Susanna. Her grandfather's grandmother. Her own progenitor. Lauren wanted to crawl into the painting, seize those elegantly curved and yet strong hands, and wrench the truth from those rosy lips that were parted in satisfaction, at a spell well-cast, perhaps, or at a demon lover well-used.

And how many truths were there?

Morgan le Fay. Titania with gossamer wings and a languid, come-hither look. Guinevere removing her crown, distractedly, as though it were no more than a hairpin amidst her luxuriant tresses. Helen of Troy against an anachronistic battlement, the tower's own, looking out to sea in both hope and dread. St. Bride draped demurely in her green cloak, a tiny flame in her dark eyes acknowledging her pagan roots, and the pagan rites that she had not forgotten.

Lauren felt the heat of that flame in the pit of her own stomach, melting her limbs, teasing her senses, as though she was feeling music rather than hearing it. And she heard nothing except an almost subliminal pulse less in her ears than in her heart. The sea.

Her own voice seemed loud and crass. "You could get a fortune for these, though you'd have to go through a dealer."

David didn't answer.

"Beckwith used a darker and more defined line than Weir, right? And Weir used a more saturated color. Like the painting downstairs. Catherine's—is it *Dream* or *Destiny*, anyway?"

David didn't answer. She turned to see him standing before the mirror, his slender body, taut as a bowstring, reflected dimly in the mottled glass. His head was turned. He wasn't looking at his own reflection, but at something behind him. And the angle wasn't right for him to be looking at her.

Lauren took a step toward him. "David?"

"I was driving about the country, not knowing what to do with myself. I stopped at Thurso Tourist Information for a ferry schedule, thinking, I suppose, that if I kept traveling, I might—escape. But the Orkney ferry had already sailed. I walked into the town, and found Charles's shop, and photos of Blackness Tower on his wall."

Lauren stepped closer to David's back, so stiffly braced his own sergeant major would have looked sloppy, trying to see what he was looking at in the mirror.

Nothing. His own reflection was no more than a ghostly shape in the glass.

"I drove to Black Ness. I walked round the tower. The front door was barricaded, but I broke in. Mice were nesting in Margaret's piano and birds in Gideon's chimneys. But this room, with the paintings propped in a corner like orphaned children, and the bed and the mirror, the ones Catherine knew, and Susanna, this room is where it happened."

Lauren saw the place, sad, quiet, cavities filled with relics of lives gone to . . . But only the bodies had gone to dust. The lives lingered.

The flame in her stomach flared, radiating heat into her cheeks. The very air seemed charged, each mote of dust an almost invisible flake of silver in the fragile light, eddying not around her but around David, as though he exuded a force field. A force field sucking her down as surely as a whirlpool a ship. She stepped closer.

"I stood here, in front of this mirror, which was so decayed and dark I saw little more than my own movement. And then I saw her, behind me. The hair, the lips, the tilt of the head. Catherine. Susanna. You."

"A ghost? A vision?" Every follicle in her body stiffened and reached toward him, tingling.

He turned around, lifted the fall of hair from the side of her face and cupped her head in his hand. His eyes were focused both on her and beyond her. "I never saw her again, not like that. I'd say I imagined her, except I knew nothing about her, not then. Not until I saw the paintings, and researched the place. Not until I knew what to do with myself."

She waited.

"I was meant to set Blackness Tower to rights."

Well, yes. And yet . . . "You said you were here because of a dream," she whispered, following the guidance of his hand, tilting her face toward his, toppling slowly toward his chest.

"Because every night since I saw you in that mirror, I've dreamt of you. Your hair loose or piled on your head. Wearing a ruff and a stomacher, or a kimono exposing the back of your neck. Playing the piano. Embroidering. Walking away from the tower and up to the chapel. Again and again." His whisper was a caress on her face.

She shivered. With delight. What else could it be, when he repeated her own dreams back to her? And she surrendered to it.

"I've dreamed about Blackness Tower for years. And then my grandfather got a calendar with a photo of it, and I came to see what my dreams mean." She gulped, but went on to the end. "And now you're part of the dream."

"I've hoped since the moment I saw you standing by the chapel that you'd say just that." His lashes fluttering, he bent his head and kissed her, gently, delicately, so that she felt the air moved by his motion and his breath mingling with hers as much as she felt the firm, soft flesh of his mouth, his parted lips, the tip of his tongue barely touching hers, trembling with vitality.

And with a gasp that was almost a sob, she felt herself slip-sliding into David Sutherland's abyssal blue eyes, where mysterious creatures swam, and where a woman could drown.

CHAPTER SEVENTEEN

Lauren swam up from deep water. *This guy is spooky,* she warned herself, even as she leaned against his chest, his ribs an iron cage beneath her hands.

I can't get involved with him, she told herself, even as he took her hands and kissed them.

He led her out of the room, past Persie crouched like a pincushion in an alcove, and back down the spiral staircase.

But I'm spooky, too. Like my ancestors before me. And of all men, David understands. I don't have to hide any more, not from him.

Her knees wobbled. His long fingers laced around hers supported her steps, and his arm against hers buoyed her up so that they walked shoulder to shoulder.

"There's one more room for you to see," David said. "The cellars."

She'd only been joking about dragons in the dungeon. But she didn't protest when he opened a door in the antechamber, revealing a second staircase below the first, one that spiraled into the throat of darkness.

He snapped a switch on the wall, and somewhere down below a few watts of light changed blackness into shadow. "Mind your step."

Close behind him, hanging onto his hand, she stepped mindfully down stone treads dished by centuries of footsteps. The air of the vaulted chamber at the bottom was cold, damp, and stale, thick with the wet-dog odor of decay. Lauren tried breathing through her mouth, but that coated her throat with scum.

A few wine bottles reposed in a rack intended for a much greater number. A pile of oozing black bricks in one corner must be peat for the fireplace. They should have been sprouting mushrooms, the glow-in-the-dark kind.

The place was tidy, for a dungeon. Lauren wasn't sure what she'd expected, Halloween spooks? "What did this place look like when you first got here?"

"A midden. You'd have thought the prehistoric inhabitants came out at night to leave their rubbish." David picked up a flashlight from the wine rack, switched it on, and shone it into the darkest corner of the room, where the curve of the vaulting reached the unevenly set flagstones of the floor. "See those rusted bolts in the wall?"

"Shackles for a prisoner?"

"Yes. The landowners, the lairds, had the right of pit and gallows. If you fell afoul of a laird, you were finished."

"Yeah, there's a letter from James Mackay at the library saying just about that."

The light played over the stacked stones, thin slabs of the local slate that had first been fitted together—when? James Mackay built on the foundations of a Norse tower. These stones looked even older, stained, moldy, flaking away. "Are those words carved on that stone?" Lauren asked.

Grasping her hand even more tightly, David directed the light onto two lines of rough, square letters scraped into the flat side of a stone.

The first line read, *Padric Oneil 1588.*

Lauren jerked back, but David's hand caught her. "Oh my God," she exclaimed. "He *was* here! There's a Patrick O'Neill listed on the manifest of the *Castillo Negro*. As a *platero*, a silversmith. The silver skull pocket watch— watches, not just mine—they're Spanish-made."

David's mouth opened, shut, and finally said, "I'll be damned. You don't mean Calder's right!"

"What's the second line?" She leaned closer to the scratches, which, however gray they were, seemed white against the darkness of the stone. "*Timor mortis conturbat me.*"

"The fear of death confounds me. Or upsets me. I've even heard it said, 'The fear of dying scares me to death'." David's dry laugh echoed from the low ceiling, returning as a cry of sorrow. "An infinite jest, isn't it, that the name O'Neill turned up here, to haunt me."

"People can be haunted, as well as places."

"Yes."

Lauren glimpsed a movement from the corner of her eye. She glanced around, but nothing was there that hadn't been there a moment before. She'd seen a mouse, she told herself. Persie was napping, and the mice were playing.

David pulled her against his side and turned off the flashlight. The stone letters faded into shadow. "This chap here, how did he die, then? Hanged, beheaded, chucked over the cliffs? A bloody shame, if he survived the shipwreck. Or did he survive the laird's justice as well, to die in bed?"

"And after all that, is he the body in the grave with Susanna?" Lauren's voice sounded hollow.

"It's not possible. The stratigraphy . . ."

"You said there was enough weirdness to go around, here."

David's arm crushed her. "Yes. And that confounds me."

The walls leaning together, the chill oozing from the ancient stone, the heavy air—Lauren felt her shoulders bowing beneath grief and depression, just as she felt David's arm chilling and hardening and the breath growing shallow in his body. And she felt the slow tremor in the stones beneath her feet, the thrust and retreat of the sea against Black Ness.

Abruptly, with a sudden intake of breath, David turned away from the wall and its message carved by a dead hand. Stowing the flashlight, he escorted her back up the treacherous staircase, switched off the feeble light, and shut the door.

The antechamber seemed brilliantly lit compared to the cellar. Compared to Lauren's most recent dream, when she had seen David as Gideon Bremner and herself as Susanna. Surely the Bremners had used oil lamps as well as candles—her dreams were not replaying past events but interpreting them, re-casting them. Was that how the Sight worked? It always rendered true visions, according to the letter in the library files, but truth could be relative, if not actually distorted.

And David's dreams, were they extraordinary Sight or common ghosts, if ghosts could ever be common?

Her thoughts stumbling as badly as her feet, she let him guide her past the curtain and into the sitting room, where he switched on two nice, bright electric lamps. He sat on the couch and pulled her down beside him, his fingers laced with hers, her hand balanced on his knee.

She breathed in the clean air and eyed the piano, now silent. The basket was still piled with neatly coiled yarn and thread. Today the needle was inserted in the stretched fabric of the sampler. Was it David's hand that had done that, or the invisible touch of one long dead?

This is no metaphor.

The clean sweep of David's profile turned up toward Catherine's portrait. Susanna as Catherine raised the silver skull the way Susanna as Morgan le Fay raised the rose petals above her cauldron of fire, as offering, as evidence.

Yesterday Lauren had held up the skull. Now it was gone, taken by someone for reasons she couldn't fathom. Just as she couldn't fathom the dreams that now thrilled and frightened her as well.

"Tell me your dreams," said David, and his gaze lowered to meet Lauren's.

She told him of her recurring dream of Blackness Tower, and how it had widened and darkened since she arrived, so that she was seeing visions—the shipwreck, the figure on the tower and in the cemetery, the funeral coach, the antechamber. And David himself. You and me, he'd said. Assembling a puzzle was the least of it.

His eyes moved from the painting to her face, thoughts glinting in their depths.

"There's one thing I didn't dream," she concluded. "The first night I was here, the watch started up all by itself. I didn't know it worked. It hasn't worked since. And now it's gone."

His brows lifted and his eye sparked. "It's more than an artifact, I expect. It has meaning."

"Sure it does, if only to me. But whatever it means to anyone else . . ." With little sparkle, she went on, "Maybe Patrick O'Neill made the skull, maybe he didn't. But he was here in 1588, and obviously didn't make too good an impression on the laird."

"James Mackay, Catherine's husband."

"Most of the Armada survivors who landed in Scotland got back home safely. Even though Patrick was Irish, that shouldn't have hurt his chances here. But James's letter says something about dispatching the 'rag' that wasn't drowned—all by the will of God, of course. What if . . ."

"Patrick found himself a neglected wife, estranged from her husband over spiritual issues, the sort of issues that have never failed to provide excuses for murder, especially when you factor in the Seeing Gift." David looked back up at the painting. "Who was murdered then? Catherine, as Rupert Beckwith wrote? Or Patrick? Or both, come to that?"

"Maybe James arranged for their disappearance. It's easy enough to say, oh, so-and-so left the country or was lost at sea."

"Mariota Simison put it about that Catherine's lover had been a selkie, to salve her reputation. An outlander from the sea, and a seal-man—that's not so great a stretch of imagination."

"Mariota was the maid and the go-between, right? Where did I see her—oh, in the appendix of Bremner's *Life and Times*. Did Margaret write that part?"

"I've got her book about Catherine and the Psychical Society. She leaves little doubt she's the artistic and literary one, not Gideon. She seems to have raised Beckwith from a pup, for all she was almost the same age."

"You have a copy of *Catherine Sinclair and the Matter of The Seeing Gift*? I was hoping to get one from Charles Innes. I assume he's not going to take a dislike to me, not when he made sure I got Gideon's book."

"He's pleased you've come," David assured her. "If he'd never taken a liking to me, and told me about Blackness Tower, we'd not be sitting here."

And what if I looked like my mother's side of the family, small and dark? Would we be sitting here then?

"How many coincidences, congruencies, happenstances, whatever, does it take to make a pattern?" Lauren asked aloud. "Maybe I was called here, maybe you were, but . . ."

"Some things," said David, "you can't explain, you can only feel."

What she felt was the warmth emanating from his body, and the pins and needles of his presence, like the fine spray of sea water in a storm. What he wasn't feeling was her. He wasn't even teasing her palm with his thumb, like in her dream. A perfect gentleman, her grandmother's generation would have said, even as her own moaned, *hot!* and warned, *fixer-upper*.

Not that she wasn't a fixer-upper herself. Still, she wasn't easy about baring her soul to him, a much riskier nudity than that of the body.

"I came here," she stated, "to find Susanna's lover, my great-great grandfather. I think we can safely assume he was not Patrick O'Neill. Or was Patrick even Catherine's lover? Does Margaret say?"

"No, she repeats the story of the selkie is all. What interested her was the Seeing Gift. And what she called elemental presences here at Black Ness."

"Ghosts and fairies. Seers. All fodder for the Psychical Society."

"You're a Seer as well, descended as you are from Susanna, and her from Catherine." His smile was more indulgent than ironic, aware not of himself but of her.

What had she wanted, for him to criticize her, argue with her, put her down? Or put her on a TV show? She shook her head, committing herself to nothing. "Was Susanna a Seer?"

"Margaret thought so. She was a bit jealous, I think."

"Of Susanna's Gift—if you can call it that—or of her beauty, or did Susanna have something going with Gideon rather than with one of the artists? Power as an aphrodisiac and all that."

"Best you read the book for yourself. Although it's maddening, using people's initials, implying, alluding. We forget how much more open we are these days. Perhaps too open." His face darkened, no doubt thinking of the newspapers analyzing the strength in his trigger finger.

His hand clasped hers so tightly she was losing the feeling in her fingers. Gently she withdrew them, pressed his thigh with what she hoped was an encouraging grip, and stood up.

The painted Susanna lifted the skull, reflected light leaking between her fingers. Lauren's feet were so cold she tottered rather than walked toward it, and peered up at the brass plaque on the bottom of the frame. It gleamed, polished since yesterday. Polished in honor of her return. Polished like the silver-gilt of the missing skull watch.

Catherine's Dance.

"Dance?" Lauren asked, feeling as though the title had mutated before her eyes.

"Sorry?" asked David, pulling himself to his feet. "Oh, the painting. 'Catherine's Dance', yes. Weir based the painting on Rupert Beckwith's poem, where he speaks of Catherine dancing."

"Maybe it's symbolic—she's dancing with Death." Lauren managed to look away. "You said you were dreaming of me. But you must have been dreaming of Susanna, after seeing the paintings. Or Catherine, although who knows what Catherine looked like?"

"Rupert Beckwith's book includes a sketch of her, copied from a drawing in the chest. I'll leave Calder to pronounce on its authenticity. Suffice it to say, Susanna was the very spit of Catherine."

"That seems less likely than me being a dead ringer for Susanna, but . . ." *Give up. This is a rationality-free zone.*

She moved her chilled feet towards a bookshelf that filled the space between two windows. "Do you have a copy of Beckwith's poem, too?"

"Ask to see Charles's copy—he keeps it in a locked case."

"I will, thanks."

"You'll find Beckwith was a better painter than poet. His poem looks to be a lost episode of Tennyson's *Idylls of the King*. It's titled 'Blood Red Falls the Rose'."

"The painting of Morgan le Fay in her sacred circle, that's his, right?"

"Yes, with the same title."

"What was his source material? Old manuscripts? Local legend?"

"Perhaps he dreamt of Catherine, and thought her his muse."

"Maybe so. Maybe he was in love with Susanna, or Susanna playing Catherine. You were saying yesterday that he's probably my great-great grandfather." She stepped up to the window, her arms tight across her chest. Without David next to her, the room was cool, if not raising gooseflesh with otherworldly music or unexpected paintings, not now.

This day was dim, made even more uncertain by the ripple of the old window glass. A thick mist or a thin rain blotted the horizon, so that Lauren wondered if she'd really seen the hills of Orkney the day before, not to mention blue sky, blue sea, and green land between. Well, sky and sea might now be gray, but the turf was still green. It sloped down to the pink-tinted sand of a beach, edged with slate slabs like the broken battlements of Camelot and cupping the waters of a bay. St Bride's Hope, a natural harbor tucked into the southeastern side of Black Ness.

She'd never walked there in her dreams, just to the north, where tall cliffs stood above the sea. Where the waves surged, tripped, fell, and shattered into froth like tattered lace against the stony backbone of the Ness.

A man wearing a posh leather jacket strolled out onto the headland and posed like a conquistador surveying a map of the Americas. Magnus.

Past him glided a vertical pole—oh, a mast, set into a low-sided ship lined with colored roundels. Cool, Lauren thought. A replica Viking ship for *Paranormal Files*.

The dragon-headed prow lifted and the waves pushed the ship onto the beach. Brawny men clad in loose belted garments leaped out. Swords and spears gleamed dully in the shadowed light. And then women emerged as well, carrying baskets and children. They weren't playing conquerors but settlers, drawn to this place that was ancient even then.

Magnus turned and walked away, not without a casting a sharp glance up at the tower.

When Lauren's eye shifted back to the beach, she saw nothing, not one splinter of wood, not one shred of fabric, not one footprint.

David came up behind her, shielding the chill trickling down her back. "What do you see?" he asked, and his hands closed on her shoulders, steady, snug.

"A Viking ship. I saw it, but then it wasn't there."

"Right," he said, not at all sarcastically. "A time slip. Other lives interleaved with ours. Visions given by the uncanny and capricious powers, the elemental presences, here at Black Ness. You sense them more clearly than I do. You were meant to come here."

She inhaled, exhaled, and her living breath fogged the rippled glass of the window, erasing the view. She was meant to come here. Maybe the watch was meant to be lost. But she wasn't going to give up on free will, not yet. Susanna's son John had claimed his free will by running west.

"Except for that movement in the mirror, I've seen only dreams," said David, his words stirring her hair against her ear. "Dreams and nightmares as well. Though who's to say that our dreams, good or bad, aren't another existence? Not when your dreams brought you here, so that together we can set Blackness Tower to rights."

"You've set it to rights," she murmured. "All the plumbing and masonry and stuff like that."

"Its body's restored, but its soul's not yet healed."

"Soul?" And yet she knew what he meant. She knew the place was wounded the way she felt David's wound. She knew it was wrong the way she'd sensed the wrongness in her own father.

John Reay's silence was a curse on the family tree, twisting its limbs, stunting its growth. How much farther back did that curse go, here, at the place where his silence began?

"I came here to right a wrong, yes. But just naming my great-great grandfather, that's not going to be enough, is it?"

"I suspect not."

"So what are we supposed to do, then? Wait for fate to send me another photo? Wait for destiny to bring back the watch?"

His hands flexed and loosed on her shoulders, rubbed down her arms, wrapped around her waist and pulled her back against his taut, wiry body. "Listen. See. Sense. And we'll be told when the time has come to act."

"And what to do, and how to do it?"

Out to sea, a cruise ship slipped slowly by. People sat at tables with pots of tea and little cakes, viewing the harsh coastline, shivering in mock fear as the waves made their teaspoons dance. For a moment Lauren saw herself sitting with them, watching the hollow of St. Bride's Hope, the green hillock of Black Ness, the spike of the tower and the tiny lump of the chapel, now swarming with bright insects—watching them all dwindle and disappear over the horizon into the past. Leaving her here, standing in the window of Blackness Tower.

If not free, then not alone.

David's hand trailed up her body to her hair and lifted it away from her neck. His mouth touched her nape, the sensitive spot. The sweet spot, where she sensed the uncanny. But there was nothing uncanny about the sparks that coiled down her limbs and flashed off her fingertips.

She felt her face flush, as red, no doubt, as the rose petals in Susanna's hands. And yet even as her mind told her body to turn around and embrace him, her arms across her chest tightened rather than loosened and something in her flesh shriveled, like fingertips too long under water.

David, a wounded soldier, a sailor of dreams, a demon lover.

And distantly, in another galaxy, repeated thuds rattled the front door.

CHAPTER EIGHTEEN

With a huff of laughter that tickled her ear, David released her. "Weeks pass without my seeing a soul here—not a living one, at the least. But the last few days . . . Well, dubious as I am about Calder's charms, or Anderson's, come to that, rest assured that yours are positively enchanting. The book's on the shelf there." He headed towards the antechamber.

Enchanting, Lauren thought. Beguiling. Seductive.

Fearsome.

Her warm right hand, the one David had been holding, settled the hair on the back of her neck. Her eyes scanned the classic novels and old adventure tales on the shelf. There it was.

Catherine Sinclair and the Matter of the Seeing Gift was a slender volume bound in tooled leather, the end papers printed with a delicate paisley, the edges of the pages gilded. Lauren didn't recognize the publisher: Andrew Taliaferro, Canongate, Edinburgh. Never mind the condescending article in the newspaper, the name on the spine was Margaret Bremner, not Mrs. Gideon Bremner. Neither was it Margaret Maiden Name, whatever that had been.

Lauren carried the book toward the antechamber, its cold leather cover much less pleasant against her palm, if significantly less fraught, than David's hand.

He stood next to the marble-topped table holding her coat. His clear diction, military-sharp, cut the Scots accents emanating from Ewan's two student emissaries, Jason and a weedy lad who looked too slight to lift a mattock, let alone his end of the Spanish chest.

As David maneuvered the boys and the chest toward the open door, Jason said, "My mum, she's telling me to apologize for the bonfire. It was just a bit of fun, mind."

"Aye," said the other. "And that pillock from the library, tell her to be apologizing as well. Turning up like that and ticking us off—you'd think she had better things to be getting on with."

"Those wheels, they'd never have set the turf afire, too wet, eh? Just as well she caught a bit of an ember. Next time she'll be minding her own business. Ow!" Jason banged the chest—and, judging by his cry, his hand—against the side of the door.

"Have a care," barked David. "And mind your manners as well. That's Mrs. Gillock to you."

Oh, Lauren got it. "Pillock," meaning idiot. But whatever Rosemary was, she wasn't an idiot, even if she had burned her arm on the kids' bonfire. It wasn't her who'd been shrieking like a banshee.

"And you, Miss Reay," said Jason from the corner his mouth, unable to turn around. "Dr. Calder's asking you to stop by the dig so's he can have a word."

Did Ewan have periscopes for eyes? Or had one of the students told him she was at the tower? "Thanks. And if y'all have a minute . . ."

The boys stopped, and their ears perked toward her.

"Why build your bonfire here at Black Ness? Why not closer to town?"

"It's always been here," Jason said.

"Since Bremner's time," amended David. "He'd have his servants build the fire, and bring out tea-tables, and they'd watch the sunset, pinkies properly extended, no doubt. Off you go. I'll be down straightaway." He shut the door on the boys and turned back to Lauren. "I see lads that age and feel like a centenarian."

"No kidding," she said. "What was that about Rosemary?"

"Her name lends itself to the joke, unfortunately."

"No. About her trying to break up the teenager's party. They were burning wheels?"

"Home-made Catherine wheels, a sort of flaming pinwheel, named after the martyr. The last bit of Lammastide tradition to survive—or that Margaret was able to revive, I expect—with the appeal of playing with fire. The lad's right, the turf's too wet to have burned."

Lauren remembered a Fourth of July before the enactment of draconian rules regarding fireworks, when she'd run round and round the house with sparklers in either hand and set her mother's dry Bermuda grass on fire. Grandpa had moved pretty spryly that night, dousing the grass with the garden hose, if not quite as quickly as Lauren herself had moved when her bare foot landed on a hot sparkler she'd dropped moments before.

That had been soon after her father's disappearance. She'd sat there in the twilight weeping for him, neither her mother's nor her grandfather's reassurances enough to soothe the burning wound of his desertion.

Then, she hadn't yet dreamed of Blackness Tower, let alone of David. Where she was again playing with fire, albeit on the brink of the sea. The drenching warmth in her stomach was giving way to an acid coffee reflux in her throat. "Catherine wheel."

"The name's a nice bit of irony."

She walked on into the kitchen, collected her bag, and placed Margaret's book inside next to *Life and*

Times, which was scabrous by comparison. When she returned to the antechamber David held out her coat. "My jacket's upstairs. If you'd like to get on, have that word with Calder . . ."

And collect a few wits, she added silently.

He was watching her again. Nothing had changed in the intensity of his gaze—she was simply getting used to it. To like it, almost. "You don't trust me, do you?" he asked.

"It's not a matter of trust, exactly. Maybe it's a matter of—well, belief. Faith."

There was the off-kilter smile again. "Caution goes a long way. So does reason, such as it is. Carry on listening and seeing and thinking as well, and when you've answered your questions—when you've answered my questions, come to that—I'll be waiting for you."

"Fair enough. Just remember that I've only got two weeks here. Less, now."

The smile faltered. "I shan't forget that, never fear."

"I wouldn't say *never*." Lauren's face relaxed into a lopsided smile of her own. She let him settle the coat over her shoulders, then turned and kissed his cheek, her lips sensing the skull beneath the skin.

"I'll catch you up at the dig," he told her.

Where, she thought, she'd have to be careful not to look at him and blush.

She stepped out into the courtyard and strode past teeming red roses through the gate and away, as though she knew where she was going. It wasn't until she heard the solid thunk of the door behind her that she stopped.

He understood. He didn't think she was an exhibit. He didn't think she was abnormal. And yet there was something profoundly disturbing about the man. Although profound disturbance might be in the place, the tower, the headland itself. Something had gone wrong here.

Any place people lived with their lusts and greeds and jealousies, any long-inhabited place would have its wounds. It just so happened that this place's wounds were her own. Whether that made it her responsibility to heal them, with or without David—he was expecting a lot, wasn't he, when she had such a short time here.

What was that soft but insistent noise, like repeated grunts? The students playing around?

No, she established with a glance toward the chapel, they were sitting with their backs to the wall, eating their lunches. Jason and the other boy were just joining the others, while Bryony and Ewan settled the Spanish chest in the middle of a startlingly blue plastic tarp. A squat man wearing a baseball cap hovered over them, what looked like a video camera tucked beneath his arm like a swagger stick. Magnus's troop, singular.

Lauren stepped off the path onto the springy turf and strolled toward the edge of the cliff, following the odd barking noise. It grew louder, echoing like faint subterranean hounds on a trail.

"Seals."

She looked around to see Magnus walking toward her. His hair sagged damply and the shoulders of his jacket were beaded with fine water droplets.

"They're lounging around below the cliffs," he went on, "and the fissures in the rock amplify their voices."

She stood where the grass waved above thin air, the rich black dirt beneath falling away over the stacked slate of the cliff. Far below several brown and gray shapes like flabby torpedoes lay on a stone shelf washed by the waves. The stone where the waves had smashed a Spanish galleon—masts broken, deck heeling, hull crushed, men cast into the water or against the rocks. She heard the scream of rending wood, the cries of the doomed men, and the howl of the wind.

She heard seals barking and the rise and fall of the waves, slapping, swirling, sucking.

Magnus stepped up beside her. "You have to wonder how anyone would look at a seal and think it was a mermaid or a selkie, though I suppose a selkie just wraps himself in seal skin and is actually sexy beneath."

"Well, they do have big liquid eyes and cute whiskers." She leaned a bit farther, half-expecting to see splintered timbers lodged between the teeth of the rocks.

"Whoa, careful there." His outsized hand grasped her upper arm through the thickness of Emily's coat and pulled her back from the brink.

"Thanks." She blinked, more lightheaded from her conversation with David than from the height. Emily had said there was no need to attribute a fatal fall to supernatural agencies, but then, there were all kinds of vertigo.

Steadying her feet, she withdrew her arm from Magnus's clasp and started back toward the path to see David just crossing the bridge, headed toward the dig. He had to have seen her standing with Magnus. She awarded him a point for being more possessive of the Spanish chest than of her.

"I saw you in the window of the tower. You all right? You're looking a bit feverish." Magnus fell into step beside her, his face guileless.

She tried a diversion. "You'd have a field day in there, assuming there's anything your instruments can register." Considering his own eyes never registered the ghost ship.

"Picking up some weird vibes, huh? Ghosts, fairies, earth energy, all of the above?"

At least Magnus, unlike Ewan, didn't make cracks about fools and their ghouls. "Or maybe none of the above. What are those birds?" She pointed to the black and white birds with long orange bills, once again sitting in a circle in the nearby field.

"Oystercatchers. St. Bridget's birds, appropriately enough."

"I thought they looked like executives at a board meeting. Maybe the early settlers thought they looked like prelates at a conclave. Those beaks, though . . ."

"Comic relief," said Magnus.

A sheep grazed too close to the circle of birds and they took wing, spiraling up and away with their evocative cries. Lauren felt again her dream of the funeral coach accompanied by those cries. And she felt something else, something behind that dream, behind all the dreams, a souvenir not just of death but of love.

She didn't look around at the tower. She sensed it behind her, as much thrusting up through the earth as settling down in it, watching her walk away and knowing that soon she'd be walking back.

There was the site of the bonfire, grass already closing in around the blackened stone and burned roots like a scab. She imagined the walls of Blackness Tower growing inward, filling the interior with stony scar tissue.

"What's with the fire?" asked Magnus.

"Some local kids having a Lammastide rave-up, according to David. Your pal Rosemary Pil—er—Gillock broke it up. That's why she has a burn on her wrist. Or did you notice that?"

"Oh yeah," he replied, and, staging his own diversion, "Lammas is Lughnasad, a harvest festival, right? I was thinking about doing a show about the old quarter days.

Not that they're a big deal now, not to the general public, except for Samhain. Halloween. All Saint's Eve. I guess the old churchmen decided if they couldn't beat 'em, they'd join 'em."

"To everything there is a season, and a time to every purpose under heaven. Or in sight of Tir nan Og." But now the islands were hidden behind a misty veil.

"The February quarter day is Imbolc, sacred to the pagan goddess Brighid. Now prettied up as Candlemas, St. Bridget's day. Spring and growth and, well, lambs and March hares and other fuzzies have been here all along, but Easter hasn't. Candlemas is the counterweight to Lammas, I guess, sowing versus harvesting. Birth versus death."

Magnus had done his homework, hadn't he? But then, he'd said that he wasn't just talent, reading a script.

They walked across the bridge and side by side started climbing toward the chapel. She might get used to walking up to the chapel for real, too. In the time she had here.

"Some people still think the quarter days are times of great power," he went on, "when the misty veils between worlds slip away and all that good stuff. Like you said, though, it's not necessarily anything my instruments can register. Damn it all anyway."

Or not, Lauren thought. Since Black Ness was doing a dance of the seven veils for her as it was, she was perfectly happy to have missed any quarter days, thank you.

David had taken up a position on the far side of the tarp. Despite his hands thrust into his pockets, he was standing at attention. His gaze, part amused, part bemused, intersected Lauren's. She made a sideways face at Magnus—*he followed me home, but I don't want to keep him.*

The man with camera looked around. "Magnus! This looks to be a good scene!"

"That's Vince," Magnus told Lauren. "Great technician, could make a Faberge egg out of chewing gum. Picked him up in Liverpool."

While the misty rain—or rainy mist—had cleared, the air held water like a washcloth and the sky was a blanket of gray tucked into the horizons. The students appeared damp and dilapidated. Today it was a young woman who was seated to one side, her expression woebegone, one foot propped up on a box. She must have twisted her ankle in a rabbit hole.

Steadying his hat, Ewan cast a suspicious glance upward, probably wondering if threatening the clouds with the furled umbrella lying ready at his left hand would keep them from raining into the chest. At his right hand, Bryony readied camera, plastic bags, and notepad, taking no notice of either Magnus or Lauren, who stopped at the edge of the tarp.

"Right." Ewan's oddly metallic eyes marked David, motionless. Vince, camera ready. Magnus pulling his PDA phone combo from his pocket. Lauren standing in Magnus's lee. The students peering over the rims of bottles and cans. "Grand opening, it is." And he flipped back the lid of the chest.

CHAPTER NINETEEN

The hinges squealed on a note that reverberated in Lauren's teeth. The camera whirred.

Like a surgeon working his way through a patient's abdominal cavity, Ewan began producing items from the dark, faintly smoke-scented interior of the chest. "Pottery bits from an amateur archaeological collection, picked up from the ground here or dug with complete disregard to provenance, by way of being the state of the art in those days. Grooved ware, beaker ware, Unstan ware—the same sort of pottery turned up on Orkney.

"Ah, bone. Horse teeth, most likely, or deer. Another bone. Left zygomatic arch from a human face. A poor Neolithic soul separated from his head by the neighbors, could be, or a souvenir from this burying-ground, good God-fearing Victorian folk having a taste for death."

He passed everything to Bryony without looking around, but she didn't miss a hand-off. She bagged and labeled, apparently unaware of Vince's camera dallying on the black strands framing her rosy cheeks.

Ewan gestured and the camera rotated back to the chest. The wooden one, not Bryony's, which was in any event concealed beneath several layers of sweater and raincoat. "If we're after doing this at all," he said to Magnus rather than Vince, "we're doing it right."

"You're the boss," said Magnus, his teeth bared but not smiling.

"Flint arrowheads. A carved stone ball." Ewan handed Bryony a baseball-sized sphere carved into flattened discs and engraved with concentric circles like a target. "We've never worked out what these are, and I'm hating to default to 'ritual object' without evidence, but they're nicely done. One thing they're not is models of atoms made by some Neolithic Einstein." He shot a cautionary glance toward Magnus.

Magnus shrugged—*who me?*—even as he played his PDA like a musical instrument.

"Three bits of polished quartz. Pretty, but again, purpose unknown."

David took a half-step forward. "Quartz pebbles are piled round Newgrange tomb in Ireland. And loads of other ancient sites. They had a purpose."

"We dinna ken what it was, do we now?" Ewan retorted.

"An intelligent guess never goes amiss."

"I prefer intelligent hypotheses, Sutherland."

There wasn't anything in that chest that David didn't already know about, Lauren told herself. But then, Ewan was the trained scientist. David was . . .

David was.

She wrenched her gaze away from the landscape of his face and followed the small stones from Ewan's hand into Bryony's. Despite the clouds, they glowed with light.

Ewan opened a large pouch of thick, greasy-looking paper. "Here we have sketches, maps, and the like."

"Gideon Bremner's plans and elevations of the tower," David said.

"Noted." Ewan handed several meticulous pen and ink drawings to Bryony, who slipped them into plastic bags. "This looks to be older, a sketch of a woman in sixteenth-century clothing, labeled in sixteenth-century orthography, 'Catriona Sinclerr'. Catherine Sinclair, married name Mackay—Scots women often kept their maiden names."

He looked up at Lauren, frowning.

"Whoa," said Magnus, turning toward her as well. "Another one."

"That's the sketch copied in Rupert Beckwith's book." David was speaking to Lauren—she sensed his words breaking like waves across her face—but he stared at the drawing, not at her.

Bracing herself, she craned her neck to glimpse three indecipherable words above penciled eyebrows, dark eyes, long nose, full lips between a cap and high collar. Even Ewan noticed the resemblance—and promptly dismissed it, handing that sketch, too, to Bryony with the instruction, "Find the translation of that inscription. Looks to be Gaelic."

"*Dannsam led fhailas*," Bryony read aloud, and stowed the paper away without comment.

Vince's lens panned past Lauren's face—thanks, she thought—and re-focused on Ewan.

"Sketches of the original earthworks, likely from the sixteenth century as well." He considered half a dozen thick, slightly ragged, sheets of paper. "Well now. Anderson . . ."

Magnus leaned forward. "Present and accounted for."

"Here's something for your program, something factual. Assuming these sketches are accurate and not period fantasy, there were some right impressive stone rows and rings here, and what looks to be tombs or even half-buried Neolithic houses like those at Skara Brae. The foundations of the old Norse tower are planted to one side, just at the boundary of the older structures."

Lauren leaned forward as well, catching a glimpse of roughly drawn circles, mounds, curving lines. And the solid, deliberate rectangle of what was now Blackness Tower.

David didn't budge. When it came to the drawings, he was way out ahead of Ewan, wasn't he? Or was he? A crease appeared between his eyebrows, as though he was working out yet another puzzle.

Ewan went on. "My preliminary survey was indicating substantial remains beneath the ground. If this drawing's accurate, this site might surpass the Neolithic sites on Orkney—the Ring of Brodgar, Maes Howe, and the like. Or Jarlshof on Shetland, a site built up over centuries. No surprise there, Caithness has loads of grand megalithic sites." Ewan nodded firmly and smiled broadly, perhaps seeing Plan B, brownie points in academic circles even without *El Castillo Negro*. Although Plan A was looking better and better.

Oh. Had David ever told him about, well, the name and the dour message in the dungeon were graffiti, in the technical sense.

"No surprise the early folk built themselves more than flaiks or fences," Ewan concluded. "The slate bedrock in these parts splits into natural building blocks."

Stones left undressed and powerful in the chapel walls and the perimeter fence. Stones left harsh and similarly powerful in the thousand-year-old foundations of the tower, where the rock was still strong enough to hold the iron bolts shackling a prisoner. One who'd survived fire in the English Channel and drowning in the Pentland Firth, only to be immured beneath the earth. Only to die, in the end, as everyone died.

Lauren tried to catch David's attention, wondering if he was thinking of the psalm about love being as strong as death, but his eyes, narrowed in thought, were trained on the last sheet of paper in the bottom of the chest.

Vince panned from chapel to tower and back—visual aids being helpful to the customers. Collecting their bags and cans, the students encircled the proceedings, pressing Lauren inwards so that she stood at the edge of the tarp, her shoulder lodged against Magnus's sleeve.

Magnus glanced at his watch, perhaps wondering how tightly he could edit his video. "Mounds and rings? There are the origins of your ghost and fairy stories. Your ghost *as* fairy stories."

"Goes without saying," murmured David.

Ignoring them both, Ewan lifted the last paper toward the brim of his hat and peered at it so closely his eyes almost crossed. "Well, well, well," he said, his words coming out on a low whistle.

"Aye?" prompted Bryony, plastic bag open, marker pen poised.

"Again, assuming this sketch can be trusted, there looks to have been a Troy Town here. Not too surprising, you see them on the Scandinavian coasts."

"A what?" Lauren asked, even as she felt Magnus stiffen.

David's chin moved up and down in a nod and his forehead smoothed. "A maze or labyrinth. The name 'Troy Town's' likely from the medieval period. Charles thought there was one here."

"Whether that's what's represented in this sketch . . ." Ewan began.

"A maze has dead ends and is meant to confuse," Magnus interrupted. "A labyrinth has just one path, to the center and back out. Or so the spiritual-path crowd use the terms today."

"You're the expert, are you?" David asked.

"Sort of one, yeah," replied Magnus.

"Most—" Lauren waited for Ewan to say 'normal people', but he went on, "—of us take 'maze' and 'labyrinth' as synonyms. You see them all over the world from all eras, aye, and they were put to ritual use, aye, as well as social use, and aye, the facts have long since been muddled by New Agers and the like." Ewan looked up at first Magnus and then David from beneath the brim of his hat, as though they were personally responsible for the muddlement.

David's lips parted, but before he could speak, Magnus grinned. "Cool! Supposedly Glastonbury Tor was a sacred labyrinth. Or Stonehenge or even Callanish. A writer at the time of Julius Caesar wrote about a spherical or spiral temple, depending on the translation, in the land of the Hyperboreans. At the back of the north wind. I did the show about Glastonbury, since everybody does Stonehenge and Callanish is way the hell out in the Hebrides."

David's eye caught Lauren's. His suppressed smile was probably at Magnus trotting out his expertise. Well, she had some of her own. "There's a tile labyrinth in the foyer of a big church in Dallas, based on the medieval one at Chartres in France. You see them in hospital gardens, places like that. People use them as meditation aids."

"One man's woo-woo being another man's spirituality." Magnus was leaning so far forward, the better to see the drawing Ewan held, Lauren was afraid he was going to topple like a felled tree.

"Trends are always coming and going," Ewan said. "And explanations as well. Once you're past the basic astronomical orientations of some tombs and circles, it's all subjective. Fancy. Folk tales."

"Folk tales can be useful," said Lauren. "One of the stories about Black Ness is about musicians and dancers changed to stone for playing on Sunday."

"Yes, quite." David managed to get a word in. "Memories of pre-Christian ritual."

"That's speculation," insisted Ewan. "We've got no way of knowing the origins of the tales, or the symbolism intended by the monument-builders. Though I'm granting you that the sketch here, it's titled 'The Maiden's Dance'."

"All right! Troy Towns and labyrinths were also called dancing floors." Magnus put out a boot to steady himself and a paw to take the drawing.

Ewan held the paper toward Bryony, but she didn't see it, preoccupied by the massive jeans-clad thigh now a foot from her nose.

Lauren intercepted the drawing. Inked lines mapped the entire headland, sea to one side, bay to the other, the tower and its uncompromising right angles planted between. Curving lines filled the rest of the area, long, short, connected and not. Yes, if you squinted and applied imagination, taken together the shapes suggested a unicursal maze. A single-path labyrinth. And in the center . . .

Like Ewan, she raised the paper to her eyes. What had the artist intended that splotch to represent? Maybe an idol of some sort. Maybe a human face. Or maybe it was no more than a blot of ink, smeared by an errant raindrop.

Why, she wondered, hadn't David mentioned any of this to her? She'd actually compared the tower to a maze and commented on the painting of Morgan le Fay in her magic circle. Ewan would say this was all a matter of belief, but it wasn't the level of belief required by ghosts and the Sight.

David's gaze, pensive to the point of somber, lifted from the now-empty chest to Lauren's face. *"Catherine's Dance."*

"Sorry?" asked Ewan.

"That's the name of the painting at the tower, where Susanna's posing as Catherine holding the skull watch."

Yeah, Lauren thought. And when she'd asked about it, David had fobbed her off with something a lot lamer than the facts. What? Did he think she wouldn't know what he was talking about? He'd talked about it with Charles.

He'd talked about *her* with Charles, hadn't he?

Quelling a stab of disappointment—David himself had extolled the virtues of caution—Lauren turned the angle of her shoulder toward him and his fathomless blue eyes and handed the drawing to Bryony, who whisked it into a plastic bag.

"Oh aye, the watch," said Ewan. "That's why I'm after having a word. Hang on."

The watch, Lauren repeated. She'd lost it. She was going to have to tell Ewan and Magnus. Once again she gulped down her anger, her fear, her grief, all of which sat uneasily with her doubt.

Pulling a pen light from his pocket, Ewan peered into the chest, inspected the inside of the lid, turned it around and went over the hinges, the joins, the bottom, millimeter by millimeter. Bryony started organizing the plastic bags into a couple of boxes, while the students drifted away back to the dig, show over. Or at least at intermission.

Ewan sat back and told David, "It's not modern, I'm telling you that. Nor is it stamped 'property of *El Castillo Negro*', more's the pity. Muggins here was imagining the papers shedding light on our anomalous burial, but no joy there, either. I'd be thinking you or Anderson here arranged it all to spite me, if you could have done."

Magnus guffawed.

"Why should I do that?" David asked, brows angled ever so slightly upward.

No one answered, least of all Lauren.

"Jason, Giles," Ewan directed, "help Bryony get these things to the van."

Jason and the weedy wonder reversed course. Silently, without looking at Ewan, Bryony distributed the goods and led the boys off toward the parking lot. She was being deliberately silent, Lauren decided, either as a reproof to Ewan or because she didn't give a damn, not any more.

He looked after her, face as immobile as that of the weathered angel on the Bremner monument, lacking only the lichen. Lauren could feel David's somewhat warmer gaze on the side of her own face. He sensed something was stuck in her craw. Well, let him wonder.

Magnus ran his forefinger horizontally beneath the fringe on his chin and the top of his turtleneck. *Cut.* Vince lowered the camera and then, as rain began to sift down, cursed and thrust it into the school bus-yellow nylon bag at his feet.

"Take five," Magnus directed.

The bag beneath his arm, Vince ambled away, crouched over a match and a cigarette, and settled down next to the wall.

Magnus moved on. "We've got to get things set up at the tower, right, David? Lauren, we're going to run our tests tomorrow night. You know, when the powers of darkness come out and everything. I really need to tape you standing next to that portrait."

"Next to the portrait," David repeated. "You didn't mention that."

"Sure I did," retorted Magnus.

Lauren felt the rain drops coursing off the outer layer of her hair, with the occasional cold trickle onto her scalp. Well, he couldn't tape her holding up the skull in Susanna's pose, as he'd originally intended. And she would have to think about being costumed in a long dress—David might like that. He might like it too much.

"Portrait?" Ewan turned around, braced his hands on his hips, and cocked his head, not aggressive, but not likely to be moved, either. Rain dripped off his hat.

"Catherine's Dance, up at the tower. Though she's not dancing." Magnus made a dismissive gesture. "Whatever, Lauren here's a dead ringer for Susanna, who posed for the painting. And if that sketch is any indication, Susanna looked an awful lot like Catherine."

"The sketch's not necessarily sixteenth-century," said Ewan, even as his gaze swiveled to Lauren's face. "You're descended from Susanna, a wee bit of a resemblance, that's not so odd."

"What part of 'dead ringer' do you not understand?" asked Magnus.

"Coincidence," Ewan riposted. "There's only so many ways a human face fits together."

With a glance at David—the crease between his eyebrows had reappeared—Lauren plunged into the fray. "What about something that isn't a coincidence? Patrick O'Neill, the *platero* from the *Castillo Negro's* manifest. His name and the date fifteen-eighty-eight are carved in the dungeon of the tower, with a Latin phrase meaning, 'The fear of death upsets me'."

"*Timor mortis conturbat me*," David added, tight-lipped. He'd probably wanted to tell Ewan about that himself. If ever.

Silver glinted in Ewan's eyes, and then they dulled again. "Someone likely carved the name and date into the stone recently. I'll be having myself a good look at the patination of the cuts—by your leave, Sutherland."

"Be my guest."

"Say what?" Magnus grinned, teeth flashing like a lighthouse. "A dungeon? An inscription? Sweet!"

"So who knew about Patrick and carved the name and the date?" Lauren asked Ewan. "Where's that manifest been all these years?"

"Rosemary's been requesting copies of documents from London. That's not to say someone at Bremner's salon didn't have the equivalent, and was carried away by the story. Like the modern-day folk building their re-creation labyrinths . . . Damn!" Ewan spun around and charged into the graveyard, snapping, "Come along" over his shoulder.

Magnus made an elaborate bow. "After you, Lauren. David."

Shrugging, Lauren walked beside David into the graveyard and past the Bremner angel. This time she saw no apparitions, just gaping black hole after gaping black hole, gravestones lying flat and tied to braces, narrow trenches like fissures making a grid of it all, with the students as colorful data points.

David's expression was pained but stoic. Archaeology was destruction, after all.

Ewan was kneeling between Susanna—and her silent companion's—empty grave and the main door of the chapel. Above his head the giant stones framed a trapezoidal doorway that opened not only into the metaphorical holy refuge but into the physical cold, wet, empty stone-lined chamber. One that resembled an above-ground dungeon. Or a tomb.

He was not crawling penitently into the sanctuary. He was scraping the edge of the massive slab of the threshold. Freed from its mud matrix, the honey-gray slate made a sill over a dark hollow.

Yesterday he had told Lauren that the stone's face was so weathered, it must have been above ground for long years before being recycled into a doorstep. Today his knotty forefinger indicated the mark beneath the weathering that looked like a thumb print. "See here? It's a wee maze. Having the same design here and on the sketches might be significant."

Not a coincidence? Lauren bumped heads with David and Magnus as they bent over to look, veered aside with mumbled apologies, then bent warily again.

The huge stone was deeply incised with a set of concentric circles, like those on the small stone whatsit . . . No, these lines were arranged so you wove a path, looping back and forth, from a break in the rim into the center.

"There you go," said Magnus. "There's your single-path labyrinth, just like—well, almost like—the way all the stones and mounds and stuff are arranged in the drawing."

"Exactly," David said, with another firm nod and even, this time, a thin smile.

"Here's a representation of a labyrinth, at the least. Of several, almost." Ewan's trowel traced arcs and spirals wending their way across the stone, their crevices still packed with dirt. "The local Stone Age, Bronze Age, Iron Age folk thought it all had meaning, but we've got no idea why."

"They felt it had meaning. They knew." David spoke not to Ewan but to Lauren, as though they were fellow conspirators.

Yes, she thought, even as she met and then shied away from his meaningful look. They knew it the same way she'd known about Blackness Tower. Reay. Caithness. They knew it the same way she knew David, and yet at the same time found him an utter stranger.

The tickle on the back of her neck was a raindrop that had found its way down her collar. Wasn't it? No. When she straightened, she realized the rain had stopped. A spectral sun gleamed through a thinning patch of cloud.

"There's a theory that the stone remembers," Magnus was saying. "That is, the silica in stone can function like a recording tape. You think you're seeing a ghost, but all you're seeing is a re-enactment."

"What of ghosts in forests, then?" David asked. "Or ones on ships?"

Ewan raised his voice. "This door's oriented a bit north of west. There's a fair amount of variance in orientation, mind, especially in churches this early, and I was thinking it was no more than happenstance. Or even accident, the builders missing out true west. But if the chapel's related to a megalithic site, then Black Ness likely has astronomical purposes as well, marking out the divisions of the year for the ancient peoples, like Maes Howe on Orkney oriented to the winter solstice sunset."

"Finding a major new site would make up for you not finding evidence for the Armada ship," David told him.

Magnus added, "Or not admitting the evidence you have, rather."

"Speculation," said Ewan. "Coincidence."

Ewan's rich vowels and half-strangled consonants seemed thick as honey compared to Magnus's low-carb, fat-free generic American accent. And both made completely different music—a reel and light jazz, respectively—from David's clipped accent, which like Mozart or Bach was exact and delicate at once, in no way as lushly romantic as the paintings he guarded.

What had Patrick O'Neill's voice sounded like? Had he even spoken the same language as Catherine or had he indeed been, like a selkie, speechless? What about Mariota Simison or her descendants, one of whom might perhaps have been Gideon's servant Harold? Had the Simisons had a different accent from the Sinclair, Mackay, Bremner lords of the castle? Who had spoken a variety of English, who had spoken Gaelic, who had spoken French, the common tongue of the sixteenth century?

Had Susanna had a low, resonant voice or a little-girl powder puff? Had she ever giggled? Or had she smiled back at Francis Weir and Rupert Beckwith, *knowing*.

Stepping away from the rim of the vacant grave, Lauren turned her back on the chapel door and the circle of men and looked to the southwest. The blue-gray bulges of mountains realized themselves from the gauzy mist, taking their place on stage. She looked to the north. The gunmetal sea rolled away into a pewter sky, surrounding this little land with vast indifferent gulfs like those of time itself. She looked to the east. The tower stood, shoulders hunched, against mist like cotton wool.

It was only illusion. She was standing at the center of the visible world, Lauren told herself, just as it was only illusion that the room with the old bed, and the old mirror, and the living, breathing paintings was the center of Blackness Tower.

But someone else, a lot of someone elses, had believed there was no illusion. No metaphor. Otherwise, why would they have sweated and struggled to raise stones, to arrange them and carve them, and then, years later, to bring them down and hide them from sight if not from memory?

Something was wrong here. Something was broken, allowing other times and places, allowing dreams, to leak into this world. Had first James and then Gideon's removing the stones broken some ancient design here at Black Ness?

David would say yes. Magnus would say sure, why not. Ewan would laugh.

But even if the destruction of the original stone pattern originated the wrongness, how could it be repaired? Should David hire a squadron of earth-moving equipment to put all the stones back where they'd been— assuming, as Ewan kept saying, that the drawings were accurate?

She suspected neither James Mackay, with his modern protestant no-nonsense ethic, nor Gideon Bremner, with his equally modern materialistic point-of-view, had carefully numbered each stone as it was dragged away, or each wall where it was buried.

Reconstruction wasn't possible. Healing might not be possible, either. David's puzzle might never be assembled.

The tingling on the back of her neck flowed down her back and legs and ran down into the ground that squished like a sponge beneath her shoes. Now the chill she sensed was quite physical. Surely her face was pinched beyond recognition, like her stomach, empty.

And what she felt was helplessness in the face of a task she was only now beginning to grasp.

CHAPTER TWENTY

"Earth to Lauren," said Magnus's voice.

Oh. The men were standing in a row. Brown eyes below damp red hair, gray eyes below the rim of a hat, blue eyes below a high, clear forehead—all were focused on her, though the blue eyes were the ones that seemed to be seeing her face at the center of the labyrinth.

Surrendering yet again, she squared her shoulders, lifted her chin, and forced a wan smile. "You wanted to see me, Ewan?"

"Aye, that I did. Have a look at this." He produced a white cardboard box from a plastic tub sitting just inside the chapel and extended it toward Lauren. Stepping closer, Magnus leaned over her shoulder, while David stood aloof, but not without craning his neck.

On a bed of white cotton lay a dull, blackened set of false teeth distorted into a flat shoehorn and filled with scrap metal. Warmth bloomed in her cheeks and died again. "That's the jaw and works of the second skull watch. The one that fits the cranium you were showing me yesterday."

"That's it in one. It turned up in Susanna's grave, next her coffin. And next the rabbit's burrow I was expecting, after finding the cranium in one. I was hoping to compare it to your watch before I send it away to the lab in Stirling, see if it's the same design or not."

Magnus inhaled. David did not.

"And I'm not considering whether it was made by the Patrick O'Neill on the manifest."

Magnus exhaled, rolling his eyes.

David finally took a breath, lips pursed, and turned expectantly to Lauren.

Through clenched teeth she said, "My watch was stolen last night. Taken out of my bag in the living room of my cousin Emily's house. The thief broke a window. We reported it to the police."

Magnus's jaw dropped. Ewan's eyebrows disappeared beneath his hat.

"That's all the thief came for. He left my money and my passport and everything behind. He took my skull watch, the only thing I had of Susanna's."

"Who knew you had it?" Ewan enfolded his clockwork jaw in both hands.

"Who didn't? You, all the students, Rosemary at the library—she was eavesdropping when I showed it to Magnus."

"Yeah, she was," said Magnus, and looked down at his feet.

Not so happy about your alliance now? Lauren asked him silently.

"You've left someone off your list," Ewan said. "Sutherland knew you had the watch."

"Yes," David replied, the sibilant cut short. "What are you implying?"

Ewan backed off. "Nothing. Nothing at all."

Thinking yet again, *Men!* Lauren forced her teeth apart far enough to ask Ewan, "Did you find your missing file?"

He scowled. "No."

"A good thing Rosemary made copies for me, then."

"Aye," he replied, although whether he was dubious about librarians with fingers in multiple pies, Lauren couldn't say.

"Did you find any other artifacts in Susanna's grave?" she asked. "Jewelry or anything?"

"Nothing save the clothes she was wearing, a black dress, it looked to be, and a few hairpins." Ewan's gaze strayed to Lauren's hair, its waves tumbling damply over her shoulders, and his frown eased a bit. "Hair outlasts the—well, hers is still—if not so bright as yours, mind."

Oh, Lauren thought.

David glanced toward the tower, and for once she knew exactly what he was thinking, that the hair in his mourning brooch was still russet, still soft. Soft as his own dark hair, shifting in the wind, exposing and revealing the back of his neck. She wondered if his nape, too, tingled at the uncanny, and if his throat tasted like his lips, sweet and savory at once.

From across the field Bryony's voice called, "Ewan! The lorry's arrived!"

"Well then. Keep me informed, eh?" Replacing the lid on his box and thrusting it into the interior pocket of his windbreaker, Ewan called, "I'm coming just now."

He strode through the graveyard and down the hill. A miniature pickup truck trundled along the path from the parking plot, its wheels cutting oozing gashes in the mud to either side of the footpath. Every inch the Alpha Male, Ewan stepped forward and began waving it in to a landing.

"Transport for the coffins." Magnus tucked his phone back into his pocket and headed for the gate. "Vince! Up and at 'em."

Vince rose from behind the wall, unlimbered the camera, aimed and fired.

"That's it, then," David said, and as the gleam in his eyes touched her again, Lauren felt herself blush. At least she'd held off the blush until they were alone. Sort of—who knew what still lurked in the old graveyard and its older chapel?

She asked him, "Why didn't you mention all the earthworks, the labyrinth and everything? You've had plenty of time to study the drawings, to walk the headland—to talk about it all with Charles, for that matter."

"Ah." His expression went so still that for a moment Lauren expected him to offer his name, rank, and serial number. Then he smiled and frowned simultaneously. "Yes. I've been studying the earthworks as well as a dozen other subjects. Asking questions. Working out the puzzle. You can't expect a full accounting of everything on such short acquaintance."

"But on such short acquaintance, you assume we were meant to fix the place up? Together?"

"It's not so short an acquaintance as all that. Dreams . . ." His gaze thudded down to his feet. To the same pair of boots he'd been wearing yesterday, now coated with a lot less mud.

Yeah, it was all a puzzle. She took a step back, catching herself before she fell into an open grave. "Well, you've got an appointment with Magnus, and it's my turn to talk to Charles."

"Perhaps he'll be a bit more forthcoming with you." David peered up at her from beneath his brows, the smile just edging out the frown.

"I'll call you, okay? If this time you'll answer the phone."

"Okay."

Almost dancing—a step here, a step there—Lauren made her way out of the graveyard. Somewhere a sheep baaed. Somewhere else a gull called. She felt rather than heard her stomach growl, although physical food would satisfy only part of her hunger.

At the gate she glanced back. David was standing where she'd left him, near the place she'd seen a ghost holding both the skull watch and her scarf. The scarf he'd rescued. The watch he'd held.

She waved and smiled, he waved and smiled, and she went on.

He'd wanted her to listen, see, and sense. To ask questions. So she was. As for being told, that was fine for him in his tower, with time enough to wait for revelation. Maybe with her arrival, the excavation, even the TV show, matters were coming to a head, but then, it was her head matters were coming to.

She'd call tonight and see if David kept his promise to pick up the phone. She'd see if after time away from his eyes, his empathy, his touch, she could decide whether he was more compelling or frightening.

Lauren started down the slope, then made a sudden right turn.

Susanna.

Around the corner of the wall, Lauren found the row of coffins, so decayed as to be almost shapeless. The loose bones piled in wooden boxes seemed grim and dark. They shouldn't be disturbing, she told herself. They were just—remains. But still she visualized empty eye sockets looking around at the sound of her steps and bony forefingers beckoning.

At least the male ghosts, visions, whatever they'd been, hadn't actually been beckoning. Even the one in the graveyard, who'd been holding the now-vanished silver skull. Or perhaps the now-tarnished one.

"That one," said a voice at her side.

She jumped.

"Sorry," Magnus said. "Ewan showed me that, quote, anomalous burial, unquote, and pointed out Susanna's coffin. That one."

His gesture reminded her of Dickens's Ghost of Christmas Yet to Come, directing Scrooge toward the grave that waited to embrace him. *The grave's a fine and private place* . . .

She looked up to see David loping across the bridge, fleeing back to his castle under siege.

She looked down at the disintegrated wood of what today's funeral directors tried to pretty up as a "casket," but what was still a coffin. Behind the blackened wooden scraps she glimpsed a shred or two of what might once have been a white silk lining. White silk, like the wedding dress Susanna had never had. Or white like bones bleached by either sun or sea. And the dress she wore was black and bloodless, not like the scarlet she'd worn at least once in life.

A brass plaque barely adhered to the lid of the coffin. While discolored—where was David's brass polish when you needed it?—it was still legible. *Susanna Mackay. 1870-1907.*

Just the facts, no effusions like the verses on the Bremners' monument to give Lauren any hints. Not even a "rest in peace."

"And that's the guy, there," said Magnus. "There's a story for the show."

"I'm sure there's an explanation."

"So am I, but I'm hoping it's one that'll make Mr. Scientist flip out."

Funny how she felt a lot more sympathetic to Ewan and to David when she wasn't actually dealing with them. Stepping away from Magnus, Lauren inspected a plain, even shabby, wooden box. Its lid was ajar, revealing the same dark, sodden rag she'd seen yesterday. A cloak. Perhaps the cloak worn by the man in her vision, a man either with no face or with David's.

She bent closer, so that she made out the brown bones colored by the peat in which they'd lain without benefit of coffin, over the years become one with the cloth, the cloak, that had wrapped them. Patrick? Or someone else, probably piled without benefit of clergy, either, into the loose dirt of a fresh grave, in the middle of the night, to conceal . . .

A murder.

She braced herself, but saw nothing, heard nothing. If that stroke of either imagination or insight had any meaning, no ghosts stepped forward to tell her so. But she had already seen the ghost, the lost spirit. Perhaps Magnus was right, and it—he—was lingering because he wanted the truth about his death revealed, not to mention a decent burial.

Lauren turned away from the row of coffins and boxes, and started down the hill. Cold. Tired. Tasting the bitterness not of defeat, not yet, but most certainly of mortality.

Again Magnus shortened his stride to walk beside her. "Ewan's going to send the guy's body for analysis, just like he's sending the chest, the drawings, the second watch. Just scientific exhibits. At least ghost stories treat the dead as real people, having feelings."

"Yes," she said. "They do."

Ewan and Bryony were supporting the limping girl into the passenger seat of the pickup. The driver had already made himself comfortable with a newspaper and a canned drink. Vince was still taping.

Magnus gave him a thumbs-up signal, but stayed at Lauren's side. "You know what's funny? Well, not funny ha-ha. The graffiti in the cellar of the tower. The fear of death upsets me. You'd think that the fear of death was perfectly normal, wouldn't you?"

"Another reason for ghost stories? Reassuring ourselves that some part of us survives death?"

"I'd like to know that some part of us survives."

She shivered as though an icicle slipped down her back, not certain survival was a good thing.

Magnus put his arm around her and pulled her close. "You're not used to this climate, are you? You want me to take you back to town for a meal? Ah, cancel that. It's almost time to hassle with Sutherland again."

Time flies, Lauren thought, when you're watching the world wobble around you like a top running out of momentum, its circles becoming ellipses.

And she thought, what's up with these hip guys and their goatees, anyway? Red whiskers made a shield-shape around Magnus's mouth but his cheeks were clean-shaven. He looked as though his head had been dragged through a slit too small for it, scraping off the rest of his beard.

But the goatee was more attractive than the bristling shrubberies of Susanna's day. And the goatee had been fashionable back in Catherine's day as well, as tastes cycled in and out, up and down. Like the taste for labyrinths.

"Lauren?" Magnus asked. "What is it with you? You keep zoning out."

His arm was heavy as a yoke. She sensed only the chill of his leather jacket, not the warmth of the body beneath, no matter what a fine strapping body it was.

David's lean, wiry body had trembled in her arms. She pulled away from Magnus. "Sorry. I've got a lot on my mind. That should be in my mind, shouldn't it? Language, it's funny."

"Yeah. More of the funny stuff that's going on here."
And he didn't mean funny ha-ha. "I blew any chance
with you, didn't I, when you overheard me talking to
Rosemary, there on the sidewalk outside the book
shop."

"You knew I heard you?"

"I realized that's what must have happened when
you brushed me off at the library with that crack about
blackmailing Sutherland and funny stuff going on and
everything."

"Sorry. I know you weren't threatening to expose
David's incident, accident, in Northern Ireland."

"He told you about that, huh?"

"Honesty," she said, "is usually the best policy."

Magnus grimaced. "Okay, okay. Listen up. Rosemary
used to work for a genealogical researcher in Edinburgh.
Scotland's Folk."

"Scotland's Folk?" That was Mr. Hawkins's company,
the one Grandpa had used.

"She fell over some dirt about my parents and taxes
due on their antique dealership—in fact, they left the UK
to avoid paying taxes—I'm not saying there was actually
any accounting fraud, it was just . . . Well, they're dead
now, died before their time." His gesture was anything
but dismissive, his right hand clenched over his heart as
though holding it together.

His dark eyes were steady, intense. If he was faking
sincerity with that statement, then he deserved an Oscar,
an Emmy, and a Tony, all tied up in one package. "I'm
sorry," she said.

"Thanks. That's more than Rosemary's ever said.
She threatened to make a big stink about the tax thing,
get Inland Revenue on my case, if I didn't help her out.
You know what they say, there's no such thing as bad

publicity, but damn it, the last thing *Paranormal Files* needs is a big, let's throw this guy out of the country, tax scandal."

"The sins of the fathers," Lauren said, half to herself. Any sins in her ancestry did not, so far as she knew, involve something as mundane as taxes. "So what does Rosemary want from you?"

"A story about Blackness Tower. Now, this minute. I mean, she first e-mailed me saying this place is the real McCoy—or Mackay, as the case might be—but everybody says that. So I said, I'll get back to you. Then she pulled out her secret weapon, the tax thing. Sutherland might expect his own past to come back and bite him, but she was talking about my parents' pasts, damn it."

"Why does she want you to do a story at all, let alone now?"

"Something about shining light into dark corners and cleaning things out. She believes there are ghosties and ghoulies and everything up here. Whether she believes all my electronics will detect them, your guess is as good as mine. And I'm not making any guesses. Or even intelligent hypotheses." He glanced back over his shoulder, toward the enigmatic face of the tower. "She told me about the kids and the bonfire. It was wrong, she said. They were wrong."

"Yeah, there's a lot of wrong going around," Lauren said. "But you're not exactly a willing accomplice, it sounds like."

"Would you want to get into bed with Rosemary Gillock? Metaphorically speaking," he added hastily, raising his hands.

Lauren smiled, if thinly, at that.

"Seriously. Mare scares me. She's off, somehow, worse than Sutherland is off. She's leeched onto him, too, you know, and onto Ewan, and now you. She's putting together some scheme, I bet, but what, I don't know. I don't know what the hell she wants from Black Ness."

"Verifiable paranormal phenomena? Same thing you want?"

Magnus thrust his hands into his pockets and hunched his shoulders as though he, too, had at last become cold. His gaze moved past Lauren's, to some distant sight, and for a moment she thought fear moved in his dark eyes. And not just fear of Thurso's busybody librarian.

When his gaze returned to her face, it was steady as his voice. "You said you were picking up a weird vibe here."

"No, you said that. There is something here, though. I've . . ." Lauren threw her hands in the air. She was too cold, too hungry, too worn down, to keep her mask in place. Not now, when answers were more important than secrecy. "I've been dreaming about Blackness Tower. For years, before I even knew it was a real place. I've seen, I don't know, ghosts or visions here. That body buried in Susanna's grave, I think it's the Irish *platero*, O'Neill. I know that doesn't make sense, but . . ."

"You're clairvoyant?" Magnus's stance shot upright and his eyes glittered like sparks blown from the kids' bonfire. "I knew the genealogy stuff wasn't enough motive. Nor my own self, which has been known to appeal to the opposite sex."

Clairvoyant? Well, that was as good an explanation as any, that the sensitivity was in her, the receiver, rather than in whatever was transmitting. Whoever was transmitting. That would explain why the Seeing Gift wasn't given—or inflicted on—everyone. "What gave me away?"

"Hello? You're in the portrait?"

"I had no control over that." She took a step backward.

"We need to devise some tests, something that will demonstrate . . ."

"Never mind," Lauren told him, and walked away. She shouldn't expect empathy from someone who was in the business of publicity. If anything, he thought she was *too* normal.

"Hey," Magnus called. "I didn't mean . . ."

"Magnus!" called Vince. "It's past time we were getting ourselves to the tower."

A muffled curse, and Magnus called, "Lauren, I'll talk to you later, okay?"

She waved a languid hand over her shoulder, but didn't look around until she was at the top of the hill next to the car park.

Grass lay like a slightly ragged green blanket over the headland, concealing hills and hollows like the sensitive ones in her own hand, the ones dream-David-Gideon had caressed, the ones the real David had held so tenderly. He understood. But she didn't.

Now Magnus and his henchman were headed for the tower, barbarians at David's gate. What if Magnus had talked Ewan's file out of Bryony? But then, Rosemary was only too glad to spread the word. No need to suspect him of anything underhanded with that.

But his late and obviously lamented parents had been in the antiques business, something she should have guessed from his knowledgeable comments on the skull watch. That the watch had gone missing a few hours after he'd handled it was just—wait for it—coincidence. Right?

An arrest for theft wouldn't do much for his show, either. And yet if she didn't quite have faith in David, she definitely didn't trust Magnus, Rosemary's victim or not.

The students loaded the coffins into the pickup, each layer wrapped in a black tarp, just bundles of mortality, no more. Ewan directed operations while Bryony balanced her laptop on the truck's fender, recording each deposit. They would transport the coffins into Thurso under cover of darkness, so as to avoid any public displays of impiety. Or to prevent the townswomen from gathering along the roadside, keening like banshees.

No. Banshees were harbingers of death, not mourners of the past.

The bedraggled wool bundle that yesterday had lain against a stone wall was now gone. Maybe the sheep really had been sleeping. Maybe a shepherd had dragged it away. Maybe the students had added it to their mortuary pile. Not thinking of lamb chops, Lauren walked back to Emily's car, started the engine, and turned the heat to full Saharan blast.

Yes, she'd been meant to come here, to Black Ness, to the tower on its headland. But she'd been called by more than the uncanny powers David evoked. Human manipulation had called her, too, long before human hands stole her watch. Would those hands be content with theft, or was she going to turn around and find them waiting for her? She locked the doors of the car.

In the fog gathering inside the windshield, she visualized Rosemary's sharp tongue licking stamps and affixing them to a brown envelope containing a calendar. But even if Rosemary learned about Grandpa from Hawkins at Scotland's Folk, she had no way of knowing about Lauren's dream. Of knowing that the calendar would lure her here.

Lauren turned onto the main road. As the windshield cleared, the clouds clotted, exposing rifts of sky. In the distance, a ray of sun like a searchlight illuminated a patch of field, brightening it into a glowing emerald green almost too bright for mortal eyes. A fairy color, perhaps. The color of Tir nan Og.

Something was wrong at Black Ness, something greater than an August bonfire, but it sounded as though Rosemary was less interested in righting wrongs than expunging them. Exorcizing the tower. Cleaning out pockets of darkness like David had cleaned out rat's nests. If so, would that make her Lauren's adversary? Having an antagonist would imply that Lauren herself was a protagonist, with or without David as sidekick.

She'd wanted to find the meaning of her dream, and she'd done just that. Now she had to deal with the consequences.

She was starting to sweat. She turned down the car heater, even though the interior of her body was still cold with a dread that couldn't be measured in Fahrenheit. She'd feel better with some food in her stomach, she assured herself.

Unsure of her legs—they felt like spaghetti—she drove past Ewan's hotel and Emily's house and after casting back and forth along one-way streets, found a parking place by the Co-op grocery store just off the main drag. She bought a sandwich and a soda, and sat in the car fueling her body with slimy tomato, harsh yellow cheese, cardboard bread, and chemical-flavored fizzy water.

Gulls hopped around the parking lot scouring the remains of other meals. People walked along with their pale faces turned to the brightening sky, clutching their raincoats and umbrellas just in case. Anticipate the best, Lauren told herself. Prepare for the worst.

Wrinkling her nose at the smell of the old book in her bag, she replenished her lipstick and tugged a comb through her hair. Then she popped two breath mints, the sharp burst of cinnamon almost bringing tears to her eyes.

All right. Keep on keeping on. Don't give up. And other validations.

She walked around the corner and down the street past Emily's shop to the one labeled "Charles Innes, Bookseller." A hand-lettered sign inside the glass pane of the door read, "Open." A bell jangled as she opened the door and jangled again as she closed it. The odor of musty paper and decaying leather washed over her, the scent of *Life and Times* exponentiated.

From beyond the maze of shelves stepped the wizened frame of Charles himself, balding head glowing in the light of the single bulb, glasses reflecting the daylight diffused by the dusty front window, opaque. His lips parted in a smile, revealing the jagged rim of his upper teeth.

She opened her mouth to speak, but he spoke first.

"Hello, Lauren Reay. You're here at last, then. And not a moment too soon."

CHAPTER TWENTY-ONE

Lauren's mouth hung open, as empty as the interior of the chapel.

"It's ever so good to meet you. I'm Charles Innes." His voice held none of the querulousness of age. While reed-thin, it was as crisp as David's.

Her brain whirred, sending off sparks but gaining no traction.

He stepped forward, his angular body threading the shelves. His eyes materialized behind his glasses, pale brown eyes, neither light nor dark. Grandpa's eyes had looked like that, late in his life, the dark brown eyes of his early photographs fading with age, like writing in an old manuscript.

"Aren't you a lovely lass, now. The very spit of Susanna. And of Catherine as well, I expect." His smile seemed less threatening when she saw the softness in his eyes, and yet his words weren't exactly reassuring.

Oh. Of course. "Emily," Lauren croaked, then cleared her throat of acid and cinnamon. "And David, too. They told you I'd arrived. And why I came."

He nodded. "Quite so."

"You've seen 'Catherine's Destiny,' er, 'Dream,' er 'Dance,' at the tower."

"Yes. You've brought the skull pocket watch back, have you? And lost it again?"

"It was stolen." For centuries its owners had kept it safe, until Lauren became its owner, and betrayed it . . . She should save her anger for whoever had betrayed her.

Past Charles's shadowed shape, the brightly-illuminated alcove at the back of the store was hung with pictures of all sizes. Now Lauren saw the painting, large as the original, but, as Ewan had said, ham-handedly done. It was no more than painted lines, no soul. And Catherine-Susanna-Lauren's face was fuzzed out and unreadable, like the face of a ghost.

Charles turned to follow the direction of her gaze. "Young David Sutherland tried his hand at copying some of the Blackness paintings, but gave it up as a bad job. His talents lie in building, not copying. Acting rather than reacting."

Surely that wasn't a dig at his tragic reaction to Bridget O'Neill in Northern Ireland. Indignantly, Lauren replied, "He's done a wonderful job restoring the tower."

"Yes, he has done that, and quite intuitively, before he discovered the old plans."

"The old plans of the building, you mean, not the old plans of the earthworks on the headland."

"He brought the drawings of the earthworks to me, asking for books that would help him understand what they meant. I sold him several, including Margaret's book."

Judging by David's thoughtful pucker as Ewan explored the drawings, and his comment about Charles being less than forthcoming, he still didn't understand. Yeah, the more questions you asked, the more you got. *Listen, see, sense.*

Lauren indicated the bag on her shoulder. "I've got Margaret's book here. But I thought she was writing about Catherine and the Sight and the Psychical Society."

"She was that, yes. There's no writing about that without writing about the ancient remains on Black Ness." Stepping past her, Charles turned the sign on the door to "Closed" and threw the dead bolt. "Let's have us a chin-wag, Lauren. And a cuppa."

He shuffled back to his den. Lauren followed, slowly but not reluctantly, peeling off her coat.

The air in the shop seemed thick and still after the fresh air of Black Ness, and yet it wasn't stuffy but sheltered, buffered from stark reality by the pages of books. She stepped in Charles's steps, finding no dead ends, just plenty of distraction in the cornucopia of names and titles. But she didn't have time to plunge into the shelves and explore the dust of the ages, not now.

"The Psychical Society," said Charles. "Encouraged into existence by Margaret in 1882, the year before her husband began the revival of Blackness Tower and disturbed the *genii loci*, the spirits of the place. As Catherine's husband had disturbed them, and disrupted the patterns that held them."

"The ghosts, the fairies in the mounds," said Lauren, not bothering to tell herself that this guy was spooky, too. Any previous definition she'd had of "spooky" was totally inadequate.

"Reformers and farmers have been toppling the old stones for millennia, although they'd usually leave one upright. All over Scotland one sees solitary standing stones, chipped by the passage of farm equipment and cursed by the farmer as an obstacle. But they still stand. Even James left a few stones, a hint of patterns in the turf. But not Gideon. In his hubris he deemed the stories no more than superstition, and so tore the stones down."

Charles switched on a hot plate beneath a kettle. He opened three tea bags and stuffed them into a pot, then laid out two cups and saucers. Lauren knew they were fine china from the way they glowed, like translucent bone. And by the way they rang when his hands knocked them together. Grandpa's hands had shaken like that, too, towards the end.

"Please, sit down," Charles said, and turned to a glass-topped wooden display case.

Lauren sat in a plastic chair that was angled away from the picture-laden wall.

Across the alcove hung a small pendulum clock, worn and faded. The tick tock that marked the passing of time sounded like water dripping, and like dripping water, it wore away the thickest stone or the tallest tree. Or the treads of a spiral staircase at Blackness Tower.

A gleaming new carving knife lay on the counter next to the teapot. That must be the one Emily had traded Charles for *Life and Times*. Why didn't he keep it upstairs, in his kitchen? Did he think he needed a weapon? Emily had said that Thurso wasn't a high-crime area—until her own house had become a crime scene.

"Emily gave me Gideon Bremner's book. Thank you very much for letting her have it."

"It's important testimony." Charles removed a small book from the display case and closed the lid. "So is this, Rupert Beckwith's poem, 'Blood Red Falls the Rose'. You've seen his painting of Susanna as Catherine playing Morgan le Fay."

"Oh yes. It's beautiful. Is that how he saw Catherine, with her Seeing Gift and all?"

"He saw her as powerful." Giving Lauren the book, he turned to the tea kettle just as it started whistling.

The spine of "Blood Red Falls the Rose" was too narrow for the title, but it was embossed in gilded letters on a suitably crimson leather cover. The pages were cream-colored and almost cream-textured, printed with an ornate Arts and Crafts style font. The woodcut frontispiece was based on "Catherine's Dance," except here the skull watch was not obscured by a blaze of light but was rendered in such detail Lauren felt its ghost resting, cool and heavy, in her hands. Deep inside the book was the copy of the drawing from the chest.

Ah, the publisher was Kelmscott Press, William Morris's company. 1895. That was the year Margaret's book was published. Had she facilitated publication of her pet poet's book, after his—less departure than disappearance, Lauren supposed.

She read the first page. "The moon was low, the wind was shrill, upon that northern shore, where the barrows lay a-dreaming near the keep with its dark lore. Twas then her demon lover rose and to her bower crept, cruelly never swayed by her beauty as she slept."

Wincing, she set the book on the desk. David was right, Rupert had been a much better painter than poet. She pulled *Life and Times* and *Catherine Sinclair and the Matter of the Seeing Gift* from her bag and arranged all three books in a row.

"If you'd like to read Rupert's poem, I shan't charge you a penny. Return it when you've finished." Charles handed her a cup of tea and sat down in the desk chair, an aging wooden number that squealed as he leaned back and drank from his own cup.

"Thank you. Have you read all three books?"

"I have done, yes."

"Rupert's book was published in 1895. But the salon fell apart when he left in 1891."

"His papers remained, as did his paintings." The steam from his cup momentarily clouded Charles's glasses, once more making them seem opaque.

"What did he mean by 'demon lover'? Catherine's selkie?"

"I expect," Charles said slowly, "he intended that sobriquet for James Mackay."

"But James was Catherine's husband . . . Oh. Maybe the emphasis was on 'demon' rather than 'lover'. Although who knows how they originally felt about each other."

His glasses transparent again, like his faded eyes, Charles turned his gaze upon Lauren. And watched her the way David watched her, thoughtfully, warily. Waiting. For inspiration? Or for an explosion? But she wasn't the one with the answers.

She was living the anxiety dream of taking an exam she'd never studied for, she thought, and gulped her sweet milky tea, almost burning her tongue.

"Catherine's lover was reputed to be a selkie, yes," said Charles. "That was a conceit put about by her lady's maid."

"Mariota Simison."

"Mariota Simison. It was not a conceit likely to fool her husband, who, possessing the Seeing Gift as he did, knew exactly what was happening. And he did not take kindly to being cuckolded. When he himself killed one of his tenants while hunting—we presume accidentally—he seized the opportunity to stitch up the lover, and accused him of murder."

"And the lover had no alibi because if he admitted he'd been with Catherine, her life would have been toast. That put him between the devil and the deep blue sea, didn't it?"

"Indeed. James intended it thus, to punish the lover and Catherine as well. But the lover fled to St. Bride's Chapel and claimed sanctuary. James, with the zeal of the convert, said he owed a Catholic chapel no respect. He dragged the lover out and clapped him in irons. And in that manner, James Mackay broke the laws of two separate but not necessarily disparate spiritual traditions."

"Two . . . Oh. He used his Sight for evil, to frame the lover for murder." What a story, Lauren thought. "Is it all in the poem? Is it true?"

"Yes, to both."

Bearing in mind that even to archaeologists, truth was subjective. "What happened to the lover? Did James have him judicially murdered, as that letter of his implies?"

"The poem ends with the man languishing in the dungeon of Blackness Tower remembering the sunlight and green fields of his youth."

"His life flashing before his eyes, in other words. So how did Rupert Beckwith know the story, or enough of it he added things like the green fields?"

"One assumes the transmission of local legends." Charles lifted his cup and set it between his wrinkled lips.

Well no, one didn't, not any more. Lauren was growing more and more impatient with nebulous "local legends" as the source of Catherine's story. Someone, probably Charles himself, was sitting on old letters or manuscripts, ones that would make Ewan's reputation. Or else the ghostly sound-and-light show at Blackness Tower was scripted a lot better than the coming attractions she'd seen so far. If so, that would get Ewan's goat—and make Magnus's reputation.

"Was Catherine's lover the Patrick O'Neill who carved his name in the dungeon of the tower?" she asked. "Did he survive the wreck of *El Castillo Negro*? They rescued him from the sea, like a seal. He must have had his charms."

In the Victorian death coach, he'd had dark hair and a dark goatee and David's blue eyes.

"*Timor mortis conturbat me*," said Charles. "That's a common medieval refrain, used most famously—as Rupert could have told you—in 'The Lament for the Makars' of 1506, an elegy for lost Scottish poets."

Lost Scottish lives, Lauren thought.

Someone tried the door of the shop. She looked around, but Charles didn't. Gravely he refilled his cup and held the teapot over hers. "No thank you," she told him. "I'm pretty well caffeinated for the day. And probably most of the night. I don't always sleep, as it is."

"To sleep," he murmured, "perchance to dream."

Lauren felt David's breath stirring her hair, and his hands pressing into her shoulders, and his lips brushing hers so lightly a spark leaped between them. *Perchance to dream.*

His expression completely neutral, implying nothing, Charles withdrew the teapot and sat back down.

Lauren willed her hair, and with it her nerves, to settle down. A touring company of *Hamlet* must have come through town strewing bits of verbiage like handbills, that was all.

Although Charles was a shrewd old man, just as shrewd as David, who had guessed—no, who had known—too much about her, the descendant of Susanna and of Catherine, too, through the son she bore her lawful wedded lord before she'd begun her dance with love and death.

Emily had told Charles about her strange visitor from the west, but there was a limit to what she knew. Maybe David had flapped that anything-but-stiff upper lip of his and told Charles about Lauren. About him and Lauren, together. It wasn't as though she'd asked him not to betray her confidence—he was, after all, an officer and a gentleman. Who had resigned his commission in disgrace. For something that wasn't his fault.

Charles chimed his cup gently against its saucer, recalling her attention. "*Timor mortis*. We should be upset about the fear of death, for death is not fearsome. It is merely a translation to another world. Usually no more than the spirit crosses over, but at times, very rarely . . ." His creased and crepey face turned up in something that was as much a grimace as smile. "Yes, Catherine's lover was Patrick O'Neill, from Wexford and Santiago de Compostela. The very talented craftsman who created the silver skull watches in Spain and who sketched a lovely picture of Catherine whilst here in Scotland. Before it all came to—an end."

Feeling more than a little breathless, Lauren asked, "What happened to Patrick? What happened to Catherine?"

"She died. Patrick died. James died. They're all gone."

Lauren was starting to miss Ewan's skeptical repartee, especially since he was outnumbered in this part of the world. "Well, yes, but it was a long time ago. How do you know all of this?"

"Everyone dies," said Charles. "Eventually."

She couldn't argue with that. She considered the trio of books, strange bedfellows. "All this about the ancient remains and the artists and even O'Neill—it's fascinating. It's important to the history of Blackness Tower. But I came here to find out about Susanna, not Catherine."

"Ah yes. Susanna." Charles stood, picked up Lauren's saucer and his own, and set them down beside the tea kettle and the containers of tea, sugar, and milk.

"How did she die?"

"She went walking along the cliffs on St. Bridget's Day. No one knows just when or how she fell, but her body was washed into St Bride's Hope the next morning."

"She fell." Lauren felt again that dizzying gulf of air where the grass shredded into nothingness, and small feminine feet pirouetted across her grave. "Was it an accident . . . But you just said, no one knows."

Charles peered at his own hands, as though puzzled to find them at the ends of his arms.

"February second. The first day of spring according to the old quarter days. I thought the Bremners only stayed at Blackness Tower in the summer."

"So they did. But Susanna had been born and raised in Caithness. She refused to leave. And with posing for the artists and bearing a child out of wedlock, she had no other place to go. She looked after the tower with her sister Florence and Florence's husband. And with her own son, though he was quite young when she died."

"Fifteen. Just a kid. I guess he never knew who his father was."

"Oh, I imagine he knew." Charles considered the arthritic curl of his fingers.

"Gideon died the same year," Lauren prompted. "1907."

"He and Margaret returned from the south to attend Susanna's funeral. He was quite ill, and passed on soon after."

"What's with the Burns poem on his monument? 'A man's a man for a' that.' That's an egalitarian epitaph for someone who wrote what he did in *Life and Times*."

"Like Dickens's Scrooge, Gideon came in time to repent of his sins."

"After seeing ghosts at Black Ness?" Lauren wasn't sure whether she was joking.

"Perhaps," said Charles, "one could put it that way."

Yeah, I bet one could. Lauren leaned forward. "So can you tell me who my great-great grandfather was? Who was the father of Susanna's son?"

He straightened, even though his shoulders still curved forward, and turned his seamed face to her. "Yes. I can tell you. While Rupert Beckwith was Susanna's lover, after he left her she turned to Gideon for comfort. And he was the father of her son."

"Oh. Well." Lauren's breath escaped in a sigh. There was her answer. Funny, how that answer now seemed to be little more than a dud, a damp squib, a fizzling sparkler.

Charles watched her, a slight smile playing along one side of his mouth. "Lauren, it's good to meet you at last . . ."

Footsteps echoed from above, a brisk tap of heels like a beat to quarters sounded on a snare drum. Lauren looked up. Charles turned around so abruptly he tottered, then seized the back of the desk chair. With a quick, "If you'll excuse me, please," he disappeared through a curtained doorway.

Lauren heard the treads of a staircase creaking, and his steps growing slower, and his labored breath. Then a door opened and shut, and she heard nothing more, no more steps, no voices, only a distant strain of music.

Okay. Gideon Bremner had had an adulterous affair with Susanna. Had Margaret known John's secret identity? No wonder he bugged out to greener pastures and freer air the year his parents died.

She picked up Margaret's book and opened it. ". . . Deuteronomy 27 tells us, 'Cursed be he that removeth his neighbor's landmark,' just as Proverbs 22 says, 'Remove not the ancient landmark, which thy fathers have set.' And we must not forget Exodus 20: 'And if thou wilt make me an altar of stone, thou shalt not build it of hewn stone, for if thou lift up thy tool upon it, thou hast polluted it.' An intriguing turn of phrase, that, not 'make for me an altar' but 'make me'. Our Semitic ancestors knew then, as did our Celtic ancestors of whom Catherine Sinclair was a sterling example, of the living stone that calls us home four times a year."

Lauren closed the book. If Margaret were still around, she'd be a natural for *The Paranormal Files*. Especially with that hint in *Life and Times* about the Psychical Society manipulating evidence. Something that was still happening, to no happenstance or coincidence whatsoever.

So why had Susanna died, just there, just then? Had she jumped? Or had someone pushed her, eliminating a rival or lover past her sell-by date?

Murder.

But Margaret had an alibi. So did Gideon.

A sterling example of an ancestor. Sterling silver, ha, Lauren thought. But the watch was silver gilt. For a moment she played with an image of Emily, the telephone to her ear, nodding and smiling as P.C. Liddell reported the recovery of the skull watch and the apprehension of an adversary.

The warm tea, the warm room, the successful completion of—well, part of her mission—should have loosened that cold knot in her gut. But no, the chill still prickled through her senses.

Lauren pulled herself out of the hard plastic chair and turned around, and saw that she was being watched— by countless photographed windows and countless photographed eyes.

Amid photos and sketches of the countryside, buildings, and several generations of the royal family hung the photos of Blackness Tower that had beguiled David, old and new pictures of dereliction, old and new pictures of restoration, even a copy of the drawing from the edge of the old map, without dragons.

Interspersed were photos of Blackness Tower's cast of characters, beginning with a snapshot of David himself. The angle of his head as he looked up at the tower, the waves of his dark hair softening the cliff of his forehead, his level brows, all caught at Lauren's heart. She touched the photo with her fingertip, tracing the oval of his face as she'd walk the first steps of a labyrinth.

And there was her great-great grandfather, in the same studio portrait that was in the front of his book. Gideon and the amazing beard—gack, think about getting a mouthful of that during a kiss!—hung next to Margaret and the ten-tons-of-feathers hat that shadowed her face, revealing only thin, tight lips and a glitter of eyes.

Next to them hung a photo of Susanna.

Lauren bent closer. Her movement reflected in the glass covering the photograph, so that the sepia features seemed to move, the lips almost speaking, the eyes wary. *Talk to me*.

But it was only a picture. Of her identical twin. Her dead ringer. The silent face at the center of the labyrinth.

Yes, Susanna had been beautiful, Lauren thought with all modesty due her own looks. The painters had worshiped her with their pens and brushes and Rupert with his body, even, although Lauren would like to know why he dumped her and headed out for the Mediterranean. He could not love her so much, my dear, loved he not artistry more?

Okay, that wasn't the exact quote, David wasn't here to correct her.

Maybe Susanna had dumped Rupert. Either way, with the painters making so much of that beauty, no wonder she attracted the laird's eye while the laird's wife carried on with her woo-woo. Or maybe Margaret was collateral damage. As was James Mackay, in a way. And that generation's Simison, Mariota, who had probably herself come to a vengeful end.

Now Lauren had attracted the laird's eye. Except David was into the woo-woo part of her mission, her dreams, her calling. He wanted them to set Blackness Tower to rights and repair the damage done to the dancing floor. He wanted them combine all the patterns into one.

Human beings had a natural tendency to look for patterns, she told herself. That was the basis of woo-woo of all colors, genders, and national origins. Patterns created out of nothingness.

She looked away from Susanna's dark, guarded eyes to see last year's Tourist Authority calendar. Remembering the envelope and the hospital room, Lauren flipped through it—Edinburgh Castle, Ardnamurchan Point, the Eildon Hills in the Borders, a triple peak with fairy stories of its own, drowsing in a golden August light.

What? Lauren pulled the calendar from the wall and turned through it, page by page.

August was illustrated by a photo of the Eildons. There was no photo of Blackness Tower in the entire calendar. Someone—Rosemary?—hadn't just sent a calendar to Grandpa, he or she had made one up especially for him. And why substitute the photo of the Tower in August? For the same reason Rosemary had insisted Magnus stage his investigations right away?

It all had something to do with the Celtic quarter days once celebrated, now devalued, in this ancient landscape.

It all had something to do with the date of the wreck of *El Castillo Negro*, the catalyst for betrayals ranging from Catherine's of James, and James's of his Seeing Gift, down to the theft of Lauren's family talisman. Down to Lauren herself, and the expectations riding on her back.

Now it was her hands that shook, as the chill in her gut thickened into a glacier. No, Charles wasn't being forthcoming. He wasn't even here to answer questions.

She managed to get the calendar back on its tack, stubbing her toe as she did on a slab of rock, like a gravestone, leaning up against the wall behind her chair.

Carved into the smoothed but not polished honey-gray surface of the stone, in short knobbly lines like skeletal finger bones, were the words: "Ghosts! there are a thousand million walking the earth . . . some half hundred have vanished from it, some half hundred have arisen in it, ere thy watch ticks once . . . we not only carry each a future ghost within him; but are, in very deed, Ghosts!"

The words stitched on the sampler at the tower, and the words written on the scrap of paper in the folder at the library—those had to be part of the same composition. We are all spirits, we are all apparitions, this is no metaphor.

This is a pattern.

Lauren's upper teeth indented her lower lip. If someone wanted to send her a message, an e-mail would have worked just fine. This had to be happenstance, coincidence, manipulation by human forces . . .

She knew what it was: a pattern devised by what David called powers and presences, intended to bring her and the skull watch here. The watch that had been taken from her before she could . . . "Do what?" she asked aloud.

August. Blackness Tower. Reay. Caithness.

The clock on the wall tick-tock-dripped. A truck passed in the street, a reminder of the contemporary world. Behind both sounds lay silence stirred faintly by strains of music, music that went around and around and came out where it went in.

Lauren reached for her bag. She'd had enough input, it was time to process. She'd leave Charles a note and come back later.

There, in front of her eyes, hung a color snapshot. Two people stood in front of a banner reading, "Halkirk Highland Games August 3-5 1993." They were smiling, their heads bent together, shoulders touching.

The man's short-cut hair gleamed brown, russet, and gold in the sunshine. His eyes were dark, and shadowed despite the light. His smile was broad and white and kinked at the sides.

Donny. Donald Reay, Jr. Her father. Four years after the divorce and his disappearance. In Halkirk, just up the road from Thurso—Lauren had seen the road signs.

And the woman who stood beside him, who stood so closely, so companionably beside him, was a darker-haired, smoother-faced, slimmer-formed . . .

Emily.

CHAPTER TWENTY-TWO

Lauren's dusty, gritty fingertips flew to her mouth, suppressing her gasp. *Emily? Emily!*

Her elderly cousin had fed her and consoled her and all along she had *known*. This morning she'd said, *I'm sorry I let this happen*, her voice echoing in the void left by the missing watch.

"Yeah," Lauren said under her breath, "I bet you're sorry. Did you stage a robbery and take it yourself?"

Suddenly the shop was cold as a meat locker, and as claustrophobic. "Mr. Innes?" Lauren called toward the ceiling.

At first she heard nothing. Then a faint voice, thin and crisp as frosted reeds, answered, "I'm sorry to desert you, dear. Come again. Please come again, and soon."

Lauren had no idea whether she was coming or going. She swept the three books into her bag, zigzagged toward the door, then remembered Emily's coat and went back for it. After a bad moment when she couldn't turn the knob on the bolt, the bell jangled and she escaped into the street.

She almost catapulted into a woman with a pram, maybe the same one Magnus had almost slugged the day before. His dishonesties were starting to look more and more insignificant, Lauren thought, muttering apologies and shrugging on the coat. As for David . . .

David would understand. He'd sympathize. Spooky recognized spooky.

Lauren paused in the doorway of Emily's shop, questions frothing on her lips. But amid the cutlery, the kettles, the tea towels, all the ordinaries of daily life, Emily was dealing with one customer while another waited his turn.

The shop was open tonight until seven. Now it was a quarter to five. She'd have to talk to Emily at home. "Home" being relative—right now, Blackness Tower with all its airs and disgraces would be more homey than Emily's little house, where cardboard covered a broken pane in the kitchen door.

Okay, okay, give Emily, too, the benefit of the doubt. Maybe she hadn't known who Donny was, maybe it was just a chance meeting at the Games.

Or maybe Rosemary wasn't Lauren's adversary at all. Maybe it was Emily who had been directing her steps. Maybe she'd coveted the skull watch ever since Grandpa told her about it. Maybe, all this time, she'd known where Donny was.

Narrowly avoiding colliding with more good citizens of Thurso, Lauren ran into the parking lot. She piled into Emily's car—Emily's coat, Emily's car, Emily's house— and sat with her hands braced on the steering wheel.

Gulls spun overhead like bits of cloud in a clean, blue sky. After a time Lauren started hearing their squawks, the same ones Susanna had heard, and Catherine, and the ancient men and women who labored to build patterns in stone, melodies in the key of time.

She'd been called to Blackness Tower in spirit. If she turned up there in body, carrying her suitcase, David would take her in. He'd make room for her beneath the cat-furred comforter. He'd even leave her alone beneath the comforter, if she asked.

And yet, in the night, in the darkness, warm flesh against warm flesh would hold the shadows at bay.

David was Charles's friend. Charles was Emily's friend. The photo was on Charles's wall. The old man had been almost affectionate. "You're here at last," he'd said.

A puzzle. A pattern. Listen, see, sense. Go back to the house and take it from there.

Lauren took several deep breaths, loosening her shoulders, expanding her chest. She started the car and drove with exaggerated care out of the parking lot and around the corner, past the library, the book shop, Emily's store, the restaurant. Just beyond the right-angle turn in the main drag she spotted a man walking along the sidewalk, a broad-brimmed, slouch-style hat on his head, an old pullover clinging to his broad shoulders, a canvas bag dangling at his side.

Ewan. Someone honest. Someone sane.

Lauren tooted the horn and hit the brakes. "Are you going to the hotel? Can I give you a lift?"

"Thank you kindly." He opened the door, doffed his hat, and climbed in.

Only then did it occur to her to look behind her, but no, she hadn't caused a two-car pileup. Decorously, she accelerated. "Where's your van?"

"Bryony's driving the Spanish pay chest and the anomalous burial to Stirling for analysis. The cemetery dig's finished, nowt left but moving the monuments. We've had only one last surprise."

"Not another, ah, anomalous burial?"

"Not an extra body, no, but a missing one."

"What?"

"We've opened the graves in the Bremner plot. No surprise there's no actual burial in Margaret's—her body was never recovered. What's odd is that the coffin in Gideon's grave—and a right posh one it is—is filled with rocks, scraps of raw slate and building blocks jumbled together. There's no body at all."

"That's weird. Sounds like a story Magnus was telling me, about the Reverend what's his name who was kidnapped by fairies."

Ewan's snort was polite but pointed. "I'm saying odd, not loony."

L is for Loony. L is for Lauren. She suggested, "The parish register says there were funerals for Margaret, Gideon, and Susanna. Gideon died soon after Susanna. She fell over the cliffs, did you know that?"

"Ah," Ewan said. "Ah, no, I didna know that, though I'd noted—features . . ."

"Bones broken like matchsticks?"

"Aye. I reckon she died on the instant, if that's any help to you."

Was it? Lauren didn't know.

There was Thurso Bay, wave after glistening wave rolling into the beach and breaking in a tangle of foam. In their colorful wet suits, several surfers resembled confetti sprinkled over the water.

"Gideon might have been buried with his mother's relations in Glasgow or England," Ewan went on, "with a funeral or memorial service for the servants and the local folk. He had no heirs, mind. The exhumation permission came from a descendant of a cousin in Canada."

"Yes, he does have direct descendants. My great-grandfather was his son with Susanna."

"Eh? Is that so?" Ewan swiveled toward her. "What's your source?"

"It's a who. Charles Innes. He has to have some letters or an old diary or something. He knows too many details."

"Ah, so you've tamed Mr. Innes, then. Nothing like a pretty face," Ewan said lightly, and turned away, but not without a sideways gleam of his eyes.

A recognizable face, she added to herself. "So now you're going to excavate the chapel and the headland?"

"That I am. Nae worries, I'd already got a permit from Historic Scotland for the entire site. Sutherland needed asking, aye, and was stroppy as usual, but in the end he's resigned himself to having his place turned topsy-turvy."

Or put to rights, not that uncovering the wretched remnants of the stone designs would help—heal a wound. Lauren guided the car into the hotel parking lot and loosened her choke hold of the steering wheel.

"I've had no lunch the day," Ewan went on. "If you'd fancy joining me for an early meal, you could have yourself a look at the drawings from the chest, still warm from the library copier."

Had Rosemary's interfering hand run off those copies, inspecting each one as it slid into the tray? Magnus didn't trust her. David didn't trust her. It was Ewan who might be her pawn. Ewan's digging up the headland and applying scientific analysis to the remains might exorcize the spirits of the place. So might Magnus applying not only science but celebrity.

The footsteps above Charles's shop. They'd sounded familiar, those of interfering feet. "Was Rosemary at the library?" she asked.

"No, I didna see a hair of her head."

So La Pillock had—what? Come in a private entrance to Charles's apartment, knowing her steps would draw him upstairs and away from Lauren? He and Rosemary must have been having themselves a real nice little confab.

If Ewan was Rosemary's pawn, what was Charles? Her knight, moving at unexpected angles?

What am I? Lauren asked herself.

"Lauren?" asked Ewan.

"Yeah, thanks, a hot meal sounds great. Except I'm up to here with tea. You think they'd sell me a glass of beer?"

"They would do, aye, but in that event you'd best be leaving the car at Ms. Brodie's house. We've got strict drink-driving laws in these parts."

"Oh. Okay. I'll be right back."

Leaving Ewan to make his way toward one of the boxcar-like cubicles behind the main hotel building, Lauren drove to Emily's house and parked the car. She unlocked the front door and stood in the entrance hall, every sense alert.

Nothing, just silence, shadow, and the faintly metallic odor of fry-ups past. In the living room, Emily's mantel clock struck five tinny blows.

She hung Emily's coat in the closet, then walked upstairs. In the bathroom and bedroom, none of her things had been disarranged. If Emily had come home and searched Lauren's belongings for more talismans, more goodies, she found no evidence of it.

Here was her chance to search the house. She walked into Emily's bedroom and surveyed the possibilities—dresser, wardrobe, night stand, tufted bedspread hanging all the way to the floor. Without touching a thing she went back downstairs and considered Emily's desk in the corner of the living room, but didn't open a single drawer.

That was the problem with being the good guy, she thought. Good guys had to have scruples. She'd have to start out by telling Emily, openly, honestly, *I saw a photo in Charles's shop.*

Not the best place to keep an incriminating photo, was it? Maybe neither he nor Emily knew who Donny was and it was all very innocent and Lauren was living in a glass house of her own construction—moi? dreams? spooky?—and was busily throwing stones that shattered windows.

She inspected the floor inside the kitchen door. Had Emily swept up all the glass particles? No, one glinted beneath the edge of the cabinet. And another one lay beneath the stove.

Opening the back door, Lauren checked over the stoop with its thick mat and flower pots. No glass. So the window really had been broken from the outside. One point for Emily. Although she might have stepped outside, depending on how devious she was, not that devious was a word Lauren would ever have associated with Emily.

And never mind devious, what about motive? That was one thing Emily didn't seem to have. If Rosemary wanted David to renovate, Magnus to investigate, and Ewan to excavate, what did Emily want? What did Charles want, for that matter? Did he, like David, think that Lauren—the current version of Susanna and Catherine and the current owner of the skull watch— could heal, mend, repair a place? Not a broken window or a toppled wall, a place.

What no one was asking her was whether she even wanted to try.

Lauren stepped back into the kitchen and locked the door, even though her velvet casket and its metal metaphor were already gone. Even though the wide-open landscape outside the window, hinting of new lands and strange customs, now seemed a lie.

The light winked on the base of the phone, indicating a message saved on the answering machine. Would

Emily, with her shaky grasp of modern technology, realize Lauren had listened in? She'd have to debit herself a point, for dumping a scruple, but . . .

She pressed the button even as she thought of Rosemary's ear pressed to her own phone, listening in.

David's refined tenor emanated from the tiny speaker. "Emily, ring me after you close up this evening. I've shown Lauren about the place, and yes, she's been dreaming."

Lauren felt a cold draft on the back of her neck, where the touch of his lips still prickled.

"We can trust her," he concluded, and with a whir and click, the machine fell silent.

CHAPTER TWENTY-THREE

T he floor seemed to gather itself beneath Lauren's feet, curl forward, and break like the waves in St. Bride's Hope. She grasped the back of a kitchen chair for support.

Trust? David had the gall to talk about trust? And "we"—there was a pronoun he threw around pretty easily. As for those kisses, what man wouldn't grab a kiss, cop a feel, given the chance? The encounter hadn't been a meeting of soulmates at all.

And she'd considered running to his arms tonight, thinking he'd understand, and sympathize, and together they would repel the darkness. But now it looked as though the only person in the entire county she could trust was Ewan. Who was waiting for her at the hotel.

Lauren wobbled to the sink and splashed cold water on her colder cheeks. Her stomach didn't so much grumble as shimmy. Food. Drink. A nice logical conversation. Then she'd tackle Emily.

As for David, tackling him was still on her agenda, but "tackle" now had a different meaning.

By the time Lauren's long, impatient strides—you'd think the bad guys, however ill-defined, were gaining on her—returned her to the hotel, Ewan was waiting bareheaded by the main entrance. Funny, how with his hair slicked down his ears seemed to be two sizes larger. His hand clutching his bag was scrubbed clean, the skin pink and raw, knuckles scraped, fingernails rimmed with dirt.

Normal, she instructed herself as she stepped past him into the building. She was greeted by the murmur of a sound system playing a saccharine version of "Caledonia," Dougie MacLean's homesick hymn to Scotland.

She heard her father's clear baritone singing the chorus, "Caledonia, you're calling me . . ." Words that had proved prophetic.

Normal. She stretched her taut lips and aching jaw into something resembling a smile. "Why don't you wear gloves while you work?"

"How'd I feel anything then, wearing gloves?" Ewan replied. "Here we are. Table by the window."

Lauren expected the audio track to segue into "Feelings," but it didn't.

The glassed-in porch of the hotel framed a vista of town, field, sea, and sky, anchored to the east by the striated red mound of Dunnet Head, the northernmost rim of Britain. The rolling blue waters of the bay glinted in the sunshine, but across the Firth the horizon was still cloudy. Perhaps Orkney was there after all, a thickness in the mist like an unformed idea, changeable as Lauren's assumptions.

She pulled her awareness back into the room. Ewan was looking at her as though she was the scenery. Him too, huh? "You went up to the tower to ask David about excavating. You saw the original portrait."

"Oh aye, with Sutherland doing the honors. You are the very spit of Susanna."

"There's a photo of her in the book shop that's even more startling. I look just like her, yeah. It's almost enough to make you believe in reincarnation."

"Reincarnation's the transmission of the spirit, not the physical body." Ewan lowered his gaze to the menu.

Thanks, thought Lauren.

She's been dreaming, David had said.

You don't trust me, do you, he had asked her. *It's more a matter of faith*, she'd returned.

Faith. The sins of the fathers, and the great-great grandmothers. She wanted to sink beneath the table and whimper. She wanted to abandon the watch, grab her suitcase, and head for the nearest airport.

Instead she gave Ewan her order: shepherd's pie and two veg. As for beer . . .

"Dark Island," he recommended. "From Orkney, just across the water. Nowhere near as strong as Skullsplitter."

"Skullsplitter might be a bit too apt. Here, let me throw in some money. I've still got that, even though someone ripped off my watch."

Ewan headed for the bar to place the order and get the drinks. The Muzak segued into an even more saccharine version of "The Water is Wide," all tremolo and quaver. Lauren dug through her bag. When Ewan returned, she traded him her copy of *Life and Times* for a tall glass brimming with dark, froth-flecked liquid. "Here's the book. I should have given it to you at the dig."

"No problem. Thanks for sharing."

She picked up her condensation-damp glass and dinked his. "Slainte."

"Cheers," he returned, and drank thirstily.

The ale was rich, smooth and sharp at once, and reminded Lauren of the dark peaty soil of Black Ness. She could almost chew it. She'd never be able to drink ice-cold, watery light beer again, she told herself as the tense muscles in her neck and shoulders tingled and then eased.

Wiping his mouth, Ewan leafed quickly through the book.

"I didn't see anything in there about *El Castillo Negro*, sorry," Lauren told him.

"Gideon mentions an Armada ship, but not by name. I've got a copy of the page. Something about a local legend."

It was her turn to snort, not just at local legend, but at local games and local liars.

"Here it is. '. . . and so the ship, that had set out in such a great company beneath the banners of Spain, a company intended to change the world, found a solitary, watery grave at its very edge, beneath the banner of Scotland. The shipwreck and the consequences following upon it marked a moment where history intersected myth, if myth obscured by the fogs of our northern coasts and discerned only in faintest outline through the eyes of those who could, however distantly, see.'"

"The eyes of those who could see," repeated Lauren.

"That's likely a reference to Margaret's work with the Psychical Society."

"Considering she probably wrote most of *Life and Times* herself. Here are her and Rupert Beckwith's books, too, though Beckwith's is about Catherine and Patrick O'Neill." She laid the two books on the table.

Ewan looked at her, not them. "Patrick O'Neill? The *platero* from the manifest?"

"And the name carved in the dungeon. Supposedly he was Catherine's selkie lover."

"I'll not be wasting my time on that sort of local legend," he said, and leaned over to tuck *Life and Times* into his own rough-and-ready bag. When he straightened, he held two file envelopes, one of them sporting a dirty footprint. "One of the lads, Giles, he's confessed to handing the original sixteenth-century files over to Anderson."

Magnus, Lauren thought, with a queasy swirl of strong ale in her empty stomach. So he *would* stoop to underhanded methods to get a story.

"Just by way of having a look, Anderson was saying, and he'd be putting the file back in the van straightaway. Goes without saying it's still missing. And that I've put a flea or two in young Giles's ear." Ewan shook his head.

"So Magnus didn't believe you were telling him everything you knew about Black Ness."

"Because I was not telling him anything he was wanting to hear. Sutherland's saying Anderson's staking out the tower tomorrow night, hoping for bogles. Good luck to him." Ewan took another swig from his glass, and swished the ale around his mouth as though cleansing it. "And aye, I've gone and apologized to Bryony about the file, my hat in my hand. Just as I'm apologizing to you, now, for doubting your motives when you first turned up. And for what I was saying about Sutherland. He's steadier now, resigned to his fate, like as not."

That made one of them, then. "That's okay," she told Ewan. "Everything's kind of happening at once, isn't it?"

"You've got that right."

At least, she thought, he'd given her the answer to a secondary question, even though that answer further lowered her opinion of Magnus. Had anything her compatriot told her been the truth, other than his not trusting Rosemary to share all her resources with him? And he hadn't gotten much out of Charles either, although he'd at least been admitted to the old man's fiefdom.

Carefully not saying, *speaking of Patrick*, Lauren asked, "Did you find out anything about the anomalous burial? Can you date it?"

"As yet, we've got the associated artifacts is all, but they're all from the Armada time period. The crucifix. The clothing—a padded peasecod doublet, jerkin, breeches, paned trunk hose, low shoes with heels, buckled garters, lace collar and cuffs, buttons and hooks—the lot. The cloak's Spanish style, short with a hood. We've even got two coins of Felipe II and one of James VI."

Oyster catchers flew up from the field across the road, emitting their eerie cries. Ewan's face turned to follow them. His profile was blunt, candid, down to earth. Literally.

Lauren sipped her beer, letting the liquid trickle down her throat and its consequences ooze into her body. "And the clasp on the cloak is silver."

"Cloak clasps are not typical of the time period, but not all that unusual, either."

"If the man was a silversmith . . ."

Ewan slapped the topmost folder. "It's not O'Neill. The stratigraphy is wrong. All wrong."

"What isn't?" Lauren asked beneath her breath, and, louder, "You said maybe the body was a guest from a fancy-dress ball at the tower. What if it's Gideon himself, dressed like, say, the Duke of Medina Sidonia? Maybe he got swept up in a recreation instigated by the artists."

"Good thinking, that," Ewan said with a nod. "But the body's that of a young man, no older than thirty. And I'm not seeing Gideon sneaked into a previously dug grave, whether that grave was Susanna's or not. A grave dug years after the artists gave it up and went away."

"I was wondering if it was a quick, secret burial. A murder victim."

"Well . . ." Ewan was saved from committing himself to that theory by the arrival of the food, each dish carried separately by a teenaged waitress using dishtowels for hot pads.

Lauren hadn't realized she was hungry until she started eating. She matched Ewan bite for bite, swallowing the hot buttery mashed potatoes, the succulent meat and gravy, even the bland but fresh Brussels sprouts and carrots, nectar of the northern gods. Heat melted the edges of her cold dread and cushioned the raw ends of her nerves.

The sounds of other voices rolled against her ears and receded as people sat down at other tables. On the sound system, several sopranos sang a sprightly tune. "As I came down through Dublin City, at the hour of twelve at night, who should I see but the Spanish lady, combing her hair by candlelight. First she tossed it, then she brushed it, on her lap was a silver comb . . ."

Weird, Lauren told herself, and mopped her gravy with a piece of bread. "Weird comes from wyrd, doesn't it? That means fate, which comes back around to fey with an 'e', and then to fay with an 'a', for fairies. And that probably relates to the word 'faith'. Somehow."

Ewan shoved his plate to one side, picked up his glass, and peered at her quizzically over its rim lined with foam like that on a beach marking the turn of the tide. "Aye, that's the derivation of the words."

Fate, she thought. John Reay, born Mackay, had fled, but fate had come back to bite not only his son, but his grandson and his great-granddaughter. Not Catherine's dance, not Susanna's dream, but Lauren's destiny. Heat rose into her cheeks.

A half-smile playing at the corners of his mouth—what? did he think she was getting a bit of a buzz?—Ewan opened the second file and fanned the copies, stark white and uniformly sized, across the table.

Lauren considered the sketches, the stones forming the ancient patterns, the face of Catherine Sinclair. Her own face, looking back at her. *"Dannsam led fhailas?"* she asked, tripping over the unfamiliar words.

"The Gaelic inscription translates as 'Let me dance with your shadow.'"

The words prickled along Lauren's limbs like David's lips pressing hers. *David, why?* The memory of his kisses twisted beneath her ribs, close to the spot where every thought of the stolen watch festered.

"Dance?" she repeated, just a bit too loudly. "Catherine's Dance? The Maiden's Dance? That's almost seductive—I mean, Catherine was no maiden, with a husband and a lover, supernatural or not . . ." She had no idea where she was going with that. Lowering her volume, she tried again. "Have you seen Beckwith's painting of her as Morgan le Fay casting a spell in her magic circle? That's where he got the title of his poem, 'Blood Red Falls the Rose.'"

Ewan said, "No, I've not seen that one."

"Let me dance with your shadow. Shadows as shades? Ghosts? Magnus isn't completely out in left field talking about ancient rites, you know. Heck, some people still believe in the ancient earth religions. Look at the neo-Druids . . ."

Ewan's gaze darted upward. Someone moved at Lauren's elbow. Without looking around, she thrust her empty plate in that direction. But it didn't disappear.

"Good evening Miss Reay, Dr. Calder," said a precise voice.

Lauren looked up so quickly she almost dislocated her neck. Rosemary Gillock loomed over the table.

CHAPTER TWENTY-FOUR

Rosemary was dressed to kill in a dazzling white blouse beneath a black velvet vest with silver buttons, and a long skirt in a Mackay tartan, black, green, and blue. Black tower, its green headland, the blue sea. The pattern's thin yellow stripe, Lauren supposed, was the one that would run down her own spine if she did run for the nearest airport.

She met Rosemary's smile, thin red lips over pearl-like teeth, with one just as stiff. "Good evening."

"Going dancing, are you?" asked Ewan.

"I'm attending a retirement party for one of our media specialists. You're consulting over your work, I see. It must be getting on well." Rosemary's face was turned toward Ewan but a flash from the corners of her eyes indicated she was asking Lauren, who she knew very well had just gotten an earful from Charles Innes.

"Fairly well, thank you." Ewan's voice cooled into courtesy. "Have you got any idea why there's no body in Gideon Bremner's grave?"

Rosemary's sagging lids closed so far her eyes became blue slits narrower than her glasses. Her smile didn't waver. "My goodness. What a surprise," she said, in a voice that showed no surprise whatsoever. "You've got Margaret's and Rupert's books, I see. Poor deluded souls, they were. But what's . . . Oh, my, what a lovely drawing of Catherine. Patrick O'Neill's hand, is it? A very fine hand, in several meanings. She played the slut for him, mind you. As Susanna played—well, that's all in the past. Have a grand evening, the both of you."

With a last calculating glance at Lauren, Rosemary turned and clicked away.

Sure, blame the victim, Lauren thought. Catherine and Susanna had both been trapped by powerful men.

Or had they? Rupert Beckwith's painting of Morgan le Fay did not suggest a lack of power. Neither did Weir's painting of Catherine holding the skull like a crystal ball. As for Susanna, nothing was truly past, as Rosemary herself knew all too well.

Two tartan skirt and kilt clad couples strolled toward the door, one man saying with a laugh, "I've not danced since Margaret Thatcher went flying about on her broomstick." They were welcomed by a burst of music played on accordion, fiddle, guitar, drum, whistle.

A ceilidh or party band. Donny had played in a local version of one, doing "Streets of Laredo" and "Waltz Across Texas" as well as Scottish and Irish melodies. Most people sneered at accordion music. Lauren had to swallow back tears.

Ewan's gray gaze moved from the party back to the table. "How'd Rosemary know who that was? Aye, it's not necessarily a sixteenth-century sketch, but still . . ."

"What?" Lauren looked down at the table top.

One of Bremner's elevations of the tower lay across the bottom of the portrait-sketch, hiding the legend "Catriona Sinclerr." But Rosemary had known who the woman was, and whose hand had so lovingly drawn her face and presumably added the provocative Gaelic inscription.

"Charles must have shown her the copy in Rupert's book," Lauren said.

"Ah. No doubt." Lacking his hat, Ewan tipped his empty glass at her, then resolutely set it aside and arranged the copies in a tidy stack. He leafed through "Blood Red Falls the Rose" and made a face.

Lauren peered down into her glass. A few drops of amber liquid puddled in its depths. Okay. Bottoms up. Closing her eyes, she poured the dregs into her mouth and let their flavor seep through her senses.

When she opened her eyes, Ewan was watching her, not wary or even frightened, the way Charles and David watched her, but definitely curious. Wondering, perhaps, what made her tick.

"The Neo-Druids marching on Stonehenge at the summer solstice, you were saying. And the Beltane festival on Calton Hill in Edinburgh. They're creating their rituals from whole cloth—the last traces of the ancient earth religions died away long since. Alexander Lindsay, of the 1540 chart of the Pentland Firth, he wrote in his *A True Account of the Natives of Northern Scotland* of old customs lingering at Ladykirk, of worshipers paying their respects to the stones as they went in to the chapel, of them lighting fires about the old tombs at Lammastide. But all later travelers were writing was of a curse on Black Ness."

"Maybe that's because James Mackay damaged the old stone patterns. Maybe he did it deliberately to stop people from paying their respects to the stones."

Ewan's right eyebrow lifted doubtfully. "We're only certain that the earthworks were marking out a sacred space, marking a boundary between this world and the next, as all religious sites do."

If rarely as effectively at Black Ness, Lauren thought, and for a moment she felt giddy. The ale was stronger than she'd bargained for.

She focused on picking Ewan's brains. "And then Gideon wiped out the last remnants of the pattern. Margaret tried to save the sacred space, but she couldn't. The old customs became nothing more than fodder for the artists. Well, and for the local teenagers, although whether their Lammas bonfire is a geni-genun . . ." The word wasn't coming out right.

"A genuinely ancient survival or Margaret's re-creation?" Ewan asked, and this time leafed through Margaret's book. "Good question. We've got loads of good questions."

"Only some of my questions are our questions, mutual," Lauren said, and then stopped, pressing her lips together. The ale had loosened her tongue. With David, her tongue had been freed, both symbolically and physically. As, perhaps, Catherine's tongue had been freed, along with the lacings of her dress, along with the belt of Susanna's kimono, except Susanna had traced the path backwards, from the selkie lover to the laird, the true demon of the piece, although that was medieval folklore, to say the devil was a cold lover.

Her assumption that the women had no control over their own fates was no more valid than Rosemary's view of them.

Ewan was smiling at her again. She hoped to heaven he wasn't reading her thoughts in her no doubt slightly crossed eyes. Eyes, the mirror of the soul. And it was the soul that Saw.

"The consequences following the shipwreck," she said. "Betrayal, lies, murder, the boundaries of the sacred space violated. Did it turn into a blight all at once?" Where had she heard "blight" recently—oh, Magnus's TV show. Haunts, hags, and blights, he'd said. "Or did the powers corrupt slowly, one insult at a time?"

"Eh?" Ewan had no idea what she was talking about, did he? Or what she wanted from him. And yet he gamely gave her answers, such as they were. "If you're wishing for an ancient survival, you could be looking across to Orkney. It's been no more than a century since young boys went away with torches or candles on February second, calling an ogress from the old burial mounds. In Scottish tradition they'd be calling the crone aspect of the triple goddess, the winter hag, and burning her effigy on a bonfire."

"But Susanna fell and was drowned, she wasn't burned. And like Catherine she was a mother, not a maiden but not yet a crone, either. She should have died on Lammas, that's the harvest festival. The death ritual. Maybe a rebirth ritual—who knows?"

This time it was his left eyebrow that quirked. "Susanna? Catherine?"

Lauren lost the thread of her thought. The dishes vanished from her elbow and footsteps padded away. A lively jig spilled through the doorway and flashes of tartan whirled past. "They're dancing a Strip the Willow, right? Like a Virginia reel, where each dancer spins around the others."

"Right."

"I read somewhere that dancing around a Maypole's a remnant of an old dance, where the dancers wove in and out around a central point."

"I've heard that as well. May Day's the old quarter day of Beltane, the beginning of summer."

The quarter days. Lammas, Samhain, Imbolc, Beltane, almost her own birthday . . . Wait a minute. She shared her birthday with John Reay. May 7. Within a gestational window that would have opened on August 1: Lammas. Was that when Susanna and Gideon had gotten together?

And Susanna died on February 2. Those must be powerful days at Black Ness, when tides in the affairs of men were taken at the full, or however Shakespeare put it.

Again Lauren found herself holding the thread but not the thought. She rearranged her lips and tongue and tried again. "Walking a labyrinth is like a dance, weaving in and out. I did the one in Dallas with a friend. You go right, you go left, sometimes you brush by each other, other times you're facing in opposite directions."

Ewan nodded. "That design's based on the one at Chartres, is it? That's a later, more complex pattern, larger and tighter than the old Troy Town mazes, with the paths folded back on themselves. But then, there's fashion in labyrinths like in anything else—ancient times, medieval times, Elizabethan, Victorian, modern times, they're all . . ."

". . . represented at Black Ness!" All right! She was onto something after all! Lauren leaned across the table, fanning out the sketches. "See, right here. You said yourself, there was a labyrinth at Black Ness. The tower's on one side and the chapel the other, like entrance and exit—no, the same place should be both. Like bookends, or like weights, holding it all down."

Ewan didn't look at the drawing but at her, a laugh lurking at the corners of his eyes and lips. "Speculation's right amusing and all, but where the evidence runs out, there you're obliged to stop speculating."

No, that's where you start. That was Ewan's beef with David and with Magnus—they kept right on speculating. Magnus wanted to find, and David had found, something that really was paranormal, beyond explanation. Ewan would cling like grim death to some sort of explanation, even if that took a greater leap of faith than surrendering to the mystery.

As for her beef with David, and with Emily, and even with Charles and Rosemary, there was more to it all than the shape of the labyrinth. Than the shape of time. She sank back in the chair, letting go of the moment's inspiration, whatever it had been.

A movement behind Ewan's back drew her eye. Ah, a flashy red sports car was pulling into a parking space. Magnus unfurled himself from the interior and, without looking right or left, let alone at the magnificent scenery, held his cell phone to his ear and strode into the hotel. So his ends justified his means after all. Lauren wasn't surprised.

The evening light grew richer, thickening like honey, and the sea shone like bronze. Where it met the crystalline violet-blue of the sky rose the purple wave of Orkney, it, too, a mirage, a Fata Morgana. Like Lyonesse or Numenor, a drowned land seen only in memory. And yet a white ship, an ordinary ferry boat, was advancing steadily from those same islands. If she wanted, Lauren could pay the fare and in a few hours walk the concrete streets of Stromness or Kirkwall.

She'd been called here, manipulated and tricked. And yet she had wanted to come to the end of the world and glimpse the blue-tinted peaks of the next. To hear the cry of the white gulls and the whisper of the wind and the waves. To feel David Sutherland's mouth against hers.

Her cheeks burning as though she stood next to a bonfire, she said, "I'm sorry I missed Lammastide. It would have been good to just—be here then."

He was still suppressing a laugh. Not an unkind one, but a laugh nonetheless. "You've not missed it."

"What?"

"Nowadays we're marking off the divisions of the year with a calendar dating from Roman times, taking note of the solstices and the equinoxes only because they're labeled on a piece of paper. Ancient peoples, though, here in Caithness, in Orkney, in the Americas, everywhere, they measured out time by direct observation."

"Yeah, we're cut off from the night skies by the lights of our cities. We've lost touch with creation," she said, trying to hear his words beyond the soothing lilt of his voice.

"The Celts didna divide the year just into quarters, midsummer and so forth," Ewan went on. "They divided it into eighths. The day falling halfway between the spring equinox and the summer solstice, for example, is Beltane."

"The first of May."

"So it is, now. But the people aligning their earthworks, their stones, their tombs astronomically, they were not using our calendar. It's only later, much later, that folk went to looking at that piece of paper and said, ah well, Samhain, that's November."

Once again Ewan tidied up the papers spread across the table. "The equinoxes and solstices are tied yet to their actual astronomy, but not the quarter days. Lammas is a harvest festival. On August first in these parts, the harvest is getting on, no problem with the date. But the first of August's not at all equidistant from the summer solstice and the fall equinox."

Frowning, Lauren visualized a calendar. "It's about ten days off, isn't it?"

"In 1582, Pope Gregory adjusted the Roman, the Julian calendar, which had slowly gotten away from accurately marking the seasons. The calendar leapt forward ten days. Starting first of March 1700 the difference was eleven days. Britain didna change till 1752."

"That's right, I knew that, George Washington and that crowd, their birthdays have to be adjusted."

Something not cool but cold, like the tip of an iceberg, slipped into Lauren's lower belly. The warmth died out of her cheeks as though as two frigid hands clasped them. That wasn't the answer she was looking for. And yet, at the same time, it was. Tides in the affairs of men—and women. "We're not past the date actually marked out on the ground, in the ground, are we?"

"It's tomorrow night," replied Ewan, adding with a chuckle, "When Anderson's hoping to ambush a ghostie or two."

Living stone that calls us home, four times a year.

The voices, the music faded to a hum in Lauren's ears. Tomorrow night. Did Magnus know the significance of tomorrow night? Or did Rosemary, who'd stooped to blackmail to get the man in place, not just in the right month, but on the right day? Was that what she'd meant, telling the teenagers that their bonfire on the first day of the month was wrong?

And what about Grandpa's calendar, with August singled out by its photo of Blackness Tower? If Rosemary had meant to get Lauren in place, too, she'd gone about it very casually.

It was Charles who, thanks to Emily, had told Lauren she was here at last, and not a moment too soon. It was Charles who had last year's calendar on the wall of his shop. It was Charles who, like David, talked about dreams.

Ewan was talking. "I'm planning on setting up my instruments as well, though I reckon mine are a bit more reliable than Anderson's. The chapel's oriented to the north of west, and might be indicating a sight line on Lammas sunset—or Beltane sunset, come to that. I could be working it out on a computer, mind, but for the academic journals it's best to be standing on the spot as the sun goes down, assuming you've got clear skies. And we're having a full moon as well, at the northern end of its eighteen-year cycle, another moment ancient folk observed. There's a fine coincidence for you, that this year we've got both at once."

Coincidence. The setting of the sun and the rising of the moon. The moon, an ancient symbol of the female and her cycles of birth, blood, and death. Patterns in flesh and stone.

The swing and sway of "The Misty Mountains of Home" flowed from the ceilidh. Lauren glimpsed Rosemary's spare figure in the doorway, watching. Waiting.

Turning her back—her nape was protected by the fall of her hair—Lauren looked out the window. The ferry was just gliding into the harbor, gilded by the evening light.

She looked down at Catherine's face, her eyes guarding secrets, her lips parted to reveal them, no more than ink on paper, and second-generation ink on paper at that. Still, Lauren touched that face, her fingertips sensing the vital flesh beyond the surface of the paper. Susanna had become Catherine, and like her had danced on a circle like the face of the full moon. *Ladykirk*.

"Lauren?" Ewan asked.

She hadn't heard his last three sentences. She tried to smile, but her lips seemed numb, and her voice slurred. "I've been dreaming about Blackness Tower. I've dreamed about *El Castillo Negro* smashing into the rocks. I've dreamed I was Catherine, or Susanna, or both."

His smile was gentle and his eyes twinkled. He enclosed her hand between his warm, calloused hands, protecting it the way he'd protected the tarnished silver jaw of the second watch. "We've all dreamt about the place and the people. The stories are right powerful. But that's all they are, stories and dreams. They canna hurt you."

His voice wasn't slurred at all. Any good Scot could handle his alcohol. She remembered her father putting away glass after glass, with each one growing more combative, like Gideon's face in his photo. When she had too much, though, she got silly. And she said too much, providing comic relief to people like Ewan.

How did David react, drinking his whiskey in the company of ghosts? Quieter, darker, deeper?

More apt to betrayal?

Gently she pulled her hand away from Ewan's. God knew he had more good will than anyone else she'd encountered here. But he just didn't understand.

CHAPTER TWENTY-FIVE

No doubt concerned about the way Lauren's eyes were rolling independently of each other, Ewan grasped her elbow and walked her out of the hotel.

The world seemed very quiet after the buzz of voices and the competing strains of music, the ongoing drone from the sound system and the bursts of melody from the dance. The air seemed cool, fresh, and clear. The sidewalk felt like a tightrope, so that she had to balance carefully between sea and sky. "I'm sorry," she said. "I usually handle my booze a lot better than this."

"Nae worries." He supported her across the street.

"If Bryony's got the van, how will you get out to Black Ness tomorrow?"

"On the bus with the students. Bryony's coming back on the Saturday."

Emily's house rose up in front of Lauren's eyes, its facade glowing in the sunlight, its flanks sunk in shadow. She scrabbled through her bag—oh, the books, Ewan had put them away for her, that was nice—and after studying her iPod, handed him the door key.

Smiling, he opened the door and returned the key. Smiling, he escorted her into the living room and sat her down on the sofa. Smiling his pleasant indulgent, smile— she wished he'd go back to the tight-lipped hostility of the moment they first met, to make her rejection of him easier—he asked, "Are you all right on your own?"

"I'm fine, thanks."

"Here's the number of my mobile." He produced a slip of paper, wrote several digits on it, and tucked it into the outer pocket of her bag. "See you the morn, then."

Tomorrow and tomorrow and tomorrow, she thought, but all she said was, "Thanks."

His steps padded away. The front door closed. Emily's clock struck seven. The shop closed at seven, but Emily had said something about taking stock. How long did Lauren have, not only before the confrontation with Emily, but the one after that, with David?

After a moment of rumination, Lauren decided she had long enough to read Beckwith's poem.

Propping herself in the corner of the couch, she pulled out the book, admired the craftsmanship in its package, exchanged a stare with Catherine's sketch, and started to read. *The moon was low, the wind was shrill, upon that northern shore, where the barrows lay a-dreaming near the keep with its dark lore.*

No literary criticism, Lauren told herself, not now. Just the story, ma'am.

Catherine's demon lover crept up on her as she slept, intent on justice skewed by revenge . . . Flashback. On the shores of St. Bride's Hope, beneath an August moon, a shadowy figure shed his sealskin and, with the aid of a hooded maidservant, slipped into the tower.

Eyes met, hands touched, hearts beat as one, and love was made, if for the most part only verbally. But what verbiage! Just as Rupert's painting harked back to an earlier era, so did his language, evoking Shakespeare and the King James Bible, if lacking the skill of the one and the inspiration of the other.

Rupert described Catherine lying across the huge antique bed in what in his time was the artists' studio.

He described evil, twisted James Seeing that handsome, talented, gracious Patrick was the love of Catherine's life. He described Mariota Simison, the stolid maidservant, facilitating their meetings.

What lunacy led Mariota to stick her neck out like that? Oh. She had a guilty passion for James. She wanted to get rid of Catherine and her pagan ways, dancing among the stones, forsooth, so that James would make her his wife.

Was that no more than Rupert's hypothesis? Or did betrayal run in the Simison family? As for what ran through the Mackays and the Reays, how about stubbornness, sensuality, spookiness, and sticking out not only your neck, but your entire body?

Patrick was dragged away from the chapel and chained in the dungeon, where he scratched his name on the wall while dreaming of the green fields of his youth and Catherine plotted his escape, only to have James work his—unspecified—revenge on her. End of story.

Maybe Rupert didn't know whether Patrick escaped, or what James's revenge had been, although he didn't hesitate to provide other no doubt imaginary details even as he skipped over such unpleasantnesses as what the place smelled like.

Lauren's head lolled against the back of the couch. The story was oddly non-corporeal, she thought, disembodied, as though the characters walked through a painting. Her original dream, the one repeated night after night, year after year, had felt the same way. A story from the past, no more than distant memory. And then she'd come here . . .

Jerking back into wakefulness, she set the book on the couch beside her.

David was right, Rupert had read his Tennyson. In "Blood Red Falls the Rose" he described each scene in luscious visual detail—the white shape of Catherine's naked body reflected hazily in the mirror, James's hunting dogs streaming across the frosty moorland, Patrick running to the chapel through a November fog that distorted his surroundings into nightmare, colors running and shifting . . .

Colors that shifted and ran down the canvas, each different shading of the scarlet, red, crimson dress requiring a separate stroke. The silver-gilt pocket watch was no longer cold in her hand, but warm, smooth, hard, its chime thrilling with vitality. And it began to bleed.

The blood drops became rose petals, wafting down from her hands into the cauldron. His gaze caressed her face and throat and hands. His paint-daubed fingertips lifted first her hair and then the hem of the dress. Each shading of her moans and cries, hurriedly muffled, required a separate stroke of an instrument even finer than his brushes.

"Dannsam led fhailas," whispered his voice, his breath tickling her ear, and the shadows cast by the candle swayed to the ebb and thrust of his body, and of hers rising to meet it.

The dark wood canopy of the bed dissolved and became the blue sky, and in the depths of that sky she saw metal tubes with metal wings, like great silver cormorants, human faces peering from holes in its flanks. She Saw the future even as she saw her own body reflected in the dark wavering glass of the mirror, a mermaid in the depths of the sea, and suspended above her his blue eyes and the dark beard framing the deep curve of his lips.

Footsteps rang along the corridor and a sharp, precise voice called through the keyhole, "My lady, he comes."

He knew, he had Seen, just as she had Seen what would happen—the fog, and the racing footsteps of pursuit echoing eerily from the concealed cliffs, and her own skirts wrapped around her legs as she ran down from the tower, and in her ears the cries of her own child, the child of her demon lover, for her line must go on, out of the womb and into the tomb in the eternal dance of time.

"He is gone," she murmured.

The demon's long beard was soft and warm as down against her breasts. "Hush," he whispered hoarsely, "I'm here with you, at last."

And again the precise voice at the keyhole spoke, but this time it said, "I know what's going on. I don't need the Sight to know."

She Saw not her own white body in the depths of the glass but a tall, slender young man with dark hair and smoke-blue, stone-blue, sea-blue eyes. He wore trousers splotched with brown and green as though he'd been rolling in a bog, and the elbows and shoulders of his brownish-green pullover were patched with squares of fabric shining like satin. And he was watching *her* in the mirror while behind him the room was all dust and darkness . . .

"Lauren."

Remembering, she called him back from the shadow, and he came, his cloak wrapped around him, but the path twisted back upon itself, and led away from the center, and this time he went down to death and did not return. It was the music that remained, trickling along her senses like a fine wine down her throat, flooding and retreating like the sea . . .

"Lauren, wake up."

She Saw him in his white lace and she Saw him in his white collar and cuffs, and she Saw metal ships plying the Firth, great fires roaring in their bellies. But still ships were sucked down by the whirlpools, the spiral witch-traps, the circles of time.

If I'm guilty, I'll float and you'll burn me. If I'm innocent, I'll sink and drown. Where's your justice then? What you will, my lord, I see your own death ere the year turns.

Sagging eyelids beneath a hood passed her left to right. Thin red lips beneath a feathered hat passed her right to left. And behind her thronged the ghosts, the fairies, the spirits, calling her name. Catherine. Susanna.

"Lauren, you're dreaming, dear. Wake up."

With a muffled cry, Lauren opened her eyes. Rupert, Patrick—the dream-memories mellowed in her stomach like butter and chocolate. And what about Gideon? Was he merely a sperm donor, once Rupert had gone?

The face before her was a woman's, with apple cheeks crumpled in a frown, clear blue-gray eyes, wiry silver hair above a blocky body. She knew who it was. Not someone she'd Seen. Someone real, in this reality-challenged world.

Emily was sitting on the couch clutching Rupert's book in her gnarled hands. Watching.

Closing her eyes, Lauren willed her heart to stop hammering and her ragged breath to smooth. The dream ebbed, draining from the tidal pool of her mind and its strange, temperamental entities. She'd Seen through Susanna's eyes and through Catherine's. She'd Sensed through their skin. She'd been called to complete the task neither woman had accomplished.

She had to walk the damaged labyrinth, the maze that had been corrupted from a place of comfort to a place of fear. She had to restore it. Alone.

Emily was sitting beside her wearing a concerned face, the false one of her two faces.

Lauren struggled to sit upright, it being hard to get up on her high horse when she was positioned like an upended turtle.

"You've been dreaming," Emily said, each crease of her frown shaded by weariness.

"No kidding I've been dreaming. All along. But you know that, now."

"Donald, your grandfather, he sent me a sketch of you as Guinevere—oh my, that gave me such a turn. And Charles as well, when I compared the sketch to Susanna's photo. Were you dreaming, he asked, were you Seeing, but I didna know. And then I had the note from your mother, that Donald had passed on. Crossed over."

"You didn't waste any time telling Charles about me, did you?" Lauren heard her voice rising. She didn't care. "But you never bothered to tell Grandpa about his son, my father, with you here in Thurso in 1993."

Emily set the book on the coffee table and folded her hands in her lap, fingers tightening and loosening. "Charles was saying you'd stopped in. You've seen the photo, then."

"Hell yes, I've seen it."

"Donny spoke of his daughter. Like your grandfather, he thought the world of you."

If not enough to stay with her. Never mind some rationalization about her and her mother being better off without him. Lauren punched the pillow behind her as though adjusting it to suit her back.

"We had no address for you," Emily went on. "It wasn't 'til the man at Scotland's Folk sent on the letter from Donald Reay Senior that I knew who Donny Reay had been."

"Had been?" Lauren's voice caught. "You mean he's gone?"

"Aye." Emily dragged the word out, letting it drip onto her knotted hands. "Why go telling Donald such bad news, when he'd already come to terms with his loss?"

"But you sure could have told me."

"About Donny? Aye, I could have done that, but telling you of Donny meant telling you so much more."

"Ghost stories, ancient earthworks, healing the tower. Yeah, that's just a little bit more."

"How'd I know you'd understand?" Emily asked, her frown twisting even tighter. "You didna tell me about your dreams, did you now?"

"You'd laugh at me. You'd think I was a nut. You'd think there was something wrong with me, like Ewan thought about David."

"Aye," said Emily. "And what would you have been thinking of me if I'd spoken, eh?"

"Yeah, I get it. Mutual assured destruction."

"Destruction, oh aye." Emily seized Lauren's arm and leaned toward her, her gaze more intense than her grasp. "Donny stopped in the shop, we had us a blether, we discovered we were related through Susanna. He was dreaming of her, he said. I didna know much, not then, but I told him everything. And because of that, I lost him. We lost him."

Lauren eased her arm away. Emily was telling the truth, she sensed it, she *knew* it, and yet she wanted to stay angry. Anger was better than fear.

Emily closed her eyes, sighed, opened them. "I was hoping you didna dream. That there was no task waiting for you. And yet, if you've not been dreaming, then, well . . ."

"Nothing gets fixed?" Lauren stood up. "Be right back. Don't go away."

Stepping very carefully, as though over slip-sliding beach sand, she walked upstairs to the bathroom. Some tides waited on no one, man or woman.

She splashed water on her flushed face and was surprised steam didn't rise from it. She snapped her brush through her hair, more to buy time than because she cared how she looked. She knew how she looked. Catherine's face gazed back at her from the mirror. Susanna's face gazed back at her. "I'm me," Lauren told them. "I have some of your memories, but I'm not your reincarnation. I'll do what I can to make everything right, because that's why I came here to begin with, but I'm still me."

And she didn't like being used. But there was no point in raging at Emily. She might just as well rage at fate.

Lauren walked back downstairs reconstructing her conversations with her cousin. Emily wasn't lying now, and never had been. She'd tried to draw Lauren out. Give her an opening. Set the trap and see if she walked into it . . . But no. This ambush had been set in motion over four hundred years ago, when a Spanish galleon wrecked at Black Ness.

She'd better listen to what Emily had to say, if she wanted to survive. Unlike her father, who had not.

A shadow moved in the kitchen even though Emily was still sitting on the couch, no doubt the leaves of a tree outside the window, shifting against the last gleam of the setting sun.

Taking a deep breath, Lauren sat back down. "So the Simisons, they're, like, guardians?"

"Not so much as that. We're no more than local folk who've always seen to the tower and those who lived and died there, but who've never lost their wits over it, any of it." Emily's frown had eased, and while her hands were still folded in her lap, she was no longer wringing them in agitation.

"Except for Mariota? She was on James's side."

"That's what Rupert's saying in the poem. But the truth of the matter is, she pulled Patrick from the sea, she loved him, and yet Catherine took him for her own."

"Mariota was on her own side, then. Okay." The book's cover glowed in the gathering darkness. Lauren's hands splayed against her own twill-clad thighs, hanging on for dear life to the only person she could really trust. "Whose idea was it to send Grandpa a calendar with a picture of the tower? Charles, testing him and me as well?"

"Aye, it was Charles, using a photo of David's, though he's only telling me this now. It was me suggesting to Donald he send you here."

"And bring the watch, right?" Lauren asked sharply.

"Charles was wanting to see it, he said, with his interest in antiques. I didna know." Emily looked around the room as though reassuring herself everything was as usual, there.

Lauren tried another deep breath. There—that breath actually sank down to her abdomen. "Charles said he'd been waiting for me, that I was here at last, and just in time. In time for what? Lammastide? Is that why he put the picture of the tower in August? Or was that just—" She almost said *coincidence*. "—chance?"

"You've missed Lammas."

"No, I haven't. Ewan was telling me the calendar was changed in seventeen-something. The astronomical Lammas is tomorrow night. With a full moon at its northern point, even."

Emily's head tilted and her eyes glinted. "Is it now?"

"That's when the spooks come out at Black Ness. We're going to have a blowout, Ewan, Magnus . . ." David, Lauren thought, and her thought leaped like moisture off hot iron.

"I'm wondering," said Emily, "if that's what Charles was intending, then. Lammas, and a full moon, and you and all."

It was the all that stuck in Lauren's craw. "What's Charles's stake in this, anyway?"

"I'm thinking he's had dreams himself, he's Seen everything, past and future as well—not that he's confiding in me. I'm mostly guessing from what little he has told me."

"But why would he dream about the tower? He's not related. He's not living there, like . . ." Charles was David's guru. No wonder David was leaving infuriating messages on Emily's machine. "Then there's Rosemary 'Knowledge is Power' Gillock, who feels it's her civic duty to exorcize the place."

"She's a queer one, Rosemary. Not the sort who dreams, is she?"

So what sort did dream? Sloppy, doubtful people, probably.

"I'm sorry, Lauren." Emily knit her brows, and her voice thinned. "We didna know if we were doing right, by you or by the tower. There's been an illness and a curse on the place all these years. We didna want to lose you to it, having already lost Donny."

They'd lost Donny, Lauren thought, just about the time she began dreaming of Blackness Tower. The skin at her hairline puckered, as if from the stroke of a phantom fingertip. Choking down a sudden lump in her throat, she asked, "How did he die?"

"I'm not thinking he's dead."

"What? But you said . . ." No, she herself had said. Her fingernails dug into her legs. "So where is he?"

"Nowhere."

The pucker expanded into a shudder and gathered between Lauren's shoulder blades. *Death is merely translation to another world*, Charles had said. *Usually no more than the spirit crosses over, but at times, very rarely* . . . "Come on. You're not telling me he's trapped in a fairy mound. In the labyrinth. Not a ghost, not a spirit, still in his body and alive."

"That looks like being the only explanation. Like you, he was called here, if only after years of roaming the world, viewing stones and ruins 'til at last he found the ones in his dream."

Until he found the ones that echoed with his music. "That was before . . ." Lauren licked her dry lips and said the name. "David bought the tower."

"Aye, that it was. The place was not ready then. I was not ready, for all the stories my granny told. Then, I didna know Charles had hold of many more threads than I've ever suspected. Not 'til Donny lived here and played his music, and Charles began confiding in him. And Donny mingled his dreams with Charles's tales."

"And he . . ." She couldn't think of him as "Dad" or something similar, but he was still her flesh and blood. All too solid flesh and liquid blood. "He decided he could repair the broken boundaries. But he failed. Just as he always reached and fell short."

"He went away to Black Ness on the first of August. My cousin Tam, whose farmstead was there afore it burned, he saw him walking down from the tower toward the chapel."

Like in my dream.

"He never came back. The police, they got up a search party, they went through the tower and along the cliffs. Nothing. That's not to say he couldna have gone into the water. Or run, for that matter. That's what I was thinking, for years. But now Charles is saying that Donny was trapped. And the guilt of it on his head and on mine as well, for Donny would never have tried the labyrinth without our tales sending him there."

Emily gazed down into the empty cup of her hands, her shoulders slumped.

"He fell into shadow. Neither light nor dark. Neither dead nor alive." Lauren stroked her hair back from her face and thought of Ewan finding Susanna's hair, still there in her grave. But Susanna herself had gone on. Even if traces of her spirit lingered, she wasn't trapped in shadow.

That's what was lurking on the rim of her nightmares. Shadow. Catherine tried to save Patrick, and lost him to time rather than to death. Was that what had happened to Rupert, too, his hand slipping away from Susanna's and into—what was it, limbo? A parallel dimension? The Twilight Zone?

And yet, in her dream, he had gone down to death.

Lauren felt a trailing end of thought, of imagery, flick past her, but when she tried to seize it, it was gone.

John Reay had nightmares he refused to explain. So did Donny. Perhaps his were all the stronger because his father Donald had lost all memory of dreaming. She wondered whether Grandpa got into genealogy to begin with because Lauren herself did dream. And because of his grandmother's skull watch.

"Donny, Charles, David, they've all come, and they've all played their parts, and now you're here, asking the questions that want asking." Emily fanned the pages of "Blood Red Falls the Rose," so that it emitted a brief odor of mold, like a tomb opening and shutting. "Lauren, I canna explain the half of it. I canna *know*, not as you can. You were saying yourself, we're by way of making this up as we go along. Just now you've got the near-sighted leading the blind, and it's you who's the near-sighted."

"Right." Lauren fell back against the couch. Her brain hurt. Her senses hurt. She was at last getting answers, but the only reason they weren't utterly insane was because of those senses, the ones that had been both dreading and anticipating all along.

We, Emily had said, presumptuously. "So where's my watch, anyway?" Lauren demanded, her voice breaking. "Did you take it?"

"No," said a polished tenor voice, and she spasmed upright.

David stood in the doorway, his shoulders braced back as if on disciplinary parade. He held her red velvet box in his hands, not lifting it up, like Susanna in "Catherine's Dance," but extending it outward.

CHAPTER TWENTY-SIX

The silence was broken only by the tick of the clock on the mantelpiece, its small dinks not as resonant as the stones-falling-down-a-well tick of the watch. After a long minute, time enough for several hundred ghosts to vanish and rise again, the clock whirred and struck. Nine P.M. and all was not well.

David.

Distantly, Lauren sensed Emily groaning and standing up. A switch clicked, and a warm glow eased the twilight. Footsteps strode briskly away.

David.

A breath hung like a cocklebur in her throat. Forcing it down, she dragged her gaze away from his taut, pale face and turned toward the far corner of the room.

Footsteps came toward her. The couch heaved. His hand appeared in her peripheral vision holding the box, its velvet the scarlet of Susanna's dress. The dress that Rupert had pushed aside, so that he lay in a billow of red like a warrior weltering in blood.

On the bed David had shown her. In the room where they had kissed.

The warmth in her stomach vanished like a snuffed candle, leaving a trail of smoke so acrid it made her eyes water. She hadn't realized her fists were clenched until she forced them open to take the box and lift the lid.

The lamplight gleamed from the stylized silver face, familiar as her own. Familiar as Catherine's and Susanna's, if they had been adorned with fretwork and engraved mottos. The watch's empty eyes gazed into unfathomable space, its teeth parted on the subliminal murmur of, "Remember that you, too, will die."

And then what? Would her soul go on to that peace beyond comprehension? Would her poor shred of a spirit wander around trying to finish its task? Or would all of her, her shell and its poorly-contained psyche, be caught between life and death, in oblivion? Like her father, rushing in where angels feared to tread.

There was that skein of thought again, teasing the back of her mind and whisking away.

She closed the lid, reached for her bag, and tucked the box inside it, just as she'd done at Blackness Tower. Just as she'd done at the library, when Magnus had called the watch "old fella," as though it was a former acquaintance, while his new acquaintance Rosemary stood sentinel.

Exhaling the breath that had been stuck in her chest, Lauren turned her gaze upon David.

He looked evenly back, his troubled eyes the color of smoke drifting across the sea, his lips thin, his chin tucked.

"Listen, see, sense. Assembling a puzzle. Righting wrongs," she hissed. "And all the time you knew. What the hell were you doing, testing me? What kept you from laughing at me when I said I couldn't see you breaking and entering?" Her right hand flew up and batted at his chest. His long, strong, cool fingers closed, both firm and gentle, around her wrist, and shivers ran up her arm.

"I didn't know what was happening," he told her, "not until the last two days. Nor did I break and enter.

It was Charles who broke the window and nicked your watch, when Emily told him it was here, and that it was in danger. That you were in danger."

"Oh." Lauren sagged, then reminded herself she should be feeling not relief but anger. She jerked upright again and yanked her wrist away from his grasp. Crossing her arms and hunching her shoulders, she said, "Charles called here last night, didn't he? Emily told him we'd just been looking at the watch, right here on the couch. Was it good luck or bad that I left it downstairs?" Although, she added to herself, she now had larger things to frighten her than the thought of Charles in her bedroom.

"She didn't know he'd taken it, not until this afternoon, when we had it out with him."

"So you didn't do it. Fine. But you're still playing stupid games with me, just as you've been doing all along."

His voice rose. "No, I've been working my way through the puzzle with you. I've had a bit of a head start is all."

She stared into the far corner, where the shadows lay thick as wool.

"Yesterday, when I saw your face—when I recovered from seeing your face—I rang Charles, but he already knew about you from Emily. I had to know what was happening." He paused, and when she didn't reply, went on, "I apologize for hurting you. But you showed the watch to Magnus, and Rosemary saw."

"Yeah, I went to lunch with Magnus. I didn't know that counted as suspicious behavior. What, did you think I'd let him sweet talk my family heirloom away from me?"

"It wasn't until the next day you told me of your dream."

"I dream, therefore I can be trusted?"

"You dream, therefore you're in danger." It was David's turn to take a deep, almost ragged breath. His weight shifted. "You listened to the message I left on Emily's answerphone."

"Yes, I did."

"I was defending you, Lauren." From the corners of her eyes she saw his hand lifted toward her, palm up and empty, in the universal gesture of peace.

She turned away. "I guess it was all right for me to show Ewan the watch."

"He's a decent chap, if small-minded and a spot over-ambitious."

"And he's got a watch of his own, even though it's in two pieces. It's not like I have the foggiest idea what to do with mine." She glanced at her bag. The red box winked in the opening like a tongue between lips. Red lips, red fabric, and the shine of silver . . . The image evaporated.

David was insisting, "Rosemary, however, can't be trusted, and Magnus is a loose cannon."

"Who the hell gets to decide who's trustworthy and who isn't? Charles? The mastermind? Who is he? Why do y'all trust him?"

"All I know is that he's never lied to me or to Emily."

Lauren whipped around and darted a look like a spear thrust at David. "Y'all have never caught him in a lie, you mean."

David's grimace conceded the point. "No one else understood, until you came."

Her coming was a catalyst like the shipwreck, destined since that day. And Ewan's coming, and Magnus's. What had she been thinking about critical mass? She knotted her limbs even more tightly around her soft underbelly.

No one else understood. "I bet the watch was in Charles's shop while I was sitting there."

"In his desk drawer."

"All the things I sense when I don't want to, you'd think I'd have noticed that!" She willed herself to take two deep breaths. "I'll tell you what I did notice. Rosemary was upstairs in Charles's apartment, and he went up to talk to her. Maybe they're working together, did you think of that?"

"Yes, I've thought of it. But then, I've overheard them quarreling about the stones and the Ness."

"It was when Charles was upstairs fighting or plotting or whatever he was doing with Rosemary that I saw the photo of my father with Emily. You've seen it, haven't you?"

"I didn't know the man was your father until this afternoon, when I collected the watch."

"Charles couldn't bring it to me himself? At least you and Emily have the guts to look me in the eye."

"I expect his row with Rosemary left him exhausted. He's not well. Although he means well," David added hastily.

"Yeah, everybody means well, even Rosemary." She bent double, her stomach almost cramping. "When Emily wasn't here this afternoon, you called her at the shop, right? She told you Charles spilled a few beans to me, and you told her that yep, I was dreaming away, and so you all decided to generously let me have my watch back."

"Charles knows much more than he's telling any of us, and yes, before you ask, I'm not best pleased with that."

"No kidding," Lauren returned. "There's good reason he named the cat Persephone, isn't there? Queen of the Underworld, daughter of the Goddess of the Harvest?"

"Oh yes. He'd been going on about a labyrinth, but it was only today Ewan confirmed that it's really there. I realized the Lammas date on my own, but hadn't connected that up with the full moon." His voice was a wisp of sound, harp strings humming to the stroke of those phantom fingertips. "In any event, the labyrinth needs treading. To what consequence, I don't know."

"My father tried walking the labyrinth. He fell into shadow." Her voice quavered, too.

"He was on his own. He was a man. He Saw, but he didn't Know." David's hand now lay between them, not limp but poised on the dark fabric of the couch. His eyes focused beyond her, on the shadows, the far wall, the ceiling, the clock on the mantel, and finally returned to her face. "Lauren . . ."

Surrender, murmured the indefinable something in the back of her mind.

Again she looked away, massaging the ache behind her eyes, shutting out that seductive, compelling stone-blue, sea-blue gaze. So what if she smeared her make-up. By this time she probably looked like an electrified raccoon.

Damn the man, he scooted closer so that the soft cushions of the couch tilted her toward him. She sensed the fresh evening air caught in his sweater and a hint of sun-warmed barley on his breath. He'd had a drink before he drove into town. Before he'd called Emily and it all hit the fan. If he'd been stopped by P.C. Liddell or another of Thurso's finest, he'd not only have had alcohol in his bloodstream, for the last part of his journey he'd have had a stolen antique in his pocket.

Appeasing the secular authorities was far down his list of priorities right now.

He had come into the house while Lauren was sleeping. While she was dreaming the dreams that ran in her bloodstream like whiskey, and with similar effect. He had stood over her, reading her visions in her open mouth and tumbled hair.

Surrender . . .

"And there I was last night, while Charles was ripping me off, upstairs dreaming of Gideon in your body, or you in his, something . . ." She almost said "disturbing," but a crackle in the air between them, the scrape of a match, clarified the far from unpleasant physical nature of the dream.

"Since I've lived in the tower," David said, "I've dreamt I was Patrick or Rupert. It's hard to tell who is who. The woman's always you, though."

"No, it's always a woman who looks like me," she corrected him. "I dreamed I Saw you in the mirror, looking back at—her. The one time you actually saw a ghost."

"Yes," he said again, as though trying to coach her into repeating the word. He pulled her hand away from her face. "Lauren . . ."

She let her hand rest in his, telling herself that the gesture was no more than a handshake, of no consequence. Never mind her hand fitting his perfectly, each mound of flesh nestling into a corresponding valley. Never mind the anger draining from her body and leaving her shaky.

"That bit about 'this is no metaphor' on the sampler on your hearth," she said. "I found a piece of paper with something about 'we are spirits shaped into bodies' in the file on Second Sight at the library. And there's a carved stone in Charles's shop."

"Sweep away the illusion of time," said David. "Compress our threescore years into three minutes. Are we not spirits, that are shaped into a body, into an

Appearance, and that fade away into air and invisibility? This is no metaphor, it is a simple fact: we start out of Nothingness, take figure and are apparitions. Ghosts! there are a thousand million walking the earth . . . some half hundred have vanished from it, some half hundred have arisen in it, ere thy watch ticks once . . . we not only carry each a future ghost within him; but are, in very deed, ghosts."

There was another *we*, if second-hand. "Yeah," Lauren said. "That's it."

"It's cobbled together from Thomas Carlyle's *Sartor Resartus*, and goes on about tones of Love and Faith and the mad Dance of the Dead, and the morning air summoning us home. It was a favorite of Gideon's, Charles says, once he realized the significance of Blackness Tower, not so long before his death. He felt that Carlyle must have visited here, and been moved to write that passage."

Again she felt an indefinable tingle, the touch of a ghost, a fairy's breath. It wasn't so much her skin as her mind that broke out in gooseflesh.

Chasing ghosts and fairies, Magnus had pointed out, was chasing spirituality. Even Ewan recognized the spiritual significance of old stones, if at arm's length. Maybe Margaret had finally gotten through to Gideon. Maybe his conversion, so to speak, had nothing to do with Margaret. Who had tolerated her husband's mistress under the same roof for fifteen years.

The mistress who was bound there by her child, who had no place else to go.

"Susanna stitched the sampler?" Lauren asked.

"She was working at it when she died. Every so often I'll find another stitch or two completed, just as I'll hear her playing the piano."

"She was a Seer. Even more than Catherine, she didn't belong to this world. Catherine was powerful, but Susanna was inspiration. No wonder the artists loved her. No wonder Rupert loved her, and Gideon, well, whatever Gideon felt."

"Charles tells me he loved her as well," David said. "Though I suspect Gideon was also exercising what he saw as his right to her body."

Lauren remembered the beard soft against her breast, and shivered. "She died falling over the cliff, and her body washed up in St. Bride's Hope. Did Margaret push her? Did Gideon? Did she give in to some fey mood and jump? What happened to Catherine? Did James tie her up and throw her into the ocean, excusing his lust for revenge by saying he was testing her for witchcraft? She sank, I guess, like Susanna's body sank, and she drowned. So they were both proved innocent, much good that did them."

"Charles says that before Catherine died, she predicted the hour of James's death, and so it happened. Emily's granny says that before Susanna died, she rowed with Gideon and cursed him with shadow."

"With shadow," repeated Lauren. "Both curses violated the contract of the Seeing Gift. Just where and when did *I* sign on that dotted line? Why do *I* get to pick up the pieces?"

"The pattern of Catherine's life was recreated in Susanna, if a few turns further into the labyrinth, and the patterns of both their lives are in yours, if even further along the path."

"Fine, but I'm not going over any cliffs. And I'm not cursing anyone, either. I'm me, even if Charles used Emily to bring me here. Even if you didn't realize what you were luring me into."

"You came here, Lauren, because you chose to come. To answer the call. Even so, there's still time to say it's none of your business and go home."

"And dream about the tower the rest of my life? Dream about you?"

One corner of his mouth crimped at that.

Quickly she went on, "Just because you bought the place doesn't mean it's your business."

"I was called here, if in a different way. I've become a part of Blackness Tower. My dreams prove that. You said yourself, it's a matter of belief, of faith not just in ourselves, but in the events that have brought us . . ." She expected him to say *together*, but he said, ". . . all here, now. Things happen, Emily says. Things change, through no fault of our own."

And there was *us*, and *our*. "You missed that one," she told him, and couldn't quell a smile, uncertain though it was.

"Sorry?"

"'The fault is not in ourselves but in our stars.' Shakespeare, not Emily."

"Ah, yes, quite." His lips softened into a smile and he seized her other hand.

Dishes rattled in the kitchen. They'd no doubt been rattling all this time, but she just now heard them. Emily was making tea, leaving Lauren alone with David.

Alone, period.

She'd gone from thinking she had no adversaries to thinking everyone was her adversary. Now she'd come almost full circle, to find only one name left. "Rosemary and her knowledge. Yeah, knowledge is good."

He nodded as though he actually followed her thought.

"Ewan and I saw Rosemary at the hotel, dancing. Probably dancing as though she was following a chart, even though a Strip the Willow is a much safer dance than a reel along the rim of time."

"Yes." David's smile turned up at the corners, hopeful, while the creases cut in his cheeks consigned the hope to parenthesis. "Lauren . . ."

"So what happens next, it's up to me?"

"As Tolkien says in *The Lord of the Rings*, you can't choose the time you live in, only what to do with the time you're given."

Of course David would be able to quote that, too. "That's the chance everyone gets, whether to dance or fall on their face or both. Whether to turn tail and run, or enter the labyrinth. Alone." She tightened her grasp of David's hands. They were no longer cool but as warm as though he'd been holding them to the fire growing in her belly.

"Lauren." His voice dropped into a lower register. "If you mean to go to the dancing floor, if you mean to walk the labyrinth, let me come with you. Let me dance with your shadow."

CHAPTER TWENTY-SEVEN

Lauren stared. But of course he knew the meaning of the Gaelic legend on Catherine's sketch. He had dreamed he was Patrick and Rupert, murmuring endearments into waves of russet, brown, and gold hair.

She sensed the words on his lips just as she sensed his vital presence at her side. *Let me dance with your shadow.*

"You don't mean that as a double meaning," she told him.

"Not just now, no." A lift of his eyebrow set double meanings aside for later. "I'm offering to walk with you tomorrow night. When the veil between worlds parts."

This guy is nuts. But I am, too. That's who I am.

She said, "Yes. Please."

Released from its brackets, his smile blossomed. The light in his eyes drove back the dusk. And this time she slipped without a splash into the aquamarine depths of David's gaze, and gave herself up to the beguilement of his smile. David's smile, not Patrick's, not Rupert's. Her choice.

She was clutching his hands so fiercely she felt his bones shifting. She loosened her grip. With a soft laugh, he kissed her, and she leaned into the heat of his mouth—if he was branding her, so be it.

In the recesses of her mind and body and spirit she heard yet again "The Water is Wide": *There is a ship and she sails the sea, She's loaded deep as deep can*

*be, But not as deep as the love I'm in, I know not how
I . . .* But she was neither sinking nor swimming. She was
flying, and she was no longer flying solo.

The rattle of dishes grew louder, and Emily appeared
carrying a tea tray. Releasing Lauren's hands, David
leaped up and helped settle the tray on the coffee table.
The pile of cheese and tomato sandwiches next to the
teapot and cups explained Emily's long stay in the
kitchen, assuming she'd been spreading butter with a
toothpick and trimming crusts with a spoon.

She sat down on the chair next to the couch and cast a
searching glance from face to face. David was no longer
pale but flushed, and Lauren knew by the heat in her
cheeks she was, too. Smiling as though to say, *my work
here is done*, Emily started pouring and serving. "I've
left a message for P.C. Liddell, telling him it was all a
mistake, the watch has turned up. The broken window
needs explaining, but all's well for the moment."

Is it? Lauren refused food. The shepherd's pie and
Dark Island beer lay in the pit of her stomach like
ballast. "What am I—what are we—supposed to do, at
Black Ness, tomorrow night? How do we get into the
labyrinth? Is there a door at the back of a wardrobe, or a
rotating stone in the chapel? What steps do we take once
we're in there, and I don't mean just dance steps?"

"You've not read Margaret's book yet, then," said
Emily, and bit into a sandwich.

"When have I had time to read Margaret's book?"
Lauren softened her retort with a skewed smile not
unlike David's.

"She speaks of a blocked-up doorway in the tower,"
he said, "and of an old country dance called 'Binding
the Threads'. She says each is symbolic, but we can try
taking them literally."

"That's a change, taking something literally."

Emily chuckled. "The skull watch is literal. Charles is certain it's playing a part."

"He'd have to, to go through the whole charade of stealing it until he was sure I checked out. Although there are two watches. Three. The third one's in Spain. I guess they were made there."

"Patrick made religious artifacts for pilgrims to buy and offer up at the cathedral at Santiago de Compostela—the shrine of St. James, ironically enough. A money-making business, religious artifacts, then as now."

The warm sweet tea in Lauren's stomach roiled. *Patrick didn't die. He was trapped in a dysfunctional labyrinth.*

Emily finished off a sandwich. "The two skull watches came down in Susanna's family—the Mackays had no fear of the other world. But my grandfather, Harold Simison, he buried one of the watches in Susanna's grave, thinking it an evil influence on the family. And not without reason. Ewan's found that one. John kept the other one, and that's the one you've brought back to us, Lauren."

"One of my earliest memories is of my grandfather cleaning it, and my father watching." Lauren heard each male voice, rising, falling, circling. She saw both faces—all three if you counted that of the skull—illuminated by the light of Grandpa's desk lamp, stark against the darkened room.

And now both men were gone, one into death and one into shadow.

Even though she hadn't touched it, the watch chimed in her bag. And, in answer, an echo of her own voice coiled through her mind. She remembered what she'd said to David beneath the portrait of Susanna imitating

Catherine raising the skull: *It's easy enough to say, oh, so-and-so left the country or was lost at sea.*

She frowned, groping after the trailing end of that elusive thought, feeling it kiss the tip of her mind the way David's lips had kissed hers . . .

The doorbell dinged. Emily bounced to her feet. "Who's that? It's gone half past nine."

David swiveled to watch her walk across the room and into the hall. Lauren's frown of concentration curdled into a glower of frustration.

The front door opened. Emily exclaimed. A thin, strained male voice answered in slightly outdated, veddy proper English, "I do beg your pardon, but I found myself unable to rest until I spoke with young Lauren."

"Charles," David said, shooting a glance at Lauren that was more cautious than puzzled.

"Yeah." She wasn't sure whether she was relieved or angry that he'd turned up.

"I've sent the taxi away," Charles went on, "hoping young David will see me home. That is his vehicle in your drive, I presume."

"Oh aye." Emily appeared in the doorway at Charles's side. For a moment Lauren thought he had formally offered her his arm. Then she realized Emily was supporting his uncertain steps to the easy chair. He less sat down than collapsed into it, pulled a handkerchief from the pocket of his coat, and mopped his face. "I say, it's a warm night."

No, it wasn't, Lauren thought. Even the interior of the house was cool.

David glanced from Charles to her and back again, his eyebrows tightening, the color draining from his cheekbones.

"I'll fetch another cup," said Emily.

"Thank you, no, my stomach's not quite the ticket—I overindulged at my supper, perhaps." Charles's voice thinned to a thread. He replaced his handkerchief but his hand remained pressed against his breast. His face was the color of ashes and his eyes gleamed from the shadowed depths of his eye sockets like will-o'-the-wisps, frail and furtive. And yet, like will-o'-the-wisps, they drew Lauren's fascinated attention.

"I must apologize to you, Lauren, Miss Reay, my dear child, on so many different levels. I owe Emily here, and David as well, apologies for not being entirely open, but there are great things at stake here, as I discovered to my grief and guilt when I unwittingly sent Donny into the labyrinth."

It was Donny's choice to go, Lauren thought.

"Well, all things come to an end." With a sharp intake of breath, Charles massaged his shoulder and neck.

"We should be driving you to hospital," said Emily, with an alarmed look at David.

"Yes." David stood up.

"No," said Charles. "Sit down, lad, and listen to me."

Sitting down, David reclaimed Lauren's hand. She squeezed it, knotting her fingers with his, tugging on that tantalizing skein of thought and pulling it in, as though from deep water.

Charles watched her. "I hoped to see you succeed at your task, Lauren. A young lady of such impeccable breeding, with Mackay and Sinclair and Bremner blood. No wonder men have given their lives for your avatars. But you've Seen that, have you? I've never had one jot or tittle of Sight or even Dreams, but you have a full measure. I should never have feared for the skull watch, only for you. Only of you, in a way."

"Yeah. What if I blunder into the labyrinth and make things worse?"

"No," said David. Perhaps he really believed that—he took her other hand as well.

"Young Magnus is harmless," Charles went on, "and the archaeologist chap, and Rosemary, well, we must not judge Rosemary too harshly, for in the end, she, too, is powerless."

They did lack any real evidence against Rosemary, thought Lauren. She herself held the evidence. She herself was the witness.

"I believe that the watch," the old man said, "carries resonances of Catherine's power."

"It does. Susanna tried to use it, and failed. We'll see if I can figure out what do with it. And what it costs me." Lauren faced him, chin up. It seemed as though another voice than her own issued from her lips, and yet it was her voice, tinted with an outlander's accent and the blood of another family—practical people, her mother's Breton and Norman relatives, salt of the earth and the sea.

"People have been sucked into the labyrinth," she said. "And people have been spit out. Catherine tried to hide Patrick in the maze, but he got lost there. Susanna dreamed him out again. That's why the body buried above hers is dressed in sixteenth-century Spanish clothing. It's Patrick O'Neill's body, but he didn't die until three hundred years later."

The clock ticked. Night pressed against the windows. Not one set of eyes blinked.

"Rupert Beckwith knew about James, Catherine, and Patrick O'Neill because he *was* Patrick. Poetic license had nothing to do with it."

David's lashes fell over his eyes and rose again, curtains parting to reveal a limitless landscape. "Another turn of the labyrinth, eh?"

"Yes." Charles diminished, shrinking into the chair.

Emily waited beside him the way Mariota had waited beside James. The way Florence, a Simison by marriage, had waited beside Gideon.

"Catherine loved Patrick. Susanna loved Rupert. Both variations on a couple broken apart by a jealous husband or lover or even wife." The voice at the keyhole, Lauren thought. *I know what's going on, I don't need the Sight.* Was that Margaret spying not on Susanna and Gideon, but on Susanna and Rupert? "Although Rupert disappeared in 1891, his body wasn't buried until 1907, when Susanna died. And when Gideon die . . ."

The "d" of the past tense plunked down through her mind, not lightly as drop of water upon stone, but heavy as a body toppling off a cliff. The tangled thread of her thoughts, her memories, her dreams, jerked tight, and she Saw. Not just the gleam in Charles's eyes, but who he was.

The old man smiled at her. David pressed her hand, offering her his own strength. "Ewan," she said, and cleared her throat. "He told me this afternoon. There's no body in Gideon's grave. The coffin is filled with rocks."

"Ah," said David.

"Rupert wasn't the only person who knows an awful lot about the past. So do you, Charles."

"Oh," Emily said.

Charles's smile tautened into a grimace of pain. "I knew you'd know. You'd See."

"You remind me of my grandfather. I thought at first it was just because you're old, too, but . . ." She was Seeing, past the walls of the room, the boundaries of the mundane, into a shadowy distance filled with indistinct figures and flashes like reflections from silver—she was spinning, circling down into the whirlpool of time, the rush of water loud in her ears—she was dancing, treading the dark fantastic—she was still drunk, and yet she'd never been more sober.

Giddy, Lauren hung onto David's hand. Both hands. His forearms, rigid as steel, steady now that he'd found his center. Charles's eyes glowed before her, beacons on the cliffs luring her to salvation and to disaster both.

"You're Gideon Bremner. You're my grandfather's grandfather. You were Susanna's lover. No wonder you wanted me to have *Life and Times*. No wonder you've been watching me as though I was her come back again. And yet I'm your great-great-granddaughter." She shuddered, feeling those trembling, crepey hands stroking her as they'd once stroked Susanna. But then, over a century ago, they had trembled in lust at last fulfilled. "You know what happened in 1588 because Patrick as Rupert told you. When you realized he was the ghost of Blackness Tower, you realized how wrong you'd been, how small, how narrow. You realized how little your own ambitions mattered in the sweep of time. And now you want—what? Absolution? Or just to get it all off your chest?"

Charles was watching her as he'd once watched his own face in the mirror, bearded and vital. Now he held power over only his shop. He was aging naturally, now that he'd returned from a timeless Otherworld.

"I slipped through the doorway," he said, "thinking I could control the ancient maze the way I'd controlled everything else, my workers, my wife, the young woman in my care. Patrick O'Neill, who survived blood and storm only to die at my hands for no more reason than my jealousy."

"You told Susanna he'd walked out on her," Lauren stated.

"Yes. In reality his body lay in the cellars, moldering away whilst the household went south for the winter, whilst Susanna herself went to her Simison relations, until spring came again."

"And when Susanna died—also at your hand . . ."

"No," he protested. "I returned to Blackness Tower secretly, to talk to her beyond my wife's ever so keen hearing. To tell her I meant her son, our son, for my old school in England, for my footsteps. But Susanna cursed me—and not before time, I deserved cursing—and she leapt, not into shadow but into death. Her act freed John from his bonds to me, for I could never admit he was my own. But I am bound to her, still."

"You buried Patrick's, Rupert's, bones in her grave."

"Yes." Beads of sweat trickled down Charles's face and he mopped them away. "And then I stepped into the labyrinth to defy her, but her curse and Catherine's came upon me. I slept but even then I could not dream. And when I awoke, time had passed for me just as it had for Patrick and for her, seamlessly, soundlessly."

Like Rip van Winkle, Lauren thought. Who had cited that story, Magnus? The pieces of the puzzle had been there all along.

"And now," Charles said, his voice fading to a murmur that David and Lauren both strained forward to hear, "I'm old, as I should have been long ago."

Old? He was dying. His life was ebbing right before their eyes, and yet he smiled as he sank into the chair, his hand on his breast as though making a vow. Nothing like the grand gesture, the self-dramatization of a man of his time, larger than life but smaller than death.

Emily hurried toward the kitchen. Beyond the surge of waves in her head, currents of time washing the shores of Black Ness, Lauren heard her phoning for an ambulance.

Charles gasped for breath. "David, the stones called you, and you prepared the way for Lauren. Together you'll undo the damage we've all done, and heal the wounded path and seal its boundaries. And I—well, I have seen the tower renewed and hope return."

"Hope?" Lauren gulped and croaked, "If Patrick came back, if you came back, why can't Donny Reay come back? I can't restore a life lost. Can I give my father a second chance at living?"

"I returned the same year Donny arrived," whispered Charles. "He and I, we were both called home, one through time, one through space. The uncanny forces at Black Ness, the ancient presences, they are capricious as they are relentless, and yet they can be led not to justice but to mercy. Or so I hope and pray."

"Yeah, me too." Lauren's voice broke and her thought dissipated down what seemed like a cold wind swirling around her skull.

David released her hands, laid them gently in her lap, and knelt beside Charles's chair.

She dragged herself up and sank to her knees next to him, at her great-great-grandfather's side. They appeared, she thought, like a couple kneeling before a priest to receive a blessing. A blessing that he had woven from more than one curse.

She had found him and she had lost him in the same moment. She would never be able to ask him what it was like waking up in another era, when he had no foresight of it. She would never see Susanna and John through his eyes.

She took his clammy hand, a hand that had once commanded man and industry, now fragile as a bird's wing. She looked up at his bloodless lips in a gray face, lips that were still smiling.

"Charles," David's voice said. "Charles, stay with us."

"The paramedics, they're just coming," said Emily's voice.

Lauren couldn't move. Her sensations sank lower and lower, past the cold, hard lump in her abdomen, oozing down her legs and into her feet, so that her knees seemed to sink through the carpet, through the floor, through the foundations, into the earth itself the way Blackness Tower sank into the earth, the way a grave first opened and then closed in the dark moist earth of Scotland.

With a moan she hardly recognized as her own, Lauren released her great-great-grandfather's hand, slumped against David, and gave up her mind to a dusk teeming with misshapen creatures. Ghosts, fairies, selkies. A ship, a skull. And a familiar and yet strange face, thin red lips smiling in satisfaction.

CHAPTER TWENTY-EIGHT

T he firm but gentle hands raising her up and sitting her down on a soft surface were real, not visions. So were the approaching siren, suddenly cut off, and the voices and footsteps.

Then Lauren sensed no more than her own breath until, after what seemed like more years than Patrick had languished in the labyrinth, the voices and footsteps retreated. Blunt, efficient fingers pressed something smooth and hot into her hands. A cup of tea.

Long, limber fingers guided the cup to her lips. Sweet and fragrant, the tea filled her mouth and slipped soothingly down her throat.

Her throat, Susanna's throat, Catherine's throat. Throats that issued words. Throats kissed by James, by Gideon, by Patrick and Rupert singly and in combination.

David. He had yet to kiss her throat, nibble her ears, tongue the angle of her jaw, but she felt him doing so just by looking into his eyes, like looking into the mirror at Blackness Tower.

Behind the clean angles of his face, edged by a strand of dark hair, first Emily and then the room materialized. Lauren heard her own voice, spun thin. "The stone pattern and the Seeing Gift. That's only two of the three aspects of Black Ness gone wrong."

"There were the misbegotten love affairs as well," said David.

Susanna and Catherine had each been one turning point of an eternal triangle, an infernal tangle, that was never resolved. A triangle, a harsh, pointed figure set on the sweeping arcs of the labyrinth. But David was both laird and lover, not a corner but a curve.

"If we make it through," Lauren said, "if I don't foul everything up and make Scotland drop into the sea, if we don't pop out and find Star Fleet Academy built where Dounreay is now, if we can bring my father out of the darkness . . ." And what would I do with him, then? she asked herself. Would *he* be healed?

"Shhh." Emily hushed her. "You'll be needing a good night's rest, the both of you. Just now, I'm following Charles to hospital."

"No, I shall," David told her. "You stay with Lauren."

Lauren hadn't realized his arm had been tucked behind her back until it slid away. Yes, someone had to go with Charles. She might be his blood relative, but it was David who was his chance to redeem Rupert's death, beginning with the cat named Persephone.

David's lips whisked briefly across her cheek. His face, its sobriety mitigated by a secret smile, receded. His steps dwindled and the front door shut.

After a long moment of silence, Emily said, "Well. It's been some evening, and no mistake."

"Yeah." Once again Lauren hauled herself to her feet. The room shimmied, but it didn't whirl her into a dance.

She tucked Rupert's poem into her bag, next to the watch. Was Rosemary still dancing at the hotel? Was Ewan comparing his geophysical surveys to the maps from the Spanish chest? Was Magnus honing his ghost detectors and writing his script?

Magnus, harmless. Rosemary, powerless. And yet, Charles had said something . . . She frowned, losing yet another strand of inference, another image-string, and yet, with so many weaving and knotting in her mind, what was one more gone?

Charles had never quite been of this world. Was he now laid out on a bed, his fragile shell monitored, chained up by wires, tied down like a technological sacrifice? Or was David watching as a nurse covered the old man's face, obscuring it at last?

What birth date had David given the paper-pushers? Not 1842. Something in the 1920s, maybe, when Grandpa had been born to Gideon's son, John Reay, a free man still bound to Blackness Tower.

Had anyone called a clergyman to ease Charles into the next world? But he had made his confession, he had eased his own way.

"Good night," Lauren told Emily, and climbed the stairs.

Numb if no longer cold, she showered, brushed her teeth, and inspected her face, three faces, in the mirror. She opened the box holding the skull watch and set it on her dresser. "Go ahead. Tell me something."

It sat mutely, its empty, sunken eyes watching her.

Sleep? *Yeah, right.* Cracking a window for fresh air to relieve the acrid, antiseptic, sickroom taste that lingered in her mouth, Lauren propped herself up in bed and opened *Catherine Sinclair and the Matter of the Seeing Gift.*

"Ah times, ah manners," the book began. "Here, now, as the nineteenth century with its wonders of modernity strains toward the twentieth, we reflect upon the marvels wrought by our forebears . . ."

As David had said, the book was maddening. Margaret had used initials, implying, alluding, shrouding her own birth and antecedents in a cloud of obscurity. Except for the last name of the uncle who had given a very young Margaret in marriage to Gideon.

Simison.

Lauren sat up straighter. So despite his belief in blood and social class, Gideon had found not only Blackness Tower in Caithness but a bride as well. Margaret must have been a relation of the Harold who was Susanna's brother-in-law. Class could be as complicated as DNA.

There was the story of Catherine and Patrick again, told much more astringently than in Rupert's poem, if also more forgiving of the supernatural element than in the appendix of Gideon's book. That being something else she'd never get a chance to ask Charles about.

Margaret went on about teaching Rupert how to speak properly, as though he were a male Eliza Doolittle. Had she known he was Patrick O'Neill, speaking Irish Gaelic and Irish English from three hundred years earlier? Like *Life and Times*, was "Blood Red Falls the Rose" co-authored by Margaret?

Lauren skipped ahead. Aha! There was the bit about the country dance, "Binding the Threads." Like any code, now that she knew the key, it wasn't hard to decipher. Catherine, the seer, the witch, had left the pattern behind the way weavers marked out their tartan setts on a stick, here the red, there the black, and through it all a thread of silver.

Susanna had seen and heard. She had Known. But she had been neither strong enough nor bold enough to do more than summon Patrick back to life. And when she lost him for the second time, her spirit was crushed. Away with the fairies, Susanna.

Other than engendering John—and she might have felt little pleasure in that, only obligation—Susanna's role had been to channel Catherine's devices to Margaret, so that Margaret could drape them with ambiguity and convey them onwards through her book.

Just one more thing. Where was the door into the labyrinth, the one Charles said he had entered? By definition, there could be only one, an entrance and exit combined . . . Well, no. He'd said something about a wound. She herself had imagined a leak allowing other times, other dreams, into this world.

Lauren glanced up, thinking she heard the skull watch chime in unison with Emily's clock downstairs, which played its tinny melody and then struck once.

One A.M. Time had turned the corner into Lammas an hour ago.

And when I awoke, Charles had said, *time had passed for me just as it had for Patrick and for her, seamlessly, soundlessly.*

"Who was *her*?" Lauren asked aloud.

Downstairs, the doorbell sounded, and in its echoing resonance Lauren heard again a faint chime from the skull.

Emily's steps padded past her door. Leaping up, Lauren huddled on her robe and followed Emily down the darkened staircase into the even darker entrance hall. Then light glared, inside and out, and Emily peered through the window. Lauren didn't need her "It's David back again" to know who stood on the porch.

In her fleece robe, fluffy slippers, and pincurls, Emily looked like a gnome. When she opened the door, she hung back. Lauren, in her flannel robe and socks, her hair spilling down like sunlit cloud, didn't hesitate. She stepped out into the puddle of light where David stood, his expression set, his complexion wan, his tail of hair stirring uneasily in the wind. That chill wind, sea-scented and heather-tinged, washed over her, splashed through her mind, and dripped down her back.

"I looked over as I passed," he said, "And your lights were still switched on."

"Charles is gone," said Lauren.

"You're needing no Sight to see that, are you?" Emily said around the door.

David nodded. "His heart gave out. Gave up, with the weight lifted from it."

"And he didna fear death, not now."

"His face was turned to the light." David's voice shook. "He said a few words, there, at the end, but all I caught was 'mare.' A name? And he passed away, very gently, with a smile."

Mare, Lauren thought.

"Mare?" In the narrow aperture, Emily's eyes glinted with grief, and yet Lauren was reminded of another set of eyes, glinting with satisfaction outside the Quiet Room in the library.

Mare. Pins and needles swept from Lauren's shoulder blades down her arms and through her thumbs. The man at the hotel, the one going into Rosemary's dance, he had called Margaret Thatcher a witch. In the local dialect . . . "What was Gideon's wife's name?"

"Margaret," said Emily, pronouncing the name Mairgret. "You're reading her book. Why . . . ?"

David's hands grasped Lauren's upper arms, steadying her, waiting.

Lauren's palms tingled, remembering the supple tooled leather of the book, a skin tattooed with two-thirds of the name of Margaret Simison Bremner. Who had not only left the country, but who had also been lost at sea. Whose face Lauren had Seen and whose voice she had Heard.

"Charles said about being trapped in the labyrinth, 'Time had passed for me just as it had for Patrick and for her.' Catherine walked the labyrinth, but was never trapped there. Neither was Susanna, if she walked it at all."

Emily shook her head. "You're not meaning—not her, too. Not a third one. Not . . ."

"Mariota. Margaret. Rosemary." The names spilled from Lauren's lips. "Mare."

"Of course," said David, the words hissing through his teeth. "He said not to judge Rosemary, that she's powerless. Not harmless, powerless. Knowledgeable but powerless. And frustrated."

"Mariota followed Patrick into the labyrinth," Lauren said. "I've been thinking of her as middle-aged, like Juliet's nurse, but if she'd been in her teens in 1588 . . ."

"She might have returned and lived as Margaret for many a year, returned again and only now, as Rosemary, reached her fifties."

"Into the labyrinth not once but twice. That would give you some kind of complex, all right. We'll have to tell her about Charles."

"I'll phone her the morn," said Emily.

"I don't think we need to worry about her turning up tomorrow," Lauren said. "Worry about what happens when she does turn up, yes."

"Now now, none of that," Emily said. "You've been called. We've all been called, even Rosemary. Time's come full circle."

"Yes," Lauren said, because it was much too late to say *no*. And because David held her arms, and her hands pressed against his chest beneath his jacket so that she sensed the beat of his heart.

Emily smiled. "You're all right then, are you, lass? And you, David? Good night, then. Try and rest. The morn'll be here soon as may be." Leaving the lights on and the door partly open, she withdrew, and her steps faded up the stairs.

Lauren looked into David's fair, keen face, the ocean-deep eyes looking at her. "It's not like I'll actually be sleeping."

"Then dream something useful," he told her, and pulled her so snugly against his chest she felt his heartbeat reverberate in her entire body. His lips were cool, then warm, then hot, his mouth eager and yet shy—just the teaser now, the taste, a hint of grain and brine on his tongue, like a fine-tuned musical instrument plucking her senses.

With a grimace that was part wry smile and part anguish, he spun around, strode down the walk, climbed into his Range Rover, and was gone.

Lauren stood on the porch embracing herself, trying to hold in the warmth of his body, and watched the red taillights disappear. What would be worse, she wondered, to lose herself in the labyrinth, or to lose David, now that she'd found him? She could set the place to rights, and yet lose the person. She could fail in more than one way.

Had David felt this way when he stepped onto the Irish streets, just before he spun around at a sudden noise?

She shut the door, turned off the lights, and climbed the stairs. She lay down on her bed and stared at the silver skull grinning in its scarlet bed.

Beyond the silence of the house, of the town, of the night, Lauren heard the surge and retreat of the sea, like the blood in her own body. Blood red as taillights, as velvet, as Rupert's book, as Catherine's rose petals.

Rosemary had no paranormal powers, no. But still she knew more than anyone else. She had recognized Patrick's sketch of Catherine because she'd seen it done.

She lost Patrick to Catherine, and Rupert to Susanna, and now she used every man she encountered. Charles, Gideon—she had once been his wife, quarreling over destruction and restoration at Blackness Tower. Perhaps they had been quarreling over it this—yesterday—afternoon.

Margaret had wanted to save the stones. She had wanted to heal the running sore that was Black Ness. As Rosemary, now, had Margaret changed her mind? Did she want to exorcize Black Ness of those same elemental presences she'd once worked to preserve?

Lauren frowned, trying to remember if Magnus had actually told her those were Rosemary's motives or if she had simply assumed they were. And even if Magnus had told her, was he right?

The erstwhile Mrs. Bremner had told the kids their bonfire was wrong. They had the wrong date, yes, but they were also committing sacrilege, like using an altar for a pool table.

Once again it all circled back to Mare. Whether she'd heard them directly from Catherine or through Susanna or both, had she written the patterns, the setts, whatever they were, down accurately? She knew where the doorway was, an entrance guarded not by dragons but by ghosts. But when she appeared at Blackness Tower tomorrow, would she help, hinder, or merely watch, still on her own side?

Lauren's eyelids filled with sand. Lord Reay had spun ropes of sand, pink sand like that at St. Bride's Hope, a blush of color like the harling on Blackness Tower, belying its name.

She fumbled for the switch on the bedside lamp. The room plunged into darkness, and then the darkness thinned in the glow of light from the window.

In its box, the silver cranium gleamed like a crystal ball held up in Susanna's hands, raised in Catherine's hands, lifted in Lauren's hands toward the sinking sun, the rising sun. A beam of scarlet and silver glanced out, and crossed a second beam, and a third. Inside the sacred space stood three women with one shadow, and a man beside them, among them, who gazed gravely from eyes as blue and deep as the sea.

She moaned, twitched, and turned over, and slipped into a dreamless sleep.

CHAPTER TWENTY-NINE

In reality, not in dream, Lauren climbed toward Blackness Tower. The clear morning sunlight cast its shadow across the uneven lumps and broken lines of the headland like a knife aiming at the undefended flank of the chapel.

Persie imitated a gargoyle on the topmost parapet, unconcerned by the precipitous fall to the cobblestones below. Beside her, before the coffin-shaped void of the open turret doorway, stood a man. Pale face, dark hair flowing, white collar.

He lifted his hand and waved. Lauren waved back. Had she once seen the ghost of Patrick Rupert standing there? Or had she foreseen David watching for her arrival?

With a flash of teeth whiter than his collar, he turned to the doorway and vanished. But something lingered behind him, a shape and a shadow in the air . . . No, that was gone too. The cat lay there alone.

Imagining David's steps on the spiral staircase, echoing like the pulse of the house, Lauren stopped and looked back at the chapel. It was now alone on its hillside, within its boundary, a variation on the hope of life after death.

There the ghost of Rupert Patrick had saluted her with the silver skull watch and her own scarf. His remains would get a proper burial now, she and David would see to that, although how Ewan would ever explain his time-confounded grave, she had no idea.

Lauren felt as though she were eyeing ancient images caught in crystal, the way a lock of Susanna's hair was captured in the mourning brooch in the antechamber. Students filled in the excavations around the chapel, their voices and the clump of their shovels faint and far away. Beyond them, the sea lay smooth as a mill-pond. A brightly-painted lobster boat left a wake straight as an arrow. Gulls called, cormorants dipped, oystercatchers circled, sheep baaed.

And there was Ewan, his hat pulled well down, working his way around the headland. Armed with his canvas bag, a clipboard, a compass, and a handful of plastic flags on long wires, he crossed the shadow of the tower left to right, then right to left. Rabbits loped away before his steps like dolphins riding a bow wave.

The labyrinth was intrinsic to the earth itself, Lauren thought, the fences and mounds merely marking its presence. She had Seen the Norse settlers landing in St. Bride's Hope, drawn to a place already known. But if Ewan found comfort in believing the lines caused the sacred space, rather than vice versa, more power to him.

The door at the base of the tower opened. David raced toward her and they met in a fierce embrace, each spinning around the other. But they did not yet have world enough and time, nor a fine and private place, to indulge the flesh as it should properly be indulged.

Lauren pointed at the shadow of the tower. "There's a spiral cut into a boulder somewhere in the American Southwest. A crevice between the stones piled up in front of it is just wide enough that a dagger of light crosses the spiral on the solstice. And on the equinoxes there's a dagger on either side."

"Emily swapped Charles a dagger, a knife, for his own biography."

"I saw the knife in his shop. Cold steel. Iron. Was he going to try and break the spell holding himself, or Rosemary, or Donny, even, the way Robert Kirk asked his cousin to use a dagger to free him from fairyland?"

"Perhaps he was. Though he's free now, in any event." They stood side by side, hand in hand, shoulder to shoulder. Closing ranks. "You told Calder about Charles, did you?"

"I called him right after breakfast and offered him a ride. He was glad to hear the skull watch wasn't really gone, and sorry to hear Charles was. The rest of the way here he lectured me about his work at the graveyard. Caithness District Council's moving the best-preserved of the grave monuments to the town museum. But the Bremner angel's going to the main cemetery, not that anyone's going to know that it'll be marking Gideon's grave after all."

"'In that sleep of death what dreams may come?'" asked David.

"Charles said he never dreamed at all, like Grandpa."

"So he did. And now you're the last of their line. So far."

Death and rebirth? Into the tomb and out of the womb? Lauren wasn't going to touch that, even with David's bemused smile caressing her face.

"I called Magnus, too," she told him "but he didn't pick up. He beat me out here, didn't he? His car's parked next to yours."

"Yes, he and the other chap turned up before I'd eaten my breakfast. They're crawling about the tower with their gadgets. I told him of Charles."

"And he reacted the same as Ewan, right? Oh gee, what a shame?"

"Yes, if with somewhat more feeling, I should think. He doesn't know about the watch yet. I saved that for you."

"Thanks," Lauren told him. "Emily called Rosemary and told her Charles was gone. All Rosemary said was, 'Thank you for informing me' and hung up. I'm wondering now about Margaret's book, whether those are the genuine access codes to the labyrinth or not."

"Knowledge being dangerous as well as powerful," said David. "We shan't know until we try."

"If we can find a way in. Like Charles said, she mentions a doorway in the tower."

"That blocked door on the second floor was barricaded when I arrived, and has been for the past century, I expect. I didn't have it opened—the measurements showed no space inside for more than a medieval latrine shaft set into the thickness of the wall. And Margaret makes very little of it, not that I knew what I was searching for when I read her book."

"But you knew who."

"Yes," he said.

Funny, Lauren thought, how what had once given her the creeps in his manner now seemed comforting. She no longer had to explain, to defend, her own creepiness. Maybe they were soulmates after all.

She looked again at the shadow of the tower. It could be an arm and hand extended in longing, not a weapon. And the fragile, feathery strands of mist floating in it weren't actually there—they were seeping from another dimension. Ewan walked right through one and never broke stride.

David was gazing back at the tower. "I've got a hammer and chisel ready for a go at the door."

"That can't always have been an entrance, though, just since James's tower was built at the edge of the original pattern. And there's the sunset, and the skull watch, and . . ."

"And you."

"And me." Lauren closed her eyes and opened them. No, she wasn't dreaming, not now. She wondered suddenly if there were another way to lose David—by not fulfilling the expectations of his dreams. Or by refusing to share the expectations of hers. Pressing the strong yet graceful hand she held, she said, "Maybe we'll see the main entrance when Ewan suddenly disappears."

David laughed.

Ewan was working his way closer, planting his flags as carefully as an acupuncturist inserting needles into his patient's vital meridians. His gaze was averted from Lauren and David almost nestling in each other's pockets. That clasp of his hand last night was just friendship, then, she thought. Or it was now.

From the open door of the tower came a yelp in a Liverpudlian accent. "That wire's hot, Magnus, fer chrissakes!"

"Sorry," returned Magnus's voice. "I thought you'd switched off the current already."

"You've been dozy all morning. Pull your finger out and pay attention." Vince's grumbles trailed away.

Footsteps thudded over the cobbles and Magnus burst through the gate. Today he was in full Viking mode, head down, shoulders coiled, features set in a scowl of something between determination and exhilaration. He stared at Lauren, shifted his gaze to David, then bared his teeth in a congratulatory smile. "Good going, Sutherland. But you know American girls, always a pushover for a Brit accent."

"Come off it, Magnus," Lauren said.

"Correct me if I'm mistaken, but I believe you want my permission to set up your equipment in my house?" Releasing Lauren's hand, David draped his arm around her like a sixteenth-century gallant settling his cloak onto his lady.

She shot him a mock severe glance, and he retreated half a step but left his hand resting lightly on her shoulder. It was his tower, his dreams, his resolution—he wasn't going to be cut out, whether the ending was good or bad.

Magnus spread his hands. One of them held not an olive branch but a small camera. "Hey, whatever. I just came out here to check the angle of the sun and that shadow."

The shadow was growing shorter as the sun rose higher, as though the tower swallowed it. Magnus raised his camera, squinted, shot, considered the results, and repeated. "First thing this morning, the shadow was almost touching the chapel. I figure it will touch it tomorrow. And with the chapel door pointing northwest, you've got a sunrise-sunset right angle, with the hypotenuse the coastline."

Lauren waited for some conclusion, maybe about *El Castillo Negro* being drawn into the mysterious Caithness triangle, but then, Magnus didn't know what she and David knew.

"I wonder about Stonehenge," Magnus went on. "I mean, everybody stands inside the ring of stones to see the sun rise over the Heel Stone, but what if that's not what the builders intended? Maybe you've got the priests and the other big shots inside the holy of holies, yeah, but then, what if you organized the entire tribe *outside*, so when the sun rises you see the shadow of the stone penetrate the circle? Pretty darn sexual image there, you know. Fertility rites and stuff."

"Are you suggesting something of the sort here?" asked David, with a glance upward to the window of the mirror room and studio.

"Who knows? Maybe the tower was built in this position to replace the equivalent of a heel stone. All right!" Magnus nodded approvingly at his latest photo. Stowing the camera inside his leather jacket, he left his hand resting there, à la Napoleon. His grin wavered, turning sheepish. "Lauren, all bad feelings aside, okay? I've apologized to Ewan for not bringing back that folder and causing a problem with Bryony. If there's anything I need to apologize to you about . . ."

"What do you want?" she asked, not without a chuckle.

"I told you yesterday. I want you to pose in front of the painting. I had a red dress overnighted from a theatrical supply place in Edinburgh."

Her chuckle chilled into ice water, dripped off David's suddenly stiff fingertips, trickled down her back. A red dress. Like Susanna's. She felt the corset tightening around her waist, the fabric lying cool, smooth, heavy against her legs.

"It's a shame about the skull watch being stolen," Magnus went on, "but maybe we can borrow the top half of Ewan's—he's still got it, he says. Or . . ."

"I have the watch." Lauren reached into her bag and pulled out the box. She flipped up the lid. The sunlight glinted off the skull like a paparazzo's flash. "It was—it wasn't really stolen, just misplaced."

If she'd told Magnus it had been dropped off by a UFO, he wouldn't have heard. He stood transfixed, a silver flicker in his dark eyes, his empty hand falling from inside his jacket.

The sudden reflection attracted Ewan's attention. He marched up to the group outside the gate and said, "Ah, there it is, then. Bryony's got the jaw in Stirling. Fine work. If that O'Neill chap made the skulls, then he was quite the artist."

Oh yeah, Lauren thought, he was an artist, all right.

"What did you make of the graffiti in my cellar?" asked David.

Magnus cleared his throat. "You mean the guy's name carved in the stone?"

"It looks to be genuine. And Bremner speaks in his book of finding the words there when he arrived. I'm thinking Magnus here will be making extra photos and sharing them with me, for my paper on the wreck of *El Castillo Negro*, just as I was sharing my files with him." Ewan's gray eyes focused on Magnus. Lauren could almost hear the slap of duelist's gloves across the red goatee.

Magnus assumed his best "Aw shucks" expression. "Of course. I'm always glad to help out the academic side."

"Lends him a spot of respectability." David murmured into Lauren's ear.

She grinned.

"Vince and I are setting up in the cellar," explained Magnus, "the sitting room, and the bedroom upstairs, the one with that kickass bedstead and the other pictures. We've got everything from your basic candles, thread, and sticky tape—to detect movements, right?—to state of the art stuff, laser thermometers, an EMF meter, an ultrasonic unit, even a negative ion detector, all tied into a computer."

"And all this is in aid of what?" asked Ewan.

"Temperature changes, electric fluxes, static charges, noises only animals can hear—there's a reason they're more sensitive to the paranormal."

"Right." Removing his hat, Ewan wiped his forehead on his sleeve.

"Come on, you're a scientist."

"Exactly."

"Science says that what appears to be matter is energy, and what looks solid is actually waves. And you knock a few ghosts?" Gesturing toward the tower like a maitre d' indicating the best table in the house, Magnus started for the door. "Come on in, take a look, give us the benefit of your expertise. And when you're done staking out the labyrinth, I'll tape it. Tonight really is Lammas, huh? Is that cool or what? We'll pick up some vibes this time, I know we will."

Ewan tucked his hat beneath his arm, along with his drawings and remaining flags, and fell into step beside Magnus "Neither the pattern nor my survey's complete, not by a long chalk. I'm after applying to the University for an excavation grant—there's a lovely chambered tomb just in the center of the pattern. The site's more a Neolithic cathedral than a graveyard."

Magnus and Ewan disappeared into the tower, unlikely bedfellows. But then, their ambitions overlapped.

"Please help yourselves," David called after them.

"A cathedral," murmured Lauren. "Burial mounds line the curves of the labyrinth the way tombs line the aisles at Canterbury or Westminster Abbey. It's a place for rituals of more than death."

"I reckon that's what the ancient peoples were about, oh yes."

David's hand was still steady on her shoulder, still warm, but it didn't dispel the little shivers puckering her spine. "Have you given Ewan permission to excavate?"

"More or less. Details to be worked out, papers to be signed, etcetera."

"There goes your hermitage."

"And not past time. Ah, here's Emily."

A blocky figure appeared over the hill, crossed the bridge, and strode toward them. Emily carried a large basket and wore a glower of determination. "I've closed the shop for the day, told the clientele that things needed doing elsewhere."

"I've got your car," said Lauren.

"Sandy from the taxi service was owing me a favor—his wife special-ordered a set of dishes, then returned it. Here's food enough for lunch and dinner both if you lot dinna go at it like pigs."

"Thank you," said David.

By dinnertime, Lauren thought, she'd want bread and water. Or nectar and ambrosia. She imagined herself back in Dallas, at a sushi or coffee bar, admiring Nicole's new shoes or groaning at Rachel's dating misadventures. She wanted a cappuccino. She wanted a taco. She wanted her own apartment with its known quantities.

She wanted David, and the resolution to her dreams, and to set things right, whether or not that included saving her own father.

"I tried phoning Rosemary again," Emily was saying, "but she didna answer. She's not come to the library the day, nor cried off with an excuse. You've not seen her?"

"Not a glimpse," said David.

Her glower intensifying, Emily walked on toward the tower. "I'll set up in the dining room."

"Well then." David's arm wrapped Lauren's shoulders again. "Allowing for British Summer Time, the sun sets at 9:14 and the moon rises at 9:30."

"And by then we'd better be on stage." Lauren sensed a movement high overhead and peered upward, afraid she'd see Persie falling from the skies and yet, presumably, landing on her feet. But it was a raven peering beadily back at her, whether real or spectral didn't matter. "Magnus is right, you know. Animals do seem to be sensitive to paranormal stuff. We saw Persie looking at that blocked door—was it just yesterday?"

"She sits in the paneled bedroom looking at the paintings as well."

The paintings. Not the poem titled "Blood Red Falls the Rose," but the picture.

Lauren felt her hair entwined with a golden cord. She felt the heat of the flaming brazier beneath her hands, and the tiny kiss as each red rose petal fell from her fingers. She felt draperies swirling around her body, exposing hints of pale flesh. She felt grass cold between her naked toes, and power leaking upward through a circle carved in the turf, like a cut in living flesh welling with blood.

"Lauren?" David asked. "Don't start without me."

She blinked. The sun shone in a blue sky. *Not yet.* "Let's collect some rose petals," she told him, her voice thin as a silk thread and taut as a filament of steel.

CHAPTER THIRTY

The evening sunlight spotlighted Blackness Tower like an actor posing for his big soliloquy. Lauren, the understudy frog-marched into the lead, gazed out over the parapet. A slight breeze teased her hair just as David's presence beside her teased her senses.

Below, the blue sea shattered into lace against the honey-gray rocks. The shadows cast by the long, low rays of the sun threw the coil of the labyrinth into relief. The turf rose, fell, disappeared and rose again, the buried mounds beads of a prayer far older than the rosary. Each of Ewan's tiny flags threw its own shadow, pointing from the now deserted chapel toward St. Bride's Hope.

The deep blue horizon again suspended Orkney in mid-air, as it had on the afternoon, years ago, Lauren had arrived. Jet-lagged, spaced out, she'd been more sober then than any time since. Especially today.

She and David had filled two vases with roses, he thankfully resisting any mutters about gathering ye rosebuds while ye may, Old Time it was a-flying. Lauren placed one vase in the haunted bedroom. David put the other on the mantelpiece in the living room.

They had walked across the headland with Ewan, nodding at his litany of felled stones and slab-sided cairns echoing beneath their feet. They'd helped him set up his computer in the dining room, next to the sandwiches and salads and scones.

Magnus and Vince had quibbled over the placement of their electronic ghost traps and Magnus and Ewan had squabbled over why ghosts wore clothes. Ewan had crouched, his cell phone to his ear, speaking gently while Bryony's soft voice emanated from the tiny speaker.

They had returned again and again to what Lauren called the third floor and David the second, where the stone-filled doorway dead-ended not just any alcove, but one across from the room with the bedstead, the mirror, and the shrouded paintings. When David announced he'd be opening the door that night, Magnus grinned and said, "Way to go!" while Ewan allowed that a professional archaeologist might be useful on the occasion.

Persie had prowled the corridors. More than once she crouched before the door, the entrance, the gateway, her shoulders peaked and her tail coiling right, left, right, left. Only once did David try to touch her, and received a deep-throated growl in return.

Persie must be seeing shapes in her peripheral vision, too, Lauren had told him. And silently she wondered if any of them was Donny's trapped spirit, calling for help, or if he was too far gone to care.

Every time Lauren had touched the tile-like slates choking that doorway she felt an exquisite tingle, so that by the time the sinking sun glazed the northwestern sea, her skin was gathered and tucked as the fabric of the dress Magnus expected her not only to wear, but to be recorded wearing.

Now, atop the tower, she breathed in the warm damp air scented with land and sea and peat smoke, free of the acrid reek of Vince's cigarette. Ewan stood on her left and Magnus stood on David's right, leaving them in the middle like referees. Far below, Emily sang, "The water is wide, I can't cross o'er, neither have I wings to fly . . ."

Her voice barely stirred the bated breath of the evening. When Magnus glanced at his watch and murmured, "Eight-fifteen, an hour to go," he might just as well have shouted.

Was that a solitary figure standing among the abandoned monuments in the chapel burying-ground or just another phantom? Lauren squinted, and decided she was seeing the lonely angel on the Bremner monument, a testimony to time and misinformation. *Who can find a virtuous woman? A man's a man for a' that.*

A cry resounded through the tower. "Vince!" exclaimed Magnus, and led the charge into the turret doorway and down the stairs.

Spewing invective, Vince sprawled over a couple of stone steps just down the hall from the blocked door. "The floor rose up beneath me feet and over I went."

Emily came panting up from the kitchen. "What's happening?"

"He tripped." Magnus retrieved the video camera from the floor and checked it over, leaving Emily and Ewan to raise Vince to a sitting position. "Unless," Magnus went on hopefully, "you were pushed by invisible hands or saw an Elizabethan lady walking into the blocked door or something."

"No," said Vince. "I'm telling you, the floor . . . Yow!"

"He's hurt his arm," Emily said, and to Vince, "Is that painful? Is that?"

Vince's cursing reached new levels of inventiveness.

"Is it broken, then?" asked Ewan. "Bad luck."

Yes, Lauren thought with a glance from Emily to David, it was.

"I'll drive him to hospital." With Ewan and David providing leverage, Emily hauled Vince to his feet, which he managed to keep, if unsteadily. "Magnus, help me get him to the car park."

Lauren handed over the car keys, then tagged along as the three men and Emily maneuvered Vince down two flights of stairs to the antechamber. "I'll lend a hand," Ewan offered. "I'm away to the chapel for photos of the sunset." He retrieved his camera from his canvas bag while David distributed coats and jackets and opened the front door.

With a grimace bracketing contriteness and frustration, Magnus set the camera on the marble-topped table. "Looks like it's only you that's hurt, Vince. Good thing you've got a head like a football helmet."

"I was meaning to stay with you," Emily said to Lauren beneath her breath.

"I know I'll be all right," Lauren lied.

Emily wasn't fooled. "Have a care, dear," she said with a firm pat on Lauren's forearm, and to the others, "Come along, the man's needing attention."

David and Lauren watched as Emily herded Vince and his lopsided supporters across the courtyard. At the gate, Magnus spun around so abruptly he almost threw Vince and Ewan with him to the ground. "Lauren, get your dress on. I'll tape you in front of the portrait soon as I get back, then David can do his thing with the chisel. Opening a blocked door right at the witching hour, more or less. That'll make a great scene."

David shut the door before she could reply. "Cheek," he stated.

"Nerve? No kidding. But he's right, it's time to put on the dress." Lauren eyed the doorway leading into the living room. She'd avoided that room all day, putting off the moment when she would not just look up at Catherine and Susanna's portrait for the third time, she would do so claiming her role as their heiress.

"You're not obliged to do as he says," David reminded her.

"Doing what Magnus says is the least of it."

"Yes." David's voice was brittle as porcelain, his smile forced, his eyes shuttered.

He's frightened, Lauren thought, and he doesn't want me to know it.

Well, that makes two of us.

In silence, side by side, they climbed to the haunted bedroom, the heart of the house. The large flat box holding the dress lay on the bed, on the century-old bedspread, keeping company with Lauren's bag, Margaret's and Rupert's books, and the skull watch.

Lauren had modeled in period dress. A Victorian corset with its multiple strings and eyelets or a Tudor bodice with rows of finicky hooks held no mysteries for her. But her designated assistant, Emily, had just disappeared on an errand of mercy. David, now . . .

He threw all three shutters open so that the room flooded with light. The red roses glistened, still dewy. Each carved tendril on the bedposts cast a shadow on its neighbor. The blotched surface of the mirror shifted and shimmered like a pool half covered with floating plants.

Let's get this over with.

Lauren opened the box and stared. Scarlet silk embroidered with gold and silver resembled flames rising from the bed.

Trust Magnus to find a dress the exact color of the one in the portrait, if decorated with leaf shapes. And, she saw as she lifted it, the dress was cut like the blue one in the Morgan le Fay painting or the kimono she'd worn in her dream, the fabric stitched into a bodice and draped into skirts, but not tortured into tight folds. She wouldn't need a corset after all. Good. She might want to breathe.

"It's lovely," David said, and, stiffly, "I'll wait outside, shall I?" He creaked across the floor and stepped into the hall.

Lauren suddenly felt very alone, and yet, at the same time, felt that cobweb-across-the-skin sensation of being watched. She glanced toward the canvas rectangles beneath their dust covers. Guinevere, Titania, St. Bride, Helen, Morgan le Fay—Susanna as Catherine as Morgan le Fay—they had already strutted their moment in Vince's spotlight and now stood aloof, if not exactly silent, not if the murmur in her ears was long-ago voices rather than the nervous purl of her own blood.

She shed her shoes and socks, sweater, blouse and jeans, but retained her bra and underpants. In their thin, micro-fiber embrace, she might just as well have been naked. If the cold air and the cold floor hadn't drawn actual gooseflesh on top of her extrasensory pucker, then the chill of the long chemise and silk dress would have.

Shivering, she settled the dress around her torso and smoothed it across her thighs. A zipper would have been helpful, if anachronistic. Instead, a dozen buttons ran up the back. She called, "David, I need you to do me up."

She turned away from the door, only to find herself facing the mirror. The scrying glass.

Dimly, as in deep water, she saw the autumn foliage of her hair and her face and neck white as marble. She saw the dress decorated with coils of silver-gilt thread, looping and turning. She felt her ribs compress beneath a willow-stiffened bodice, a triangular stomacher, a whalebone corset.

Footsteps came toward her. A second image moved beside hers—a white shirt beneath a sweater, exposing a pale throat, and jeans outlining firm hips and long legs—a white open collar beneath dark lapels—a white ruff over a jerkin . . .

She spun around with a gasp.

"It's me," David said hoarsely. Grasping her shoulders, he turned her away from the mirror.

That left her facing the bed.

His cool, firm fingertips stroked her back from shoulders to waist. She shivered again, this time as fire rose into her cheeks and sank into her belly. She felt a tug as he fastened the lowest button, and the second.

He stopped. His hand slipped inside the dress. His other arm lifted her just as she spun toward him, so that in one quick, intricate dance step, they fell onto the bed. Scarlet billowed. The old wooden bed frame groaned. Lauren smelled dust, the fragrance of roses, David's scent of soap and wool, and the mulled wine odor that was both the spices of the orient and the coppery scent of blood.

Power and blood intermingled. The spiral path, the door to another dimension.

His hand caressing her flank was hot, her lips against his were hotter. In another moment he'd lift the hem of her dress—her knees parted in welcome—it had been a long time, too many springs and harvests, too many risings of the sun and settings of the moon and turnings of the tide. The voices murmured, interlaced ghosts, James Catherine Patrick Susanna Rupert Gideon . . .

No. I'm me. I know who I am. I perceive myself.

The sensations flowed away from her body like warm tears down a gravestone, evaporating into a stillness, a calm before a storm. "It's me," she said, and gently pushed David away.

World enough and time, and only two people in the bed, and the past an inspiration but no longer a burden.

"Ah. Yes. Quite." With a shudder he pushed himself up and to the edge of the bed.

From far down below, a door crashed open. "Hey, kids!" Magnus bellowed. "Let's get it on!

"Let me dance with your shadow," said Lauren to David's wry smile, and surprised herself with one of her own. She *knew* in that knowing that was Feeling, that was Seeing. And if the outcome wasn't as she intended, as they expected, so be it.

He gave her his hand, no less strong but now cool, and buttoned up her dress. Together they walked across the room to the window—fresh air, light, the sea lapping intimately at the land. And Ewan standing beside the chapel, his hat pushed back, his camera ready to record the sun slipping below the horizon, into Tir nan Og.

"Yo!" shouted Magnus. "Let's do it!"

"Hang on!" David shouted back.

Lauren took the skull watch from her bag. It nested in her hand, hard and cool as a seeing stone, chiming gently. The reverberation of that note flowed down her limbs and through her bare feet to the floor. And deep in the house, something answered.

David offered Lauren his arm. They walked away from the sunlight streaming into the bedroom and down to the living room. Which faced east, not west, and thronged with shadows that rendered the roses the deep crimson of blood. But Lauren Saw the rising of the moon, and the room filled with a silvery light in which danced the shadows of what and who had once been, the shades of roses long gone.

Persie crouched on the hearth eyeing the half-completed embroidery and the basket of thread. Magnus crouched over a laptop computer eyeing the cat. At a brief arpeggio from the piano he glanced around. "All right!" He looked back down at the screen and his face fell. "Crap. Nothing."

Nothing to record except what the senses felt, heard, tasted, except what the mind remembered and the heart held tight.

Gliding on her bare feet, Lauren walked beside David to the portrait and released his arm. She threw her head back so that her hair fell like brocade around her silken shoulders, and lifted the skull in both hands as an offering and a testament.

The face in the portrait looked toward the window, the ship, destiny. It was her face, her spirit double, an omen not of death but of the helix of memory. The aroma of roses and mildew wafted to her nostrils. The ceiling lights and the glare of Magnus's camera reflected off the skull.

"Good," he crooned, "nice, keep it up, baby."

"She appears," said David, "to be a grown woman."

The skull took on a red-tinted glow. In it Lauren Saw the child Susanna, her hair pulled back in braids. She sat reading beside a vast fireplace, the one in the now-burned farmstead, perhaps. Beside her sat a teenage Mariota, wearing a cap and ruff, her skin smooth, her eyes wide and avidly watching Susanna's lips as they moved, pronouncing the words trippingly on her tongue, no doubt.

And Lauren Saw the same fireplace, and a mature Susanna, her hair free, throwing rose petals into the flames with a dreamy smile upon her lips. Beside her knelt Patrick O'Neill, jerkin, cloak, and all, in the attitude of a student to his teacher, or a knight to his lady.

Mare. The sun was setting. She wasn't here. And yet Lauren could See her eyes in the gleam of that fireplace, where Susanna had led first Mariota and then Patrick across the boundary of three hundred years.

"That's a wrap," said Magnus. "Let's head on upstairs."

Lauren lowered the skull. Her hands trembled, not with fear but with effort. The chime rang like a tolling bell. Her hair fell into her face and she scooped it away.

From the basket Persie fished a skein of twisted gold thread. "Well done," said David. He unhooked the thread from her alabaster claw and twined it through Lauren's hair, tying it back from her forehead. Then he pulled a rose from the vase, checked it for thorns, and tucked it into her bodice. "There you are, the very image of the sorceress."

"I'm no sorceress," she told him, and gravely took his arm again. *I'm a vessel.*

Magnus, arms full of electronic arcana, followed them back up the staircase. The corridor lay dark beyond the mote-filled beam of sun shining from the bedroom. Two glints at the top of the stairs behind them were Persie's golden eyes, quickly extinguished when she faded into shadow.

David raised his chisel and chipped at the crumbling mortar between the slabs of slate barring the doorway. Magnus lifted and lowered a couple of remotes, checked the cold blue screen of his computer, looked at his watch. "Nine o'clock. If the bogles are going to come out, they need to do it now."

Lauren stood to one side, motionless as her portrait, the watch steady in her hand. Ewan would probably have conniptions, but he wasn't back yet and they couldn't wait. It was time. Time had come. Time . . .

And yet something wasn't right.

With a scrape and a patter of particles, David pulled out and set aside the first freed stone. A palpable darkness oozed from the cavity behind.

The light of the video camera shone out again, a harsh, flat light, not richly multi-dimensional like the light spilling across the corridor. Had James Mackay planned for Lammas sunset to shine directly into his bedroom windows? The light beam hit the wall to one side of the alcove, illuminating freshly-painted but featureless plaster. Maybe he'd intended that dead end, too.

David removed another stone, and another. The blackness behind the barricade gathered rather than retreated. Beyond, Lauren glimpsed raddled gray-brown stone, dust, and lichen.

"There's something symbolic in an old latrine," said Magnus. "Ashes to ashes, dust to dust. Shit to shit, I guess."

"It's not a latrine after all." David added another block to the pile. "It's a spiral staircase."

"It is? Sweet!" Camera poised, Magnus stepped closer, thrust his fist into the opening, then jerked it back. "Ow! There's still a stone there. Or ice, even."

"Not a bit of it." David pushed the chisel toward the blotch of darkness. It bounced back. "But there's a barricade, it seems."

"Like a force field? An invisible curtain?" Magnus waggled his fingers.

The beam of sunlight shimmered. Those were not dust motes floating in it. Those were fairies, childhood visions of the world within and ahead cloaked in gossamer and light. Those were fairies, the awe-inspiring inhabitants of Faerie and their death-dances past and future.

Lauren remembered the light reflecting off the brooch holding a skein of Susanna's hair. She remembered her dream—the silver cranium gleaming like a crystal ball held up in Susanna's hands, raised in Catherine's hands, lifted in her own hands toward the sinking sun, the rising sun. A beam of scarlet and silver glancing out, crossing a second beam, and then a third.

"We need to reflect the sunset into the hole," she said huskily. "Is the cranium from Ewan's watch in his bag downstairs? And we'll need something else, a third reflective surface—I've got a hand mirror in my bag . . ."

"No," said Magnus. The light motes danced in his eyes, spinning wildly.

David glanced back, past his thigh-high pile of loose stone. "No?"

"I'll get Ewan's skull." Magnus set his equipment against the far wall, close to where Vince had fallen, and galloped off down the staircase.

David removed more stones, each sliding with a squeak and settling with a clink.

There. Except for a low parapet of slate and mortar, the doorway was clear of stone, if clogged with darkness. From far below came a fetid breath. Lauren thought of Patrick Rupert's body moldering away like a piece of discarded meat, while Gideon and Margaret chased the sun to the south, while Susanna sat abandoned beside the fire with her sister, or perhaps with her parents in Strathnaver, winter gales crying in the chimney and her fatherless son crying in her arms.

Magnus bounded back up the stairs and extended Ewan's cardboard box to David. "You use this one."

David set down his tools, wiped his hands on his jeans, and opened the box. Inside, the mutilated watch glowed fitfully.

Muttering, "Here we go," Magnus reached into the inside pocket of his jacket and pulled out a cloth bag. Blue, teal, turquoise satin rippled with light, light that faded when he produced another skull watch.

Engraving, fretwork, humorless rictus grin—it was identical to the other two. It only appeared smaller because the hand that held it was so large.

"There were three," Lauren said, gazing at Magnus with wild surmise. "Patrick made three."

"That's the one from Spain," said David.

Magnus lifted it into the beam of light. It flashed red and silver. With a gulp, he said, "My parents bought it from a private owner the day before they were killed in the Madrid train bombing. When Rosemary told me about Ewan finding the skull here at Black Ness, about there being another skull in Susanna's family, I knew I had to come. I knew I had to come now, this month, because there's something weird about Lammas sunset, she said so. She said that four times a year, things happen."

Lauren's breath escaped in a long sigh of comprehension. Her eyes moved from Magnus's flushed face to David's taut features.

"The tax stuff, it's true. But it doesn't have anything to do with Rosemary." Magnus raised and lowered the skull, sending darts of light up and down the corridor and across his own rigid grin. "I don't know what she wants. Me, I want proof that life exists after death. That a bomb or a bullet or some nasty disease, that even just the cycle of time, that that's not the end."

Lauren laid her hand on the clenched muscle of his arm. "I don't think that's something you can prove. You can only feel. Tolkien wrote, 'We are not bound forever to the circles of this world, and beyond them is more than memory.'"

Magnus stared at her.

"All we can do here, tonight, is walk through the valley of the shadow of death . . ."

"And fear no evil," David concluded. Drawing himself to attention, he lifted Ewan's cranium into the beam of light that struck from the bedroom doorway, so thick and bright it bleared out any view of the bedroom within.

"Now," said Lauren. "It's sunset." She raised her family talisman into the ray of brilliance.

His grin becoming a grimace of determination, Magnus held his skull steady.

The reflections of all three glanced out, wavered, swayed, and melded into one in the center of the doorway.

CHAPTER THIRTY-ONE

The reflected light glared like the setting sun, past gold, past red, to pure white, so bright that Lauren could only watch through her eyelashes.

Brilliance flared inside the aperture, and the shadows fled. Then, between one breath and the next, the sunlight disappeared and the reflected light died away.

Dazzled, Lauren blinked. The gentle luminescence of dusk flowed through the corridor and into the open doorway. Twilight, nightfall. The gloaming, the Scots would say. The darkness before the dark before the dawn.

Magnus's shuddering exhalation broke the silence. Easing his skull back into its bag, he replaced it in his jacket with a pat on the leather as though he tucked a child into bed.

David gazed at Lauren over the skull cap still gleaming faintly in his hands. "We're between sunset and moonrise. Shall we go?"

"Yes." As one, they set their artifacts on the topmost stone of the pile. As one, they stepped toward the open door.

Magnus snatched up one of his remotes and pointed it into the shadow. The tiny red light of a laser sparked against the worn stone. "Hey, I'm getting a lower temperature reading in there."

"Cold air's being sucked up the shaft," David took Lauren's hand.

"I'll follow you down with the camera," Magnus said.

Lauren looked around at him. "No you won't. You'll stay here and tell Ewan and Emily where we've gone. Tomorrow he can go after his ground truth. Tonight, we're walking the labyrinth."

"Say what?" asked Magnus. "The labyrinth? For real?"

"And if we don't come back," David said, "use the photos of my good side in your program."

"Don't come—what?" Paling, Magnus stepped back from the verge. "The valley of the shadow of death, huh? How about I wait for Ewan and Emily here. I'm kind of fond of the circles of this world."

From far below or far away, Lauren heard voices rising and falling in a melody of languages. Calling her.

She knew where she was going. Not alone, and with her eyes open.

"What about a flashlight?" Magnus asked.

"We'll have light," she answered.

David stepped over the low wall into the aperture and bounced on the balls of his feet. "The landing's solid, but small. Here you are."

His hand braced her over the sill. Her bare feet pressed into the broken bits of mortar and she winced, but the cold welling up from below was more painful— and exhilarating. The thrum of the sea flowed through the stone and through her flesh and bones, to chime inside her living skull. She smiled.

Darkness gathered in the ceiling of the small cylindrical chamber. Perhaps she saw tiny eyes glinting there. Perhaps she saw the stars coming out. It didn't matter. Right now, her gaze was turned not toward heaven, but toward earth.

The wedge-shaped stone steps spiraled, steep and narrow, downward into the throat of shadow. Gathering her skirts in one hand and lacing the fingers of her other

hand with David's, she eased herself sideways down one
step at a time. The odor of decay thickened in her mouth
and nose and then dissipated.

The harsh glow of Magnus's camera light swept back
and forth, up and down. Then they rounded the curve of
the staircase, and the caustic gleam faded away. They
should be passing the second floor, Lauren told herself,
heading toward the first, where the steps would slip
invisibly down beside the living room fireplace, behind
"Catherine's Dance."

The age-stained stone of the walls grew transparent
and disappeared. Her next step carried her from gritty
slate to chill grass, its stalks caught between her toes.
A sea breeze teased her cheeks, played with her hair,
stroked her arms and legs between the folds of the
dress. St. Bridget's birds called, as they had called for
thousands of years before the gods had names.

Beside her, David stood tall and lean. So did the
monolith before them, the first of a row of stones not just
standing but leading on into the twilight.

Meeting the determined blue gleam of David's eyes,
she looked back and saw no stairs, no tower, only a low
doorway of one massive stone bridging two others that
opened into a small grassy mound.

The stone walls lining the cellars of Blackness Tower
were the stone walls of an ancient tomb. The site of the
tower had never been more than a leak in the vessel of
the labyrinth. Or a mouth giving tongue to the mysteries
of the site. *Timor mortis conturbat me.*

As one, Lauren and David stepped forward. The light
grew rather than faded, so that their shadows rose from
the darkness to parallel those of the stones.

"It's Black Ness," David murmured. "I recognize the
contours, the hill, the bay, the sea."

"Is it Black Ness as it once was, or is it neverland?" she replied, but he had no answer.

Their voices echoed eerily. Somewhere off to their left came a scraping sound, like metal on stone, but when they stopped, held their breaths, looked and listened, there was nothing.

To the northwest, the horizon ran the red of a bleeding wound, but overhead, stars emerged from an indigo sky. To the northeast, a lustrous glow flowed upward. The melody of voices diminished and rose again, now blending with the ebb and surge of the sea, now rising above it. Then the music of a flute spilled through the cold, still air, so high and clear Lauren felt each follicle on her body tighten and nod in response. And yet the music was that of her own senses quivering.

"Binding the Threads," she whispered, and took both of David's hands, his warm, vital hands that fit hers so well. Humming the melody she heard in her head, she led him weaving between the stones, going in where they had come out, as scarlet sunlight waned and silver-gilt moonlight waxed.

The row of stones doubled in and doubled back, and with it a line of cairns. David and Lauren followed the path, a living shuttle joining the weft of the earth to the woof of the sky. The inscrutable smile of the moon peered over the horizon, tinted red. Smiling, Lauren caught the gleam of David's answering grin—step, turn, sway. They were making love, meeting, parting, spinning together and separately along the stone scroll that curled inward to the center of the labyrinth.

In the clear, cool, but not indifferent moonlight, Lauren saw the long mound of a chambered tomb, covered with grass and studded with tiny flowers. Its end opened before them, two earthen ridges tapering down from either side like opened arms or spread legs, framing a cobblestoned courtyard. The heart of the dancing floor.

At its back two great stones leaned together like the horns of a crescent moon. Between them gaped a doorway, not into nothingness, but into a darkness shot with glitters.

Breathless, David panting beside her, she stepped over the massive stone threshold carved with coils and curves and miniature labyrinths like human thumb prints, and into a round antechamber. Its corbelled slate roof narrowed upward. Its side passages weren't impenetrably black—in them thronged wavering tendrils of pale smoke and dark shadow, slim as thought, humming like plucked strings. And yet there was nothing . . .

No. A human shape huddled just inside the door. A man. Releasing one of David's hands, Lauren knelt at his side.

The man's short-cut hair gleamed brown, russet, and gold in the moonlight. His eyes were closed, shadows above his pale cheeks. His lips opened on a slow, uneven breath.

Donny. Her father. She remembered his face as though she had seen its living lines only yesterday. She had forgotten his face, and it was a stranger's.

Biting her lip—Donny!—Lauren placed her hand on his arm. His living arm, the flesh warm beneath his windbreaker jacket.

He stirred. His forehead pleated in a frown. He groaned.

Lauren glimpsed his nightmare. It wasn't a horror movie's rotting corpses, as much a *memento mori* as the skull watches. It was that of tasks forgotten, of loved ones in peril, of love lost. Of helplessness and hopelessness in the face of forces within and without.

It was the distortion of living, not the certainty of death, that soured a dream.

Gently, Lauren shook her father awake.

His dark eyes opened and filled with shadow. Recognition moved in their depths. A whimper escaped his throat. His dry lips parted. "Susanna?"

"It's me, Lauren, your daughter."

"My daughter's a little girl in braids. A fatherless child—oh!" His eyes cleared and he raised himself on his elbows. "Lauren. Oh Lauren, I'm so sorry."

"So am I," she told him, and brushed his clammy forehead in a kiss.

With a searching look at Lauren, one she returned with a slight nod, David released her hand and grasped Donny's shoulders. "Come along, sir. We'll get you out of here."

Briefly Donny focused on David. Even more briefly, he smiled. Then his eyes rolled back and moaning he slumped to the earth.

Together Lauren and David pulled Donny to his feet, where David draped one of Donny's arms around his own shoulders. Together they turned away from the unformed dreams and faded memories thronging the depths of the tomb, the womb, and walked toward the guiding row of stones.

Outside, the circle of the moon had shrunk and was partially obscured by cloud. More clouds rose from the sea and gathered across the headland, each clot of vapor reflecting a pinkish glow.

"Fog. We'd best hurry." Limping with the weight of Donny's clumsy steps, David started toward the closest standing stone. Its shadow faded and died.

"The stones weren't arranged that way when we came in," Lauren said.

"They're pointing the other way now. All we have to do is retrace our steps."

"But we didn't come in the entrance. We came in the side."

"We'll find the entrance, then. At the chapel, I expect." David looked around. "Keep close to me, the fog . . ."

The fog closed in, prickling on her throat and feet. "David?" She blundered toward a tall shape and found herself embracing a stone, slick with ice. "David!"

"Lauren!" His voice reverberated from the stone and she spun around. Her feet were so cold she stumbled into another stone. Her exhilaration curdled into terror— hopeless, helpless . . .

The murmur of voices was no longer human. She heard the bark of seals ringing in caverns below her feet. She heard the deep-throated baying of dogs and the thud of hooves upon the turf.

The tower must be that way. And then, past the tower, all the way to the entrance, the exit—please God, please St. Bridget, let David and Donny be waiting there.

Something rushed by her in the fog and she squeaked. *Calm down, it's only a bird.*

She knew where she was. She knew where she was going. She placed one foot in front of the other and paced across the grass. If she could just lift the fog like a curtain, like the hem of her dress, she'd once again see the moonlit headland and the ancient stones like columns in a cathedral, marking the path. She'd once again see David.

She hadn't lost him, he was in front of her, with Donny.

What if, helping Donny, he wouldn't be able to get back out? He would never leave the man behind. He'd be trapped, like Patrick, like Mariota Margaret, like Gideon . . .

The noises around her expanded, contracted, blended into a confused clamor. A light seemed to hang around her, glowing very faintly on the billows of fog. Surely she was walking down from the tower—yes, there was the burble of the stream, and water so cold it seared her feet—she was walking uphill again toward the chapel, toward sanctuary.

She had dreamed this, she told herself. She knew where she was.

But the baying and the galloping hooves were drawing closer. James's hunters were chasing her. She had no sanctuary.

She ran, and her skirts wound around her legs, tripping her up so that she fell headlong onto concealed stones. Pulling herself up, she ran again, faster, her breath stuttering with terror . . .

The ground fell away beneath her feet. Her body tipped forward, her dress fluttered, and she hung suspended between one breath and the next, between earth and heaven. A rent in the fog revealed the sea below, the rim of each wave glinting in the moonlight, and below the water the shadows of drowned sailors swaying in a dance of death.

Catherine dropped into the water trussed by her power, and her spirit never broke free. Susanna turned her back on power and leapt for freedom, but her spirit stayed bound to the labyrinth.

Lauren was closer to birth than to death, she had found her father, she had found herself. She could wait!

But still she fell, and her lips parted in a wail . . . A hand grasped hers and jerked her back so forcefully she went sprawling onto the turf.

Before her face every blade of grass was lined with a silvery sparkle. She lifted her head to see the fog contracting, so that the surface of the sea mirrored a setting moon, but the land was still obscured.

The legs before her were not the jeans-clad limbs of either David or Donny. They were clothed in black corduroy and ended in black sensible shoes. Beside a black sweatshirt, a hand curved into a talon held a long carving knife. Cold light trickled from its blade. *Quite a nice one, Solingen steel.*

Gasping, Lauren looked up so quickly she almost dislocated her neck.

"Good morning, Miss Reay," said Rosemary's precise voice. Her eyes were narrow glints of bitterness behind her glasses, and her thin red lips squirmed with bile. "You'll be needing this." And she turned the handle of the knife toward Lauren.

"What?"

"Don't be as stupid this time as you've been twice before. What I've fought and struggled to learn, you've known all along. You've got the lineage, you've got the strength. Use them."

"I'm not Catherine. I'm not Susanna."

"No matter to me, lass. It's the third time round, and the last. Do it right this time, before the blight takes us all."

Lauren pulled herself to her feet and the knife from Rosemary's hand. Its handle was hard and cool to her touch.

The pristine northern air filled her chest. The fog rolled back, exposing the desecrated stones lying in the turf like broken teeth. A warmth beyond chill flowed from the earth through her body, drawing her back erect and her shoulders up.

I know who I am. And why.

"Yes," she said. Turning her back on Mare, she walked toward the great tomb outlined against the fading stars.

Some healings were done by a laying on of hands. This would be done by a laying on of feet.

Her skirts floating around her legs, she climbed to the roof of the grave and planted her feet on the living grass. The moonlight was so bright she cast a shadow. It glinted on the blade she clasped.

She plucked the rose from her bodice. The petals fell blood red onto the tomb, incense purifying a holy site.

Rosemary watched her from the cliff top. Somewhere David, too, might be watching, still burdened with Donny. Somewhere the inhabitants of the real world passed through an ordinary night, oblivious to the blasted heath lapping at their toes.

The moon slipped below the northwestern horizon, pulling its luminescence after it. In the darkness before dawn, a hush fell over land and sea.

Bending, she swept the knife in a circle around her, cutting a black oozing gash in the green turf. From it streamed upward a multitude of glistening tendrils, coiling and parting like smoke. Like withering roots. Like unraveling threads.

Voices whispered just beyond Lauren's hearing. The notes of flutes, harps, pipes wove into an intricate melody, swelled through her body, and died away into no more than a resonance deep in her ears. In her mind. In her soul.

The shadows, dark and light, feathered upward and disappeared into the dawn, the pitiful leftover remnants of malice, self-righteousness, greed, envy, that had formed a deadly whirlpool in the center of the maze.

She knew now that destroying the stones, the shape of the labyrinth, had done nothing to harm it, any more than burning a church would destroy the Scriptures. Malevolence had broken the bounds of the sacred space.

Betrayal had corrupted it. Disrespect for the ghosts that thronged its spiral had fouled its very memory.

Rosemary could never have exorcized it.

But I have healed it! Struck by a bolt of fierce joy, Lauren raised her arms to the sky and laughed.

The wind freshened, sighing in satiation. A rosy glow flowed up the northeastern sky, pulling the incandescence of the sun behind it, and the humps of Orkney materialized between shining sky and shining sea like the first earth formed after Creation.

Again the shadows cast by the long, low rays of light threw the labyrinth into relief. Now, though, it coiled around her and away from her. Each stone, each mound, each slate fence glistened, transparent, the ghosts of Black Ness.

Like pain, like sorrow, the joy ebbed. Lauren drooped, shaking. But there was surrender, and then there was surrender, and now was not the time to give up. David and Donny were lost. Rosemary watched.

Lauren stepped down the side of the mound, which was considerably flattened from a few moments before, and offered Rosemary the knife.

Slowly, as though wondering what the trick was, Rosemary took it. "I told Charles, yesterday afternoon, to leave well alone. I distracted him from giving you the knife and the answers as well. If you were meant to come here, you would do." She shook her head. "But you've not earned your way in, as I have. You've been given the way."

"Given?" Lauren retorted. "The gift of Sight, you mean? Yeah, it's led me on a heck of a chase. That's not exactly something to be jealous of."

"Perhaps not." Rosemary's lids sagged, then lifted again over a chill glitter. "Catherine, Susanna, they died cursed, and their shades haunt me."

Haunt *you*? Lauren wanted to demand. And yet she saw Catherine taking Patrick from Mariota, Susanna taking Rupert and then Gideon as well from Margaret, David finding the plans of Blackness Tower in the library, his back turned, unaware.

A cold, fresh north wind made her hair and her skirts into the rippling flags of an expedition departing home port. *David*. She looked across the headland where the shades of the old stones and the lines of the labyrinth faded in the sunlight. She saw no one. She Saw no one. *Please tell me they didn't go over the cliff!*

She swung back to Rosemary. "So how did you get in here?"

"The first time I blundered in, a child chasing a hopeless love. The second time I entered deliberately, weary of struggle."

"And the third time?"

"Intent, belief, knowledge," Rosemary said. "I clasped the coattails of the sorceress, and when the boundaries trembled for you, I stepped through as well. Entering, it's much easier than leaving."

"I'm not . . ." Whatever she was, right now she had powers Rosemary did not. But they weren't enough. Lauren scanned the headland, trying to sense David's presence, trying to See. Nothing. "We get out by following the thread of the shadow, out through the chapel, right? The holy gateway."

"You don't know all the answers?" Rosemary's thin, white face was purged of all resentment, but her tongue was still tart.

"Don't be stupid. I am not Catherine. I am not Susanna. Whatever spirit moved them stirred me as well, but we only passed on the labyrinth walk. You know a lot more than I do, Mare. Hell, it never occurred to me to bring a knife, did it, even though we were talking about it!"

Across Rosemary's features flitted the ghost of her satisfied smile. "Was it Charles told you who I am, then? Or were you given that, too?"

"I was told, yes, but not by Charles. Catherine and Susanna in their destruction sowed the seeds of a new beginning, and you were part of that. You've always been a part."

Rosemary stooped as though finding her body too heavy to sustain, turning the knife over and over in her hands. Lauren was reminded of David contemplating the blood on his hands when confessing to killing Bridget O'Neill. *David* . . .

"Did you kill Rupert?" she asked.

"Yes. Charles told you he did it, didn't he? Controlling to the end, he was."

"If you couldn't have Patrick, if you couldn't have Rupert, then no one would, is that it?"

"Don't judge me, not when you have David."

Please let me have David, Lauren thought, even as words stirred in her throat and drew her erect, so that she looked down on the woman bent in pain before her. "I'm not judging you. This place is. Charles hoped that the powers, the forces, would be led to mercy rather than justice. I think they have. They have repeatedly given you the chance to find the redemption Catherine and Susanna never found. Until now. Until I released them."

"I came here tonight thinking this to be my prison."

"Don't be stupid, Mare. You've got a home in Thurso. You've got work in the library. Charles may be gone, but you've got friends. You were dancing with them last night."

Rosemary stared at the knife in her hands.

"Go on and live the rest of your life. Help people gain knowledge. And maybe you can help them gain wisdom, too. God knows," Lauren added in her own slightly quavering voice, "I could use some myself."

"Indeed." Rosemary looked up, her pale lips constricted with a smile that might, in time, achieve satisfaction. "Come along, then."

And from across the headland, David's voice called, "Lauren?"

CHAPTER THIRTY-TWO

Threading the maze, treading multiple dimensions, Lauren and Rosemary traced each turning of the pale, attenuated stones and their accompanying cairns. They walked past the doorway of the tomb that was the foundation of Blackness Tower, now blocked by a fall of stones and closed forever. They waded the peat-stained, amber-colored stream and climbed the low swell of land where the chapel had once risen and where it would, in time, arise. They came to the low pillars of rock that marked both the beginning and the end of the labyrinth.

A pale, wild-eyed David sat on the lee side of the northern pillar, his body bent protectively over Donny, asleep on the turf.

At their steps he leaped up, saw Rosemary, and recoiled. She lifted her hands, one holding the knife, the other empty, and after a long, keen stare—he was not and never had been Patrick or Rupert—she said simply, "Mr. Sutherland."

Elbowing Rosemary aside, Lauren touched his face and chest and embraced him.

"I thought I'd killed you," he said hoarsely. "I let you go, and you disappeared, and I thought you'd fallen. Then I heard your voice chanting words I didn't recognize, and I knew . . ." He buried his face in her hair and hung on, a shudder wracking him from toe to crown, from stern to stem. "All I could do was follow the stones until they ended, here, and wait for you to come."

She started to tell him she hadn't chanted, but it didn't matter. "Everything's all right now," she told him, and released him, but not without taking his hand.

Rosemary's spare figure stood against the sunrise, casting a long shadow. She wasn't smiling. "The gate will open for you. Shall I lead the way?"

"Be my guest." Lauren leaned down to take Donny's cold limp hand as well.

His hand was too cold, too limp. A dead weight. His eyes weren't shut in sleep at all. Her calmness whirled to panic. "Dad, Daddy . . ." She still didn't know what to call him. "Donny!"

David bent over him, touching his throat and chest. "Lauren, a moment ago he was muttering beneath his breath, something about spirit and gifts."

"Can't you do CPR or something?"

"No." Rosemary spoke as precisely as she ever did. "He's given up the ghost. Let him go."

Lauren sat down, hard, on the grass beside her father's body. His face was calm, its lines more peaceful than she'd ever seen them in life. Her jaw ached, her eyes filled, and then eased, but she had already cried for him, years ago.

She couldn't have him back, either as he'd been or as she'd imagined him. He'd waked long enough to recognize her, to speak to her. That had to be enough—as Charles had said about the tower renewed before he, too, found his freedom.

"I'm sorry," said David. "I should have . . ."

"No guilt," Lauren told him, her voice trembling. "No regrets. We saved him, we just couldn't bring him back to our world."

Again Lauren kissed her father's cold forehead, and then she let David raise her to her feet.

She leaned against his side, forming her body to the shape of his. His face was drawn to its minimum, the flesh taut over the shapely bones, and yet his lips eased into a sad smile. "He's buried properly, just here, where he learned his music."

Rosemary's narrow eyes behind their narrow glasses considered Donny's body, and Lauren pressed against David. Her nostrils flared and her lip curled. But all she said was, "Come along then."

She stepped into a grassy bowl that lay between the pillars of rock. She stepped through it, so that her feet and legs slipped through the turf, and her shoulders, and her head. With a jerk, Lauren fell toward her, circling down the side of an earthen whirlpool, her limbs tangled with David's, his breath caught in her hair, her body elongating beside his. *Don't let go . . .*

Her consciousness slipped away behind her and fell toward her. Through shadow and sunlight and moonlight, through the earth and out the other side, she spun into the blue of the sea and the sky. Into the blue of David's eyes.

She was standing inside the chapel, clasping David's hand as he stood beside her, like a bride and groom after the marriage ceremony.

Rosemary, the matron of honor, stood on the spiral-carved threshold. At her feet, the knife shone clean and silver in the morning light.

It really was morning. And yet they'd walked down the staircase only minutes earlier.

Lauren and David stepped past Rosemary into the trench-filled, grass-trampled interior of the graveyard. Two rabbits peered at them from beside the wall, then leaped away, white tails twitching. Persie sat at the base of the Bremner angel, unconcernedly washing her face. An orange lifeboat plowed through the waves toward the blue-tinted peaks of Orkney. White gulls called.

The walls of Blackness Tower blushed in the tender light of dawn. Its shadow, tinged with silver, reached across the coiling shape on the headland to caress the flank of the chapel, binding not threads but stones.

A cold, clean, north wind, one that had never before touched human nostrils, caught Lauren's scarlet dress. It billowed like a sail, exposing her limbs to the chill. She shivered, her knees beginning to knock and her teeth chatter, and her strength drained away.

"Right." His chin setting, his lips thinning, David peeled off his sweater and pulled it, warm from his body, down over Lauren's. He seated her in the shelter of the doorway and pressed his lips against the top of her head. "Be back in a tick, love. Mrs. Gillock. And here, Persie, earn your keep." He picked up the cat and set her on Lauren's feet. Then he ran, down from the chapel and toward Blackness Tower.

The cat obligingly assumed the shape of a tea cozy. Lauren wiggled her toes in the blessed soft warmth of Persephone's fur. She had the feline stamp of approval, then. Good.

Lacing her arms across her chest, Lauren let her head fell back against the stone wall. Her stomach squirmed. Breakfast. And a nap in a warm bed beside David, beside his long, lean, vital body, so that he'd be there when she awoke.

Rosemary folded down beside Lauren, the knife between them like a lethal bundling board.

It wasn't cold steel that had lanced the festering wound. That was only the final touch. It was her asking questions, tying the threads, loosing the knots. *Intent, belief, knowledge. The stones remember.*

Mare remembered. "Why Gillock?" Lauren asked.

"Why not?"

Why anything? "You found Patrick on the beach, the sole survivor of *El Castillo Negro*. You nursed him back to health. But he fell in love with Catherine."

"I was a servant. She was a lady. She had borne her husband a son, she had done her duty by him. What is love, in a marriage? Nothing."

"I don't believe that. My parents loved each other. They would never have been hurt so badly if they hadn't." She closed her eyes and saw Donny's quiet face. He was really gone now. Now she could forget her anger with him, and feel only grief.

Her mother wouldn't believe the truth if Lauren told her. No one would believe the truth about Charles or Rosemary or . . . "Catherine put Patrick into the labyrinth to save him from James."

"On the eve of his execution," Rosemary said, her words slurred but her face turned toward the light, "she ripped open the side of the labyrinth and he was drawn in. She would have done better to let Patrick die, for saving him cost her own life."

"Even though she sank, so was proved innocent," said Lauren.

Rosemary's laugh was hollow, echoing in the hollow hill beneath the stones of the chapel. "I had seen Catherine with her flowers and her knife at the foot of the tower stair, making of it not a priest's hole, but a priestess's. I was accused with her. Fleeing, I, too, was sucked down to perdition."

Perdition? But yes, it would have been. "Catherine used Patrick's two skull watches to open the cleft, didn't she? That's why I had to bring mine back, to close it again. Or were all three watches here in—it was January of 1589, wasn't it, when James wrote that letter?"

"Yes. James kept two of the watches, and returned the third to the Spanish ambassador in Edinburgh along with the contents of the pay chest. He was richly rewarded."

"Good work, Rosemary, getting all three watches, and me, and everyone else, here at the right time."

Rosemary shook her head. "It was Charles's work, and mine, and it was fate. Destiny. Powers, call them what you will."

It was her choice, Lauren thought, what do with that will. With what she had been bequeathed. And she thought of Donny lying beneath turf, beneath stone, in the other world he had always inhabited. Free.

"Before Catherine," she asked, "did people use those quartz crystals that Ewan found in the Spanish chest? Or did they need a key?"

"No. The labyrinth was always open, welcoming all and releasing them again. Until James and Catherine unbalanced it, corrupted it, made of it a sinkhole." Rosemary's entire face sagged, not just her eyelids, covering eyes that saw so much without ever Seeing.

No, Lauren thought, the distribution of gifts wasn't fair. To either of them.

Through the door of the chapel she saw the sunlight spreading across the northwestern horizon, at the back of the north wind, into the west where the world ended. "So what's it like to live in the sixteenth century? In the nineteenth?"

"The past is another world," Rosemary replied.

"Yeah, it would be. You did well adjusting to each new world."

"When I first emerged, Susanna was visiting her sister, who had married one of my folk, a Simison of Black Ness. She was a child, but she recognized me. She took me in hand and brought me along well enough that I was able to make an advantageous marriage, intending to set things to rights. But Gideon was having none of it. I was forced to work around him by way of the Psychical Society, and with my writing and his. And then, having seen the labyrinth disgorge one incarnate soul, Susanna raised one of the skull watches and dreamt Patrick from it as well."

Rosemary had tried to do it all over and get it right, but again it had all gone wrong. Fate. Destiny. Coincidence. "She taught Patrick, too," Lauren said.

"It was I who created Rupert Beckwith," replied Rosemary, her lip curling again, like a withered leaf. "Who developed his artistic talents and who guided his words. Who laughed when visitors said he lacked the Irish gift of blarney, for he seldom spoke."

"He kept quiet because he was afraid he'd be caught out."

"Yes. We had one difficult moment, when Oscar Wilde asked him what mutual friends they might have had in Ireland."

Lauren looked around at Rosemary's sharp profile, now dulled by long use. "That's right, all sorts of notables visited the tower. Including Wilde. Cool."

"He was inspired by his visit to write *The Picture of Dorian Gray*. I'm surprised he could exercise enough self-discipline to write anything at all."

"Messy souls, artists," said Lauren wryly. Patrick Rupert, Donny . . . "What happened with you and Rupert, anyway?"

"He was still Patrick. He loved Susanna, even though she was no more Catherine than you are either woman. He loved her despite what I had done for him in two separate lives. And Gideon, he loved Susanna as well. I was too strong, and he preferred her more—yielding personality."

There was surrender and there was surrender. Lauren petted the cat, evoking a rumbling purr. David would make her purr as well, when the time came.

"Gideon was organizing our autumn move to London. No one was at the tower save the two of us and Rupert. He donned his old Spanish clothing to paint a self-portrait, to add Patrick to his depiction of Catherine as Morgan le Fay. Seeing him, I remembered. How I remembered. It was . . ." She grimaced in pain. "Too much. When Rupert passed me on the stairs—well, bad luck, that, passing someone on a spiral staircase."

That superstition was a memory of the ancient dance. "You tripped him. And he fell."

"I'm not sure I intended that, but it happened. He fell at Gideon's feet, his neck broken as surely as it would have been by James's hangman." Her grimace ebbed, as did the color from her eyes, leaving them bleak.

"And you hid his body in the cellar. With no one in the house, no one would notice the—ah, the decomposition process. And there he stayed, reduced to bones inside his Spanish clothing, until you and Gideon buried Susanna."

Rosemary' fists clenched on her lap, knuckles white, wrists corded, so that the edge of old burn writhed. "Gideon had his revenge on me. He told Susanna Rupert had deserted her. Her spirit left her, then, and when Gideon claimed her, she did not resist. She bore him a child."

Lauren raised her hand, then set it down again without reaching out. Rosemary was so cold, so reserved. Private. Like David had been, until his dream came true. "The child was my great-grandfather. John Reay, who was born a Mackay."

"Gideon swaggered and preened. He had begotten a son! But I refused to play his game and pretend the child was mine. I threatened divorce—that would have been a greater scandal than his seduction of an artist's model. Still, he had plans for the boy, intending to take him from Susanna and send him south for an education."

"But she defied him at last. She threw herself over the cliffs even as he tried one last time to grab her. By then, John was old enough to resent Gideon's power over him, so with his mother gone, he made a break for his freedom. I can see—I can understand that," Lauren amended hastily. And yet she had Seen John's flight from bitterness into bitterness all her life. Donny had been trapped by it long before he'd been trapped in the labyrinth.

"Ranting, angry, Gideon defied the labyrinth and was trapped. I staged a funeral for him."

"Ah. That's where the 'a man's a man for a' that' came from."

"Yes." Rosemary's mouth turned up at the ends, clenched as tightly as her hands. "I lingered on a few more years, but in the end I followed. I left instructions with Harold Simison to seal Catherine's doorway behind me. What irony that the ship I supposedly sailed upon sank, as the *Castillo Negro* sank, so that the Simisons had no need to build any elaborate fictions round my disappearance."

"That was a stroke of luck," Lauren said dryly.

Rosemary darted her a sharp glance, but said only, "When I found myself once again stumbling out into this chapel, I wept at my resurrection."

Again Lauren raised her hand in sympathy, and let it fall. The strange powers and elemental presences here were capricious, yes, and yet . . .

"It was Gideon who found me. Charles Innes, he had become. Tam Simison, Emily's cousin, had helped him ease into this world—less than a hundred years on, that was no great burden compared to what Patrick and I . . . Well, that's as may be. It was only as Charles that Gideon learned who I was. Then he was no longer the stamping bull, the selfish bully, against whom I had struggled, though he still played the laird. He convinced me that we were meant to return."

"You went to work for Scotland's Folk so you could trace John's descendants. It was just luck or coincidence or something that my grandfather was tracing back the other way. And here we are. Your plans worked out at last."

"A pity that after so many years, Charles didn't survive one more day." Rosemary slumped against the chill slate slabs that were young compared to the buried and broken stones of the labyrinth. In the delicate, even frail, sunlight, her features seemed aged beyond her physical years.

"A pity my grandfather didn't live a few more months. A shame that my father, well . . ."

Persie pricked her ears. Lauren lifted her ten-ton weight of a head. She heard voices, recognizable voices, David's refined consonants, Magnus's flat vowels, Ewan's thistled diction. And Emily's comforting tones supporting them all. If there was a hollow ring to the footsteps crossing the turf, she couldn't hear it, not now.

"I never said thank you for saving my life," she told Rosemary. "For breaking that particular thread, there at the cliff."

Rosemary looked around at the approaching voices and sighed. "Perhaps Susanna owed her death to me. Perhaps Catherine did as well. Perhaps I owed them both my death. But still I live."

This time Lauren did press Rosemary's frigid fist between her hands, warmed by David's sweater and the sunlight. "Wisdom and knowledge seem as good a goal as any," she said, and struggled to her feet.

From the corner of her eye, she saw Rosemary smile, perhaps in gratitude rather than satisfaction, but she couldn't really tell. And she saw the woman's clenched fists loosen, her fingers roll open, and let go.

Then the others were on them.

CHAPTER THIRTY-THREE

D avid supporting her from behind, Lauren let Emily slip her own athletic shoes onto her feet. "Thanks."

"Nae worries, dear. Or are you worrying?" Emily looked long and hard into her face. "David's told me about Donny. I'm sorry."

"He's all right," Lauren replied, and between Emily's strong arm and David's, she walked out of the chapel.

Magnus engulfed Rosemary and aided her faltering steps. "So did you get what you wanted?" he asked her.

She considered a long moment before she replied, "Yes."

Ewan looked around at the trenches, the remains—everything was still ship-shape, assuming the ship had been wrecked—and said to Rosemary, "You're here as well? I was thinking I saw you standing by the Bremner monument yesterday afternoon. What's all this in aid of? Lauren?"

"We spent all night out here," Lauren told him. "We were re-creating ancient rites. You know, walking the labyrinth, closing the old tombs, all that good stuff."

Magnus's brows went up and Rosemary's down. Ewan snorted. "Ah, you're taking the piss, I reckon. Pull the other one while you're about it."

"It's not a joke any more than it's a metaphor," said David.

"Not a sensible answer between you," Ewan replied. "Away with the fairies, the both of you."

No kidding, Lauren thought.

"Madness," Ewan went on, "passing all the night in that dress, and no shoes on your feet! Anderson, you and your taping's got a lot to answer for."

"I don't think so," Magnus said.

"And you, Sutherland, it's your own property, aye, but taking down the wall on your own, no idea what you're missing out—still, that's a grand bit of staircase, running down just by the fireplace in your sitting room—it likely ran on down to the cellars, once upon a time."

"Once upon a time," said David. "Let's get back to the tower, shall we?"

"It's gone six o'clock," Emily said. "I'm cooking us a proper breakfast, eggs, sausage, bacon, beans, tomato, toast with lashings of butter and jam and honey. Come along, Rosemary, Lauren, we'll set you to rights. Oh, and Vince's arm's not broken at all. There's a stroke of luck for you."

No kidding. Smiling, leaning against David, Lauren walked down from the chapel and up to Blackness Tower. His unshaven jaw prickled against her forehead and the undiscovered country of his body and spirit tingled in her Sight. From his other arm, Persie looked across the headland, whiskers poised like antennae sensing currents beyond human comprehension.

Magnus's dark gaze shifted from the back of Ewan's head over the top of Rosemary's limp permed curls, to Lauren's face. "All I got beyond a few weird readings was you in front of the picture and then galumphing down that staircase in a long dress and bare feet. Nothing else registered a fricking bleep-censored thing. Although I know what I saw," he added, eyes wide, teeth gleaming in a grin. "You went down the staircase and hours later came out here. And the mirror cracked, all by itself, a ginormous fissure running from corner to corner. Abso-fricking-lutely cool. Thanks."

"You're welcome," Lauren returned.

And, beneath her breath, Rosemary said, "Yes, you are, at that."

Within moments, Lauren found herself seated on the living room couch, bundled in a comforter and nursing a hot cup of tea. A small table beside her held a plate of rich, delicious, filling food. Persie lay on the hearth in front of a fragrant peat fire, exuding peace as only a cat could. Lauren's family skull pocket watch sat on the mantelpiece, shining in the light of the morning sun, ticking.

Rosemary sat in an armchair on the far side of the hearth, a cup in one hand, a piece of toast in the other. In the sunlight the furrows in her face slowly eased. She was, Lauren thought, a drowned land rising from the waves.

Emily looked past the curtain hanging in the doorway. "More tea? Toast? No? All right, then." Her eyes twinkled, her apple cheeks glowed.

Lauren smiled at her cousin, then up at her great-great-grandmother's portrait. *Catherine's Dance.* The intensity of its sunset colors was muted by the light, which instead emphasized the subtle ridges and whorls of paint beneath the varnish, the bones beneath the skin. The labyrinth beneath the turf.

In the paintings, Catherine and Susanna remained forever young, beautiful, and strong. They had reached Tir nan Og. David would never sense their ghosts again.

Lauren herself would have to play the piano—it had been a long time since Donny had guided her fingers in "The Water is Wide," but she could find the notes again. As for the sampler on the hearth, maybe she could eventually finish that, binding the threads.

O Death, where is thy sting? she thought. *O Grave, where is thy victory?* Those weren't the words original to this place, but they had come here soon enough, and the meaning was the same, always the same.

David sat down beside Lauren, holding not a bottle of whisky but a cut-glass decanter that reflected little rainbows into her eyes. Gravely he poured a dollop into her tea, then held the decanter over his own cup. With an infinitesimal shake of his head, he put it down without pouring.

A fixer-upper, Lauren thought. *Yeah, that makes both of us.* She sipped, and the sweet tea warmed her stomach while its keen undercurrent rose in an amber vapor to her head and formed the thought, *Now what?*

Ewan's and Magnus's voices emanated from the dining room between the chimes of cutlery, clashing, combining, clashing again, plotting astronomical data, future excavations, the promotional opportunities of Patrick O'Neill's name carved in the cellar.

"I'm digging a moat," said David, "so I'll have a drawbridge."

"Ewan won't be happy with you messing up the stratigraphy," Lauren told him.

Maybe they could throw Ewan a bit of bone, like the human bone he'd found in the Spanish chest—which might actually be a relic of Patrick Rupert straying out of place as well as time—by theorizing that the body was Rupert Beckwith's, and that he'd dressed in period Spanish garb to paint Patrick into "Blood Red Falls the Rose." That was true, after all, if not Ewan's ground truth.

Rosemary's head fell back and her eyes closed. Lauren wondered if she ever dreamed.

And Lauren wondered if she'd ever dream again.

"I've got plane reservations in—nine days, something like that," she said, even as she settled into the circle of David's arm.

"Well then, we've got some territory to cover before then." His hand captured hers. His long, limber fingers teased the hills and hollows of her palm, the friction sending a warm thrill up her arm. She gasped, her tired body waking with pleasure, and she felt warmth rising to her cheeks.

"Just one thing," she whispered. "Can we spend a couple of days on Orkney? It's not really the next world, I know, but . . ."

"Yes," he said, and with a soft laugh, "My mum said I'd never meet anyone in this godforsaken place."

"She was wrong on both counts." Lauren traced his jaw line with her lips, the sandpaper kiss of his stubble sending a wave of delight all the way to her toes.

His own breath growing a bit short, he said, "When you get back from America—if you come back . . ."

Fair enough, she thought.

"I found a sixteenth-century ring in the windowsill of my bedroom, not the old bedroom, the studio—the room I made over for myself. If you'd like to have it . . ."

"No, thank you. Maybe, eventually, you can get me a new one. A ring with an interlace design, one that's ours alone."

He smiled, the creases in his cheeks resembling the curving stones guarding the center of the labyrinth, as perfectly balanced as the scales of justice.

She laid her head against his shoulder, and traced a spiral on his hand, and gazed up at the portrait of her ancestors, two in one.

Once she had doubted that her dream of Blackness Tower had meaning, and believed the people who told her it was only imagination, as though imagination was ever nothing.

But now she knew.

"I'll come back," she told David. "I always come back here."